USA Today bestselling auth.............................., is read in multiple languages around the world. Enjoy sweet romances as Emily Murdoch, and steamy romances as Emily E K Murdoch. Emily has had a varied career to date: from examining medieval manuscripts to designing museum exhibitions, to working as a researcher for the BBC to working for the National Trust. Her books range from England 1050 to Texas 1848, and she can't wait for you to fall in love with her heroes and heroines!

Regency Whispers

Regency Whispers:

The Wallflower Academy

EMILY E K MURDOCH

MILLS & BOON

First Published in Great Britain 2024
By Mills & Boon, an imprint of HarperCollins*Publishers* Ltd,
1 London Bridge Street, London, SE1 9GF

www.harpercollins.co.uk

HarperCollins*Publishers*
Macken House, 39/40 Mayor Street Upper,
Dublin 1, D01 C9W8, Ireland

ISBN: 978-0-263-32332-0

LEAST LIKELY TO
WIN A DUKE

For my parents,
Who encouraged me to write when I couldn't.
For my husband,
Who emboldened me to write when I wasn't.
And for my wonderful readers,
Who told me to write even more.

Lastly, to PB, PB, BB and BB.

Chapter One

This was absolutely the last place Miss Gwendoline Knox wanted to be—not that she had any choice in the matter.

Murderess wallflowers were rarely wanted at home.

'There y'are,' muttered the coach driver, rather unceremoniously dropping her trunk to the ground. It rolled, mud splattering up one side of the leather case. 'Academy.'

Gwen swallowed and looked up at the large manor house, its beautiful Tudor bricks glowing in the afternoon sun. Imposing chimneys pumped out smoke and the large front door had a highly polished bronze knocker.

'But where am I supposed to—?'

The whip cracked and the horses stepped forward, pulling the coach away and leaving Gwen alone on the drive. Silence quickly spilled into the gardens.

If only her mother had agreed to accompany her, Gwen thought wistfully as she picked up her trunk, leaning slightly thanks to its weight. But that would have meant talking about…the incident. Perhaps this was best.

Besides, this was why she had been sent to the Academy. To get out from under her mother's feet, prevent any hint of scandal and find a husband. Gwen tried to push the unkind thoughts from her mind, but they intruded, nonetheless.

If Mother had been kind enough to come with me, she would not have been so unkind as to send me here.

It was an unpleasant thought, and it was getting her nowhere. The bright autumnal sun was drawing long shadows across the gardens, and a chill in the air hinted at an icy evening.

Stepping forward timidly, Gwen knocked on the door, which was immediately opened by a footman in blue livery.

'Miss Knox,' he said smoothly. 'Miss Pike is expecting you.'

Gwen was certainly not expecting the hall she stepped into, conscious of the mud she was spreading into the magnificent space. High ceilings, a beautiful red carpet, and landscape paintings along the walls: the very picture of elegance.

'Ah, Miss Knox!'

A smiling older woman, perhaps nearing fifty, was approaching rather like a battleship. Gwen took a step backwards.

'How pleasant to make your acquaintance,' said the woman, who could only be Miss Pike. 'The Wallflower Academy welcomes you.'

'And no one will miss you there!'

Her mother's parting words rang through her mind.

'It's not as if women like you deserve happy endings, do you? Not after what you've done...'

Gwen winced. It was bad enough to be labelled a wallflower by one's own mother, but to be sent to such a place! It was scandalously embarrassing.

'I do not want to be here,' she said, the words slipping out before she could stop them.

They did not appear to offend Miss Pike. 'Of course you don't,' she said with a broad smile, waving her hand as though opinions mattered little. 'And you won't be alone.

Matthews, please show Miss Knox to her bedchamber. The end room.'

A flurry of corridors passed Gwen by until she was standing in a small yet genteelly furnished bedchamber. A large bed, a writing desk, a toilette table and a wardrobe were the only items within it, but a large bay window looked out onto the south of the house, towards the rear gardens. She could see kitchen gardens, what appeared to be a walled rose garden, and an abundance of carefully manicured lawn.

She turned. The footman had gone. She had not even noticed his departure.

Breathing out slowly as her heart rate started to slow, Gwen sank onto the end of the bed and closed her eyes. This was not the end of the world. She would manage.

'Goodness, you look terrible,' said a cheerful voice.

Breath caught in her throat, Gwen was unable to say anything as her bedchamber door opened, and a pair of ladies entered.

'Sylvia,' said a woman with black skin and a broad smile.

She had on her arm the hands of another lady, a little older, with milky white eyes.

The door shut and flickers of panic tingled up Gwen's spine. To be so enclosed with unknown people…

'My word, your bedchamber has the most outstanding view,' said Sylvia, leaning towards the window. 'We're all jealous, you know.'

'Oh, I don't know,' said the one with milky eyes, who had been helped to the window seat. 'I don't think I would mind. I'm Marilla. You can call me Rilla.'

Gwen nodded weakly. She was always terrible with names, but she wasn't about to forget Rilla in a hurry. When had she lost her sight? How could she speak of it so calmly?

'I don't hear the new one laughing,' said Rilla mildly. 'Don't you worry about it, whoever you are. I don't—you shouldn't.'

'Gwendoline Knox,' Gwen said weakly, head spinning and in desperate need of solitude. She had risen early for that day's journey. 'You can call me—'

'Do you have any beaus?'

'N-No!' Gwen spluttered, startled into speech by Sylvia's blunt question.

She was still grinning as she leaned against the window. 'I only asked.'

'Don't hound her, Sylvia,' said Rilla.

'I'll hound whoever I want,' said Sylvia brightly. 'I've got to find entertainment somewhere in this place.'

They laughed, and Gwen smiled nervously. As long as she didn't draw attention to herself…

They were not as dull as she had expected. An Academy for Wallflowers…well, her mother had considered it perfect. The perfect place to hide someone. Gwen had tried to imagine the sorts of ladies who were sent to such a place—women no longer wanted by their families, who had tried, and failed, to make a match.

The beginning of the Season had been only a few weeks ago, and Gwen knew precisely what her mother expected of her: to keep her head down and make a good match.

But how was she expected to do so in an Academy full of ladies who could conceive of nothing worse than making light conversation with a handsome gentleman?

'Are we it?' Gwen flushed as laughter resounded around her bedchamber at her question.

'It?' repeated Sylvia with a giggle. 'Were you expecting something far more impressive?'

'Don't tease her, Sylvia,' Rilla said with mock severity. 'You forget, you've been here an entire Season! You can no longer remember how frightened you were when you first arrived.'

A slight pink tinge came to Sylvia's cheeks. 'I suppose not. Yes, Gwen—can I call you Gwen?'

Gwen would have permitted her to call her anything she liked if it meant the focus of the conversation moved on quickly. 'Yes.'

'Yes, Gwen, we are "it"—at least some of it,' said Sylvia with a grin. 'There are—what…? Five of us here now? You make six. I am least likely to be wed—'

'I think I'd agree with you on that one,' muttered Rilla.

'Daphne is least likely to say boo to a mouse—'

'She does this,' Rilla said to a bemused Gwen. 'It's her way of keeping track of us, apparently. Some ladies come and go rather quickly.'

'They…they find husbands?'

Gwen could hardly believe it. For all the wonderful references Miss Pike had sent her mother, it had been hard to fathom how the Academy could marry off so many wallflowers in such a short time.

'Oh, Miss Pike has her ways,' said Rilla dryly.

'She does know what she is doing most of the time,' said Sylvia, glancing at Gwen with a knowing look. 'So, you are here for a husband, are you?'

Gwen wished heat would not immediately flush up her décolletage, wished it would not pinken her cheeks and make her words incomprehensible.

What would she be? Least likely to form a coherent sentence?

'I—I… That is…my mother wants—'

'Oh, mothers,' said Sylvia dismissively. 'I was sent here by my mother.'

'Me by my father,' Rilla said curtly. 'Such as he is. But not for marriage. No, the blackguard believes—'

'Miss Knox does not need to hear our sob stories,' interrupted Sylvia firmly.

Gwen swallowed, curling her fingers around the blanket on the bed. The tension taut in her shoulders and neck was starting to give her a headache, and Sylvia was right. She certainly did not need the histories of the ladies who had invaded her bedchamber.

What she needed was quiet and solitude—a chance to think over all she had heard, all she had seen. All that she might now expect.

She was a prisoner here, sent by her mother after her own scandalous marriage, after the…the incident had become a fact. What she, Gwen, was going to do about it… Well, that was quite another matter. A matter that required due consideration—and she was not going to be able to think with all the noise in here.

But first, Gwen had questions which needed answering. 'What…what happens here? At the Wallflower Academy, I mean? How does she—Miss Pike—how does she… marry us off?'

Rilla chuckled. 'It's all very simple, Miss Knox. You have no need to be concerned. Miss Pike gives us lessons—'

'Lessons in how to be more interesting and charming young ladies,' Sylvia interrupted, rolling her eyes.

'Lessons on attracting a gentleman,' Rilla continued, a smile curling her lips. 'And then eligible gentlemen are invited to come and meet us.'

'View us,' said Sylvia wryly. 'Like specimens. Like animals in a zoo.'

Gwen swallowed. It did not sound particularly appealing. She had never been one to enjoy being looked at—which was all to the good, for her mother had pronounced her plain when she had first started curling her hair and pinning it up.

No, to be invisible. That was the thing. To go through life without being noticed, without attention, was all she desired.

The thought of gentlemen arriving at the Academy to look at them all, as though through a catalogue...

'I will hate it,' she whispered. 'I just want to be left alone.'

'Plenty of opportunities for that,' said Sylvia, and there was little laughter in her tone this time. 'Some of us have been here for years. 'Tis not a given that you will ever be chosen.'

Was that bitterness in her voice? Gwen could hardly tell. There had been such mischief in everything Sylvia had said since barrelling into her bedchamber.

'You will get accustomed to it,' said Rilla quietly. 'We all do.'

Gwen nodded mutely. It sounded awful. So, gentlemen would come to...to examine them.

'We have lessons on how to speak with confidence, how to stand tall, how to select topics of conversation,' Rilla explained, her hands folded in her lap. 'Music, art, languages...the normal things.'

Sylvia rolled her eyes. 'It's completely ridiculous. As though being shy, being a wallflower, is something needing to be cured.'

Only then did a natural smile creep across Gwen's face. Until now, her fears of being forced to change, to be a different person, to lose so much of who she was had overwhelmed her.

'You are not at all the wallflowers I had expected,' Gwen admitted with an awkward laugh.

Rilla grinned, her pale eyes turning in Gwen's direction. 'I am not here as a wallflower, you understand. 'Tis my father's intention—'

'And I'm not a wallflower at all, but a prisoner,' declared Sylvia with a wink. 'My father wants to marry me off without having to bring me out into Society. So here I am, stuck amid all these quiet ones. I manage to gain sufficient conversation at the official dinners, of course. You have missed the first one.'

Official dinners? Gwen's cheeks blazed with heat at the idea she had missed something important. Miss Pike's letter had said that any time was perfect for her arrival, that she should not rush her goodbyes with her family.

It had not prevented her mother from bundling her off as soon as possible…

'Official dinners?' she repeated.

Rilla smiled wearily. 'Miss Pike hosts six dinners throughout the Season. Only the very best and most eligible gentlemen are invited—though of course, they must all be accepting of a wallflower as their bride.'

As their bride.

Gwen's stomach twisted most painfully and her grip on the blanket increased.

Because that was what she was here for, wasn't it? To make a match. To be married off, cast away from her family to make her own way in the world. To be hidden amongst the most unlikely of ladies.

'And I have missed the first?'

A rather wicked smile spread across Sylvia's face. 'You did not miss much—it was a complete disaster! Oh, Gwen, it was awful. The gentlemen Miss Pike had procured were so immensely dull they did not ask us anything, nor start any conversation—and of course this lot said nothing either!'

There was a peal of laughter from Rilla. 'Speak for yourself! I tried to ask Mr Whatshisname something about the meat course, and he said—'

'"I don't speak to wallflowers!"'

Both chorused this, and then fell into peals of giggles, the loudest snort coming from Sylvia.

Gwen looked at the laughing women and tried to smile. It was all too much: too much noise, too much expectation, too much going on. Her mind clouded, her head spun. She tried to make sense of all the information she was being given, but her bones ached from the long carriage ride, and the very last thing she wished to do at this moment was have dinner with what Miss Pike considered to be eligible—

'Don't worry,' said Rilla, a smile still dancing on her lips. 'The second official dinner is this week.'

Gwen's stomach turned horribly, threatening to return the meat pie she had hesitantly accepted at the inn just a few hours ago.

The second official dinner—so soon? She would barely have enough time to settle into the Academy!

The room closed in, as if the air was running out, and Gwen gasped for breath. 'I… I need…'

'Goodness, you sound awful, Gwen,' said Rilla, a slight crease of concern appearing between her eyes. 'Are you quite well?'

Gwen shook her head, unable to speak. Then, remembering Rilla, she said, 'Y-Yes.'

'She needs some air,' said Sylvia firmly. 'A walk in the garden. I will go with you…show you the way—'

But Gwen had already risen and waved a hand. 'Oh, no, I can easily—I—I would like to be alone, if you do not mind.'

Fear seared her heart at the thought of giving offence, but Sylvia only sighed. 'You wallflowers are all the same.'

Gwen swallowed, shame flooding her veins, but a second glance at the beautiful woman showed her Sylvia had meant no harm.

It was just too much. Too many opportunities to reveal the truth.

'I have to…' Gwen tried to speak, but made no effort to continue as she half walked, half stumbled out of the bed-chamber.

It was not difficult to find her way outside. Once she had descended the staircase into the hall, she opened the front door and stepped out into the cold yet welcoming air. There were sufficient borders and hedges here, along the drive, in which to lose herself.

Her skin prickled with the cold, but at least it was cooling. Gwen paced, hardly looking where she was going, entering into one of the portions of the garden lined with hedges.

The Wallflower Academy. It was like a bad jest some-one had made in their cups, and yet it was real. She was here. The tall redbrick building loomed above her. She had no home, no friends—although that might soon change—and no idea what she was going to do with herself at these awful dinners.

If only I was not guilty of something so terrible, Gwen thought bitterly as she turned a corner, her skirts whip-ping because she was walking so fast.

Then she could have asked her mother to allow her to remain at home.

But it was not to be. She had to live with the conse-quences of her actions, and this was far more pleasant than a prison—even if the punishment included being paraded before gentlemen for their enjoyment!

Gwen's eyes filled with tears as she turned hurriedly around the next corner, the hedge brushing against the sleeve of her gown. How could she bear it? What could possibly make the Wallflower Academy endurable?

She turned another corner and walked straight into the most handsome gentleman she had ever seen.

Chapter Two

Percy Devereux, Duke of Knaresby, sighed heavily as his footsteps thudded down the front steps of the dratted Wallflower Academy.

Academy. The cheek of Miss Pike to call it such a thing, when places like Oxford and Cambridge existed in the world. Why, a finishing school concerned with dancing and decorum was hardly an 'academy', in his view.

Besides, Miss Pike was dreadfully dull. If she was any indication of the poor women sent to such a place, it was no wonder the so-called 'wallflowers' found themselves left on the side-lines of every ball and conversation of note.

The bright autumnal air shimmered with the afternoon sun, and Percy watched the merest hint of his breath billowing on the breeze. The Season had begun, and it brought with it little pleasure and less excitement.

It was only down to Staromchor's mother that he had even come at all, cornered at Almack's just days ago. A 'charitable duty'—that was what the Dowager Countess had called it.

A damned nuisance, more like.

That dinner he'd been forced to attend had been outrageously dull, and he had firmly vowed he would only drop by a few times for the look of the thing.

Still, the Academy was only a twenty-minute drive from Town, and it was not so very arduous to make the trip—as long as it was infrequent.

But when there were far more interesting diversions to be had in London—concerts and card parties and riding in the parks—it was impossible to see how he would be dragged out here more than twice in the whole Season.

Percy squared his shoulders and thanked his stars he had performed his duty without having to see a single blushing wallflower. In, five minutes with the dreaded Miss Pike, and out. Not bad.

Striding down the driveway, gravel crunching under his riding boots, Percy pulled on his gloves and tried to calculate what time he would arrive back at the Knaresby townhouse. Almost four o'clock, by his reckoning. Just in time for—

A heavy weight halted his path, so dense and immovable Percy was almost rocked off his feet. But the weight itself was not so fortunate. Down it fell, in a tumble of skirts and ribbons, and to his horror Percy realised he had toppled not some statue unexpectedly in his path…but a woman.

'Dear God,' Percy muttered, shaking his head at the irritating distraction now preventing him from reaching the stables. 'Apologies, I am sure.'

His gruff remark was ignored, however, as was the hand he offered the young lady who had so unceremoniously been toppled to the ground.

A fierce glare came from bright eyes, and unfathomably Percy's breath caught in his throat.

Then his hand was pushed aside and the young lady, dark-haired and apparently furious, rose to her feet, brushing at her skirts.

Ah. One of Pike's wallflowers.

A lazy grin slid onto Percy's face as he waited for the stammering apology he was doubtless about to receive. After all, he was a duke. And though they had not been introduced, it would be clear from his elegantly tailored coat and graceful top hat that he was—

'Why cannot you look where you are going, oaf?'

Percy blinked. The woman before him had just picked a leaf from her skirt and flicked it to the ground, not looking at him as she spoke—but she was looking at him now.

Those bright eyes he had noticed before were now shining with irritation, and a frown creased the otherwise pretty face. Lips were pressed in a rather furious expression, and the lady did not stop there.

'Do us both a favour, Mr Whoever-You-Are, and consider a little when you walk with no thought to your surroundings, for there are others in the world beyond yourself!'

After a ringing silence, the woman clapped her hands to her mouth, eyes wide, cheeks a flaming pink which was, although Percy tried not to notice, most becoming.

Her horror at her own words could not have been more evident, and Percy did the only thing he could: he laughed.

By Jove, he had not expected that! No woman had ever spoken so to him in his life. Admittedly, there must have been a few who had done it behind his back, but still... They all respected the name and the title, never speaking abruptly or disrespectfully.

This was no wallflower—she could not be. What was she doing here, at the Wallflower Academy, with such an unrestrained and violent temper?

'I—I... I do beg...' the woman stammered, her hands not leaving her mouth so her words were muffled.

If only the pink in her cheeks did not make her so alluring, Percy mused, taking a proper look at her as a woman for the first time. An elegant figure, a gown that might have seen many Seasons but was still relatively fashionable, and a large muddy patch on her behind.

A behind that was well formed, even if it was difficult to tell through the fabric…

A lurch in Percy's stomach pulled him to his senses. Now was not the time to be measuring a young lady's assets, impressive though they might be.

Still, his curiosity must be sated. 'What is your name?'

'Nothing,' the woman said hastily, turning away. 'Good day.'

For a moment Percy could hardly believe she had done so. What? No elegant curtsey? No apology for leaving his presence? No flirtatious grin, moreover, and no teasing hint at her name? No invitation for him to call again? No manners at all?

Hardly aware of what his feet were doing, Percy found himself following the woman up the gravel path towards the Academy. Which was foolishness. He was a duke! Ladies were meant to run after him, not the other way around! It was most unaccountable, this need he had to know her name…

'You must have a name,' he said reasonably, his lungs inexplicably tight. 'Everyone does.'

'It is no concern of yours,' came the swift reply over the lady's shoulder.

Remarkable… Since rising to his title Percy had been inundated with ladies, all simpering and smiling, ready to be delighted—something he hardly regretted—but this was the first to actively avoid his presence.

Perhaps it was because she was unaware of his station, his title. That must be it.

Drawing himself up as best he could, while still pacing

after her, Percy said, impressively, 'I am Percy Devereux, Duke of Knaresby.'

A strange noise emitted from the woman before him. It might have been a laugh, or a cough—he could not tell.

'My name is definitely no concern of yours, then,' came the reply.

There was nothing for it. Percy's curiosity was aroused, and despite his better judgment, and all sense of decorum, he reached out.

No woman walked away from him.

'Wait.'

His hand was on her arm, which was covered by her sleeve. There was no reason for the sudden rush of heat, the tingle in his fingers, the sense that it was he who had been knocked over this time.

Everything swayed a little. The world stayed the same, of course, so perhaps it was he who swayed. Perhaps they both did.

The woman had halted, as if unable to walk forward, and was staring as though she had been cornered by a wild dog.

Percy swallowed. He was acting strangely…far out of character. He had not come here to accost young ladies; he had not even wanted to come here at all.

What was such a woman doing at the Wallflower Academy?

'Did you come here to find a husband?'

The words had slipped from his mouth before he could halt them, and Percy found, to his distraction, that they had a rather pleasing effect. Once again the woman's face was tinged with pink, but she looked defiant.

A most intriguing look.

'I do hope, Your Grace, you do not believe I bumped into you merely to gain your notice!'

In truth, Percy had half wondered that very thing—but now she had spoken, now he heard the tremor in her voice, he could not believe it.

'If…if you could release me?' she said softly.

Percy was still holding on to her and had no desire to release her. His curiosity was still piqued, and he was certain she would run off as soon as she was unrestrained. But the connection between them… There was something there. Something he could not explain.

'Unhand me, sir.'

Sir! The audacity!

Very slowly, one finger after another, he released her.

It was like a small bereavement. The connection was cut, the world stopped swaying, and Percy found he had rather enjoyed the dizziness his touching her had produced.

Yet things were not entirely back to normal. The woman had not fled, as he had expected, but was standing before him with wary eyes and hands clasped before her.

Percy examined her. She was no wallflower. He was certain.

The first of Miss Pike's 'official dinners', as she called them, had been one of the most dull affairs of his life. Never before had he been presented with such a quiet bunch of ladies, and although the bolder one, a Miss Sylvia, had attempted conversation, it had been so stilted Percy had left before dessert, his promise to Miss Pike be damned. There was only so much a gentleman should have to do as a favour to his old governess.

He had never met anyone at the Academy like the woman before him now.

Fire lay under that shyness, Percy was sure. He had felt it when she had berated him so heartily for his inattention.

Though the sparks had disappeared, there was something still smouldering under those dark eyes of hers. Something he wanted to fan back into flames.

'Look,' said Percy imperiously, and irritation flushed through his voice, 'I merely wish to know the name of the person I knocked to the ground, that is all. Your name please, miss?'

Unless she was a servant? Surely not. Percy knew enough of good breeding and the clothes of a maid to know one when he saw one.

A tutor, perhaps, at the Academy? He had heard Miss Pike complain that she needed additional help. Was this it?

'I just wish to know you,' Percy said, trying to inject a little of the Knaresby force into his words.

The woman's gaze dropped. 'No, you do not.'

'Are you always this contrary?'

A mere hint of a smile curled across her lips. 'No.'

He chuckled as a cold breeze blew past them. The sun was setting in earnest now, and he would certainly not be back in Town as expected. His mother would have to wait.

'And when people chastise you for that stubborn streak of yours,' he said, 'what do they call you?'

The smile on her face broadened, and Percy's stomach lurched as her beauty blossomed.

Dear God. She was a marvel.

'They…they call me Miss Gwendoline Knox. But mostly they call me Gwen.'

Gwen.

A shiver went down Percy's spine—which he allotted, of course, to the cooling of the afternoon. It had nothing to do with the wallflower before him. It couldn't.

Oh, don't bother lying to yourself, he thought.

It was natural to be attracted to such a woman. She had all the features and form Society expected in a woman to be called pretty, and yet she had…more.

Putting his finger on it would be difficult. And Percy wanted to put more than a finger on her.

Miss Gwendoline Knox. Gwen.

How he dearly wished to call her Gwen. Such an intimacy, of course, would be insupportable. No noble-born gentleman would consider it. No well-bred lady would allow it.

'And now you can be on your way.'

Percy's gaze snapped back. 'Why would I want to?'

Gwen frowned, and glanced back at the manor before saying, 'Well, you cannot wish to stay here in the cold, talking to me.'

Heavens, how little she knew. Percy could see it in her now he came to look closely. The fear of the wallflower... the expectation that she would never be enough. Not entertaining enough, pretty enough, clever enough. The assumption that she would be passed by. The knowledge, deep within her, that no one would wish to know her, that any conversation would be borne of pity, not interest.

What was it like to go through the world in such a way?

'Because you are a wallflower?' he said, with a wry grin.

A flash of sharpness in her eyes, an inclination towards rebellion, then it was gone.

'Yes.'

'At this awful Academy?' Percy said, looking up at the building before him.

A stricken look overcame Gwen's face. 'Is it truly that bad? Is its reputation unfavourable? I only arrived an hour ago.'

Ah.

Percy found it a challenge to consider his words carefully before he spoke again in this woman's presence. He was, after all, a duke. Well, he had been for the last few months. More, he was a Devereux. His family had been bred for careful and considered conversation, for every word to mean something, to convey the very best feelings and hide the rest.

And here, with her, this woman who had berated him just as swiftly as she'd blushed before him, his feelings betrayed him. They offered him nothing but plain truth—something rather dangerous when a duke.

'I did not mean... Not awful,' he said. 'I merely meant... Well, what is the word?'

Gwen looked at him silently. A prickle of discomfort, not unpleasant, crept up his neck. How did she do that? Look at him as though he was merely a servant himself? As though he was not eminently superior to her?

It was uncanny. It was delightful.

'Intense,' Percy landed on, unable to think of anything better. 'Intense, I suppose, for everyone involved. Just a marriage market under a different name.'

'And you are not married?'

It appeared he was not the only one whose tongue was eager to betray its owner. Percy saw a flush cover Gwen's cheeks, but she continued to hold his gaze defiantly.

Interesting... A wallflower with a dash of curiosity as well as a temper. Most interesting... And she found him just as interesting, did she not? Only a woman interested in a gentleman would ask said gentleman about his potential wife, would she not?

Percy found to his surprise that a flicker of pleasure was curling around his heart at the very thought. It appeared Miss Knox was just as intrigued by him as he was her.

Yet it was not possible, of course, for this conversation to go further. Percy straightened his shoulders as the thought, though unwelcome, hit him with its truth.

He was a duke. She was a wallflower. Probably of little family and no real reputation, if her parents had been forced to send her here to find a match.

And Percy Devereux, Duke of Knaresby, was hardly free himself to make a choice in the matter of his own marriage. He had a duty, a responsibility, to marry a woman of excellent breeding, impressive dowry and, most importantly, respectability in Society. He needed someone far more impressive than a mere wallflower.

A shame. This Gwendoline Knox was rather starting to grow on him.

But he had a far more important focus at the moment, and he was late for old Mr Moore. His mother and the solicitor would not wait for ever. James's will had to be read.

Not that he wanted to dwell on such matters, but he was left with little choice after the way he had arrived at his title.

'No,' Percy said with a wry smile. 'No, I am not married. Not for the lack of my mother's efforts, however.'

'Good,' said Gwen. 'I mean—not good! Just…fine. Fine.'

Fine. A mediocre word from a rather extraordinary woman.

Percy saw the interest in her eyes, the desire flushing her cheeks. He watched the way she leaned ever so slightly closer, all thoughts of escaping him clearly gone from her mind.

It was flattering, of course. And it was a relief, in a way, to see the effect he had on women—even those he had rather unceremoniously accosted by way of greeting.

But that did not explain why his body was responding. Why he wished to take a step, bridge the gap between them. Why, when she shivered in the cold of the afternoon, he wished to place an arm around her and pull her near, to share his heat. Wanted to tip her head back and capture those lips and—

Percy cleared his throat.

No, that would not do.

Still, he could not help himself. A little further teasing would do no harm. 'Just "fine"?' he said.

Gwen hesitated, her gaze moving from his eyes to his lips before it fell to her hands. 'Your Grace, you must realise there is a reason I am here. At the Wallflower Academy, I mean.'

'I have no idea,' said Percy honestly. This was no wallflower, he was sure.

'I am not particularly eloquent,' said Gwen to her boots. 'In talking with gentlemen, I mean.'

'We are talking,' he pointed out.

'No,' said Gwen, glancing up with a smile she was evidently trying to hide. 'You are badgering me.'

'Probably.' Percy grinned. 'Rather fun, don't you think?'

He needed to step away. A small part of him knew that, even if it was shrinking at an alarming rate. Step away from the wallflower and return to Town.

'So, you are not here to find a husband?'

Gwen glanced back at the manor house for a moment before saying, 'No. At least, I don't... I am not desperate.'

She said the last word rather too firmly, if Percy was any judge, although he could not understand why. Surely a woman like this would have no trouble in attracting a nice gentleman? A country squire, perhaps? Someone who could keep her comfortable.

A vision of another man touching Gwen rushed through Percy's mind and his heart rebelled. In an instant the image was gone, though his hand was still clenched in a fist.

'Least likely to win a duke, though,' said Gwen quietly. 'Not after what happened at home, I mean.'

'At home?' Percy asked, his curiosity piqued once more. 'What do you mean by—?'

'I must go inside. They will be wondering where I have got to,' said Gwen in a rush. 'Good day, Your Grace. It was...'

Words failing her, Gwen turned and half walked, half ran up the drive to the steps of the Wallflower Academy. Within a moment, she was gone.

Percy stood, unable to move. As swiftly as she had entered his life she had disappeared.

'Least likely to win a duke.'

So she had said. And yet he was intrigued.

Forcing aside the desire which had so quickly blossomed in Gwen's presence, Percy shook his head, as though that would rid him of the confusion miring his mind.

Miss Gwendoline Knox. A wallflower unlike any he had ever met.

Percy smiled. Well, it was only a week until Pike's second official dinner. His invitation had so far gone unanswered. Perhaps it was time to reply and reward himself with more of Gwen. Demonstrate to her just what calibre of man she had been so quick to run from.

Chapter Three

'This dinner,' said Gwen with an awkward smile. 'We truly have to attend?'

Rilla grinned. 'It is not that bad.'

Night had fallen a few hours before, and Gwen's bedchamber had once again become a gathering place for the two wallflowers who had first welcomed her to the Academy.

If anyone had thought to ask Gwen—and no one had—she would have requested they use Sylvia's bedchamber. It was not as well-proportioned as her own, and neither did it have such an impressive view. Nonetheless, Sylvia herself was no wallflower, and revelled in the company of others.

And Gwen…

Sitting in the window seat by the bay window, Gwen looked out at the flickering torches that Miss Pike—or 'the Pike', as she was affectionately yet fearfully known by the other wallflowers—had ordered to be placed along the drive.

In mere moments carriages would be rattling along that driveway, bringing gentlemen of eligible suitability from London to dine at the Wallflower Academy. There would be conversation. There would be attention. There would be expectations.

There might even, Sylvia had teased, be some sort of recital required, when the gentlemen returned to the ladies after their port and cigars.

Gwen's stomach lurched painfully at the mere thought. *Entertainment. Diversion. Singing. God forbid.*

She had been blessed neither with musical talent nor an ear for a tune, and if she was forced to step up to the pianoforte...

Well, there would be no chance of a match for her then. And if Percy should decide to attend—

But Gwen forced that particular thought from her mind. There was no possibility that the Duke of Knaresby—which was how she should consider him—would be attending the second official Wallflower Academy dinner this evening.

Firstly, she told herself sternly, he was a duke, and had no need to hightail it to a house of wallflowers to find a bride. Goodness knew what sort of gentlemen did resort to such a thing.

Secondly, he had no interest in her. A certain curiosity, true—she had seen it in his eyes. A thirst for knowledge, however, did not translate into a hunger for...

And thirdly, Gwen thought hastily, as she tried not to recollect just how delectable the Duke's lips had looked, she was in no rush to be married. Her mother might consider her a problem unless she was darkening someone else's doorway, but she was not eager to be a wife.

'*So, you are not here to find a husband?*'

'*No. At least, I don't... I am not desperate.*'

Her cheeks flamed with heat.

'I can *feel* you worrying.'

Startled, Gwen looked over at the blind woman, who was smiling. 'You can?'

Rilla laughed. 'They really aren't that bad, these dinners of the Pike's.'

'They're not?' said Gwen hopefully.

It was only a dinner. A few hours of good food and polite if a little stilted conversation. A chance for Sylvia, the only one among them who truly wished to shine, to play the pianoforte and sing and dazzle.

And then bed.

The comfort and the sanctuary of her own bedchamber. Gwen swallowed as she looked at its current inhabitants. All she wanted was a bedchamber empty of all others, where she could rest alone and try not to think of the shocked, wide eyes haunting her dreams...

It had been a relief to discover the food was good and the beds comfortable at the Wallflower Academy. Gwen had not been sure that would be the case when she had first entered the Tudor manor, with visions of gruel and slops clouding her mind.

'You're brooding again.'

''Tis all very well for you Rilla,' said Gwen darkly. 'You cannot see all the gentlemen staring at you, wondering why your family was so desperate as to place you here, wondering why you are so unmarriageable.'

'Well,' said Rilla with a dry laugh, 'with me I suppose they can see without needing to wonder.'

Gwen laughed. She could not help herself. Rilla had been encouraging her all week to laugh when she felt like it, rather than censor herself around her merely because she was blind.

'Ah, a laugh!' Rilla grinned, her pearly eyes moving in Gwen's direction. 'You are finally becoming one of us, then, if you are able to laugh at me and with me. Took you long enough.'

'I have been here only a week!' protested Gwen with a laugh of her own, some of the tension in her stomach dissipating. 'And besides, I have never met a blind lady before.'

'Well, we're not special,' said Rilla with a shrug, placing a bracelet on her wrist. 'Which reminds me—do you have a moment?'

She was proffering a letter she had taken from the pocket of her gown.

Gwen took it. 'And this is…?'

'A letter from my father,' said Rilla, with a coldness Gwen had not expected. 'Summarise it for me, would you?'

Blinking down at it, Gwen's gaze took in a medley of affectionate words.

My darling child…hope to hear from you soon…worried for you…think of you daily…

She swallowed. Not phrases *she* had ever received in a letter from a parent. 'You don't want me to read it?'

Rilla shrugged. 'It's always the same. Never mind, give it here.'

Gwen handed it back wordlessly. Oh, to have a father alive! Or a mother who cared enough to write with such warmth, such love…

'Right, then. Are you adorned and ready to descend?'

Gwen's heart skipped a beat. Her first presentation to the eligible bachelors Miss Pike believed would be suitable for her wallflowers. Would she meet their expectations? Would she disappoint them all? Worse, would it be a repeat of the first official dinner, which Sylvia and the others had told her was such a disaster?

'I suppose we have to go?' The question was rhetorical, really, but Gwen had to ask it. 'We cannot… I don't know… Plead a cold, or a headache, or something?'

'Not if you don't want the Pike swimming up here to discover whether you are feigning,' said Rilla wryly. 'Trust me, once you have been subjected to her battery of enquiries you really do have a headache.'

What had occurred in these walls between these wallflowers before she had arrived?

But she'd had no opportunity to ask questions—not that she would have had the boldness to do so and draw attention to herself. There were plenty of secrets in her own past, after all, that she would rather keep hidden.

She would do anything but have the other wallflowers discover what she had done.

Gwen rose. She had not bothered with jewellery or adornment. This was not the time to hope for pleasant conversation. Her mind was still ringing with the words of the Duke who had knocked her to the ground and then taken her breath away in quite another manner.

The thought of conversation with other gentlemen was quite out of the question.

Chatter in the Academy rose as the wallflowers left their bedchambers and descended the stairs. Gwen's foot almost slipped on the next step. She could hear them. The gentlemen.

Gentlemen. Men.

Men she did not know and who would look at her as a piece of meat. What was it Percy—the Duke—had called it?

'Just a marriage market under a different name.'

A smile drifted across Gwen's face, although she tried not to think about Percy.

He was not wrong.

'There must be a better way for us to meet eligible bachelors,' she breathed.

Rilla laughed. 'Come on, Gwen. Spend more than one minute thinking about that. Can you imagine us at a ball? Some of us can barely talk to gentlemen, and I am hardly a suitable dance partner.'

Gwen's stomach twisted as she missed the last step and almost pulled Rilla down with her. 'I do apologise!'

'You do remember I am the blind one, don't you?' Rilla said with a laugh, straightening her skirts as she stood at the bottom of the staircase.

Gwen smiled weakly and nodded. Then, remembering Rilla would not see her expression, she said, 'Yes, I will try to remember.'

They had halted in the hall, with its impressive landscape paintings oppressive in the dim, candlelit evening. The door to the drawing room was about ten feet away. Laughter. Chatter. Men's voices. Low, deep, and utterly confident.

Something painful tightened across her chest. If only there was anywhere else Gwen could be in this moment… But no, home was not an option. No longer home, no longer a place she was welcome. She would have to resign herself to the corridors and rooms of the Wallflower Academy.

This was now her home, but Gwen knew not for how long.

'There they are,' one of the wallflowers whispered— rather unnecessarily, in Gwen's opinion.

They all stood there, as if unable to step back and unwilling to go forward. Gwen could guess what they were feeling. If it was anything akin to her own feelings it was a painful mixture of embarrassment, fury at being subjected to such a thing, and fear that the reality would be even worse than her imaginings.

'You will be married!'

Gwen's mother's words echoed painfully in her mind— the last thing she had hurled at her daughter before she had stepped into the coach taking her to the Wallflower Academy.

'You are unlikely to win anyone's affections here, Gwen-

doline, and it is time for you to find your own place in the world. Without me, without scandal following you, and without whispers of what you've done. Any misstep, and I warn you...'

I warn you.

Gwen swallowed, tasting the fear on her tongue. It was infuriating to force down all thoughts and her temper— the part of her that seemed most natural. But then, she had seen what that temper could do. She must never let it out again. Not after shouting at the Duke, anyway.

Even if she would be sorely tempted when certain ir- ritating dukes knocked her to the ground.

'It's just a dinner,' Gwen said aloud into the silence of the hall. 'Just food.'

'If that helps you,' said Rilla with a dry laugh. 'Come on. Let's get this over with.'

The drawing room was brilliant with light, compared to the dull hall. Inside, the room Gwen had seen in the comfort of quiet evenings, with silent reading and gentle conversation between the wallflowers, had been transformed.

Miss Pike truly knew what she was doing, Gwen had to admit. The faded furnishings had been improved dramatically with silk hangings, and there were velvet cushions on every sofa and armchair. Elegant books had been placed carefully around the place, as though to emphasise the wallflowers' reading habits, and someone had—surely on purpose—left a half-finished painting of exquisite beauty near the curtains by the bay window.

A bureau had been opened up to reveal a drinks cabinet for the gentlemen, and the pianoforte had been uncovered. A fire was roaring in the grate, and there were more candles in one room than Gwen had ever seen.

They illuminated...right in the centre, surrounded by a

gaggle of chortling gentlemen... Percy Devereux, Duke of Knaresby.

If it had not been for Rilla on her left, Gwen was fairly certain she would have stopped dead in her tracks. Her heart certainly did, and a painful squeeze followed as it tried desperately to return to its rhythm.

But it couldn't. It pattered painfully in her body. And Gwen could do nothing but stare at the tall, dark and grinning gentleman who was watching her with a possessive expression.

Not, not *possessive*. That was surely her imagination.

Nothing could have prepared her for this moment. It was unthinkable—incomprehensible. Had the Duke not had enough of her foolish conversation that afternoon when she had so thoughtlessly walked into him?

Gwen could not take her eyes from him, and after managing a few steps more came to a halt in the drawing room. Rilla halted too, evidently unwilling for quite different reasons to approach the group of gentlemen.

A roaring rushed through her ears and Gwen blinked, just to ensure she was not seeing things.

But she was not. In fact, it was getting worse the longer she stood here. Percy—*the Duke of Knaresby, she must remember that*—was walking over to her, with that same smile on his lips and an imperious look in his eyes.

'Wh-What are you doing here?' Gwen stammered, hating the hesitancy in her voice but unable to do anything about it, trying desperately to forget how she had yearned to see him.

It was ridiculous. What would a duke need the Wallflower Academy for? Surely he had far more interesting evening entertainments to attend?

Percy raised a quizzical eyebrow. 'Why, I am here to see you, of course.'

Heat blossomed up Gwen's décolletage and she hoped beyond hope he had not noticed. But of course he had. Or did she imagine that twinkle in his eye…a little too knowing?

'Who is it?' asked Rilla, her unseeing eyes staring at the gentleman before her. 'At least have the good manners to introduce yourself, man.'

Gwen swallowed. The situation was going from bad to worse, but there was nothing she could do to stop it.

Conversation continued around them in the drawing room…mumbled words Gwen was sure were questions being asked about her.

How did a wallflower on speaking terms with a duke arrive at the Academy?

But she could not do anything about the gossip surely circulating at this very moment. Gwen might appear to be a wallflower, but she had a good enough understanding of decorum to know her duty.

'Your Grace, may I have the honour of presenting to you Miss Marilla Newell?' said Gwen, hardly aware of each word that came out of her mouth.

Percy bowed low and Rilla dipped into a curtsey.

'Miss Newell,' said Gwen, swallowing in an attempt to moisten her mouth. 'May I introduce H-His Grace, Percy Devereux, Duke of Knaresby.'

'Duke of—? Well… Very pleased to make your acquaintance, I'm sure,' said Rilla. 'Very pleased.'

Try as she might, Gwen was unable to keep her eyes from the Duke as he bowed. She wished to goodness she had managed to resist the temptation, for the instant their gazes met he winked.

It was not heat this time, but something rather akin to it that rushed through Gwen's body. A warmth…a prickle of interest—something that drew her to him, pulling a smile across her face against her better judgment.

'Goodness, a duke,' said Rilla conversationally. 'Gwen, why did you bother coming here if you have such a striking circle of acquaintances?'

'I think we are needed over here,' said Sylvia, stepping forward hastily. 'Come on, Rilla. Your servant, Your Grace.'

After dipping the fastest curtesy Gwen had ever seen, Sylvia shepherded Rilla away and left Gwen alone with the handsome Duke.

Not that she thought him handsome. Obviously.

That would be foolish, Gwen told herself, *for he certainly does not consider you any such thing.*

But after convincing herself over the last six days that she had seen the last of the Duke, it was rather discomforting to find him not only at an evening dinner which she would be forced to sit through, but to be accosted by him the moment she entered the room…

'Well, you have made your point, turned up and surprised me,' she said quietly, so only Percy could hear. 'You can go now—back to your companions or back to Town, which is where I suppose you will go.'

'Nonsense,' said Percy briskly. 'I came for dinner, and I am very much looking forward to the conversation of my dinner companion.'

A little of the tension in Gwen's shoulders seeped away at these words. With five wallflowers, and seemingly double the number of gentlemen—the Pike had outdone herself—there was little chance she would be seated beside this particular gentleman, who made her whole body shiver whenever he came close.

A knowing smile teased across Percy's lips. 'I have, of course, applied to Pike to ensure you are seated beside me.'

Gwen's mouth fell open, and she saw with some surprise that the Duke's gaze followed her lower lip. 'You—you haven't?'

His eyes glittered. 'She's my old governess—you didn't know? She thinks my conversation would be good for you.'

Governess? It was rather difficult to picture the Pike anywhere but here. 'Your governess?'

The Duke was prevented from replying by the resounding gong echoing from the hall. Instead, he moved to her side and put out his arm without speaking, a haughty look on his face.

Speaking was not necessary; his meaning was clear. He intended to accompany her into the dining room and she was supposed to be grateful for the honour.

Entering the second official dinner of the Wallflower Academy that Season on the arm of a duke!

Gwen could never have dreamed of such a thing—would never have expected such attentions from any gentleman, let alone one with a title!

But there was something strange about this man. The pomposity was to be expected, she thought dryly, because he was a duke. There was the arrogance she'd always thought dukes would have, the expectation that anyone in his presence should be thanking him on bended knee for paying them any attention whatsoever.

Could there be any more to him than superciliousness?

Percy cleared his throat. Gwen's heart tightened for a moment, but the warmth created by his presence was spreading through her body and she could do nothing but take his arm.

'Thank you,' she said in a small voice.

He nodded.

As they stepped forward together Gwen was conscious of every eye in the room upon her, wallflowers and gentlemen alike. That must account for the strange tingling in her stomach and just below. There could be no other explanation.

And then he hesitated.

She glanced up at Percy. His eyes were roving the table. He was evidently unsure where he should sit.

Unsure? A duke? Did they not always have the greatest precedence?

His hand tightened on hers. 'I… Uh…'

'Over here, Your Grace!' The angelic tones of Miss Pike. She was gesturing to the head of the table. 'Only the best seat for our most esteemed, our most…'

Her words washed in and out of Gwen's ears unheard as Percy resumed his pace and helped her to the seat beside his.

As he did so, the wallflower opposite her picked up a spoon, immediately dropped it with a clatter onto her wine glass, and flushed crimson.

Sylvia leaned past two of the gentlemen without offering either a glance. 'All these wallflowers!'

'Hush!' Miss Pike frowned.

Gwen's stomach turned, but Sylvia merely flashed a grin. 'Rilla and I rather hoped you wouldn't be a true wallflower, Gwen, but I can see by your flush that you're just like them!'

It was all Gwen could do to smile and say nothing. Well, she had managed it, then. In just one week she had put aside her temper and faded into the background. As her mother had always wished.

They sat in silence until the first course was brought out—some sort of soup. Pea soup? Normally Gwen would not care for such a thing, but she eagerly picked up her spoon and began to eat.

If she was eating, she could not be expected to maintain conversation.

'You look very…nice.'

Gwen choked, spewing green soup across the crisp white linen tablecloth. *Nice?*

'Do not tease me,' she said in a low tone.

She was fortunate tonight. Miss Pike had evidently endeavoured to find a few talkative gentlemen, for a pair of them were having a spirited conversation about the latest horse racing at one end of the table, and Sylvia was engaged in a debate on poetry with a man three seats along.

No one seemed to have noticed her shameful soup spurt…although a footman was looking at her rather despairingly.

Surrounded by the noise of the conversation, Gwen glared at the Duke beside her.

'I am not teasing,' said Percy amiably. 'If I was teasing you…'

He put down his spoon and twisted in his seat to face her. Gwen tried to ignore him, to take another mouthful of soup, but her hands did not obey her. Quite contrary to her desire, she also twisted, the better to face the Duke.

His face was a picture of solemnity, and when he spoke it was in a low voice—so low only Gwen could hear him. 'If I was teasing you, I would say you are the most…the most beautiful woman I have ever seen.'

Scalding heat seared Gwen's face.

The cheek! Did he wish to offend her, then? Was this all some game? Some trick to entertain him?

'So that's not true, then?' she asked fiercely. The arrogance of the man!

'Oh, no, it's all true,' said Percy lightly. His eyes did not waver. 'A duke never lies. I just wanted to tease you.'

Gwen swallowed, soup entirely forgotten. How was it possible for a gentleman to make her feel like this? As though…as though her skin was waking up for the first time, tingling, aching for something she did not understand?

She glanced across the table and saw Miss Pike nodding encouragingly at the pair of them. 'You do know what the Pike will think, don't you? Now you've insisted on sitting next to me at dinner, I mean.'

Percy shrugged nonchalantly. Evidently to him the opinions of a woman like Miss Pike were inconsequential. 'Let her think what she wants. I certainly know what *I* want.'

This was ridiculous!

Gwen tried to turn away, but for some reason her body did not wish to comply. On the contrary, it wished to be nearer. Gwen found herself leaning closer, and to her great surprise Percy did not move back.

'This is ridiculous,' she said in an undertone. 'You are a duke and I am—'

'Nothing,' Percy said quietly, all laughter gone from his voice. 'I remember what you said, Gwen. And, despite my turning up here in my best cravat and most elegantly embroidered waistcoat, you are not impressed by me, are you?'

How easily they did it, Gwen thought with a shot of pain through her heart.

The way gentlemen flirted, responded so quickly, with such wit. Just like they did in novels. It was most unfair. She had no knowledge of the world, no knowledge of men or their ways. How was she supposed to spar with him?

'Impressed? No,' Gwen said quietly.

Was that a flash of anger she saw in those commanding eyes? 'Why the devil not?'

'Because you have done nothing impressive, Your Grace, save bearing a title you inherited and did not earn.'

Not for the first time in his presence Gwen raised her hands to her mouth in horror at what she had said. When would she learn that her temper had to be hidden away, never permitted to surface?

Percy did not look offended, but he hardly looked delighted. 'I see.'

'And besides, if…if my father was alive, he would ask you…' Gwen licked her lips as she hesitated, and saw with wonder the flash of desire in Percy's eyes. 'He d-died just a few months ago. Suddenly. He would wonder, as I am, why you, a duke, are noticing a mere commoner like myself?'

'I am asking myself the same question.'

'And he would ask you what your intentions are.'

It was a bold statement, and Gwen could hardly believe she had spoken it. But Percy did not look away. And even though a shiver rushed up Gwen's spine, she did not break the connection either.

'Well,' said Percy, 'if your father was alive, I would tell him.'

She laughed—and immediately clapped her hands over her mouth as most of those at the table looked at her.

It took a moment—it seemed an age—but eventually they all returned either to their soup or their conversations.

Except one.

Percy was chuckling under his breath. 'You are not really a wallflower, are you?'

Well, perhaps this is rather enjoyable, Gwen thought as she took in the handsome, strong jaw of this man who seemed unable to leave her alone.

Why not flirt with a duke? It would certainly not lead anywhere. She could consider it practice. A distraction.

'And you?' she said lightly. 'Are you really a duke? I only have your word for it, after all.'

Gwen had thought her remark rather witty, but it had a most unexpected effect on the gentleman. A shadow swept over his face, and a flash of anger, of fury, and for the first time since they had been seated at the table he looked away.

'I apologise,' Gwen said quickly. Whatever she had said, she had clearly offended him.

Percy laughed dryly. 'You do not know what you are apologising for. Do you?'

It was too much. Gwen was all at sea in their conversation—which always seemed to be the case whenever she was in the company of the Duke of Knaresby. Percy did something to her—something she could not understand but could only guess at.

She liked him. She was attracted to him. She found him most irresistible, even if his manners were incorrigible and his conversation haughty. Was this why she was acting so strangely...as though drawn like a moth to a flame?

'No,' Gwen said helplessly. 'I do not. I am sorry.'

Somehow that was the right answer. A teasing smile on his lips, Percy reached towards her and took her hand in his.

Gwen almost gasped aloud as he raised it to his lips and kissed the very tips of her fingers. Oh, to feel those lips, to feel the warmth of them... The pooling desire in her body was crying out for it. Such a simple movement, yet one so heightened with promise of more.

'Gwendoline Knox,' said Percy quietly, her hand still in his, 'when I make you do something that requires an apology, you will really need to mean it.'

Chapter Four

'Then I realised it was in my pocket the entire time! Reminds me of the time I went hunting with Buxhill and Lindham—you know them, of course? Fine gentlemen, but not so good with a horse. Did I ever tell you where I got my filly from? Lovely ride, really pleasant manner—though when I first purchased her naturally...'

Percy's chin almost touched his chest and he jerked up, sleep swiftly pushed back. Never mind that the impending slumber would have been appreciated, it would not do to be seen napping while Westerleigh chatted away at White's.

That was the trouble with the gentlemen's club, Percy thought, as he nodded vaguely at whatever the old boy was saying and leaned forward to pick up his cup of tea. It was cold.

White's was all very well—a sterling establishment, and he wouldn't hear a word against it—and yet... There was just something rather old-fashioned about it. Percy glanced about the Blue Drawing Room, where he had settled himself not an hour ago. Decorated in the finest furnishings the seventeen-seventies could lavishly permit, there was a rather tired air about the place. The leather was worn to skin in some places on the armchairs, and each of the little tables upon which the gentlemen rested their cups—tea, whisky, or other—were chipped.

In truth, Percy thought, stretching in an attempt not to show Westerleigh that he was bored by his monologue, there was nothing interesting at White's. When it boiled down to it—and the meat here was dreadfully boiled—it was all about the people one interacted with.

And when one of them was Westerleigh…

A yawn threatened to reveal his boredom, but Percy managed to stifle it just as a gap appeared in the conversation. 'Yes, indeed,' he said.

The Earl of Westerleigh nodded pompously, evidently unaware that his dull monologue was putting his companion to sleep. 'And, of course, there was nothing for it but to continue! When I spoke to the man in question, he told me…'

Percy could not have recounted precisely what this anecdote was about for love nor money, having totally lost the train of the conversation, but that was rather an advantage. It left him free to think about a more pleasant topic.

Like Miss Gwendoline Knox, for example, and the way candlelight illuminated her face when she was embarrassed—or aroused.

Percy swallowed, but saw that old Westerleigh hadn't a clue. No one in the place was listening to a word he said, and he had not noticed that his young companion had quite another thing on his mind.

A young lady with dark, almost black hair curling around her bright, expressive eyes. Eyes that had danced with confusion and mischief as they had conversed at that Wallflower Academy dinner.

And to think he nearly hadn't attended.

Percy dreaded to think how he might have spent that evening talking to some of his mother's dull friends, listening to dull tales like Westerleigh's, eating dull food…

Instead he had been treated to the most delightful display of restrained irritation he had ever seen. Why, if they had been alone, Percy was willing to bet Gwen would have walloped him for the things he had said—and quite rightly, too, in some cases.

'Gwendoline Knox, when I make you do something that requires an apology, you will really need to mean it.'

He shivered at the very thought. Oh, the things he would like to do to Gwendoline Knox… It was almost criminal, how delectable she was. Far more interesting than old Westerleigh, though Percy was not so unpolitic as to say so.

It was strange, though. Any other Thursday in Town, Percy would have expected some of his acquaintances to be here—rather than this old friend of his father who was boring him at present, his moustache bristling in the almost continuous speech.

'I thought to meself, *This is it, young chap!* Of course in those days gentlemen had far more opportunities for adventure—none of this Grand Tour nonsense you chaps dally with. No, it was to war for me, and I discovered to my surprise…'

Percy nodded. On any other day Westerleigh's new topic might have lifted him out of his listlessness, but not today.

No, unless a certain lady walked into White's, with a delicate air and a fierce temper…

Percy was smiling—a most uncommon occurrence in White's. One did not come here to be entertained. One came to escape the world. The trouble was, he did not particularly wish to escape the world today. At least, not one particular part of it.

Not that he should.

He folded his hands firmly in his lap, as though that would prevent him from being rash. It wasn't *his* reputation, after all, that would be harmed. It would be Gwen's.

Their unequal stations, her innocence, his lack of honourable intentions…

Gwen would take a great risk in just being seen speaking to him, Percy knew. The censure of Society… But then, he would risk the wrath of his mother. It was almost the same thing.

'And then I—Knaresby, old thing. Where are you going?' Westerleigh blinked in surprise.

Percy pulled his coat straight and nodded politely to the older man. 'Duty calls, my dear chap.'

'Ah… Well, duty and all that,' said the older gentleman comfortably, reaching for the glass of brandy which had been refilled subtly, without request, by a footman as soon as it had been emptied. 'Quite understand.'

Percy was impressed—because he certainly didn't understand. He could not comprehend why he was walking out of White's at this early hour, why he was instructing his man to ready his horse, and why he was directing that horse out of Town.

'Your Grace?'

In fact, he—

'Your Grace? Devereux?'

Percy halted. Of course. *He* was 'Your Grace'. It was still taking a bit of getting used to.

The demure words had been spoken by a footman in White's colours, his hands clasped together before him almost as a supplicant.

What on earth did he want?

'Yes?' Percy prompted.

The footman smiled awkwardly. 'It is only… I need to speak to your steward, Your Grace.'

Percy blinked. 'My steward?'

What on earth for? There had never been any need for his steward to be involved in his White's membership.

The footman inclined his head. 'To organise your bill, Your Grace. 'Tis a small matter...'

'Oh, that's easy enough,' said Percy, his shoulders relaxing. 'You had me worried there! Here, how much is my tab?'

He pulled his pocketbook from inside his jacket, and saw with surprise that the footman looked genuinely flummoxed.

'I... You... Your steward,' muttered the man. He cleared his throat. 'Dukes do not carry money!'

Heat flushed Percy's cheeks. 'They...they don't?'

No one had told him that. But then, there were so many hidden rules, weren't there? So many things others just seemed to do without thinking, as easily as breathing.

Whereas every breath he took was a determined gasp.

'I must speak with your steward,' the footman said firmly, carefully avoiding looking at the pound notes in Percy's hands. 'That is the proper way of doing things.'

Proper way of doing things? *Well, that's as may be,* Percy thought, as he gave his steward's name to the clearly embarrassed footman.

James wouldn't have allowed a mere servant to talk to him like that—make him feel the fool. Besides, he had never been one to enjoy 'the proper way' of doing things. Not before the title, not after.

Why else, he thought as the autumnal air whipped past him, chilling his ears and giving him a greater desire to arrive, *would I be so intrigued by Gwen?*

Why else would he be arriving unannounced at the Wallflower Academy?

It was not so far out of London that a visit was unwarranted or surprising, but as far as he knew there were no planned events this afternoon. No teas, no music recitals, no card games, no dinner—and certainly no ball.

A wry smile slipped across Percy's face as he surveyed

the old manor house as it appeared around a corner. That was a thought... Gwen at a ball.

Miss Knox.

He really needed to remember the bounds of propriety, Percy reminded himself as he slipped off his horse and handed over the reins to a stableboy who had rushed forward.

He might have called Gwen by her first name at the dinner, and he might have looked as though he wished to slowly unwrap each and every piece of her clothing, wanted to kiss every inch of her skin...

But that didn't mean he was going to do anything foolish. Except turn up here unannounced, of course.

His knock on the front door of the Wallflower Academy was therefore accidental. He had not meant to do it. His feet had just meandered to the door, and now he was there it seemed ridiculous not to knock.

Precisely what he intended to do, Percy was not sure. His thoughts were not forming properly. For some reason his heart was thumping loudly. He could hear it in his ears, feel the tight pressure in his chest.

When a footman finally answered the door, Percy astonished himself and the servant by barking, 'Gwen!'

The footman blinked. 'I beg your pardon, Your Grace?'

Percy shifted on his feet, as though that might help him remember both his manners and his senses.

You are not falling in love with a mere wallflower, he told himself sternly. *After everything you have been through to get here, you do not need any complication. You know the sort of woman you must marry. You know the criteria. You are just being polite. You are visiting the Academy. You could be visiting any of them.*

The array of wallflowers currently in residence at the Academy rushed through his mind.

Perhaps not. None of them attracted him as Gwen did. None of them drove a need in him…a want that was starting to affect his judgment.

Percy jutted out his jaw imperiously—or at least as imperiously as he could muster. 'I thought I would visit the wallflowers.'

This was evidently an unusual statement. The footman looked a little concerned, and swallowed hard before saying, 'Is…is there an invitation upon your person, Your Grace, that I could see?'

'Invitation?' repeated Percy, completely bemused. 'What would I need an invitation for?'

'Well, you see, it's a matter of…of delicacy,' muttered the footman, his boldness deserting him. 'Having gentlemen in the house unaccompanied…'tis not right…'

Percy cleared his throat, but said nothing.

The man had a point.

Miss Pike had probably created the rule after a difficult situation. One that should certainly not have occurred. A scandalous one. Involving a wallflower and a rake, no doubt.

Someone entirely different from him.

'I think, in the circumstances, you can make an exception,' Percy said, smiling and taking a step forward.

It was a step he had to immediately retract, as the footman did not budge.

'Circumstances, Your Grace?'

The man knew him and yet was determined to refuse him access! The blackguard!

'I am a duke,' Percy said pointedly.

'And I am a footman,' said the footman stoutly, not looking Percy in the eye, but rather gazing at something just beyond his left shoulder. 'I know my place, and I am sorry to say, Your Grace, my place is in here and yours is out there. Unless you have an invitation...'

Percy stared at the man helplessly. Foiled—and by a footman. no less! It was most infuriating. Just beyond this man was a woman who was bold and brash and a wall-flower. She was also shy, and a multitude of complexities Percy had still to understand.

And once he understood her he could leave her alone and get back to his primary goal this Season: finding a wife.

It was simple as that.

Understand Gwen, then leave her.

The twist in his stomach told Percy he was attempting to fool himself, but he ignored it and instead directed all his ire towards the unfortunate footman before him.

'Miss Pike,' Percy said in a cold tone, 'will hear about this.'

The servant drew himself up. 'I hope so, Your Grace.'

Muttering curses under his breath against servants in general and footmen in particular, Percy turned away from the man and walked down the steps.

It was galling to be so close to Gwen and yet be unable to see her...

A slow smile crept over Percy's face as he stepped to-wards the stables and he halted in his tracks. If he skirted around the other side of the house—not towards the stables but towards the orangery—there was a very real chance he would be able to see her.

But that would be a foolish thing to do. Something only a lovesick mule would do. Percy knew better. He would get his horse and ride straight home. That would be the sensible thing to do.

Stepping lightly across the gravel, and hoping the drat-ted footman was not watching, Percy crept away from the stables and towards the westerly side of the house where the large orangery stood. A little dilapidated now, it none-theless offered a perfect view into the dining room and the drawing room of the house.

Surely Gwen would be in one of those at this time of day…?

Highly conscious that he had no idea whatsoever what the wallflowers imprisoned inside the Academy found to fill their time, Percy crept through a rather cumbersome hedge and across a border, ruffling a rose.

Soon he found himself at one end of the orangery.

And was rewarded.

Looking through the orangery and into the room be-yond, Percy could make out Gwen and the other wallflow-ers, evidently having a lesson in dinner etiquette.

They were all seated at the dining room table with places set and a plethora of knives and forks before them. An irate-looking Miss Pike was striding up and down, de-livering a monologue perhaps not unlike the one he had been subjected to by Westerleigh.

The reactions of the wallflowers, at least, looked the same as his. From where Percy was standing, it appeared that the black wallflower—Sylvia, wasn't it?—was try-ing to stifle giggles.

Percy smiled as he watched Gwen attempting to pay attention despite the obvious tedium.

How had a woman like Gwen ended up in a place like this?

True, she was shy—but there was a real temper under that hesitancy. Her beauty, her conversation… It did not seem possible that Gwen could not find a match. Percy was cer-tainly finding her far more interesting than he should be…

He gasped. Gwen had looked up, right into his eyes, her gaze fierce, sharp, as though she had heard his thought. As though she had not approved of it.

Taking a hurried step backwards, Percy felt his foot slip on some mud, toppling him to the ground. The wind knocked out of him, he gazed up at the gloomy grey sky and wondered what it was about this woman she managed to cause someone to be tipped to the ground every time they came near to each other.

When he'd managed to right himself, brushing off as much mud as possible, Percy looked up to see Gwen red-faced and the other wallflowers giggling around the table.

Blast. He had obviously embarrassed not only himself, but Gwen too.

What had overcome him? Bringing him to the Wallflower Academy without an invitation, skulking around like a common cad, slipping over with shock when a mere glance met his eye?

He was a damned duke! He had responsibilities—duties in Town unable to be ignored. So why was he here, pulled towards this woman?

It was a question Percy could not answer, but he would soon need to.

After exchanging a few words with Miss Pike, Gwen rose, curtsied, then started towards him.

Oh, hell. What was he supposed to say? How was he supposed to explain why a duke was hiding in hedges and falling beside orangeries, all to see a wallflower he must not pursue?

'Well,' said Gwen quietly, opening the door of the or-angery and leaning against the doorframe. 'You seem to have made your acquaintance with the ground.'

Percy glared. How did she do it? There was no malice in her tone, no coquettish teasing as he had learned to ex-pect from eligible young ladies. Instead, Gwen appeared to be…earnest. Honest. It was a strange thing to see in a lady of marriageable age, and Percy found himself rather undone by the entire experience.

'I… I fell,' he snapped.

By Jove, he needed to gather his thoughts and tame his tongue, or he would be making even more of a fool of himself than he already had!

The damp from his fall had started to seep through his breeches.

'Yes, I saw,' said Gwen, still quietly.

There was mischief in her eyes, but it was held back by a reticence Percy did not quite understand.

'There is a front door, you know. I've walked through it myself. 'Tis not too arduous.'

Percy forced himself to speak. 'I wasn't permitted entry.'

Gwen stared. 'Goodness, why on earth not?'

He shrugged, as though that explained the situation. When it became apparent from Gwen's waiting expression that it did not, Percy tried to make the entire thing far more impressive than it actually was.

'I was forbidden entry because…because it was believed the place would not be safe with me in it,' he said, waving an arm expressively. 'That you wallflowers would not be safe with me. Have to fight me off with a stick, I suppose.'

Gwen's cheeks flushed scarlet and she glanced behind her, presumably at someone carefully listening in. Decorum had to be upheld. They could not be alone.

It was instantaneous. He'd crossed a line—some line Percy had had no idea was there—and she'd closed herself off.

The mischievous air was gone, replaced only by the demeanour of a quiet, uninterested wallflower.

'Well, I will say good day, then,' said Gwen, and moved to shut the door.

'Wait!' Percy acted on instinct, his desire to impress disappearing, subsumed by the need to keep her with him.

He looked down. He had placed his hand on hers, and even through his riding glove he could once again sense that strange, yet enjoyable tingling that typically preceded one of his beddings.

Percy was no innocent. He did not have to wonder what this meant. He wanted her—badly. Needed to know every inch of her…to tease pleasure from those lips now parting in wonder at his presumption in touching her. Then he'd leave her behind.

But Gwen did not know that—and it was best she never knew. Percy might take the pleasures of courtesans, but he was not one to take the innocence of a wallflower—not one under the protection of a lady as fearsome as Miss Pike, anyway.

Carefully, and slowly, as though any sudden movement might break the connection between them, Percy removed his hand and moved back.

'Your Grace, I do not understand why—'

'Come with me.'

Gwen's eyes widened, her breath catching in her throat, and Percy stepped towards her, his desire to dominate her will forcing him forward. He wanted to see the change in her as she spoke. Not just hear her words, but sense the change in her breath, feel the heat of her skin.

'I… I beg your pardon?' Gwen whispered.

'On a ride,' Percy said high-handedly. 'I have my mare here, and I am sure there are horses in the Academy's stables. Come with me. On a ride.'

For a heady moment he thought he had convinced her. Gwen examined him, her eyes appraising, and Percy felt scrutinised as never before. What was she looking for? Trustworthiness? A sense of his being a rake?

She would find both—and more besides, Percy thought with a wry smile. But what he was far more interested in was what *he* would find when spending more time with her.

Gwen Knox. There was something about her…something he could not put his finger on though he very much wished to. Something she was hiding. Something more than was natural for a wallflower.

Something that one day he would uncover.

'No,' she said firmly, though her lips curled into a smile. 'You are jesting with me.'

'I am not jesting with you,' said Percy, piqued at her immediate refusal. 'Come riding with me.'

'You came all this way from Town to ask me to go on a ride?'

'I came all this way to see you.'

Percy could think of no better way to put it. It was the truth. She had drawn him here inexorably, against his better judgement and seemingly against the wishes of the footman who guarded the door.

But he was here, and so was she.

Gwen had had no need to leave her lesson to speak with him—she had chosen to do that of her own volition. She wanted him. Percy could sense it.

The fact was it was absolutely impossible—foolish, even—for a duke and a wallflower to be conversing like this…

Well, Percy would deal with his conscience later.

'Do you not need to marry a woman of—of good fortune and connections?'

Percy blanched. The bold question from Gwen had come from nowhere, her words clear and without malice.

And she was right.

Percy wished to contradict her immediately, tell her that

his choices were his own, and he could wed—or bed—whomever he wished.

But it would be a lie. A boldfaced lie and one she would discover soon enough. Gwen had seen the need in him. For Percy certainly did need to find a wife with a dowry and a good reputation.

Needed to far more than she could ever realise.

'I see the truth in your eyes, you know. You cannot hide it.'

'I…' Percy said, but words failed him.

This was ridiculous—words never failed him. He was a master at wit and at wooing, but when it came to Gwen… she undid him. It was most unfair, for he had never wished to impress anyone more.

'Well, when you work out the answer,' said Gwen gently, 'come and tell me. I cannot help but feel, Your Grace, you are teasing yourself far more than you are teasing me. Good day.'

And with that she closed the door of the orangery and returned not merely to her seat in the dining room, but further into the Academy and out of sight.

Percy leaned heavily against the glass of the orangery—then hastily stood as it made an awful creaking sound.

This woman was going to be the death of him.

How had Gwen put it?

'Least likely to win a duke.'

Percy shook his head with a smile. *Least likely?* That was not precisely how he would have put it.

Chapter Five

Monday slid into Tuesday, which was very much like Wednesday, and before Gwen knew it she had been at the Wallflower Academy almost two weeks.

Days repeated each other in the same tired, dull routine she was already accustomed to, and it was difficult to see how some of the other wallflowers, who had been resident in the place for months, if not years, suffered such boredom.

Breakfast, and then a little light reading was expected from all the wallflowers—but not too much. Gwen had been subjected to a lecture one day from Miss Pike, on how too much reading was wont to make a woman a bluestocking.

'And if there is one thing worse than a wallflower,' the indefatigable Miss Pike had said sternly, 'it is a bluestocking.'

Gwen had spotted out of the corner of her eye a particularly irritated scowl, but no one had been bold enough to contradict the owner of the Wallflower Academy.

Which was probably all to the good. Gwen had no desire to bring attention to herself, or to challenge the fearsome Pike and have even a hint of a suggestion of returning home to her mother.

Not after the chaos she had endured at home. She had left that behind. She would never face that again.

After breakfast and light reading came lessons—something Gwen was resigned to.

Lessons. The Academy made her feel as if she was back in the schoolroom, learning her alphabet and practising her handwriting, but these lessons were irritatingly childish.

Small talk and conversation. Napkin folding. Disagreeing with one's conversational partner. Using forks and spoons. Walking with one's head at the correct angle. The appropriate way to speak of the weather. Identifying a person's rank at a distance. Music appreciation.

If Gwen had had anywhere else to go, she would have packed her things and been off within three days of arriving at the austere Academy.

By Thursday afternoon, several days after Percy—the Duke of Knaresby…she really must remember to give him his correct title—had arrived so strangely at the Wallflower Academy and played some sort of jest upon her at the orangery, Gwen could not remove his words from her mind.

'Come riding with me.'

If she was truly so desirous of leaving, Gwen thought painfully, as she sat in silence in the quiet of the afternoon with the other wallflowers, some reading, some embroidering, Rilla just gazing sightlessly into space, then why had she not accepted Percy's invitation?

A ride… Something she had forgone since she had left home. An opportunity to see some of the countryside about the place. More, a chance to leave the confines of the Wallflower Academy for more than five minutes in the garden.

It would have been heavenly.

It would have been glorious.

It would have been far too much of a temptation to bear.

Which was why Gwen was rather surprised to find herself bundled into a dog cart at this awful time in the morning.

It was all Sylvia's fault, of course.

'Sylvia, what on earth is this about?' Gwen had asked, yawning, after being dragged out of bed by Sylvia, who had already been dressed. She had got into her own gown and been pulled down the servants' staircase to this dog cart waiting by the side of the Academy. 'Have you lost your senses?'

She certainly had.

The morning air was freezing, and Gwen's mind had whirled at such an unexpected turn of events.

What was Sylvia thinking?

Sylvia's expression was sharp and determined. 'I'm not staying here to rot for ever. I don't care what the Pike says. I'm not going to be married off, and my parents won't take me back—not my father, at any rate.'

Gwen tried to follow her rapid words. 'But that doesn't explain—'

'I'm running away,' Sylvia pronounced proudly. 'On!'

The dog cart jerked forward as Gwen attempted to take in the words just spoken. Running away?

'So what am I doing here with you?' It was all she could manage.

The day was so early, her breath blossomed before them.

Sylvia grinned. 'You're no wallflower.'

Gwen swallowed. 'Y-yes, I am.'

The lie tasted bitter, but she had no choice. She could not be found out. She had to fade into the background and—

'No, you're not,' Sylvia said, quite calmly, leaning back in the dog cart as if she frequently drove such a conveyance. 'And though that place is no prison, let's be honest. Our families don't want us. They can call it an academy as much as they want, but it's just a place where unwanted daughters are left and abandoned.'

Gwen tried to think of words to counter Sylvia's argument, but she could not. Was she herself not a perfect example of this?

'No, the whole world is out there, and I am tired of being treated like a child, ordered about by the Pike as though I have no idea what I'm doing,' Sylvia said firmly.

'And so…a dog cart?' asked Gwen helplessly. 'And abducting me, I suppose? Is that the plan?'

Sylvia's grin was bold. 'All part of the plan. You can get out, if you prefer, but I thought you'd be interested in getting out of this place.'

Gwen's gaze flickered up to the tall manor house slowly disappearing into the distance.

She had no wish to be there, it was true. But where else could she go?

And Sylvia was no fool. Though she had not shared the information, she must have a plan. They must be meeting someone, wherever they were going. She must have some family who would take her.

Gwen sighed. 'This is ridiculous.'

'This is an adventure!' beamed Sylvia. 'Finally!'

It did not feel like much of an adventure when the dog cart brought them to a loud, noisy and most definitely stench-filled street. There were countless people meandering up and down, carts, dogs, a man on a horse, a woman leaning out of a window shouting something…

It was overwhelming. Intoxicating.

And the dog cart had disappeared into the melee.

'Is…is this London?' Gwen asked in wonder.

Sylvia snorted. 'This place? No, just a small town where I thought I could find…'

Her voice trailed away and Gwen narrowed her eyes. 'I thought you had a plan.'

'I did,' Sylvia said, though her defiance was lacking now. 'I planned to leave the Wallflower Academy. Now I have—'

'Sylvia Bryant, you have no idea what to do next, do you?' Gwen said, with dawning comprehension and panic rising in her chest.

She was in a strange town she'd never heard of, with a woman with no plan at all, no luggage, no money—what on earth were they going to do?

The panic started to solidify into shame. Her mother had ordered her to be obedient and not to draw any attention to herself! And here she was, bound to get into trouble with the Pike when they got back.

If they could get back…

Sylvia looked wretched. 'I… Well, I didn't expect it to be so—'

'No one wants us, Sylvia,' Gwen found herself saying, the shame and panic mingling to bring her temper out. 'We're at the Academy because we have nowhere else to go! It's not a prison if you have no alternative!'

Sylvia's cheeks were reddening. 'I never said—'

'Gwen? Sylvia?'

Against all the odds, a voice was calling their names— a voice that came from a coach.

Gwen's stomach twisted as a face appeared in the window of that coach. Of all the people—

'What are you doing here?' asked Percy brightly.

Her heart skipped a beat. This was most untoward— what on earth was *he* doing here? And how was she supposed to explain?

'It's your duke, Gwen!' Sylvia said eagerly. 'My word, do you think he could take us—?'

'He'll take us straight back to the Academy, and you

must pray the Pike hasn't noticed our absence,' Gwen said, far more firmly than she felt.

If they were lucky, they could slip back in and pretend the whole thing had never happened.

As long as Percy could be trusted to keep his mouth shut...

A lopsided lazy grin slipped over the Duke's face as he clambered out of his carriage. 'I didn't think to see you here!'

His words were directed at Gwen, who refused to meet his eye. It was going to be painful, asking him this, but—

'Can we have a lift?' Sylvia asked cheerfully.

Gwen blinked. How did she do it? Speak so boldly, without any care, to a duke?

'Sylvia,' she hissed under her breath. 'I think—'

'Oh, I'm more than happy to take you back to the Academy,' said Percy, though his gaze was firmly fixed not on Sylvia, but on Gwen. She could feel the intensity of his gaze even without looking up. 'Come on. I'll—'

'I don't think so, Y'Grace.'

Gwen looked up. A man's voice had spoken—one she did not recognise. Now she had looked up, she could see it was Percy's driver.

He looked a little embarrassed, but it was nothing to the surprise on Percy's face. 'Why in heaven's not?' he asked.

'Well, because...because dukes don't pick women up off the street,' said the shamefaced driver. 'Not in daylight, anyway.'

Heat blossomed across Gwen's chest. Was the man insinuating—?

'This duke does,' Percy said firmly, offering a hand to Sylvia. 'A gentleman always rescues a lady, my man, and in this case there are two. Gwen?'

She had no choice but to accept his hand into the coach.

Settling beside Sylvia, Gwen gave her a stern look that received nothing but a grin in reply—and then Percy himself seated himself in the carriage.

'You're running away, aren't you?' he asked conversationally.

Before Gwen could do anything, Sylvia nodded blithely. 'Gwen tried to stop me, but I was determined.'

'Yes, I can see that,' said Percy softly.

Gwen looked at her hands, clasped together in her lap, as the carriage jerked forward.

This was outrageous! It was all Sylvia's fault—running away, indeed—and Percy would never let her hear the end of it, she was sure. Why, he would—

'I think it's best,' came Percy's quiet voice, 'if we say no more about it. We'll be at the Academy in less than twenty minutes, and you can slip back in. It's still early.'

Gwen swallowed, and managed to force herself to look up in gratitude.

Her breath caught in her throat. How did he look like... like *that*?

As though it was his greatest pleasure to rescue her.

As though he had hoped for nothing more when he awoke that morning.

As though spending just a few stolen minutes with her, even in the company of Sylvia, was a gift she could have bestowed upon no more grateful recipient.

Gwen forced herself to breathe. She was seeing far more in that look than existed, she was sure.

And he was right. In an inordinately swift amount of time the Academy could be seen through the carriage window, and Sylvia's shoulders had slumped.

'Not a word,' Gwen said firmly as the carriage came to a halt.

And, most surprisingly, Sylvia obeyed.

The two of them said nothing to Percy as they descended from his carriage, nothing to each other as they slipped through a side door and walked the familiar route to the drawing room, and nothing to the wallflowers who looked up curiously as they entered.

Gwen stepped over to an empty seat after retrieving her embroidery from the box. Her heart was thundering as she pulled out her needle and examined her progress.

What a disaster the morning might have been!

'Miss Knox?'

Besides, Gwen told herself firmly, her gaze drifting over the crimson thread slowly forming a rose on the embroidery hoop between her fingers, *a carriage ride with a duke is not simple. And it was Sylvia's fault, entirely.*

And it meant something. She was sure it did. If not to her, then to Percy. Certainly to the Pike, if she ever found out.

'Miss Knox!'

Startled, Gwen dropped her embroidery hoop. It slipped to the floor with a low *thunk*, and after she'd leaned down to pick it up the mirage of the Pike before her did not disappear.

'Miss Knox, you do not attend!'

Gwen swallowed. It was one of the most common critiques she had to endure from the sharp eyes of Miss Pike: not attending.

As though it was that easy.

As though she could force from her mind the face of Percy Devereux.

As though she could forget the way he had spoken to her at the dinner, the way he had held her hand, skin to skin, something Gwen had never done with any gentleman before.

As though she could pretend she had not seen him that morning.

Their connection was something she longed for. A connection which drew something out of her she did not understand. Yet she knew where it led…

Oh, she knew.

'Yes, Miss Pike,' Gwen said hastily, conscious that the owner of the Wallflower Academy was waiting for a response. 'I do apologise, Miss Pike. I was thinking about… about the next rose.'

'Rose?' Miss Pike raised an eyebrow.

Gwen lifted her embroidery. 'Yellow or white?'

For a moment Miss Pike glared, as though attempting to discover whether there was an impertinence somewhere in the wallflower's remark.

Eventually it appeared she could find none. She sniffed. 'White. There is a letter for you.'

Her hand shot out and Gwen stared at the letter within it. Cheap paper and no seal—just a dot of sealing wax. Her heart sank, all hopes that it might have been a note from a certain gentleman disappearing in an instant.

There was only one person that letter could be from.

'You know, Miss Knox, I believe you are doing well in your comportment classes,' said Miss Pike stiffly, as though it physically pained her to say something pleasant.

Sylvia was seated behind Miss Pike, and Gwen saw her grin, and then make a silly face behind the older woman's back. Gwen stifled a laugh. She would not permit Sylvia to get her into trouble, no matter the inducement. Not even when she had dragged Gwen into a dog cart to run away from the Academy.

'But I wish you would try harder in your dining etiquette,' continued Miss Pike, a creasing frown appearing between her grey eyes. 'Really…disappearing off in the last fork lesson… I was most displeased.'

Gwen swallowed. Percy's face swam into view—that

teasing smile, that shamed expression when he'd been caught slipping over in the mud by the orangery.

He was a delight.

He was a torment.

He was a duke. Certainly not someone she should be thinking of.

'Yes,' said Gwen quietly, taking the letter from Miss Pike's hand and choosing not to comment on the negative remark. 'Thank you for your kind words, Miss Pike.'

If possible, the Pike's frown deepened as she examined her, and Gwen did not attempt to hold her gaze. It would be a fruitless task. Not only because her natural shyness did not permit it, but because Miss Pike clearly had decades of practice in fearsome gazes.

Gwen's gaze slipped instead to the roses in the embroidery in her hands, one complete, one half finished, the other a mere outline. She swallowed hard, forcing down the remembrance of that strange encounter.

What had Percy been thinking? Sneaking around the side of the Academy, looking in at them from the orangery, and then saying such strange things to her—almost flirting with her. As though she was a prize to be won, a lady to be courted, a prospective bride...

The thought was unconscionable. No gentleman would consider her a worthy match, Gwen was sure. No dowry, no real family name, no spirit or conversation to recommend her.

Only a temper which, once unleashed, could be deadly.

Her throat was dry, and no matter how many times she swallowed Gwen could not regain her composure.

She was being ridiculous.

Likely as not, dukes flirted with anything that moved. She was not special. She had not attracted him for any particular reason.

She was here because it had been impossible for her to remain at home after the scandal.

But that did not explain why he had come here, all the way from London, a full twenty-minute ride. Gwen could not comprehend it. Surely he would be inundated with invitations for parties and concerts, opportunities to visit Court, to see old friends and make new acquaintances…

What did it all mean?

'I see you have made quite an impression on the Duke of Knaresby.'

Gwen's eyes snapped back to Miss Pike, whose frown had disappeared and been replaced by an expression she could not place for a moment.

Then it became clear. Greed. Of course.

Miss Pike would be well rewarded by my Mother, Gwen thought darkly, *if she marries me off to a duke.*

It would be quite a coup for the Wallflower Academy. She doubted whether anything so wild had ever occurred in the place.

'I think you have done well with him so far, Miss Knox,' said Miss Pike calmly, utterly unable to see the flush on her charge's face—or simply ignoring it. 'I would have had you pegged as the least likely to win a duke. But I believe more conversation is required to hook him. You will need to put in more effort.'

Gwen could hardly believe those words were being spoken—and in the drawing room before all the other wallflowers, too! She could only see Sylvia and Rilla's expressions, to be sure, but if they were indicative of the others' she would soon be under a most direct interrogation.

'I cannot… I will not… I do not believe the Duke will be returning,' Gwen managed.

At least she was almost certain those words had come out of her mouth. She had intended them to do so.

'Nonsense,' said Miss Pike cheerfully. 'I will ensure he receives every invitation.'

If only she had a little bravery, a little determination—anything to force her mouth to move and her thoughts to pour into the conversation. If only she could make it clear to Miss Pike that she had no desire whatsoever to see Percy—the Duke—again.

Except she did.

Gwen could not lie to herself, even if she wished to lie to others. Seeing Percy was the only potential event of interest on her horizon—a horizon that stretched out seemingly for ever, littered with boring lessons, dull afternoon teas, insipid conversations at dinner and nothing else.

Nothing until she found a husband.

But she never would.

Gwen could confide in no one at the Academy—not yet. But she did not need the opinion of others to know that her secret would be ruinous to any potential husband, let alone a duke.

She would not put Percy and his family name through such scandal.

Not, Gwen thought hastily, her cheeks searing with heat, *that Percy was even considering her in such a manner.*

This was all Miss Pike's fantasy. She wished to see something that was not there, Gwen told herself firmly. It was not. At least, not from his side.

Miss Pike sighed. 'Why do you not go outside, Miss Knox, and read your letter there? I believe you are in great need of fresh air…you look most flushed.'

It was all she could do to nod mutely, rise, place her embroidery on her seat, and leave the room without falling over. As she stepped away the room spun, which to Gwen's mind was most unhelpful. And each step was a leaden beat against the drum of her own heart, which did not appear to be beating properly.

'You look most flushed.'

Well, it was no wonder she looked flushed. As Gwen opened the front door and stepped into the blessed cool of the afternoon's autumnal air, she tried not to think of Miss Pike's critique, her words of encouragement in Percy's direction, the gaze of all the other wallflowers and, worst of all, the letter in her hand.

The letter she knew she would have to read.

Gwen walked around the house, past the orangery, the sight of which at least tugged her lips into a wry smile, and continued across the lawn towards the ornamental gardens. The one just before the kitchen garden had a nook she had made her own, between a corner of the redbrick walls and a growing evergreen tree which gave her protection from the wind.

It was there, on a small bench which must have been placed there at least a decade ago, if the growing moss upon it was anything to go by, that Gwen seated herself and slowly cracked open the sealing wax to unfold the letter.

It was, as she had expected, from her mother. It was short, cruel, and to the point. Just like every one of the almost daily letters she was receiving.

Gwendoline,

Goodness, I have never been so entertained in all my life as when the Crawfords come to visit. Their company is most welcome now that I have removed you from the house, and their son pays me such flattering compliments—nothing, of course, my dear Walter could complain at, and in fairness it appears there is little gentlemen of real taste can do in my presence but praise it.

Why, I had to be quite forceful with the Major just last week when he kissed my hand, and in public too! I soon put him to rights, but I am sorry to say it only seems to have increased his passion.

That is the benefit of marrying a man like Walter. He recognises that my beauty cannot be diminished by his affections. I really was the most fortunate of ladies to have snared him.

The inn is doing well, though you did not ask. We are thinking of renaming it. Naturally we simply cannot let it be known as the Golden Hind any longer.

I receive very few reports of your conduct at the Wallflower Academy, so I must presume it is bad. I am disappointed, Gwendoline, but not surprised. You always were a most contrary thing.

While I have made not one, but two impressive marriages, you are lagging behind in your duty to me. When will you find a gentleman prepared to have you? I am sure Miss Pike does all she can, so it must be your deficiencies, your faults prevent it.

Remember, this secret of yours is one I could spill at a moment's notice, and if I am led to believe by Miss Pike's reports that you have been disobliging, I am willing to share it.

Even if it leads to the ruin of us both.

Keep me informed of any gentlemen you believe worthy of your attentions, if you are able to find any. I hope you enjoy your long sojourn at the Wallflower Academy.

Your Mother

PS I have redecorated your bedchamber and made it my sewing room. Why did you never say the light was so delightful? You cruel thing, keeping such a pleasant place from me.

Gwen leaned against the crumbling brick wall and exhaled slowly, but it did nothing to relieve the tension in her shoulders, which was creeping across her skin like a wire, prickling painfully, tightening her chest, making every breath more difficult.

She should not have read the letter. She probably shouldn't read any of them. She had known before the seal had been broken that it would contain words such as this. Words that hurt. Words that pained deeper than any cut.

Despite her better judgment, Gwen looked again at the letter. Each capital had been elegantly curled. Her mother's handwriting was so like her own. It was as though her own words were biting back at her.

'Gwen—I mean, Miss Knox?'

Gwen stared at the approaching figure of Percy Devereux, who was stepping around the borders with purpose towards her.

No. It could not be.

She had dreamed him up…his appearance was only a figment of her imagination. She had been thinking about him too much over the last few days, that was all. She had not expected to see him, had assumed he had returned to whatever business had taken him from London. She had dwelt too much on his face, on the way his lips curled when he looked at her, that tantalising scent that was his and his alone.

But she was not dreaming him. She could not be—not with the few other wallflowers taking a walk around the gardens staring so curiously at him.

Percy stopped before her, his gaze dancing to the letter in her hands and then back to her face.

Gwen swallowed, the tension in her shoulders spreading to her throat, making it difficult to speak. What could she say? Her mind was swimming with the harsh words of her mother, preventing her from breathing calmly, from even thinking clearly.

Keep me informed of any gentlemen you believe wor-thy of your attentions, if you are able to find any.

Well, she had certainly found one.

'A letter, I see,' said Percy. 'From your mother?'

Gwen's heart skipped a painful beat. 'How did you know?'

She had spoken too quickly—an accusation, not a question.

Percy shrugged, as though he had not noticed the fear within her. 'Well, you mentioned that your father had died just recently, and you have not spoken of any sibling. *Is* it from your mother?'

Frantic thoughts did Gwen no service, offering her no possible reply save, 'Yes.'

She had to get rid of it. Even the smallest chance that Percy might catch a glimpse of some of her mother's words… It did not bear thinking about. But she had brought no reticule.

'I did not expect to see you here,' she said as calmly as she could manage, quickly folding the letter and placing it in the one place she could be certain no one would touch: down the front of her corset. 'I would have thought you'd return to London.'

Only then did Gwen realise that Percy's cheeks had pinkened and his gaze was most inexplicably focused on her breasts.

Ah.

The action of placing something in one's corset did not raise any comment in an Academy designed for wall-flowers. They were all ladies there, and often without a reticule… Before a gentleman, however, it was rather a scandalous thing to do.

Gwen rose, her only thought to distract the Duke from the rather hussy-like thing she had just done. 'Will you walk with me?'

'Walk?' repeated Percy in a dazed voice, as though he had been hit over the head with a mallet. He blinked, then his eyes focused. 'Walk. Yes, as you wish. Walk…'

It was all Gwen could do to keep her breathing calm as she stood at Percy's side and started to walk slowly through the gardens. He was so close; if she was not careful her fingers would graze his own.

She could feel the heat of him, the intensity of his presence—or was that merely her imagination? Whatever it was, it was overpowering. Intoxicating. Painful. Thank goodness they were not technically alone, what with the other wallflowers gawping at them across the flowerbeds.

To be so close and yet not to touch…to feel the incompleteness of her desire… Gwen knew it was scandalous even to think such things, but she was sorely tempted. Just to know…

'I am beginning to think,' she said quietly, 'that you never leave the Academy.'

Percy chuckled, and picked at the dead head of a seed pod as they passed a border. 'Not with you stuck here. I prefer to be here.'

It was mere politeness, that was all, Gwen told herself.

It was foolish to think Percy would not say such a thing to any lady he was walking with.

Still. It was pleasant to hear such things.

'Ensure Miss Pike does not hear you say that,' Gwen tried to say lightly. 'She will consider you a gentleman wallflower and may seek to imprison you here alongside us.'

'I can see compensations in that,' came the quick reply.

Gwen looked aside. How was he able to do it? Was Percy an unusual gentleman, able to return any flattery with a quip of his own? Or were all gentlemen, and dukes in particular, trained in such fawning?

'It was from your mother, wasn't it?' asked Percy quietly as they turned a corner to walk in the rose garden, where a few splendid white blooms were still fragrant on the air. 'The letter? I saw the way you flushed, Gwen, I hope you do not mind me saying so.'

Gwen swallowed. 'And what if it was?'

She had not intended to be so combative, but it was difficult not to be. What did he want with her, this duke who surely had offers of far more interesting conversation elsewhere?

'Nothing. I just…' Percy's voice trailed away, and Gwen was astonished to see in his face what appeared to be genuine curiosity. 'I am interested. In the letter. In you. In— Damn.'

Gwen waited for further clarification, but it did not appear to be forthcoming.

It did not make sense—*he* did not make sense. A duke would hardly interest himself in the affairs of a wallflower—particularly one with no name and little prestige.

Yet there was something about him. Something that drew words from her Gwen could not imagine revealing to any other. Something that made her trust him more than anyone else she had ever met.

'It was from my mother,' she admitted. She paused at a rose bush, reaching out to cup a blossom. It would make an excellent model for her embroidery. 'She…she has remarried, and is rather pleased to have me removed from under her feet.'

That was putting it politely.

Gwen had to congratulate herself on her restraint, especially when Percy asked a most interesting question.

'I suppose she is encouraging you to be wed yourself, then?'

The tightness that had emerged in her shoulders the moment she had started to read the letter started to lessen. Though she could not explain it, there was relief in speaking the words aloud, even to someone like Percy. Someone who looked at her with such... Well... In anyone else, Gwen would have called it longing.

'No one wants to marry me.'

The words had been spoken before Gwen could call them back, and highly conscious that she was discussing her marriage prospects with a duke, she forced herself to laugh and continue walking through the gardens.

'I mean to say, all wallflowers are a rather difficult prospect,' she said swiftly, babbling, 'and I do not believe myself any different from any other wallflower. I merely speak the truth of the situation in which we all find—'

'Gwen.'

She halted. The single syllable from the Duke was sufficient to stem both the tide of her words and the movement of her feet.

Percy was smiling. That roguish grin she was starting to depend on more than anything was dancing across his lips. 'I would not be so sure that no one wishes to marry you, you know. I mean, not myself, obviously. I have a reputation to—Certain criteria must be met before I—'

Her hands were in his. Gwen was unsure how it had happened—she had certainly not stepped forward and reached for him. But that left only the possibility that he had stepped towards her and claimed her hands with his own.

And that could not be.

As Gwen's heart pattered most painfully in her chest, her breath short and her mind spiralling, she knew she must be mistaken.

Percy was right beside her, inches away. Why, if she just stepped forward she would close the gap between them… feel not only the strength of his hands around hers but the movement of his chest with each breath, the power of his body…

And that was when Gwen knew she was in trouble.

As she gazed, speechless, into the dark eyes of this Duke who so easily bewitched her, a desire rose within her that she could not and would not contain.

A desire she had never felt before.

A desire to be kissed, and to kiss in return.

To be held close, closer than was acceptable for a gentleman and a lady…a duke and a wallflower.

'I wondered…' breathed Percy, and Gwen shivered at the warmth of his breath on her skin. 'I wondered whether you would permit…'

His voice trailed away and Gwen unconsciously leaned closer, desperate for him to continue. In this moment she would have given him anything.

'Yes?' she whispered.

And there it was—the same desire that rushed through her veins was in his eyes. He wanted something she could not give.

'Permit me to take you on a carriage ride next week?'

Gwen blinked. There did not appear to be any teasing in his eyes, but he could not be serious.

A carriage ride with a duke?

He had said himself, just moments ago, that she was most unsuitable for him. *Certain criteria,* or something.

What would Miss Pike say? What would Society say,

seeing a wallflower from the Academy out with a duke in the intimacy of a carriage?

'How can I refuse?' said Gwen with a wry smile. 'What day suits you best?'

Chapter Six

It was not the incorrect day. Percy knew this to be impossible. He had been counting down the hours, not merely the days, since Gwen had agreed to come with him for a carriage ride.

Sunday after church, that had been the day agreed, at two o'clock. Plenty of time for Gwen to finish her luncheon, Percy had theorised, although his own stomach had incomprehensibly rebelled at the thought of food when it came to his own meal.

'And where are you going?' asked his mother sharply, as Percy pulled on his greatcoat and hunted for his favourite top hat.

Percy missed only a beat before he replied lightly, 'Oh, taking a lady out in the barouche. You know how it is…'

He smiled at his mother, a finely dressed, impressive-looking lady. She had been pretty as a young girl. Percy knew that from the portrait on the landing upstairs in their London townhouse, but she had become a far more handsome woman.

A woman who was now frowning. 'I see.'

Was it the fluttering of discomfort he felt at his mother's look, or something else curling within his stomach? Perhaps it was hunger. Percy had been unable to eat anything, despite his mother's glares at the dining table.

'I must be off, Mother,' Percy said, a little too brightly, opening the front door. 'I know you would hate for me to be late!'

'Hmph…'

That was the only sound he heard before the door closed behind him.

Percy grinned. And the grin did not fade as he grew closer to the Wallflower Academy, or when its redbrick frontage appeared at the end of the drive. Yet below the smile was something else…something that worried him.

It was a strange sort of gnawing at his stomach that recalled the sensation of hunger yet could not be the sole reason.

It was only when Percy drew back the reins and slowed his barouche to a stop outside the Wallflower Academy that he was able put his finger on precisely what it was.

Still. It was so unlike him.

Nerves?

He had never been nervous with a lady before in his life.

No, as Percy jumped down from the barouche, and admired the coat of arms so recently painted on its doors, he knew it was foolish to be nervous.

What did he have to be afraid of?

It was only a drive with the most beautiful woman he had ever met.

Only a wallflower with a temper like a tiger.

Only a suggestion to the world at large and Society in particular that he was courting said woman…a woman he could never marry.

Percy cleared his throat and attempted to push aside his rebellious thoughts. It was madness. If his mother knew he had not called upon Miss Middlesborough, or Lady Rose, or the Honourable Miss Maynard...well, there would be trouble.

Trouble for another time. For now, his thoughts and heart were filled with one woman, and as Percy strode forward to knock smartly on the front door of the Academy he was filled with the foolish hope that it would be Gwen herself who would open it.

Of course that was not the case.

'Hmm...' said the footman, in a remarkably similar tone to Percy's mother not half an hour ago. 'Miss Knox, I presume?'

'The Duke of Knaresby, actually,' said Percy, with what he hoped was a winning smile.

Neither the smile nor the jest appeared to have much impact on the footman. Indeed, it had rather the reverse effect from the one Percy had intended: the footman glowered, then slammed the door.

Taken aback, Percy turned and looked at his barouche.

He could not have mistaken the day.

He had even gone so far as to pencil the date into his diary—a most unusual event.

No other lady required such attention.

No other lady, Percy could not help but think, *was Miss Gwendoline Knox.*

The knot in his stomach had risen and was now in his throat. He should get back inside the barouche and leave. It was a ridiculous proposition to have made to a wallflower with no name and no dowry.

Percy knew what was due to him as a duke, to be sure, but he was equally cognisant of what he owed to the Dukedom.

Heirs.

The next generation did not spring out of nowhere. One had to create it, and with a woman who had the breeding and elegance one expected in a duchess.

Gwen was not that woman.

Percy hated the thought, but could not deny its veracity. Gwen was a wallflower, far below his station, with no family to recommend her nor any position in Society to protect and elevate his own.

She was, in short, precisely the sort of woman his mother would not be impressed by.

A prickle of excitement seared his heart. Perhaps, if Percy was honest with himself, that was part of the attraction. Gwen was beautiful, yes, with a temper that only flashed when she allowed herself to be provoked, and she made Percy wish to bed her immediately, if only to remove this all-consuming desire from his body.

But that could not be. His… Well, his rather unusual rise to the Dukedom of Knaresby required him to avoid all potential for scandal and find a wife with enough prestige in Society to paper over the cracks of his own respectability.

Oh, he hadn't caused any true scandals. Not really. But as a man he had been reckless, thoughtless of consequences, easy to befriend and easy to egg on… It was a miracle, really, that he hadn't got into more trouble.

And he certainly couldn't bed Gwen just to get her out of his system, no matter how much he might wish to.

Gwen was no courtesan, happy to exchange her body for coin or the protection of his name. She was different. Precious. He'd seen that in the flush of her cheeks whenever he looked at her, whenever his growing desire slipped into his words.

Percy's jaw tightened. Besides, she was protected by the iron fist of the Pike, as he had started calling her in the privacy of his mind—ever since Gwen had mentioned the nickname.

The Pike would certainly not permit any of her ladies to be taken in such a way.

No, Percy was a fool and he knew it.

As the wind rustled in the trees around him, their leaves starting to fall and their golden colouring splashing the drive with their red and yellow hues, he turned to the barouche.

This had been a mistake. He should leave before he made even more of a fool of himself.

He therefore had to perform a rather uncomfortable twist to face the Academy once again, when the sound of the front door opening and the swishing of skirts met his ears.

'Gwen—Miss Knox,' Percy corrected hastily as he almost fell over in his haste.

The smile which had already started to creep across his lips disappeared in an instant. There was Gwen, beautiful as ever, with a simple yet elegant pelisse around her shoulders. The painful lurch in Percy's stomach informed him, with very little potential for misunderstanding, that although he could neither wed nor bed the pretty wallflower, that fact did not prevent desire.

And there was Miss Pike. She stood beside her charge, a frown deep across her forehead and a glower on her face.

Percy smiled weakly. 'Ah… Hello, Pike—Miss Pike.'

Blast. If only he could maintain some sort of decorum. Percy tried not to notice Gwen stifling a giggle, nor the additional creases appearing on Miss Pike's forehead.

'Indeed,' she said, with a deference he knew her wallflowers did not often see in the woman. 'Your Grace. I have to say I am surprised—a barouche?'

Percy waited for more information, but there did not appear to be any. 'I assure you it is in most excellent repair, and will provide a smooth and gentle ride for Miss Knox.'

Damn his searing cheeks and the unexpected twist in his stomach! It was hardly Percy's fault, was it, that the innuendo was right there for anyone to see?

Gwen had certainly seen it—that, or there was another reason why her cheeks had darkened and her gaze dropped.

He really could not make her out. Sometimes wallflower…sometimes impassioned woman, Gwen was a medley of things Percy found rather intoxicating.

'I am sure it is a most impressive barouche,' said Miss Pike with a fawning laugh, 'but I was given to understand that this would be a carriage ride of a different nature.'

Percy stared. *Different nature?* Surely she did not believe him to be so much a cad as all that? If he'd had nefarious intentions, he would not have collected Gwen from the front of the Academy!

'Different nature?' he repeated, as an awkward silence crept between the three of them.

Gwen cleared her throat and spoke to the ground. 'I believe what Miss Pike intends to say is that a barouche can only carry two.'

Once again Percy waited for the rest of the explanation, but it was not forthcoming. 'I invited you, Miss Knox, and no other. Was I supposed to provide a second barouche for your companions?'

Miss Pike rolled her eyes with a smile. 'Really, Your Grace, I thought I had taught you better! I should have thought it obvious that your carriage requires sufficient room for a chaperone!'

Ah… Too late, Percy realised what the two ladies had assumed about this journey, and why Miss Pike was wearing a rather severe pelisse of her own, with no adornment of any kind.

Yes, it should have been obvious—and to any gentleman of real merit it would have been clear. Taking Gwen out on her own would be a recipe for scandal if they were spotted, and Percy could expect that someone would inform his mother immediately of the unknown woman in his company.

Alone with him. In his barouche.

But it was rarely a concern for a man of low rank, and it had never been of concern to Mr Percy Devereux, when he had been that man. It seemed a long time ago now. No woman had ever attempted to compromise him into matrimony then. There had been no point.

But now…

'Such an honour…such a pleasure to have you gracing us with your presence,' Miss Pike was saying, with an ingratiating smile on her face as she curtseyed again. 'So wonderful to…'

Percy allowed her to continue. It was nothing he hadn't heard before; the woman had been fond of him for years. Although admittedly the Pike's reverence had dramatically increased upon his ascension to the title. It was astonishing, really, just how welcome his presence was wherever he went now that he was a duke. No one had been much interested in his company before.

'Ah, there you are,' said Miss Pike, turning back to the door which had just reopened.

Percy glanced at it too, and was astonished to see Miss Marilla Newell appear, guided by a footman. Another wallflower?

'Miss Pike,' said Miss Newell firmly. 'I think you must admit, once and for all, that I hardly meet the requirements to be a chaperone. It might have escaped your notice, but I am blind.'

A shot of embarrassment flooded through Percy's bones and he looked away, even though he knew the lady could not see his gaze—but Gwen laughed and stepped forward towards him.

'Do not mind Rilla,' she said in an undertone as the

blind wallflower and Miss Pike began a heated argument in murmured whispers. 'She rather enjoys teasing people, and she is not shy at all about her blindness. It is…it is most agreeable to see you.'

Percy smiled weakly. 'Right. Yes. Good.'

'And furthermore, Miss Newell, you must consider your future here at the Academy!' Miss Pike's words had risen in volume, only increasing Percy's embarrassment at the whole situation. 'Why, you have been here three years and…'

'We could just…go…' said Gwen quietly.

Percy blinked. The wallflower had a rather scandalous look about her—a mischievous twinkle in her eye he had only glimpsed once before, when she had attempted to flirt with him at the dining table.

It did something rather strange to him. Not unpleasant—no, Percy would not describe this sensation as unpleasant. But it was…different. He had bedded ladies before…even dallied with the idea of having a mistress, before deciding it was probably more trouble than it was worth. Expensive things, mistresses.

He knew desire, knew passion.

Knew what it was to make love to someone.

But this was not that feeling.

True, it was similar—a rising stirring in his stomach that both dropped to his manhood and rose to his heart. But it was different. Warmer. Deeper. And a twinge of pain came with it…a bittersweet sort of knowledge that something was not quite right.

'We could,' said Percy with a smile. Raising his voice, he turned to the arguing ladies on the doorstep of the Academy. 'Miss Pike, Miss Newell—I promise not to kiss Miss Knox, if that is what it takes for you to trust me. I shall bring her back within the hour and we shall keep to the country lanes. No visits to Town. Will that do?'

There were splotchy red patches across both Miss Pike's and Miss Newell's cheeks.

'Well, really!' said Miss Pike. 'Percy Devereux, I have never heard the—'

'Excellent,' said Percy cheerfully. 'Come on, Miss Knox.'

To his great disappointment, Gwen was wearing gloves. And after Percy had helped her into his barouche, though there was the pleasure of being close to her, of having been of some small service, there was no opportunity to touch her again. Not as he would like, anyway.

Leaving behind the astonished voice of Miss Pike and the laughter of Miss Newell, Percy tapped the horses with his whip and the barouche moved forward, crunching along the drive.

Only then was he able to lose himself in his delectable consciousness of Gwen seated beside him. That was the real benefit of a barouche, Percy thought gleefully, as the horses settled into a gentle trot and they reached the road, taking a left to meander along a country lane. It might not offer the most comfort, nor the most elegance—but, goodness, did it offer an opportunity for intimacy!

Gwen was seated beside him, her hips pressed against his own. With every movement of the carriage Percy could feel her. His arm, now dropped to his side, nestled against hers.

It was enough to stir something hungry within him, something Percy immediately forced down.

This was not that sort of carriage ride.

'I…' Gwen swallowed when Percy glanced at her. 'I have never been in a carriage before. With a gentleman, I mean. Alone.'

It was perhaps the most endearing thing he had ever

heard. Percy saw the hesitancy in her, the nervousness at being around him, and it spurred on his feelings of power.

How delightful to be around a woman who was so easily impressed, so easily won over.

'Well, I would not concern yourself,' Percy said brightly, in an attempt to put Gwen at ease. 'I have been in plenty.'

Only as the words left his mouth did Percy see his mistake—too late. Gwen's face fell, her gaze dropping to her hands, and he saw tension creeping around her mouth as her lips pressed together.

'I see,' she said quietly.

'No, you don't,' said Percy quickly, hating himself for speaking so thoughtlessly. 'I meant… Well, there is no trick to it—no brilliance one has to offer. You just have to enjoy yourself. The responsibility to entertain is upon myself.'

A smile crept over Gwen's face at this pronouncement. 'Something you are well practised in, I would think?'

'Yes. I mean, no.'

'Well? Which is it?'

The temptation to say nothing—to sweep this awkward moment away and focus instead on the beauty of the countryside and the woman beside him, anything except be honest—weighed heavily on Percy's heart.

Gentlemen were not honest. Dukes certainly weren't. Very few occasions in their life required them to be.

It was often easier to just ignore one's feelings, push aside all and any desires against Society's expectations, and instead laugh.

Percy sighed. 'My mother arranges carriage rides for me with eligible young ladies—but you cannot be surprised, surely? I am the Duke of Knaresby.'

By God, he would have to do better. Percy hated the twisting pathetic words he had used instead of the direct honest ones he wanted to. Words ringing in his heart as well as his mind.

This is different, Gwen, because you are different. You are special. You are becoming more special to me with every visit, and I don't know what to do with myself when I am without you.

Percy cleared his throat. Words he could not say.

'In a way, then,' said Gwen, 'we are under the same pressures, the same obligations. We both live in houses with older women who are determined to marry us off.'

He could not help but laugh at that characterisation of his mother. 'Something like that, yes—only in my case... Well... What do you know of the Duchy of Knaresby?'

Gwen stared, obviously surprised.

Percy was a little surprised himself. As he directed the barouche along another country lane, not meeting a single person along the way, he wondered what had possessed him to start on this topic.

He had never spoken openly about it before.

Why now?

'In truth, I had never heard of it until we met,' said Gwen. 'Why?'

Percy sighed. 'Many reasons... My father was not the Duke of Knaresby.'

For a moment he hesitated. There was no need to tell Gwen his sorry tale, was there? Only a woman who might have a permanent connection with him needed to hear it, and Gwen was certainly not that woman.

Marry Gwen? A woman with no connections, no name, and no opportunity to better Percy's position in Society? A woman who did not fit James's criteria?

Ridiculous.

Still, he continued. 'The Duke was my uncle—my father's brother. He died along with his two sons, in a terrible accident, and just months later my brother…'

His throat tightened and he found he could not continue. *When was the last time he had spoken about James?*

Not since the funeral. Not since they had laid his brother in the cold, damp earth.

'I am sorry to hear of your loss.'

Gwen's voice was sweet, gentle, soothing to his soul.

Percy cleared his throat and found he had the strength to continue.

'I am the last Devereux—the last male in the line, anyway… I never thought I would… No man should face such a thing. My brother was the most…the best brother anyone could have…'

Percy cleared his throat once more, and blinked rather rapidly at the road ahead of them.

He was not about to permit himself to show something as uncivilised as emotion!

'He taught me almost everything I know about being a man, a gentleman,' he continued, in a rather more controlled tone. 'He was eleven years older than me, and our father died when I was very young. Indeed, my brother was the one who taught me what a gentleman should look for in a wife.'

The words hung in the air most uncomfortably, and Percy wondered what in the name of goodness had come over him.

A subtle glance at his companion showed him that Gwen had raised an eyebrow. 'Indeed?'

'Indeed,' said Percy, retreating into the haughtiness which was his fortress in difficult conversations. 'Elegance, of course, and beauty. Good manners, a good family—far more important now I have inherited the title.'

'Indeed,' repeated Gwen.

A prickle of discomfort seared across Percy's chest, but he refused to pay it any heed.

'Blonde, naturally,' Percy continued blithely. 'And a good singer, with only one sibling—'

'And here I am, an only child,' Gwen interrupted with a wry smile. 'And not blonde, to boot. Though I think I am unlikely to make a match for…for other reasons.'

Percy flushed. God above, it was not as though no other gentleman in Society had dissimilar requirements! He was just more honest about them. Did he not deserve such a wife?

'My brother taught me the criteria, and now he is gone,' Percy said stiffly. 'And the last time I saw him…'

His voice failed him. The last time he had seen James neither of them had known it would be. Just a hunting party… just an evening spent talking and laughing and drinking and smoking. As any father and son would. At times, it had been hard to recall that James wasn't Percy's father.

And what had his brother said?

'Now, you must promise me, Percival…'

Percy had grinned adoringly at his elder brother.

'Not to marry a woman who does not fit my requirements. I won't have just anyone joining this family!'

'I have no thoughts of matrimony—' Percy had tried to say.

But James had cut across him.

'Promise me, Percy. Promise me you will marry someone who fits these conditions exactly. Promise me!'

And Percy had swallowed. *'I promise.'*

'I promised him,' he said aloud to the waiting Gwen, his cheeks red. 'Promised I would marry someone he would have approved of. It was the last thing I ever said to him.'

Gwen looked at him curiously. 'Almost a deathbed promise, then?'

Percy's jaw tightened. He was not going to cry. 'I honour him by seeking out a woman of whom he would have approved.'

He tried not to glance once more at Gwen. *Blast.* A woman James certainly would *not* have approved of.

Grief threatened to overwhelm him, just for a moment, but Percy pushed it back. He would honour his brother's wishes. He would speak calmly and matter-of-factly with the wallflower, then he would take her home. This had been a mistake.

He cleared his throat. 'Neither James nor I expected that a title would be our fortune. Consequently, as you might imagine, I was not raised to be a duke, nor even a duke's brother.' Percy laughed bitterly. 'Many in Society do not consider me to have the upbringing—nor, in truth, the breeding—to be a duke. Least likely to distinguish myself, I suppose.'

'Well,' said Gwen, nudging him gently and making Percy's stomach lurch most uncomfortably, 'I certainly have not seen you display the decorum I would expect in a duke.'

Their laughter mingled in the cool autumnal air and Percy was enchanted despite himself. There was no denying it. She was beautiful, witty, kind, all wrapped up into one. But James would not have liked her because of her low breeding and lack of title, her dark hair and surely half a dozen other reasons…

His traitorous heart ached at the thought of disappointing his dead brother. Did Gwen know how rare a gift she was?

Percy pulled back on the reins and slowed the barouche to a stop. Enjoyable though the journey was, for this he wanted to be stationary. He wanted to look into Gwen's eyes…see her reaction to him.

He wanted to know whether what was sparking in his heart was sparking in hers.

'You know,' he said quietly, glancing at her, 'we are truly not that different.'

A mocking smile teased at Gwen's lips. 'Yes, I suppose so. I must marry someone—anyone who will have me. I am least likely to make a good match, let alone win a…a man's heart. Whereas you…you must wed a beautiful, wealthy, well-connected someone. Not so very different.'

Painfully conscious of her arm resting beside his own, Percy turned in the barouche towards her.

Gwen's gaze did not drop, meeting the fire of his own.

'Well, you meet one of the criteria, at least,' Percy whispered.

Something was happening. Something he could not explain and had no wish to halt.

He had to—

He shouldn't.

Drawn to her inexplicably, unable to stay away, Percy leaned slowly towards her, not moving his hands, bringing his head closer to hers. His lips closer to her lips.

He could not stop looking at them, could not understand why he was not already kissing her when this desire had grown inside him so passionately.

For a heart-stopping moment Percy was certain she'd permit the indelicacy…lift her lips to his own and claim him as he wished to claim her.

A few inches…not even an inch…and Percy stared at the delicately delicious lips which were now mere seconds away from touching his own.

Gwen pulled away.

'I don't think—W-We shouldn't…' she said breathlessly, looking away to the horses, her fingers tightly wound in her lap. 'You promised the Pike.'

Percy could hardly help himself. He wanted to ignore the world and its expectations, push aside all memories of James and what he would demand of his little brother, and instead…

He knew he should lean back, give her space, give her a moment to compose herself—but he didn't want her composed. He wanted her underneath him, begging for more, desperate for his touch.

He forced that image of Gwen away but the reality of Gwen remained before him.

Dear Lord, such a pretty temptation.

'Perhaps we shouldn't,' he murmured. 'But I want to.'

Gwen's laughter was gentle as she raised a hand to his cheek. Percy leaned into it, desperate for her touch—anything to quench the growing desires within him. But it did nothing but augment them.

'I think,' said Gwen quietly, 'that you should return me to the Wallflower Academy.'

Percy groaned. 'You're no wallflower…you're a torturer.'

'You chose your own method,' said Gwen lightly, removing her hand and clearing her throat. 'Well, Your Grace. I think it is best you take me home. Then you can return to London and seek out this perfect wife your brother prepared you for.'

Chapter Seven

'And, of course, there are many elements that might make a conversation dry. The first thing that can make a conversation dry is the topic itself. The second thing that will make a conversation dull is the primary narrator. The third thing that makes a conversation boring…'

'This whole conversation is boring,' muttered Sylvia under her breath.

Gwen tried not to giggle, though it was a difficult task. After all, Miss Pike had been monologuing about the difficulties of entering, maintaining and refreshing a dull conversation for at least ten minutes—with, it appeared, little awareness that her own soliloquy was perhaps just as dull as the conversations she was encouraging them to avoid.

'So, when a gentleman chooses a topic you have little interest in, what should you do?' asked Miss Pike, rearranging her skirts in the pew, as the large church grew busy with people and noise. 'Miss Sylvia?'

'Leave him in the dust and—'

'Now, there is nothing worse,' said Miss Pike, turning to her wallflowers and speaking over the grinning young woman, 'than a lady who is unable to show interest in a gentleman's conversation—even, as I have said, if it is most dull. I assure you there will be topics gentlemen wish to discuss which border on the banal!'

'Nothing could be worse than this lecture,' Sylvia breathed to Gwen, who was seated beside her on the pew behind Miss Pike.

Gwen was forced to turn her giggle into a cough. At least this lecture could not go on for ever—the gentleman at the front of the nave had just risen, and the vicar was nodding approvingly.

Miss Pike turned swiftly. 'Another cough, Miss Knox? I would hate to think you had caught a chill on your carriage ride with His Grace. I should have forbidden it.'

'No, no, just a tickle in my throat,' Gwen said hastily.

She was still a little unclear just how much power Miss Pike had over them, but if it was anything like she feared, the older woman could send any of the wallflowers to bed without any supper if they so much as hinted at having a cold.

And then she would have no opportunity to see Percy.

The thought flashed through her mind unconsciously. Gwen half smiled as she noticed it. Not that she had any plans to see Percy. It would be ridiculous to expect to see him again so soon after yesterday's carriage ride.

So soon after yesterday's revelations about his marital expectations. And his brother's requirements. Requirements that were understandable, in Percy's position. And even more understandable after hearing about the loss of his brother.

After yesterday's almost-kiss…

'I think I will leave you,' said Miss Pike severely. 'This wedding is one of my greatest triumphs, and I should rightly be seated behind the bride. A gentleman with two thousand a year! Any of you should be grateful even for the idea of being so well married. Good afternoon, ladies.

Enjoy the wedding, and we will continue this conversation later.'

The wallflowers inclined their heads politely as the owner of the Wallflower Academy elegantly swept across the church. Only when the footsteps of the Pike halted, as she sat imperiously at the front of the church, did all the heads turn in one direction.

Heat seared Gwen's cheeks.

All were turning to her.

'Well?' Sylvia demanded.

Gwen blinked. She could not be asking what she thought she was, could she? She would not be so indecorous, and in a church—

'Tell us everything about this duke of yours!' Sylvia said eagerly. 'And when I say "everything", I mean *everything*! Quickly... Lizzie could be marching down the aisle at any moment!'

'Do not skimp on the details,' said Rilla. 'I can do without any description of the Duke, though.'

'Speak for yourself! I need to hear about every iota of conversation, every touch, every thought that flew through your head,' said Sylvia with a laugh. 'Come on, Gwen— we will live vicariously through you! Oh, that handsome duke!'

Her stomach stirring uncomfortably, Gwen groaned, dropping her face into her hands as raucous laughter filled the church, along with a cry from Rilla that no one had told her he was handsome.

'You didn't want a description!' Gwen said into her hands.

Rilla snorted. 'You know I did not mean it!'

Other clamours echoed around the church as all the wallflowers demanded the full story, though there were a few pink cheeks as other congregants glanced over at them and the Pike glared over her shoulder.

It was all too much. Gwen had known she was a woman who found no delight in the attention of others for most of her life. But she had a temper—a temper unbecoming in any woman, let alone a wallflower.

The idea that all her new friends—friends who really hardly knew her, and who saw her as naught but a fellow wallflower, like them, with no dark secrets—wanted to hear about each moment she had spent with Percy, those precious moments...so unexpected...

If she spoke of them aloud they would surely disappear into the ether like vapor, gone like mist on a winter's morning.

'There is really not much to tell,' Gwen said weakly as she lifted her face from her hands and saw, much to her disappointment, that the wallflowers had, if anything, grown closer.

Sylvia raised an eyebrow. 'So the Duke did not invite you on a carriage ride?'

Gwen's stomach twisted. 'Well—'

'And he did not force Miss Pike to permit you to go alone, despite the provision of a perfectly good chaperone?' asked Rilla dryly.

Gwen smiled weakly. If this had been happening to any other person—anyone other than her—she knew she would perhaps be barraging that wallflower with the very same questions she was being subjected to. She would want to know all the details. How it had felt to be so singled out, to be in the presence of a gentleman with such a grand title, to feel his hand on her own, to feel him move closer and closer, inch by inch, his fierce gaze softening as it focused on her lips...

Gwen swallowed.

Her heart was not fluttering, she told herself firmly. She was merely tired.

And not tired because she had been unable to sleep last night, desperately trying to understand what on earth Percy had been about. Kissing her in a carriage? All alone in a country lane? The man had his reputation to think of, irrespective of her own!

'But Gwen—'

'Hush! Here she is!'

The organ music had changed, the sound half lost in the rush of skirts as the congregation rose. Gwen quickly joined them, peering around to see a blushing bride in a delicate pink gown walk down the aisle.

A wallflower wedding…

Miss Pike was correct, in a way. It was a triumph. Gwen could hardly believe it had been achieved, but the proof was right before her.

As Lizzie reached her equally blushing husband-to-be, and the congregation took their seats, the voice of the vicar washed over her.

'We are gathered here today…'

A wedding. Gwen had never considered—or not with any seriousness—quite what that would mean. Standing there beside Percy, vowing to—

Beside Percy?

Now, where had that thought come from?

The vows were over far more swiftly than she had imagined, and Gwen rose hastily as the clearly ecstatic newlyweds swept down the aisle in a rush of lace. The church emptied slowly and the wallflowers were buffeted about. When Gwen finally made it outside, she stepped to one side of the porch and leaned against the wall.

There. She had managed to attend a wallflower wedding without drawing any attention to herself. She should be congratulated, really.

Someone nudged her shoulder.

'A duke!' Sylvia looked remarkably impressed. 'My word, Gwen, I must admit I did not think you had it in you when you first arrived at the Academy.'

'It is not like that,' Gwen attempted to say—but it was no use.

It was quite clear the wallflowers had had precious little opportunity to see one of their own attracting any attention—now they needed to revel in all the details.

'Well, whatever it is like,' said Rilla, leaning on Sylvia's arm with a mischievous grin, 'I recommend seducing him as soon as possible.'

Sylvia and Rilla collapsed into hysterics as astonished gasps came from those around them.

'You know,' said a different, deeper voice, 'that is a wonderful idea.'

Gwen froze. Her heart stopped, her fingers turning to ice, as she turned very slowly to look past the crowd who had gathered around the happy couple, to where the voice had emanated from.

Leaning against the church door with a wide grin on his face, cutting an impressively majestic figure in coat and breeches, was Percy.

Gwen's legs quivered, and her mind was unable to think about what she might possibly do next. Run? Flee the churchyard? Flee the Wallflower Academy and never return?

There could be no other option. How would she ever live with herself, knowing that Percy had overheard such nonsense? How could she possibly return to the Academy, knowing they all believed her to be courted by a duke when she knew full well he could not offer her anything?

Worse, how would she ever be able to look Percy in the eyes, knowing he had said such words?

Sylvia's laughter had faded swiftly. The other wallflowers had disappeared, which Gwen thought impressive, for she had not noticed them leave, and Rilla was looking in his direction, he head tilted to one side.

'Do my ears deceive me?' she asked in a low voice. 'Is that the Duke in question?'

'Yes…' breathed Gwen.

How long has he been standing there?

How much of the conversation had he heard?

Gwen tried desperately to run through all the wild and inappropriate words.

His hearing even one statement would be too much, but there was naught she could do now.

Besides, if she was not careful Sylvia would start pestering Percy with uncomfortable questions. Gwen might only have known her for a few weeks, but she knew there was nothing that woman would not ask.

'Excuse me,' Gwen said quietly, stepping away from the church wall towards where Percy still stood, a wide grin on his face.

Forcing herself to ignore the whispered conversation now occurring behind her, between Rilla and Sylvia, Gwen tried to step past Percy and go back into the church. Into sanctuary. Surely nothing untoward could occur there?

He did not budge.

'Why, hello, Gwen,' Percy said, his smile still broad. 'How pleasant to see you.'

'Let me pass, please,' said Gwen.

It was most irritating. He was doing it on purpose merely to annoy her, she knew, and the trouble was it was working.

Percy Devereux, Duke of Knaresby, had a particular skill in gaining a rise out of her, and the worst of it was the sensation was not pure irritation. That would be far too simple. Added in was a medley of desire, desperation, and…

Percy straightened up only slightly, leaving a gap just small enough for her to pass through if she brushed past him.

The sensation of her gown moving against his coat would be heavenly, but Gwen attempted to ignore the thought of it. What would Miss Pike say if she saw such shenanigans? Surely she would reprimand her, and there could even be a letter home to her mother.

A mother with far too much power over her.

'Your Grace…' Gwen said, as the murmurs behind her increased in volume.

'Percy,' he said, his smile faltering. 'I think…no, I am sure… I want you to call me Percy.'

Gwen's heart had only just started racing again, and now it skipped a painful beat.

Percy? How could he expect her to address a gentleman—a duke, no less—by his Christian name!

It was outrageous. It was intimate.

It was precisely what she wanted.

'I only call my friends by their Christian names,' said Gwen with a raised eyebrow as she remained by the church doorway. 'And a friend would move aside so I could step through.'

Was he surprised by her response? Gwen could hardly tell. Her mind was whirling, trying to understand what on earth he was doing here, hoping he would ignore—or forget—Rilla's comment.

Percy nodded. 'I suppose a friend would. But I, Gwen, am not your friend.'

Gwen's stomach twisted painfully.

And there it was.

The confirmation she should not have needed. The Duke

was merely playing with her. Teasing her. She was entertainment, that was all. Really, she should be grateful to receive any attention form him whatsoever. It was far more than she had expected, and drastically more than she had deserved.

'I see,' she said dully.

'No… "Friend" would not be the right word,' said Percy, dropping his voice under the medley of congratulations and conversations about the wedding.

At least they were not alone, Gwen tried to tell herself. That truly would be scandalous.

'What would be the right word?'

His face flickered. Gwen could see the war within him between what he wanted to say and what he knew he should not.

'Gwen, despite my better judgement, I want far more than friendship from you. And friendship would not be sufficient to describe what I feel about you.'

Gwen swallowed and looked into his face. A dark sort of seriousness had overcome Percy now, and she could see a flicker of uncertainty, of doubt, that she had never seen in that proud face before.

It stoked something in her…something new.

Hardly aware where this boldness was coming from, and certain she would regret this later, Gwen stepped forward. Her chest brushed up against his and for a wild moment she felt his breathing, felt it in tune with her own. She could feel his heartbeat—although perhaps that was her own pulse, racing frantically as she moved her face to within a single inch from his.

Then it was over.

Gwen stepped through into the church, where sunlight was streaming through the stained-glass windows, and although her breath was inexplicably ragged, she was still standing.

Two small pink dots had appeared in Percy's cheeks and his hands were clenched, as though he had forced himself not to reach out and touch her.

Mere fancy, Gwen reminded herself as she took in the several people still in the church, chattering away. She was seeing what she wished to see. Percy certainly would not have desired to do such a thing. He was merely teasing.

He stepped closer and whistled. 'Dear God, Gwen, what do you want to do to me? Drive me mad?'

Gwen flushed. There was no helping it. There had been desire in his words in the doorway—there was no possibility of mistaking it for anything else.

He desired her.

Matrimony was out of the question, and it would be far better for her if she could put it entirely out of her head. The spectre of his brother would loom over his choice.

A pair of ladies ceased their conversation and moved towards the door, glancing at the two of them curiously. Gwen stepped out of their path, carefully not looking at Percy, now standing on the other side of the aisle. If Miss Pike was to find her here, with the Duke, having a private conversation…

Well, there was no limit to what the owner of the Wallflower Academy might think.

Gwen half smiled at the memory of the almost-kiss she and Percy had shared in his barouche just four and twenty hours ago. Perhaps Miss Pike would not have a completely erroneous idea of what was happening, after all…

'I have no intention of driving you mad, Your—Percy,' Gwen said hesitantly, stepping towards him and keeping her voice low. His name sounded sweet on her lips. Sweet, and yet shockingly forbidden. 'You have said I do not meet your criteria, that your brother would not approve. You were the one eavesdropping on my conversation.'

My private conversation, Gwen thought as Percy stepped towards her, closing the careful gap she had left.

Not that she would have shared her true feelings with the other wallflowers. No, Gwen was still trying to ascertain precisely what they were, and she could not yet comprehend sharing them with anyone else.

She had feelings for him, undeniably. Feelings that swirled and mingled. Fear, desire, and a need to be felt and seen and heard as she never had been before.

And they were real feelings. These were not imagined emotions after reading a novel, or hearing from her mother about yet another lady of her acquaintance who had found a match.

No, these feelings stemmed from a gentleman whose voice made the hair on the back of her neck stand up and every part of her want to be closer to him. Closer than was appropriate.

Gwen swallowed. This was ridiculous. Percy was a duke. He needed to marry well—far better than her level. Had he not been open with her, and honest about the qualities his wife would need to have? And the truth of why she was at the Academy... Well, that scandal would be the last thing a gentleman like Percy needed.

'I rather enjoyed hearing you and your friends discuss me, I will admit,' said Percy cheerfully.

A knot tightened in Gwen's throat. 'I—I wasn't talking about you.'

Percy raised an eyebrow. 'Goodness, should I be worried?'

'You should not have been eavesdropping in the first place,' said Gwen, choosing to sidestep his question. ''Tis hardly a gentlemanly thing to do. And outside a church!'

He shrugged with all the lack of care of a titled nobleman. 'If the conversation is about me, does it truly count as eavesdropping? I do not believe so.'

It was a careless counter, but Gwen found it difficult to argue with. The conversation had, after all, been about Percy.

She supposed she should be grateful she had not been overheard saying anything personal. Why, if she had even attempted to explain to the wallflowers how she felt about him...the attraction in every word he spoke, the way he had almost kissed her...and his kindness. The way he looked at her not as a wallflower, but as a woman.

Gwen swallowed. 'I think, g-given the kind of woman you must marry, and the woman I am—'

'A wallflower, you mean?'

It would be too easy to merely agree with him. Gwen tried to formulate the word 'murderess' but decided against it.

Too much honesty would be the end of her.

'Yes, a wallflower,' she said quietly. 'I just think... Well... You and I, Percy—'

'I like that,' Percy interrupted, and Gwen realised with a start that he was now merely inches away. How had he moved without her notice? She needed to step back, but her feet weren't working. '"You and I".'

There was a sound—a movement out of the corner of her eye. Gwen took a hasty step back from the Duke as a gentleman stalked past them, glaring at Percy most irritably.

'What on earth...?' Gwen murmured as the gentleman stepped out of the church.

Percy chuckled. 'Oh, he's just sore because I won a bet against him just a few weeks ago. Now, will I be seeing you for dinner?'

Percy? At the Academy for dinner?

Panic flushed through Gwen's veins like boiling tar, searing her heart and her stomach alike with painful dread.

Another dinner? She was not aware of any formal dinner that evening—and if she was going to suffer through another official Wallflower Academy dinner she would have appreciated more time to prepare.

Prepare for what, she could not think.

'There's one tonight? A dinner, I mean?'

Percy frowned. 'I had thought you would eat dinner every night.'

There was nothing Gwen could do to prevent the flush searing her cheeks. 'So…there is no formal dinner? It will just be you?'

The words echoed around the church in a most disobliging way, but there was naught Gwen could do to stop them.

Percy hesitated for a moment before replying, 'As much as I would wish it…no. The wallflowers will be there, of course. And the Pike.'

That at least forced a smile to Gwen's face. 'I… I asked you once what—what your intentions were. You did not answer me then.'

That boldness she did not recognise within herself had risen once more to the fore, and this time she did not look away from Percy's face as she spoke the words—not really a question, but a statement of confusion. A need to know more.

But the bravado typically within Percy's face had disappeared, replaced by something akin to uncertainty. He shifted his feet, and when he finally replied it was in a soft whisper. 'I don't know.'

Gwen stared. It was not the answer she had expected at all—far from it.

'I should not be here, waiting after a wedding service to see you. I should not want to—My brother would never have encouraged—All I know is that I cannot stay away from you, Gwen,' said Percy urgently, reaching for her hand. 'That I will not.'

'I do not want you to. Stay away, I mean.'

Her heart was racing, but there was nothing she could do to stop it. Was his racing too? Were the same desperate confusions whirling around his mind? If only Gwen could read Percy's thoughts and know whether this was a trick, a jest, or something more. Something deeper.

'I do not know where this is going…' Gwen breathed weakly.

Percy smiled. 'You know, for the first time, I wholeheartedly agree with you.'

Chapter Eight

It was the ride, Percy told himself as he slowed his barouche along the drive towards the Wallflower Academy.

It was the ride. That must be it. There could be no other explanation for why his heart was pattering so painfully, why he could not concentrate on more than one thing for a matter of minutes before his mind meandered again.

Meandered to Gwen.

Percy clenched his jaw as the horses trotted along the gravel drive, but he could not help breaking out into a smile.

Gwen. Well, there was no point in trying to lie to himself, at least not in the privacy of his own mind.

He knew why his body was on fire, his mind unable to stop returning to the woman who had become the reason for his entire existence since he had first seen her.

Before he knew it, Percy had found himself visiting her almost every day. Playing cards, walking in the gardens, even putting up with those awful musical recitals from other wallflowers.

His stomach lurched. He was spending, in summary, far too much time here and not nearly enough time doing what he should be doing. Seeking a suitable wife.

Even now his desire had got the better of him. Approaching the Wallflower Academy with this wild idea? It was foolhardy.

Percy could not explain to himself why it was so important that he keep returning to the Wallflower Academy, but it was becoming increasingly painful for him to be away. The new idea, of course, had come to him only an hour ago, and it should have been immediately pushed aside. James would never have countenanced it. No, tonight's plan, concocted an hour ago, just as dusk had been falling, was far more audacious.

Which was why his presence here was just as much a surprise to himself as anyone else.

Percy pulled up his barouche outside the stables to the left of the main house. He was beginning to sound ridiculous even in his own head.

A stableboy scampered out of the stables as Percy's boots hit the gravel. 'Y'Grace!'

'Hello, Tom,' said Percy with a wry smile.

It was bad indeed that he was on first-name terms with some of the servants here at the Academy. But he was one step closer to Gwen. To seeing her, listening to her. Making her laugh, if he was fortunate. To making an even bigger fool of himself than he had already, if unfortunate.

'Back again, Y'Grace?' commented the stable lad with no shame. 'You're here an awful lot, aren't you?'

Percy glared. 'Not very often, I think.'

'At least three times a week at my count,' continued Tom with little fear. 'Don't you have other places to be, a great lord like you?'

Percy laughed weakly, but he could see the boy was not speaking to flatter. It was an honest question, one he would have to answer eventually—at the very least to his mother.

For he had not yet verbalised, even within himself, just why he could not stay away from Gwen. Why his chest tightened whenever he was away, as though his very lungs were unwilling to breathe air she did not breathe.

Why, his dreams were starting to become so scandalous it was surely not right for him to be coming to see Gwen at all. Not when the last time he had seen her in his mind she had been without clothes, without shame, and desperate...

Percy swallowed. The stable boy was still staring, wide-eyed, clearly intrigued by this strange duke who considered the Wallflower Academy the height of entertainment.

And the boy was right. He did have other places to be. Places his mother was expecting him to attend to meet the very best of eligible young ladies. He needed to find a wife—one who would confirm his place in Society now he'd inherited the title.

Well, he'd soon find himself in one of those places...

'I like it here,' he found himself saying to the boy. 'Tom, look after my horses, will you? I pushed them hard on the road.'

Because I was desperate to get here.

Percy made sure he did not say that.

Because every minute I am away from this place, I cannot help but wonder why. And being away from Gwen...

Percy clenched his jaw to ensure none of those words slipped out. The last thing he needed was the whole household thinking him a fool—not just the wallflowers. A grimace covered his face for a moment as he thought of the conversation he had overheard...

'I recommend seducing him as soon as possible.'

It was difficult to know who was more the fool: Gwen, for permitting his attentions when she knew there was nothing he could do about them, or himself for continuing to return, time and time again, to the woman he craved more than any other.

Craved, but must not have.

'I'll look after them,' said Tom placidly, clearly unaware of the turmoil within the Duke before him. 'Good day, Y'Grace.'

Percy blinked. He could not stay standing in the stable all day. He had to go and be a gentleman—and whisk Gwen away from the Wallflower Academy in a very non-gentlemanly manner.

How long he stood there before the redbrick manor house, his heart thumping painfully and his mind unable to decide whether to simply return home and avoid the shame inevitably coming his way, or enter and spend as many precious minutes with Gwen as he could...

Percy could not tell. He was sliding into trouble, he knew. No other lady of his acquaintance made him feel like this, made him question himself like this. Made him wonder whether it was worth it to throw it all away, leave the title and glory behind, and make Gwen his wife.

Gwen...his wife.

It was a heady thought. Percy found his fingers tingling and he clenched them, as though refusing to permit the sensation.

He was being ridiculous. Worst of all, he was playing not only with his heart but with Gwen's. What was he doing, if not hurting them both?

'Percy?'

He started. He had not noticed her step out, attired in an evening gown for dinner. *Excellent.*

'Marvellous, you're suitably dressed.'

Gwen frowned. 'Suitably dressed for—?'

'An academy dinner, I suppose?' Percy said, unable to help his interruption as excitement coursed through him. 'Tell Miss Pike you've received an invitation to Town for this evening,' he ordered.

She bristled. 'Who are you to be ordering me—?'

'I'm no one…no one to you,' he said, the words spilling from him. 'But I want to be.'

Gwen's eyes were wide, but she disappeared back into the Wallflower Academy without another word.

This was foolishness to the extreme! Percy knew he was running a risk with this plan, that it was one he should not even be contemplating, but there was too much reward to be gained. Besides, she had obeyed him. Not that he wished to make frequent demands of her…but surely if she had no wish for his company she would not have complied?

By the time Gwen stepped out again, a pelisse hugging her shoulders and a confused expression still in her eyes, Percy had made up his mind. Society be damned. He would take her.

'Where on earth are we—?'

'I'll explain when we get there,' said Percy, certain that Gwen would argue with him if he was so foolish as to reveal all now. 'Come on.'

The journey was swift, and for some unknown reason he found their silence more comforting than any conversation might have been. When was the last time he had truly enjoyed the company of a woman like this? In a delicate, unassuming way? It was most odd.

Only when his barouche rattled down King Street did Gwen turn to him with wide eyes. 'You have brought me to London!'

'I would have thought that was obvious,' said Percy with a snort.

Her cheeks darkened to crimson. 'I just—Well… Perhaps obvious to you. I have never been here before.'

Percy could not prevent his jaw from dropping. Never been to—? But London was the centre of the world—it was where everyone was! Anyone of importance, anyway.

'Never been to—?'

'It may have passed you by, Your Grace,' came the snapping retort, 'but the world does not revolve around London.'

Percy swallowed his indignation. The way she spoke to him sometimes—as though he was nothing! Well, this evening he would show her just how a woman should address a duke.

And then, whispered the irritating voice in the back of his mind, *you'll take her back to the Wallflower Academy and never see her again? Because this is a mistake. Your brother James would never have sanctioned this!*

'Well, here we are,' Percy said aloud, drawing the carriage to a halt. 'Almack's.'

It was Gwen's turn for her face to fall. 'No, you have not…? Almack's?'

'I have indeed,' said Percy with a grin. Dear God, it was pleasant to be rich. Rich, powerful, able to do whatever he wanted! 'I'm sneaking you in, so you had better be on your best—'

'But you can't—'

'There is nothing I cannot do,' said Percy easily, jumping down from the carriage. 'You'll soon see.'

He was rather pleased with himself. Almack's was, after all, one of the most delightful and exclusive assembly halls in London. Vouchers were issued by strict invitation by the most respected in Society. To be seen in Almack's was to be a part of the *ton*.

He offered his hand, but for some inexplicable reason Gwen did not take it. Stranger still, she was glaring.

'Don't you want to get out of that Academy?' he said.

She hesitated. 'Yes, but—'

'And haven't you always wanted to see how the better classes live?'

Percy had not meant his words to wound, but he saw a

spark of anger in Gwen's eyes, glittering with the reflection of candles.

'I've seen enough already,' she said darkly.

Percy blinked. Now, what on earth did she mean by—?

'Come on, then, let us get it over with,' said Gwen with a sigh, disembarking from the carriage while studiously ignoring Percy's proffered hand.

'Over with?'

Gwen marched up the steps, leaving Percy to suddenly realise he had been left behind.

How did this woman never cease to surprise him?

She was handing her pelisse to a footman with very bad grace by the time Percy reached her. He threw his great-coat to the same man.

'Gwen, I—'

'I think you'll find it's Miss Knox here,' Gwen said, arching an eyebrow. 'I suppose you have some sort of pretence for my being here?'

Percy hesitated. He supposed he should do, but—

'Devereux? I thought it was you. It was so kind of you to wait. Your mother has asked you to accompany me.'

His heart froze. He turned slowly on his heel towards the sound of the imperious voice, and his stomach lurched painfully when he saw it was indeed the woman he had feared.

The Dowager Countess of Staromchor. Finlay Jellicoe's mother. He was a friend from childhood—a rather elevated one at the time, considering Percy had had no title, but strangely lesser than him now when it came to rank.

Percy almost laughed. The vagaries of Society could alter so dramatically with just a few deaths.

But he had certainly not intended to meet the Dowager Countess here. What was she doing—and why was she so convinced his mother had asked him to go with her?

'Come now, sir, offer me your arm!'

He felt something strange and stiff brace within him. 'It's Your Grace, actually.'

'Oh…' The Dowager Countess raised an eyebrow, looking far too amused for Percy's liking. 'I suppose it is.'

Percy felt Gwen's eyes on him, but could say nothing.

The Dowager had done it on purpose, of course. All the old aristocratic families had been astonished when he had been elevated to their rank, and some were none too happy about it.

Not that they would say so outright, naturally.

'My darling boy is sadly occupied this evening, so it was not possible for him to accompany me,' said the Dowager Countess impressively as she dropped her pelisse onto the now almost buried footman. She leaned against the cane clasped in her left hand. 'You are here to make a match, I suppose? And quite right too. Almack's is the only place to find a woman of suitable breeding. And you are…?'

Percy opened his mouth but, traitorously, no sound came out.

'Miss Gwendoline Knox, my lady,' said Gwen, curtseying low.

It was painful to watch the Dowager Countess sneer so openly at a woman she evidently believed inferior to her—and not without cause.

Percy's stomach dropped. Had he made a grave error by bringing Gwen here? And the Dowager Countess was still holding out her hand to him, as though it was natural Percy that would abandon his companion and accompany her.

'My lady…' he said aloud.

Well, what choice did he have?

'I don't know what you are doing, loitering here in the hall, we will be much warmer inside,' said the Dowager

Countess, striding on impressively now she had her balance. 'You may have my arm.'

Percy put out his own automatically—well, he was not a complete cad—but he could not help but regret finding himself in this corner.

How was he supposed to speak with Gwen now?

Just out of the corner of his eye he could see her, watching him curiously. Oh, damn it all to—

'I must say, I have been reading such dreadful things about your family, Your Grace,' the Dowager Countess said happily. 'I can see why you need to wed—and swiftly. Your brother's death...what a scandal! Have they caught the culprit yet?'

Percy's jaw tightened. 'No, my lady. Investigations are ongoing.'

'Indeed? An inn, I heard? Though where such a place could be found I do not know.'

He said nothing—not even to correct her. His mother was right, though: he needed to marry. He should not be here, should not be dallying with wallflowers when he needed a bride, and a wedding to distract the gossips of London.

That certainty did not help now—particularly with Gwen following them so demurely. Knowing her place, Percy thought darkly.

When it became clear that he was not going to speak, the Dowager Countess said, 'I thought I might see you at the Wallflower Academy, for I hear gossip that you have made yourself rather popular there.'

Percy's jaw tightened. Dear God, the speed at which rumours could spread in this town! Now he would have to hope beyond hope that his reputation was not sullied by the connection, and that he would still manage to find a woman of whom James would have approved.

He was highly conscious of the heat on the back of his neck. Undoubtedly it was being warmed by the gaze of Gwen...

'Yes, I always knew being a patroness of the Wallflower Academy would provide me with sufficient entertainment,' the Dowager Countess continued as they walked towards double doors which opened to reveal spectacle and noise as they approached. 'But I had no comprehension it would be so thrilling. They are little darlings, aren't they?'

Percy smiled weakly, but held his tongue despite great provocation.

It was, after all, most infuriating. Not only was he being forced to remain by the Dowager Countess's side—unable to speak to Gwen at all, let alone privately—but he was also being forced to endure the banal conversation of a woman who clearly considered the wallflowers mere playthings.

Playthings! He would like her to spend more than five minutes in their company, Percy thought darkly. Sylvia had a tongue that could lash just as well as the Dowager Countess's, and Rilla was sharper than half the men in his acquaintance.

'They are most eloquent women,' Percy said as they stepped into the dance hall.

Much like White's, Almack's was unchanged. He couldn't imagine it being any different from the way it had been since the first time he had been given his vouchers: the elegant pillars, the tables covered in food and large punch bowls. A set of musicians were tuning their instruments at one end of the room, while Mamas cooed after their daughters, newly entering Society, at the other.

'Eloquent? I do not believe I have heard any of them string three words together,' said the Dowager Countess impressively, inclining her head at someone who had approached in a rush of fawning. 'Apparently there is a new one to view…most interesting. No real family, of course, and no connections. No real beauty either, I'm told.'

Percy's stomach twisted painfully and he could not help himself—he looked over his shoulder at Gwen.

She was furious. The same fury he had seen when he had accidentally knocked her down was visible in her eyes, and Percy could understand why.

Not that he could say anything. Oh, perhaps a man *born* the son of a duke…who'd had a duke's education, had been taught a duke's mannerisms, pride…perhaps he would be bold enough to directly challenge a woman like the Dowager Countess.

It was, after all, mostly true. Gwen had no family and no connections. She was a most unsuitable companion for a duke. She had beauty, yes, but Percy was not foolish enough to think that sufficient.

Perhaps, if James had not died…

Percy swallowed. Then he would not have been the Duke. Wouldn't have risen to the title under a cloud of scandal. Wouldn't need his advice at all.

But he was gone.

Percy's heart hardened. He was not about to disgrace his memory.

It was fortunate indeed that the Dowager Countess had released his arm to move away and chatter with the person who had approached. He was relieved not to have to disgrace both himself and Gwen by a half-hearted breathless defence.

No real beauty? Gwen? What idiot had shared *that* message? Percy could not conceive of anyone looking at Gwen, with her dark eyes, the cleverness within their pupils, the way her lips curled into a smile when she believed she was not being observed…

Percy's stomach lurched painfully.

Not beautiful?

'Well…' said Gwen quietly. 'That is breeding.'

A rush of exasperation roared through him. 'I cannot defend the indefensible, but you should think twice before speaking in such a way of your betters!'

Speaking to anyone in such a way a few months ago… it would not even have crossed his mind.

But he had changed, somehow, and it was only now that Percy realised it. Betters? Almost everyone had been his 'better' before the Duchy had fallen most unexpectedly into his lap.

Something curdled painfully in his chest.

Now they were words he might have spoken to anyone who had uttered such a disrespectful sentence. So why did Percy feel so traitorous saying them to Gwen?

They might have been such a perfect match. Before his title, before Society's expectations, before his mother had demanded the world…

Gwen would have been perfect. Bold, clever, elegant. Beautiful. Well-born enough for a man with no real fortune and no ambitions to nobility.

Indecision washed through him.

He should leave.

He should turn around, apologise to the Dowager Countess and her companion, if he could find the patience, and leave. Take Gwen back to the Academy. Forget about her.

Percy had come not to hear gossip but to be with Gwen—to get her on her own if he could. To make her laugh if he could. To dance with her scandalously before the *ton*, who would not know her humble origins. To lean close, breathe her in, finally kiss her, taste her lips…

'My betters? Right… So long as I know my place,' Gwen said with a glare. 'Well, we are here now—unless you wish to return me to the Academy at once. What does one do at Almack's?'

A pair of gentlemen overheard her question and shot her a puzzled, disapproving look.

Percy grimaced. He felt so foolish now. What had he been thinking, bringing her here?

'I'm sorry,' he said stiffly.

For a moment Gwen merely examined him, as though she could see within his mind, within his heart. Could she see the regret? Feel the anguish of the words which had slipped out?

'You don't even know the meaning—Forget it... You are forgiven,' she said quietly.

Percy frowned, examining her closely. 'Don't know the meaning of what?'

For some strange reason, Gwen would not meet his eye. 'It doesn't matter.'

'Anything you wish to say to me matters,' he said softly, his chest painful when she refused to look at him. 'Gwen!'

There was something intangible flickering under the surface. A passion, an intellect...something more. Something he had underestimated. There was far more to Gwen's thoughts than her mere words.

Gwen continued to talk, but he could not take in a word. He had acted rashly, yes, but they were here now, weren't they? Was it better to stay, attempt to make the best of the evening...? Or return her to the Academy? And what had she been about to say?

'Your Grace?'

Indecision paralysed him, preventing him from retreating, getting out of the place, or moving forward to dance with Gwen before the floor grew too crowded.

After all, there was always the danger that his mother might change her mind and attend tonight...

'Per—Your Grace?'

Percy blinked. Gwen was looking at him with a rather strange smile.

'I said, are you ready to accompany me in the next set?'

Percy swallowed. He should not even be countenancing such—

Fingers, warm and certain, slipped into his. He looked down. Gwen had taken his hand.

'I know I shall never come here again,' Gwen said in a low voice as the musicians played their opening notes. 'So I think it only right you dance once with me before we leave.'

His stomach relaxed and his heart sang as his eyes met hers.

Gwen.

It was criminal, the way he was being tempted. By God, Percy knew full well that he should leave. He certainly should not tempt Gwen's temper again. Once unleashed, it made her as fearsome and as eloquent as any man, let alone any lady of good Society.

Percy's feet took him closer, unconsciously. A flush crept across her cheeks.

'Well?'

'Oh, you must not mind His Grace,' said the Dowager Countess airily, waving a hand at Percy as she leaned away from her conversation partner. 'He is a duke, true, and far above your station, but you may speak to him if you wish.'

The colour in Gwen's cheeks was now a radiant crimson, and Percy would have done anything to help her escape. Every nerve in his body was on edge, but there was naught he could do. How could he disrupt Almack's? His reputation was only just being remade after his brother's outrageous death—he could not risk...

'I'll bear that in mind, thank you,' said Gwen sweetly,

before pulling Percy towards the set now being made in the centre of the room.

His heart was beating so rapidly he could barely hear the music—but that did not seem to matter. Gwen released his hand as she passed him, leaving him to stand in the line of gentlemen, and it was agony—agony to be without her.

This was too much…he was going too deep. He needed to step away and—

The dance began and the line of ladies moved forward. Percy's heart caught in his throat as Gwen smiled, her eyes flashing with mischief, and he knew then this was the most delightful mistake he had ever made.

He raised his hand and his stomach lurched as she met it with hers. It wasn't meant to feel like this, was it? He had danced before with countless ladies, all of them far superior in station to Gwen. At least, Percy supposed they had been. It was hard to concentrate on any other ladies now, with Gwen's hands in his as they promenaded down the set.

'You are so beautiful…' he breathed.

He could not keep the thought in; she had to know.

Gwen smiled ruefully. 'Is this the part of the dance where you compliment your partner?'

Percy swallowed. 'No, this is the part of the dance where I am supposed to find my senses.'

Because his hands burned as he touched her waist and ached as they left it. His heart was thumping so loudly he was certain she would hear it, and if he was not very much mistaken…

Oh, he would need an ice-cold bath after this.

Gwen glanced up through dark eyelashes as they stood at the end of the line, watching the other dancers promenade down the set. 'What did you expect, Your Grace, by bringing me here?'

Percy did not know. All he knew was that the mistake

was a glorious one. One never to be repeated, and so to be revelled in.

'Aren't you afraid?' she asked.

His stomach lurched as he lied, 'No.'

'Someone could recognise you…spread rumours…ruin your reputation,' Gwen said with a knowing smile as she stepped towards him.

Heat rushed through Percy as their bodies grew closer again. Recognise him? He had already crossed words with the Dowager Countess—it was too late for that. He would simply have to hope their conversation would not be mentioned to his mother.

Besides, he was not yet so famed in the *ton* to have his face noticed in a crowd.

'If they do, they will see naught but me dancing with a beautiful woman,' he said smoothly.

'A woman you cannot marry, though. Or even consider.'

'Of course not,' Percy said instinctively. 'You don't meet the—I mean…'

Damn. He had spoken without thought, giving the correct answer—the only response he could possibly give. And yet they tasted bitter in his mouth, those words which he would have said to any other woman who did not meet James's standards. And why did looking at Gwen make the words hollow?

And then the dance was over. The music stopped. Percy blinked, and heard gentle applause echoing around the room.

Gwen shook her head with a smile as she took Percy's unhesitating arm. 'I think we are agreed that I am not your future bride. So let us forget that. I had always worried I would never be able to dance in public.'

'In public?' repeated Percy, as though he had been hit over the head with a cricket bat. 'Yes…'

They were walking back to the side of the room—unfortunately, Percy saw too late, to where the Dowager Countess was now standing.

'I've never done such a thing at the Academy, anyway, and—'

'The Academy?'

Percy groaned inwardly as the Dowager Countess looked over at them.

'I know you cannot be talking about the Wallflower Academy. His Grace would never be so foolish as to risk his reputation by giving one of those girls any expectations,' the Dowager Countess said with a laugh that filled the whole room. 'Besides, they have little to recommend them, do they not?'

Bitter fire rose in Percy's throat. 'I believe the purpose of the Academy is to teach—'

'Oh, but you cannot teach the ability to talk to people, no matter what that woman says,' interrupted the Dowager Countess. 'What's her name? Miss Perch? Miss Pickle? And that must leave the wallflowers in a sorry position, must it not? Not that I am saying *you* are such a thing, Miss… I would never presume to insult you so. I mean to say, who would marry a wallflower?'

Percy could barely see, he was so furious, so desperate for this moment to be over. It was excruciating, standing before Gwen in such a conversation.

'I believe that with many wallflowers, as you call them, it is only confidence which is lacking,' he said quietly, trying not to catch Gwen's eye. 'With a little confidence—'

'Confidence comes from breeding, not lessons,' said the Dowager Countess curtly. 'Not that you'd know anything about that.'

Now it was Percy's turn to flush.

Of all the things she could have said—it was an outrage! Just because he had not been born to the Dukedom...

But he could say nothing. His mother's desire to remain in polite Society, let alone his own, required that he accepted the whispers and the murmurs about his sudden rise to the aristocracy. Why else was his mother so fixated on him making a 'proper' marriage?

'Have you nothing to say for yourself? Why are you so dull?' the Dowager Countess said lightly, flicking a finger at Gwen.

Percy's blood boiled—but he had no right to feel that way. He was not Gwen's relation, not father nor brother, to protect her reputation. He was not her betrothed and nor— Percy's stomach lurched—her husband to stand by her.

But by God he wished he was.

Mortified did not adequately explain the feeling in Percy's system, yet no words rose to Gwen's defence.

What could he say—what could he do?

Cause more rumours to flutter about London, to reach his mother's hearing, that he had fallen for a wallflower? Allow the whole of Society to believe he had been taken in by a woman who, in public, was unable to string more than two words together?

Worst of all, he might give Gwen hope that he would one day offer her something Percy knew he could never give her.

Gwen smiled coldly, no warmth reaching her eyes. 'My apologies, my lady, Your Grace, for being so devastatingly dull as to be considered a wallflower.'

'No, don't—don't say that,' said Percy wretchedly. 'Gwen—'

'You must understand, Your Grace, we are simply not prepared to speak to people of your elevated rank.'

Gwen's words were so icy she might have given his

mother lessons. Percy hated the way she spoke—without hope, without any belief that she was worth so much more than this rotten treatment.

'Do not say that,' said Percy again, stepping towards her. He wanted to be much closer, to bring Gwen into his arms, but he managed to restrain himself. Almack's was not the place for such expressions of passion. 'It is just that people of my rank, you know...we must speak the—'

'Truth?' interjected Gwen with a raised eyebrow. 'It is true. You and your kind, Percy—my apologies, *Your Grace*—look at us as like animals in a zoo. That's all we are to you—entertainment. Well, I have no desire to entertain you further today. I want to go home—I mean, to the Academy.'

Without another word, Gwen strode off towards the double doors, though she had the presence of mind not to slam them.

Percy stood there, hating himself and the situation he had allowed himself to be pulled into. Because Gwen was right. To others of his kind, the Wallflower Academy *was* merely entertainment—a way to be amused on a quiet day. His mother would certainly agree. He had been absolutely round the twist to bring her to Almack's. His father would never—

The thought halted in Percy's racing mind. Now he came to think about it, he wasn't sure what his father would have done. The man was a distant memory, faded, based primarily on the portrait of him in the hall. The man himself... It was James who had stepped into that role. James who had fleshed out the figure now living in Percy's mind, doling out judgement.

Percy swallowed. So what would James advise in this scenario?

And what was he to do with these growing affections?

Chapter Nine

'*Have you nothing to say for yourself? Why are you so dull?*'

Gwen swallowed and pushed away the painful memory from the day before and the fit of rage threatening to surface. She was not going to allow one conversation to overtake her mind, nor permit the words of one woman to colour her day.

But it isn't just one person's opinion, is it? a horrible, cruel voice in her mind reminded her, as each passing day brought more elevenses, luncheons, teas, dinners—though, thank goodness, no balls.

One after another they would continue, she knew, until she had managed to make a match her mother could be proud of.

Or, Gwen thought dully as she tried to focus on Miss Pike, *until her mother gave up hope of her marrying at all.*

How long? A Season? A year? Rilla had been here three years, she had revealed to Gwen, and her family had all but given up hope of a match.

'They have far more nefarious plans for me now,' Rilla had said darkly, only that morning, but though Gwen had questioned her politely she had been unwilling to say more.

'And the left foot forward!' Miss Pike said fiercely.

Gwen cleared her throat and moved her left foot, matching the other wallflowers in the line. That was the trouble with this particular class at the Academy. One could pretend to be attending when one was being lectured on etiquette. The ladies could have their own conversations when pretending to practise small talk. Even when learning the refinements expected at a dining table it was possible to ignore much of what Miss Pike said.

But not, evidently, in dancing lessons.

'Really, Miss Knox, I expected better of you,' said Miss Pike severely.

She was standing before the line of wallflowers in a room that anywhere else Gwen would have been described as a ballroom, though she had never seen it used in such a fashion. Still, the wooden floor was sprung, there were candelabras all along the walls and a magnificent chandelier above—at least, Gwen was sure it was magnificent. It was for the moment covered in a dustsheet.

'I do apologise, Miss Pike,' Gwen said quietly to the floor.

She tried not to notice the intrigued looks Sylvia was giving her, just to her right. As long as she prevented her mind from slipping back to the day before, when she had danced in a very different room and with a very different partner...

'Now—right hand up, palm straight, for you to meet the palm of your partner,' said Miss Pike, demonstrating.

Gwen started. She had become lost in her thoughts again—an inconvenient and all too repetitive problem of late.

That was the trouble with almost kissing dukes, she told herself sternly. And this particular duke had rather got into her head.

Still, it was not as though he had almost kissed her

yesterday—nor put up much of a defence at the Dowager Countess's words.

Gwen sighed and lifted her hand in the manner Miss Pike indicated. How they were supposed to learn to dance without partners, she had no idea. If only they could bring in a few gentlemen to dance with.

Any gentleman but Percy.

Even the thought felt like a betrayal. Though anger still roared in her veins, hot and sparking along her fingertips, she could not entirely quash the memory of his fingers on her skin, those tantalisingly unbidden desires—

She mustn't.

Yet the thoughts did not diminish.

Gwen's heart leapt at the prospect of dancing with the dashing Duke again. His hand pressed up against her, his steps following hers, that wonderful moment when he'd place his hand on her back, around her waist, and she'd look into his eyes and know...

Know.

Know what he wanted of her. What he felt.

It did not appear that Percy knew what he felt, but Gwen could not blame him. She hardly knew herself.

Besides, it was not likely she and Percy would ever dance together again. The Wallflower Academy never had balls—at least, Rilla had never known one in three years—and there was no possibility of returning to Almack's.

Gwen shivered. She needed to concentrate. Percy Devereux, Duke of Knaresby, was not her ticket out of the Wallflower Academy and she needed to remember that. If she wished to make a match—a respectable match, any match—she would need to leave Percy alone at the next afternoon tea or formal dinner and speak to other gentlemen.

Even if they did not raise her heartbeat like Percy did.

Even though they did not make her feel warm like Percy did. Did not make her long to be touched, to be held.

It made her realise he was one of the first people ever to have truly listened to her...

'One, two, three, four. One, two—Are you paying attention, Miss Knox?'

'Yes, are you paying attention?' whispered Sylvia with a wicked grin. 'Or are you thinking about that duke of yours?'

Gwen flushed. 'I am not—he is not my duke!'

'Enough talking there!' Miss Pike looked flushed herself. It appeared counting and moving was far more than her solid constitution could bear. 'Well, you know the steps now. Let me see what you can do. One, two, three, four...'

It was all rather dull, thought Gwen morosely as she stepped forward and back, lifting and dropping her hands on the correct beats. Pretend-dancing in preparation for gentlemen they'd never speak to and balls they would never be invited to.

It was all nonsense. All foolishness.

How did Miss Pike expect any of them to get married if they were never permitted to see any gentlemen truly as themselves? One could not simply transform a wallflower...

Perhaps it would be best if she did not see Percy again.

Gwen rebelled at the thought, but a part of her knew it was best. The best way to avoid pain and to reduce the agony of separation when Percy grew tired of coming here.

Because he would. He had almost said so himself. He could not marry her, could not court her—not properly. He had to make an impressive match. And she? She was a murderess. Hardly a suitable bride for a duke.

Gwen's heart contracted painfully, but she could not deny the truth of her thoughts. From today, she vowed, she would ensure she did naught to attract Percy's attention. If he even returned after that excruciating conversation between him and the Dowager Countess…

Trust her to make a fool of herself before a dowager countess!

No, from now on Percy could have nothing to do with—

'Good morning, Miss Pike…ladies,' said Percy brightly as he stepped into the ballroom. 'Practising a country dance, I see? My favourite.'

A slow smile crept over Rilla's face. 'My, my…' she said with clear satisfaction. 'Is that Gwen's duke I can hear?'

'He is not my duke,' Gwen hissed, hoping beyond hope that Percy had not heard those words—though it was too much to hope for if the grin on his face was anything to go by.

'I wouldn't be so sure, Gwen,' said Sylvia with a laugh.

'Ladies!' spluttered Miss Pike, astonished. 'Really!'

'Oh, I would not concern yourself, Miss Pike. They say far worse things about me when I am not around,' said Percy cheerfully. 'Well, we'll be off, then.'

Before Gwen could say anything, or even think about the confusion around her, Percy had leaned forward, taken her hand in his, and was pulling her towards the door.

'Off?' Miss Pike's stern voice echoed impressively around the room. '*Off,* Your Grace? Who do you think you are—stop manhandling my wallflower!'

Even with their difference in social station, it appeared the Duke could not resist a direct order spoken in Miss Pike's ringing tones.

Perhaps it was something to do with her being his governess, Gwen thought wryly as she stood, confused, by his side. All gentlemen of his class were raised by governesses, weren't they? Strong, determined, educated women, with stern voices carrying absolute command.

Perhaps Miss Pike had left her true calling.

'A problem, Miss Pike?' Percy asked mildly.

Gwen told herself she was not going to look at him—then immediately did so and regretted it. Why was the man so irritatingly handsome?

It wouldn't be difficult to resist his allure, his charming presence, if Percy was not so pleasant to look at—but as it was, she found herself utterly captivated.

He was everything she wanted.

Everything she knew she could not have.

'Y-You cannot simply abduct one of my wallflowers!' Miss Pike strode towards him, lowering her voice into a hiss, as though there were others within the room who might overhear and be shocked.

As it was, the other wallflowers looked remarkably entertained. Gwen tried not to look, but was then faced with two increasingly difficult options: gazing at Percy again, and allowing her heart to race most painfully in her chest, or looking at the ire of Miss Pike.

She compromised by staring at the floor between them.

'I cannot?' Percy raised an eyebrow. 'They are hardly prisoners. I promise to bring her back, Miss Pike, but beyond that I do not believe you can stop me.'

Once again, he took Gwen's hand in his own, and this time, with a thrill of excitement because she was both to leave the claustrophobic atmosphere of the Wallflower Academy for a time and spend time with Percy, she allowed herself to be pulled.

'Where are we going?' she asked breathlessly as Percy charged down the corridor and turned a corner.

He grinned as he glanced back. 'Anywhere but here.'

Gwen's heart soared, though there was a tinge of worry. What would her mother say if she was informed?

But there were moments—and this was one of them—

when she knew Percy understood her…really knew her. He understood her growing frustration at being cooped up like a child who had misbehaved. Why else had he taken her last night to Almack's?

Still, there was a prickle of discontent in Gwen's heart that she could not ignore as they reached the hallway and the protesting footman, who was roundly ignored by the Duke.

It had been not quite four and twenty hours since she had thrown angry words at him, and though she burned to think of them, Gwen did not regret their utterance.

She'd meant every last word.

There was too much to divide them, too much to keep them apart, even if Percy evidently did not wish it. Their stations in life and what was expected of them—and her dark past, which Percy simply could not guess—all should prevent any sort of attachment between them.

Gwen swallowed as she saw the Knaresby barouche once again stationed outside the Academy, horses snuffling in the cold air, their breath blossoming before them.

Only the smallest portion of her temper had been lost yesterday, and what had she done? Shouted at a duke, berated him for trying—and failing—to defend her from a dowager countess, then stormed out of Almack's, doubtless causing great upset and scandalous whispers.

It was a small mercy she had not raised her hand to him, Gwen thought wildly.

She was dangerous. She should not be spending any time with a gentleman like Percy, even if he was so arrogant. For his sake.

'Up you get,' said Percy briskly, lifting his hand and placing Gwen in the carriage before she could protest. 'There.' He strode around the barouche and within a moment was seated beside her. 'Off we go.'

Where they were to go, Gwen could not comprehend. Knowing not the lanes around the Wallflower Academy, it was impossible to guess. She could ask, to be sure, but after her outburst the previous day she found her words stuck in her throat.

How could she face him?

It did not appear, however, that Percy had much to say either. For a full twenty minutes, as London grew closer, they sat in silence as the hedgerows passed them at an ever-increasing pace, frost still picking at the corners of their golden leaves. They gave out as more streets emerged, and the clatter and noise of London roared about them.

Eventually, Gwen could stand it no longer. 'Where... where are we going?'

She shivered, though whether from cold or from uncertainty, she was not sure. If only she'd had time to collect her pelisse... If only she'd had time to ask more questions...

Yet time was not the problem here. Had she not, within this very hour, promised herself she would not spend any more time with the Duke who was fast securing her heart?

'I don't know,' said Percy shortly.

A thrill of horror rushed through Gwen's mind as the barouche turned a corner and rumbled down another street. She had believed Miss Pike to be far too agitated when she had accused Percy of abducting one of her wallflowers, but there was so much about Percy she did not know—huge swathes of his life she had never seen.

What was the Duke of Knaresby like when not at the Wallflower Academy? Was he taking her to his townhouse, where they would talk—where he would try to seduce her?

Gwen swallowed as her body warmed at the thought.

You are not supposed to desire such things, she told herself sternly.

Least of all with a duke who certainly could offer her nothing in the way of matrimony.

If only she had permitted him to kiss her when they had last been in his barouche…

It was a scandalous thought, but one Gwen could not help. The idea of being ravished by Percy, making love to him, his fingers on her skin… Though guilt clouded her mind, it did not diminish her desire.

A young lady should not want such things, she knew. A young lady should be chaste, and innocent, almost ignorant.

Gwen glanced at the gentleman beside her, highly conscious of his knee pressed up against hers. How would it feel if her skirts and his breeches were not in the way?

'You are cold,' said Percy regretfully, as she shivered again. 'I should have brought blankets. I did not… I just… I had to see you.'

That was perhaps the most endearing thing about Percy. When she had pictured a duke in her childhood days, even before she had arrived at the Wallflower Academy, she had envisaged an aloof, dry gentleman who never admitted fault and always blamed others.

But Percy was not like that. At least, he was sometimes. Arrogant and imperious and absolutely convinced he was in the right, no matter the subject of conversation. But at the same time he was…different. Warmer. Exactly what she wanted from a gentleman. From a husband. From a lover.

'We'll stop here.'

Gwen started as Percy nudged the horses to the side of the street and pulled them to a halt. Stop here? Where were they? And why had he brought her here?

Percy tossed a penny at a boy who was loitering on the pavement. 'See to my horses,' he said easily, 'and if they are well when I return I shall give you a crown.'

As she laughed at the boy's wide eyes, Gwen's cheeks were hot.

Here she was, in London, alone with a gentleman—with a duke, no less! What would her mother think?

'Rotten Row is just there—we'll go for a walk,' said Percy briskly. 'Come on.'

He seemed to be saying that a lot recently, Gwen thought sombrely, as she clambered down from the barouche, conscious of stares from those walking along the pavement. Well, he was a gentleman accustomed to barking orders. His rudeness was not rehearsed, but inbuilt.

'Here,' Percy said, moving his arm around her and pulling her close as he guided her forward towards what appeared to be the entrance to a great park.

Gwen's eyelashes fluttered as she was overwhelmed with the intensity of the intimacy. His warmth flooded her body as she was drawn to his chest. She could feel his heartbeat and it echoed hers—fast and frantic and untamed.

It was the most intimate she had ever been with a gentleman, and she wanted more. Unsatiated, Gwen knew that what she wanted was unthinkable. Yet it was certainly not unimaginable.

They passed through wrought-iron gates and she saw that there was, indeed, a park before them. A long path made predominantly of sand wended its way to the left, and it was there that Percy pulled her.

A number of other couples—all of excellent breeding, from what Gwen could tell from their outer garments—were walking in a similar manner.

Well, she thought wildly. *This is what it means to be a part of Society!*

How much time passed before either of them spoke again, Gwen was unsure. Her gaze drifted past the spires of churches and the roofs of tall buildings, looming against the autumnal sky. Other walkers looked at her curiously, their gazes flicking between her and Percy.

Her cheeks darkened. Of course they were wondering what she was doing with a gentleman like him!

'London,' said Percy with a sigh. 'I thought… Well, I thought it would be a chance to do something different.'

'I have never been to Town before. Except for last night, I mean.'

'Truly never been? I thought you were jesting.'

It appeared the idea was unthinkable to him, but Percy evidently had something else on his mind, for he asked no further questions.

Instead, after a minute of silence between them as they continued to walk, he said quietly, 'I must apologise for my behaviour yesterday. It was… There is no excuse. I can only ask for your forgiveness.'

There was clear tension in him as he spoke. Evidently the Duke had been punishing himself most severely for the way he had treated her and was unwilling to continue without an apology.

She swallowed. It all seemed like a dream now. The brilliance of the candles at Almack's, the silk gowns, the powdered hair, the sweeping movement of the dance…

Something of the way he had spoken echoed in her mind, and Gwen smiled. Her temper demanded that she rage, shout, even shove him to prove just how furious she was.

And she had been.

But no longer.

'You once said to me, at the first dinner we attended together, that when I had something to apologise for I would know it. You should recognise that in yourself, you know. And this…this isn't it. You have nothing to apologise for,

Percy. It was…regrettable. Regrettable, indeed. But not your fault.'

Percy sighed deeply and Gwen could almost sense the tension leaving his body. It was a surprise to see how greatly his apology had affected him, just as it had her. Why had he cared so much?

Why, if it came to that, were they in Town?

A terrifying thought struck Gwen.

He wasn't…he wasn't about to introduce her to his mother, was he?

Though the prospect frightened and intrigued her in equal measure, it soon became clear that Percy had no real idea of why he had brought her to Town at all. They meandered along Rotten Row and Gwen stared around her at London, loud and cacophonous, full of people and shouting and animals and noise.

'I thought of showing you the Queen's Palace,' said Percy with a dry laugh, 'but now I am wondering whether you would just like to stare at the people!'

Gwen's cheeks burned. 'I just—I had no idea London was so busy!'

'Far too busy, if you ask me,' Percy said with a shake of his head. 'Here, let us turn off here and I can take you through some of the busiest streets for your amusement.'

With the well-practised ease of a gentleman who had done it a thousand times, Percy guided her across the path of those well-dressed others walking along Rotten Row, out of the park, and onto the pavement of a bustling street.

Hawkers peddled their wares, someone was attempting to sell newspapers, a vicar stood on a box yelling at passers-by, and every minute another barouche or a chaise or a mail coach rushed past them.

Gwen could hardly take it all in, and fear curled at her heart. What if someone saw them? What rumours would flourish if the handsome, eligible new Duke of Knaresby was seen in public with a woman without a chaperon?

'Well, where shall we begin?' asked Percy, clapping his hands together.

Gwen laughed at her own ignorance. 'I just—Well, seeing anything, just the people in London, the noise, the excitement—'tis too much!'

Percy smiled as they started to meander. 'Truly, there is no particular spectacle you wish to see?'

'Sometimes you underestimate just how ordinary I am, Your Grace,' said Gwen with a teasing tone as they turned a corner onto a street that was, if possible, even busier. 'Most of us did not grow up as heirs to a dukedom.'

She had believed he would laugh, say something amusing about London and the people within it. What she did not expect was the dark expression that crossed Percy's face, as if a shadow had passed over the sun of his life.

'I… I thought that even if both my cousins had died without issue it would be James who…'

Gwen wished she could take back her words. Of course—how could she have forgotten? It was only by familial tragedy that his title had been inherited. How could she have been so thoughtless?

Percy laughed at the look on her face and shook his head. 'That is the trouble with you, Gwen,' he said quietly. 'Whenever I am with you I wish to remain in the present, not dwell on the past.'

'If it is too painful—'

'Oh, I can think on it quite well now,' Percy said easily, though Gwen was not entirely sure that was true. There was a catch in his voice suggesting otherwise. ''Tis only that… Well, I told you my uncle and cousins died most unexpectedly, and then my brother, and I inherited the title. But I did not mention in detail… I told you about him, my brother—my elder brother? He was a great deal older than me, so I saw little of him, and his death was quite sudden. Mysterious circumstances, to tell the truth. There were whispers of foul play, but obviously that was just talk. It was an accident. One of those accidents one can never predict.'

Gwen's heart seared with pain and she looked away. Was her life to be marked by such accidents? By these deaths of which at least one could be ascribed to her door?

She had not meant to—but then, had she? And he had died, that man. She was dangerous, that was what she was, and she should steer clear of any man she cared for.

If only she could stay away...

She had to get back. The Wallflower Academy might be dull, but it was safety. She must return.

'Gwen?'

Percy sounded astonished as Gwen removed her hand from his arm and turned around, pacing back the way they had come.

It was this way, wasn't it? Every street looked the same, and she had not been paying much attention to where they were going, most of her attention taken by the company she was keeping. She had to find her way back to the barouche...

'Gwen, what is wrong?' Percy caught up with her easily, a look of concern across his face.

'Nothing,' said Gwen, dropping her gaze so she did not have to look at him. She would not reveal the truth—not to him, not to anyone. Through a flustered breath, she said, 'The carriage—where is the barouche?'

'Gwen, come here.'

Gwen almost cried out as Percy pulled her suddenly to one side, into an alleyway she had not noticed. It was hardly wide enough for the two of them to stand in, and

Gwen leaned against the wall, ignoring its dirt, as her legs shook.

'You confuse me most heartily,' said Percy, his eyes searching her own.

Gwen could not look away. 'You confuse me every moment I am with you...'

Her breath was short in her lungs, and the world was spiralling, but for some reason concentrating on him, on Percy, kept Gwen grounded. His hands were cupping her face now, and she could not think how they had got there, only knew they felt as if they were home.

'Gwen...' breathed Percy, closing the gap between them and pressing against her, making it even more difficult for Gwen to draw breath. 'Gwen, I cannot stop—I cannot stop thinking about that kiss.'

Gwen swallowed, and Percy groaned as she whispered, 'Wh-What kiss?'

'The kiss that never was,' Percy said softly. 'The kiss we almost had in the carriage. The kiss I would take now, if you would let me. Oh, Gwen...'

It was hearing her name on his lips that did it. Overturning all her reason, Gwen gave herself up to the feelings she had so long suppressed and lifted her lips to be kissed. Percy moaned her name once more, and captured her lips with his own, gently at first.

The sudden shock of a gentleman's lips on hers was quickly overcome, and Gwen lifted her hands to clasp them around Percy's neck. And that was when the kiss deepened. He tilted her face, allowing his tongue to tease along her lips, one hand moving to her waist to pull her even closer, and Gwen's whole body tingled at the sudden pleasure rippling through her as she allowed him in.

'Gwen...' Percy moaned as he deepened the kiss, his tongue ravishing her even as his lips possessed hers.

And Gwen wanted more.

More of whatever he could give her, whatever they could share.

And even though she knew it was scandalous, kissing a duke in an alleyway as the rest of London passed them by, Gwen lost herself in the passionate embrace.

Eventually the kiss ended. Far too soon.

Percy looked into her gaze with a shaky smile. 'What have you done to me, you wallflower? You've made me want you all the more.'

Chapter Ten

Gwen tried to concentrate. She really did. And it was not a lack of willingness to pay attention, but more an inability to—

'Miss Knox! Kindly refrain from permitting your horse to meander. We are keeping to the path!'

Gritting her teeth, and attempting not to tell the Pike precisely how difficult it was to direct a horse one had only met an hour ago, Gwen tried to smile sweetly. 'Yes, Miss Pike.'

The autumnal air made their breath blossom like steam, and perhaps in any other circumstances Gwen would have enjoyed the ride. After all, it was pleasant to leave the confines of the Wallflower Academy, even if she could still just about see the Tudor manor from where they were. Mostly it was hidden by the wide oaks, their leaves almost gone, and it was almost possible to believe she had escaped the place—though Miss Pike's continuous presence rather challenged that, unfortunately.

'Ladies!'

Her heart stopped. No, not stopped—but it skipped a beat most painfully. So painfully Gwen brought a hand to her chest.

It was as though she had dreamed Percy into existence as a perfect picture of genteel masculinity, with the breeze tugging at his riding coat and a haughty yet warm smile on his lips.

Percy Devereux, the Duke of Knaresby, rode towards the gaggle of wallflowers on a steed at least three hands larger than their own. Gwen heard a gasp. For a moment she thought it had been Sylvia's, but then she realised it was her own.

'Well met,' said Percy, still grinning as he brought his horse alongside Gwen's. 'What a fortuitous chance that we meet, Miss Pike.'

Miss Pike seemed utterly lost for words. Her gaze snapped to the Duke on his horse and the wallflower he was beside.

Gwen tried to hold the woman's gaze as boldly as possible, but she could no longer do so after a few moments. How could she when she was in the presence of both the woman who had been instructed by her mother to help her find a husband and the one man she...?

But she had to put those sorts of thoughts out of her mind. It would not do even to permit them, Gwen told herself firmly.

'Y-Your Grace,' stammered Miss Pike, evidently thrown by the sudden appearance of a man of such nobility. 'You honour us with your presence!'

'So I see,' said Percy, winking at Sylvia, who giggled. 'I wonder whether you will permit me to assist?'

'Assist?' repeated not only Miss Pike, but also Gwen.

She was staring at the man who, the last time she had seen him, had been kissing her senseless in an alley before they returned to the Wallflower Academy.

Just what did Percy think he was up to?

'Assist,' repeated Percy, his smile unwavering. 'It appears you are giving the ladies some practice at horseback riding, and I would imagine the addition of a gentleman for them to speak to would greatly enhance the challenge of the exercise. Why don't I take…oh, Miss Knox, say… on a route into the woodlands, and we can practise the art of conversation?'

Heat blossomed through Gwen's body and she hoped beyond hope that it would not be obvious to the eye.

Practise the art of conversation? She would have laughed aloud if she had not been so mortified. Did he really think the Pike so foolish as to—?

'What a wonderful idea, Your Grace,' simpered Miss Pike, inclining her head as though unable to withstand such cleverness. 'Miss Knox, I require you to attend on the Duke.'

'But—'

'*Now,* Miss Knox,' came the firm direction.

And what did it matter anyway? Gwen wondered, as she gently nudged her horse to follow Percy's down a path she had never explored before. What sort of argument could she possibly put up to prevent such an action?

If she even wished to…

The voice of Sylvia echoed behind them as Gwen followed Percy wordlessly into the woodland. The trees grew closer here, obscuring house, Sylvia and the Pike until they were alone.

Gwen shivered despite herself. Alone with Percy. Again. With a man who kissed like the devil yet made her feel like an angel.

Percy breathed a laugh as he slowed his horse to walk slowly beside hers. 'Goodness, what a stroke of luck.'

'You were too bold,' Gwen pointed out, her heart pattering painfully in her chest and a smile creasing her lips despite her surprise at seeing him. 'I never would have thought the Pike—Miss Pike, I mean—would agree to such a scheme.'

'What? Because your innocence might be in danger?'

The words were shot back so quickly Gwen hardly knew what to say in response. All she could do was look at Percy, see the desire and hunger in his eyes, and swallow.

Was it just as obvious in her own expression just how dearly she wished to be kissed again?

Which was a nonsense—because where could this go?

Oh, the woodland path would undoubtedly stretch for miles, disappearing off into the wilderness. Gwen was certain the two of them could endeavour to 'get lost' if they really put their minds to it, and Miss Pike would never think to question such an excuse if it gave one of her wallflowers additional time with a gentleman such as a duke.

But after that?

Gwen's mind whirled frantically as she attempted to understand.

One more kiss, yes—but what then? Percy could hardly make an offer to her. He had made that perfectly clear...

Until he had kissed her. Then he had been perfectly *un*clear.

'Did you hear that?'

'What?' Gwen said, turning.

There did not seem to be any movement in the trees, nor any sound to be heard. But Percy was looking around, his gaze narrowed, as though expecting to see someone's shadow flickering through the trees.

'Nothing, I just thought...' Percy swallowed. 'My mother says I'm getting paranoid. Expecting people to be talking about me.'

'And they're not?'

'Oh, they are,' he said with a wry smile. 'But my mother assures me it's only good things.'

Gwen tried to smile. Only good things… That was what she wanted from Percy, but even she could not explain what she meant. *Good things.* What would 'good' look like with Percy? What was possible? They were so different. So—

'Gwen?'

Gwen started. Percy had not only halted his own horse, but hers, too. His hand had reached out, unbeknownst to her, and caught the reins of her mare, drawing her to a stop. There was a look of deep concern on his face and, try as she might, it was difficult to ignore just how handsome he was.

She smiled weakly. 'Percy…'

'Walk with me,' he said quietly, dismounting.

'But I am supposed to be practising—'

'A pox on your practising,' Percy said, holding out a hand.

Gwen hesitated only for a moment. She liked riding, but the opportunity to walk with Percy, close to him, far closer than would be possible while they were mounted… it was too much to resist.

Gently sliding from her mare, Gwen found to her utter distraction that Percy had been standing so close she was now firmly wedged between the unmoving horse and his broad chest.

Her breath caught in her throat, her gaze was caught by his own, and there was a fiery look within his eyes she had never noticed before.

Or was it simply that it had not been there before?

'I have missed you, Gwen…' Percy breathed softly.

Gwen swallowed. She should not say anything, certainly not agree… 'I have missed you too.'

This kiss was different from those they had shared in the alley. Yesterday they had been unrestrained, hot, passionate, demanding of Gwen everything she was, and she had given herself willingly.

But this was different. Softer, gentler, no less passionate but with a different flavour of desire. More reverent.

Still, it fair took Gwen's breath away, and made it near impossible for her to stand. She would have fallen if she had not been so heavily pressed between man and mare.

'Come on,' said Percy quietly.

'You have a habit of saying that, you know?'

'I wouldn't need to if you would just follow me.'

Placing her arm in his, Percy gently tied the reins of both horses to a large oak tree and started to walk Gwen deeper into the woods.

'You have never kissed anyone before me, have you?' he asked.

Gwen's cheeks immediately flared with heat. 'What makes you say—?'

'Oh, I have no complaints,' said Percy quickly. His arm tightened around her own. 'Dear God, quite the opposite... No, it's just... I can tell. Something in the way you cling to me.'

This was going from bad to worse! How was Gwen supposed to keep a calm head on her shoulders with such—such a conversation between them?

'I was kissed once,' said Gwen, the words tripping off her tongue no matter how much she attempted to halt them. 'But I did not like it.'

What on earth had possessed her to say such a thing? They had vowed, she and her mother, that they would never speak of that night—not with anyone. Not even between themselves. Not ever again.

It had been painful enough to do so the first time.

Why would either of them wish to do such a thing a second time?

But something about Percy was drawing it out of her like...like poison from a wound.

Gwen had read once about drawing out the poison when one had been attacked by a snake in the wilds of India. And was this not the same? Had not poison settled in her heart, her treacherous heart, and would she not be whole again if it could be removed?

Percy was frowning. 'Dear me, was the gentleman unskilled?'

Gwen took a deep breath. 'The man—I will not call him a gentleman—was...was forceful.'

Forceful. That was all she could manage, all she was willing to say, but even uttering the word seemed to quieten a part of her soul she had not realised had been broken.

'Forceful?' repeated Percy, and then his eyes darkened. 'Gwen, you don't mean—?'

'I am still an innocent,' said Gwen hastily, her cheeks still pink. 'He did not—But he was forceful. I did not enjoy—I did not want—'

'The blackguard—I'll cut him through! I'll call him out! I'll face him across a field at dawn!' spat Percy, and she could feel the rage boiling within him. 'The brute! Who was it?'

Gwen swallowed, remembering the darkness of that night, the chaos, the desperate need to be free, to escape from the clutches of a man who smelt of drink and pain. How she had struggled, desperate, her temper rising, outraged at his treatment, overwhelmed until she'd pushed—

'I don't know,' she admitted.

It was the truth, even if Percy glowered. 'You do not have to protect him...'

'I know,' Gwen said softly.

She swallowed, tried not to think about the crack of the—

'I know,' she repeated. 'And I do not keep his name from you to protect him. I simply do not know it.'

'No gentleman would ever—The blackguard! Is he here? At the Wallflower Acad—?'

'No!' Gwen interrupted, her heart pattering painfully still. Oh, she should never have admitted such a thing. Her temper that flared and caused such terrible things to happen. 'No, it was b-before.'

After all, how had her mother put it?

'Where's the best place to hide a murderess, Gwen? In a garden of wallflowers...'

Percy's breath was still tight as leaves crunched under their feet. 'Well, I am glad you are well rid of him, Gwen.'

It was difficult not to exclaim at this, but Gwen managed it. 'Well rid of him, indeed. It is the way of the world; I am not unique.'

'And to think it happened to you! You, of all people!' Percy continued.

Gwen's stomach twisted as he spoke.

'I remember when my brother James first talked to me about women. Told me what to look for...what to admire. Why, he was such a gentleman. He knew the ladies far better than I ever could.'

A small smile crept across Gwen's face. Something had changed in Percy. She had felt it as well as seen it. It was as if a gentle relaxing, a warmth, was flooding through him. Comfort...a sense of peace.

'You truly admired him, did you not?' she asked.

'Oh, I don't think anyone who met James did not admire him, even if they didn't like him,' said Percy, chuckling under his breath. 'He was taller than me, yet one did not feel overawed by the man. He was generous with his time—arguably to a fault. There are times, you know... times when I think I shall never live up to him. To his charm, his cleverness. His memory. Why, I remember this one time...'

Gwen's stomach slowly began to unclench as Percy chattered happily about the brother he had so clearly adored. Well, she had managed it. It was as close a conversation as she'd had about the truth, and she had not revealed the shameful end.

Perhaps—just perhaps—she could go through the rest of her life without consequences. Without having to face the awful thing she had—

'Gwen?'

Gwen blinked. Percy had halted, and her own footsteps had halted too, but she had not noticed. His expression was strange, hard to read, though intensely focused on her in a way she found most disconcerting.

'Percy?' she said.

A smile spread across his lips. 'I like it when you say my name. You weren't listening, were you?'

Shame flashed through her heart. 'Yes, I—'

'So what did my brother purchase for my last birthday?'

Gwen opened her mouth, knew there was no hope of her guessing, and closed it again. 'You know I haven't the faintest idea.'

Percy snorted. 'Well, at least that's honest. What's distracted you, Gwen?'

She hesitated before answering. It would not be right, would it, to admit to the topic that had truly entangled her mind away from his company? And in truth there was more than one distraction in her heart, and one of them was standing right before her.

'You.'

It was a simple syllable, one hardly requiring any thought. It flowed from her, from the truth of her heart, and something changed in Percy's eyes.

'You know I would never do anything you did not wish me to do, don't you?' he said quietly, dropping her arm but only doing so, it seemed, to clasp her hand in his. 'You are…precious to me, Gwen.'

The moment between them was unlike anything Gwen had ever known. Safety and danger. The heat within her meeting the cold air in a rushing twist of desire she knew she should not give in to, but—

'Kiss me…' she breathed.

It appeared Percy needed no additional invitation. Pulling her into his arms, he kissed her exquisitely on the mouth, his ardour forcing Gwen to take a few steps backwards as she clung to him desperately, her body tingling as prickles of pleasure rushed through her.

And then she was pressed up against a tree, and she gasped as Percy's tongue met hers in a tantalising tangle of lust and something deeper, something far softer. She moaned…

'Gwen,' murmured Percy, his lips moving to her neck, trailing kisses to the collar of her pelisse as Gwen tilted her head back, unable to stop herself, eager for more. 'Oh, Gwen…'

'Percy!' she gasped, unable to say anything more, hardly able to think. 'Percy, I want—'

But any specific request—even if her brain had been able to think of one—was wrenched from her mind as Percy seemed to act on her very thoughts.

If she had been able to think such a scandalous thing, of course…

While his lips continued to worship her neck she melted into his arms. This was what it should be like, she could not help but think wildly, as memories of that less pleasant encounter were overwritten by his softness, his gentleness.

There was passion there, yes, but it was controlled. Determined, but not demanding. Eager, but not exacting.

Desire rose within her…a desire which had never been

sparked before. And she wanted to tell him, show him, just how greatly she desired him.

Without a word, he seemed to know.

Percy's fingers reached for her gown. Somehow—Gwen was not sure how, pleasure having removed all senses but touch—he had pulled up her skirts past her knee, and his hand now rested on her upper thigh—her actual thigh.

Gwen moaned. The sense of his fingers on her skin was overwhelming, intoxicating, and there was nothing she could do but cling to him and hope this moment would never end.

'Tell me if you want me to stop,' Percy managed on a jagged breath. 'You understand, don't you, Gwen?'

'Don't stop...' Gwen moaned.

All thought that they might be found, discovered perhaps even by Miss Pike herself, had been driven from her mind. All she wanted was to lose herself in this moment as Percy—

'Percy!'

She had not shouted—there was not enough air in her lungs—but Gwen had been unable to help herself exclaiming as he gently brushed her curls with his fingers.

Such a jolt of decadent pleasure, such an overwhelming sensation, Gwen had never known before. Head spinning, hardly aware how she was still standing, she whimpered with joy as Percy's fingers grazed her again.

'Gwen—'

'More...' That was all she could manage. 'More!'

He needed nothing else.

As Percy's lips returned to her own, capturing both them and her whimpers, his fingers grew bolder, one of them slipping into her secret place. Gwen could see stars, feel an aching heat building in her such as she had never known before, could never have imagined her body could contain, and then suddenly—

'Percy!'

That was what Gwen had tried to shout, but her mouth had been utterly captured by the man she now knew she loved, and as Percy's fingers stroked her into ecstasy there was nothing she could do but hold on…hold on to the man she had given everything to, would give anything to.

As the pleasure slowly receded like a tide, Gwen managed to open her eyes.

Percy was gazing adoringly straight into hers. 'Gwen—'

'Percy…' she breathed, hardly able to believe she had permitted him to do such a thing. 'I—'

'Hush…'

Gwen blinked up, unsure why, after such lofty heights, Percy had had to bring her back to earth. He was looking around as if he had seen something, heard something, though what she could not—

'Gwen? Gwen, the Pike says we must return to the Academy in time for dining practice. Where are you?'

Reality was a rather disappointing thing to discover after such sensual decadence. Gwen breathed out a laugh, dropping her head onto Percy's chest, and wished they'd had a little more time. More time to talk, to kiss, to—

'Damn,' said Percy dryly, neatly capturing her feelings in one word.

'Damn, indeed,' Gwen said, the bold word sharp on her tongue. 'I had hoped—'

'I should probably take you back,' he said, sighing, allowing her skirts to fall back to the ground. 'Although I would really—Gwen, I hope that was pleasurable for you?'

'Pleasurable?' she repeated.

How could the man be in any doubt?

A flicker of uncertainty tinged his face. 'I am sorry if—'

'Percy Devereux, I could happily have you do that to me every hour, on the hour, for the rest of my life,' said Gwen quietly, pushing aside the thought that her future could never contain that. She was dangerous; she would not hurt him. And his promise to his brother would divide them for ever. 'If I could—'

'Gwen? Gwen, can you hear me?' The indefatigable voice of Sylvia came through the trees.

Percy groaned. 'Gwen, I don't want you to go.'

Her heart was racing, and the temptation to tell him she had no wish to return either was teasing her heart. They could leave. They had two horses...they could make their own way in the world...

But they couldn't. She couldn't.

There was already one scandal in her past that she was attempting to escape from. It would not do to tempt fate and cause another.

'Your Grace,' she said primly, almost laughing at the groan Percy uttered as she released him. 'I believe it is time for you to return me to the Academy.'

'Blasted Academy.'

'Yes, that one,' said Gwen with a laugh.

Oh, it was glorious to see how disappointed he was, to see how very viscerally he wished to keep her... But it was no use.

'Oh. There you are.'

Gwen whirled around, stepping as far away from Percy as she could without it being too obvious—*was* it too obvious?

Perhaps. There was an uncomfortably knowing look on Sylvia's face as she beamed at the two of them.

'My apologies, Your Grace, for disturbing you, but I am afraid Miss Knox must return with me.'

'Of course,' said Percy smoothly, and Gwen both hated and loved it that he could so swiftly act as though nothing had happened between them when everything had—everything. 'Let me help you onto your horse, Miss Knox.'

Gwen tried not to notice how her fingers tingled as Percy helped her mount her mare.

'I shall see you soon, will I not, Your Grace?' she asked in a low voice as Sylvia turned her own steed around, heading back towards the Academy.

Percy's eyes twinkled. 'Soon? Oh, very soon. As soon as I can make it.'

Chapter Eleven

The first day, Gwen did not worry. Her mind was full of memories of tantalising touches, of kisses that lingered—and those that did not.

'Gwen!'

Gwen started. A piece of fried egg slipped from the fork she had been holding before her, evidently for some minutes, her mind entirely on other things.

Sylvia was staring, utterly bemused. 'What on earth has got into you?'

'Nothing,' Gwen said hastily.

The last thing she wished to do was reveal to the wallflowers precisely what had happened between her and Percy.

He had not needed to gain a promise from her of secrecy. The very idea of sharing the most intimate moment of her life with others…

'Is it just me, or is Gwen rather quiet this morning?' asked Rilla as another wallflower helped her with her breakfast.

'I am not—'

'Silence, ladies!' Miss Pike, at the head of the breakfast table, glared at them. 'I will not have bickering at breakfast. It is far too early for all that.'

And so Gwen moved through the day dreamily, even with Sylvia's uncertain looks upon her.

The second day, Gwen did not worry either. Well, it had only been a day, and Percy surely had commitments in Town that he was required to fulfil.

He is a duke after all, Gwen thought dreamily when she was supposed to be working on some embroidery.

'Ladies should always have a talent to discuss,' Miss Pike had said firmly, that very afternoon. 'And the only appropriate talents are music, embroidery, watercolour painting or remarking upon the weather.'

The embroidery of roses that Gwen was supposed to be completing had seen no change, however, in the hour during which she and the other ladies had been seated, ostensibly at their needlework, in the orangery as slow afternoon sunlight poured through the glass.

Her needle poked into the embroidery circle but then abandoned, Gwen smiled wistfully at the thought of the way Percy had kissed her.

He must care for her. She had not expected such affection from any gentleman, so to find it from him, a man so kind, so gentle… And yet on first meeting his haughtiness! His determination that his position required the perfect wife!

It was therefore on the third day that a prickle of concern started to creep around Gwen's heart. It was, after all, a long time to go without hearing a word from the man one had shared such a scandalous moment with. A very long time indeed after one had given him one's heart—and rather more.

No note.

Gwen had looked up eagerly when the post had been brought in that morning, but her shoulders had slumped as only one letter had been placed before her, her mother's handwriting adorning the front.

Gwen had given it little thought. She knew what it would contain. More crowing over her mother's neighbours, more exhortation for Gwen to marry well—but not too well— and more vague threats about revealing their secret.

It was still unopened upstairs in her bedchamber as she sat downstairs in the drawing room, listening to the dull monologue Miss Pike was now giving the wallflowers about the correct mode of address.

'Naturally, as wallflowers, you are nervous, and therefore more likely to make mistakes,' Miss Pike was saying so cheerfully. 'The best thing to do, if you are unsure, is wait until someone else has made reference to the person in question. Then you can see...'

On the fourth day, Gwen awoke with panic settled in her stomach. Why did Percy stay away? Worse, why did he send her no word?

She had been happy to acquiesce to silence, to secrecy, but not to solitude. The rambling Tudor manor felt acutely discomforting, both home and prison.

Perhaps she should have asked him more precise questions, Gwen could not help but wonder as she stood in a line in the ballroom that afternoon, trying to follow Miss Pike's erratic instructions for a new country dance.

Perhaps she should have clarified what they would do next.

Or perhaps there was no plan? Perhaps Percy had no intention of seeing her until he was bored with Town?

The very thought curdled in her stomach.

Gwen swallowed and turned left as the other wallflowers turned right.

'Really, Miss Knox, pay attention!'

'Apologies, Miss Pike,' said Gwen quietly, her gaze fixed on the floor.

'It's that duke of hers,' said Rilla. She had a ribbon in

her hand, her sightless eyes fixed towards the sound of the wallflowers attempting to learn new steps. 'He has been away a few days, now I come to think about it.'

Gwen's heart contracted painfully.

She would do anything not to hear her new friends discuss such things!

'He has probably gone to his estate for the shoot,' Miss Pike said soothingly, and Gwen looked up to see the owner of the Wallflower Academy doing a rare thing: smiling. 'I must say I did not think you had it in you, Miss Knox, but you certainly seem to have attracted his attention.'

Heat crept across Gwen's cheeks, but she said nothing.

Why, if Miss Pike could even guess what had truly occurred between herself and Percy!

It was on the fifth day that Gwen truly started to panic. Had she upset or offended him in some way? Worse, had he discovered the truth of her past?

When that thought occurred to her, as she was reading and Sylvia read aloud to Rilla, on the evening of the fifth day since she had seen him, Gwen was certain for an instant that she was going to be sick. The very idea that Percy might have discovered her terrible crime… She was dangerous and, worse, a danger to his reputation…

'You are very quiet.'

Gwen looked up. Not a single word on the page of her book had been taken in, and she was surprised to see not only the windows dark, but the lamps lit.

'What?' she said, distracted.

'I have noticed,' said Rilla. 'Something has changed in you, Gwen, and do not say it has not, for I am quite capable of knowing when I am being lied to.'

Gwen looked at her book rather than meet Sylvia's penetrating gaze. 'It's nothing.'

Sylvia snorted. 'Nonsense.'

Could...could they tell?

Gwen was not aware that feeling the heights of ecstasy thanks to a gentleman's fingers could change one's appearance, and she had attempted to participate in all the lessons at the Academy over the last few days. They should not be able to tell she was any different—at least, not by looking at her.

'You are upset,' said Rilla quietly, 'for you have not seen your duke in a while. Am I right?'

Thankful that Rilla was unable to see the flush that was surely on her cheeks, and hoping Sylvia would not remark upon it, Gwen said, 'He is not my duke.'

'Are you so sure?'

Gwen focused her gaze on the other wallflowers talking at the far end of the room—anything rather than give credence to Rilla's words.

But she could not help it. Rilla was right, even if she did not wish to say it. Percy was hers—her duke.

The idea of her having a duke was most ridiculous, and Gwen could not help but smile at the thought. But it was true. She owned him—or at least, she owned him as much as he owned her. He had possessed her now, body and soul, and she could as easily remove her own heart as untangle it from his.

'What I do not understand,' said Rilla, 'is what you are doing now.'

Gwen blinked. 'Now?'

Rilla nodded. 'He has not been here for several days. You are clearly eager to see him. Why are you waiting for him to come to you?'

It was only when her companion said the words that Gwen realised she had no idea. Why was she here, waiting for Percy to arrive at the Wallflower Academy, when she was no true wallflower?

Just because she had been sent to the Wallflower Academy it did not mean she had to wait for her life to start, unseeingly accepting whatever hand was dealt to her.

Her life—her real life... It could begin now. This moment.

Gwen smiled at the thought.

'I need to go,' she said, rising with a swish of her skirts.

Rilla smiled. 'I thought you might. Miss Pike mentioned she would be in her study upstairs, if you wish to speak to her.'

Gwen's shoulders tightened at the thought of the lie she would have to tell, but she jutted out her chin. 'Thank you, Rilla.'

'Anything to match a wallflower,' came the quiet reply. 'It is all I'm good for at my age.'

If Gwen had thought about it, she would have remained a moment, to ask Rilla precisely what she meant. But her heart had leapt at the thought of seeing Percy, so she did not pause when leaving the drawing room, and flew up the stairs towards Miss Pike's study.

Only when she reached her door did she hesitate. She knew the room's location, naturally—she had had it pointed out to her on her second day. But she had never received an invitation—or an order—to enter Miss Pike's study before. It was territory unlike the rest of the Academy: a place for Miss Pike and Miss Pike alone.

This was where the matches were agreed.

Swallowing hard, Gwen knocked on the door.

'Come!'

The door opened into a small but elegantly furnished room, rather like a small sitting room, but with an impressive desk in one corner. Upon the desk were piles of letters and paperwork—neat piles, but piles nonetheless.

Miss Pike was seated by a small fire, knitting needles

in her hands and a rather impressive shawl trailing to her feet. Her eyebrows rose.

'Goodness, Miss Knox,' she said languidly, not ceasing her knitting. 'What a surprise. How may I help you?'

Gwen swallowed, as though that might calm the frantic beating of her heart. It made no difference.

'I… I have received a letter. From my mother,' Gwen said hesitantly.

She did not like lying. It was something she did infrequently—especially since the night that had changed her life for ever and ended a man's life.

But still, it was hardly a lie. She had, after all, received a letter from her mother.

'I would like to borrow a carriage and go to Town,' Gwen said in a rush.

Miss Pike raised an eyebrow. 'Your mother would like to meet you in Town? She does not wish to visit you here?'

Gwen swallowed.

Everything she was saying was true.

'I would appreciate the loan of the carriage, Miss Pike, but I understand if it is not possible. I will merely write to my mother to inform her.'

It was delicately done, to be sure—but was it enough? Gwen could not tell. Miss Pike certainly would not wish any of her wallflowers to write home to their families to say they were not being given the opportunity to go to Town, especially when it was to visit a family member.

'When?' came the clipped question.

'Tomorrow,' Gwen said, with reluctance.

It was too late today, but the sooner she saw Percy, the better. Her heart needed to be soothed, and he was the only one who could achieve it.

Miss Pike examined her closely. 'The Duke of Knaresby

is in Town at the moment, perhaps? And your mother? Both of them?'

Gwen swallowed. So that was what the owner of the Wallflower Academy assumed. That she was orchestrating a meeting between her mother and the Duke who had marked her out as a favourite.

'I believe the Duke is in Town,' Gwen said, dropping her gaze to her clasped hands.

A moment of silence, then… 'I have no wish to speak out of turn, but from your mother's correspondence…' Miss Pike's voice trailed off. 'Well, I do not have the impression that she is an easy woman to please.'

Heat blossomed up Gwen's chest. It was an understatement. Her mother was demanding, cruel, argumentative… and the holder of her great secret. A secret she had held over her head more than once, with delicate threats as to what might happen to disobliging daughters.

'You have my permission to borrow the carriage,' said Miss Pike impressively, not waiting for her to reply. 'Well done, Miss Knox. Well done, indeed.'

Gwen left the study quickly and quashed all concerns about lying, deceit and being caught out.

As soon as breakfast was over the next morning, she was outside and the carriage was waiting.

'Thank you,' she said breathlessly as the driver helped her up into the chaise and four. 'The Duke of Knaresby's residence, please.'

It was all Gwen could do to calm herself as the carriage rumbled along the road, slowing as the noise of London rose around it. She was almost there. After almost a week—a terribly long week without the sight of Percy's face—she was surely only minutes from seeing him. The man she loved.

'Here y'go, miss.'

Gwen started.

They could not possibly have arrived already, could they?

The driver turned and poked his head through the small opening at the front of the carriage. 'Shall I wait here, then?'

'I—I… Yes, please. Thank you,' mumbled Gwen.

She had given no thought to the driver at all, in truth. All her thoughts had been focused on one man. But those thoughts were chased away now, as she stared up at the building.

The door was imposing. Tall, wide, painted a beautiful red and with a shining brass knocker, it sat at the centre of four large bay windows.

Gwen swallowed. This townhouse of Percy's—his second home, or perhaps even his third—why, it was larger than her own home…larger than the inn itself.

A prickle of hesitation caused her hand to stay before knocking. He lived such a different life from her. In a different world…in the spotlight. Was she truly ready to risk it all—scandal, perhaps imprisonment—by drawing attention to herself and stepping into his circle?

But impulse pushed her forward and she knocked. She had to see him. She could not bear to be without him any longer.

When the door opened, Gwen said impetuously, 'Percy!'

An elderly man in servant's livery blinked. 'I beg your pardon, young lady?'

Gwen flushed. 'I—I mean… I have come to see the Duke.'

The servant, probably a butler, stared. 'Indeed? And who shall I say is calling?'

If only she had considered this beforehand. There had been plenty of time in the carriage, if she had put her mind to it, and yet she could think of nothing to say beyond the obvious.

'Say…say it is a lady.'

The butler nodded—and closed the door in her face. Gwen blinked. Was that intended as a reproof, a rejection of her request? Or was it common practice for a butler to close the door before a guest entered?

Uncertainty stirred in her stomach.

Just another example of how very different they were, Gwen thought wretchedly. The more she tried to ignore their differences in station, the more obvious they appeared.

When the door was opened again it was by Percy, who looked confused—then horrified.

'Percy!' Gwen said with a wide smile. 'I thought I would surprise you!'

It was indeed a surprise. Gwen could see the astonishment on the Duke's face. But it was mired by rather different emotions: panic, confusion, and...

And something akin to embarrassment.

Her gaze dropped and the excitement that had filled her ebbed away.

'I... I did not know when I was going to see you again,' she said, filling the awkward silence that Percy did not appear to have any wish to end. 'So I... I thought you might like to go for a walk. See the Queen's Palace, as we did not see it last time. Or...or visit any alleys or trees which are close by.'

That had been rather daring of her, it was true, but Gwen's boldness rose whenever she was with Percy. He made her more herself, somehow.

Yet the Percy she knew did not appear to be present today.

Flushing darkly, he stepped out of the house and closed the door behind him.

Gwen stared. *Was she not going to be invited inside?*

'You have to go.'

Percy's voice was low, soft, as though he was terrified of someone overhearing him.

His words did not make sense to Gwen—so little that she repeated just one. 'Go?'

'Yes, go,' said Percy, just as quietly. 'Now.'

'I… I came all this way to see you,' said Gwen, confusion twisting her heart. 'Why would I go before I have properly seen you?'

'It is a shame, but unfortunately you have arrived at a most inopportune time,' said Percy quickly, his voice low. 'I am sorry to say I have another appointment.'

Another appointment. *Of course he does,* Gwen thought dully.

It would be far too much to assume that Percy would have nothing to do today, or any day. He was a duke. There would be many calls on his time, unlike on hers.

'Go, now,' said Percy, turning her around by the shoulders and pushing her forward, back on to the pavement. 'I… I will come to see you.'

'Soon?' asked Gwen, unable to understand quite what was happening. 'Percy?'

'As soon as I am able,' said Percy, glancing back at the house as though concerned they were being watched.

Gwen looked up at the large bay windows.

Were they?

'Go, Miss Knox,' said Percy in clipped tones. 'Good day.'

The door had opened and closed again, swallowing the Duke up with it, before Gwen could say another word, and she stood there in astonished silence.

Percy did not wish to see her.

More, he had made no definite appointment day or time to see her at the Academy. Worse, there had been no declaration of love, which Gwen had not only hoped for, but expected.

A flicker of doubt circled her heart, followed by that rise of that terrible temper of hers. Gwen tried to breathe, tried to ignore the rising passion tempting her to slam her fists on the door and demand to be let in.

It was all very strange. But then, he was a duke, and she a wallflower—at least in his eyes. Perhaps this was how a courtship of this kind was carried out...

Chapter Twelve

'You mustn't!'

'I have,' said Sylvia with apparent glee. 'And there is no point attempting to talk me out of it, so don't even bother. My half-brother says this was the best trick he ever played at his club!'

Gwen stifled a laugh as she sat by the fire in the drawing room, watching the imperious Sylvia raise a dark eyebrow at the other wallflowers.

'But you mustn't!' said Rilla with a snort. 'Sylvia, you'll be caught—and Miss Pike will be furious when she—'

'The Pike could do with loosening up a little. Not all of us are wallflowers, waiting around for our lives to begin,' said Sylvia smartly as she adjusted the door, left it slightly ajar, and beamed at her creation. 'No offence.'

'None taken,' said Rilla wryly. 'Describe it to me again.'

Gwen smiled, despite herself. 'Sylvia has got it into her head to play a childish practical joke upon our benefactress.'

'Benefactress?' Sylvia snorted as she stepped away from the door and dropped heavily into an armchair. 'Jailor, rather.'

'Either way…' said Gwen hastily. Anything to avoid an argument, with Sylvia clearly feeling particularly bold today. 'Sylvia has carefully balanced a bucket of water over the door—'

'Ice-cold water,' Sylvia interrupted with apparent relish.

Rilla laughed dryly. 'You are always one for the dramatic, Sylvia.'

'Well, if not now, when?' the prankster demanded. 'Here we are, stuck inside unless we are able to catch the eye of a duke—and Gwen still won't reveal how she managed that.'

'And when the door opens for Miss Pike as she joins us before dinner...' Gwen said hastily.

The less said about Percy, the better.

She still could not get that kiss from her mind, nor the way he had spoken to her...

'The door will open, the bucket will fall, and the poor thing will be absolutely drenched.'

'I am not sure I would characterise her as a "poor thing",' said Rilla with a mischievous smile. 'Not after her nonsense yesterday about me not being able to dance. Has she even seen me attempt it?'

'No, she has not,' Sylvia said emphatically as a smile crept over Rilla's face. 'This will serve her right, I say— and all of you must swear not to reveal that it was I, or it will be the same for you when you are least expecting it!'

'You really shouldn't!' said Gwen.

But she knew well enough not to attempt to change the young woman's mind. With a smile across her lips and a knowing glint in her dark, almost black eyes, Sylvia was not a woman to have her mind changed for her.

'I'm bored,' Sylvia said dramatically. 'Bored with waiting around for gentlemen to come and view us as though we are pastries in a shop, deciding to choose which one of us to be their boring wives. I'm just trying to bring a bit of merriment into our lives.'

'Even if we wished to stop you,' Rilla said softly, 'could we?'

Gwen glanced at Sylvia, who grinned. 'No. Miss Pike will get wet—and it's only water. She can go upstairs and change easily enough.'

'Then the real fun will begin,' said Rilla, a hint of trouble in her tones. 'A card party this evening, isn't it?'

Gwen sighed. 'A card party? I truly do not understand how I will bear it. Gentlemen playing at cards…trying to pretend we are in any way interesting to them…'

Her voice trailed away. She had not thought to ask if Percy was attending. Her thoughts had wended in quite a different direction. How had he dared speak to her like that? Why hadn't he invited her inside? Had his deathbed vow to his brother finally come between them?

Then at other times—when she permitted herself to forget that he was a duke, forget the promise he'd made to his brother, forget her past—she would wonder whether they could find again that little nook in the woodland near the Wallflower Academy, where they'd shared more passionate kisses… She would think of the way he'd touched her under that tree…ponder if those kisses would ever lead anywhere…

Despite the heat of the fire, a greater fire rushed through Gwen, turning her cheeks pink and making it impossible for her to contribute to the ongoing conversation.

Rilla was laughing. 'You're acting like a child, Sylvia!'

'Perhaps I am. But I'm tired of being stuck here, tired of never getting my own way, tired of being treated like a child by the Pike!' Sylvia retorted. 'We're adults! We're ladies, women of wit…'

Gwen only half listened. If the other wallflowers knew just what she and Percy had done… It had grown, hadn't it? Grown into something far more than a lady of good repute should even conceive of!

Young ladies did not kiss dukes in carriages—and certainly not in alleyways. Wallflowers did not get taken to ecstasy after a horseback ride, with a gentleman's body pressed up against her.

Gwen had been able to do nothing but cling on for her very life as Percy had taken her on an adventure to pleasure she had never known possible…

And, worse, Gwen was certain there was more. So much more. More that she and Percy would inevitably never share.

'Shush—shush! Here she comes!'

Gwen blinked. Sylvia was waving her hands around to get the others to stop talking, and now they could all hear footsteps approaching across the hall.

Her heart leaping into her mouth, Gwen could not help but glance between Sylvia and the ajar door as the footsteps grew closer. Any moment now the door would open, and Miss Pike would receive the shock of her life!

There was indeed a startled yelp as the door opened and the bucket of freezing water fell onto the unsuspecting entrant into the room—but it was no lady in skirts unexpectedly doused.

Percy blinked through his sodden hair as the bucket fell to the floor with a clatter. 'Wh-What…? Water…?'

Gwen gasped as Rilla fell into raucous giggles. The Duke was absolutely soaked: his jacket drenched, his cravat dripping, his breeches covered in water.

'My—Your Grace!' Sylvia rose, mortification across her features. 'I did not—I thought it was—You are so wet!'

'So very wet,' said Percy with a laugh, pulling at his cravat and twisting it before him so that water ran down onto the carpet. 'Oh, dear, Miss Pike won't like her carpet being so damp…'

Rilla snorted. 'Am I to suppose Sylvia's victim is not who we thought?'

'Sylvia's victim, you say?' Percy raised an eyebrow through his wet hair and turned a sardonic look at the woman now spluttering incomprehensively. 'Is it you, Miss Bryant, I have to thank for this sudden bath?'

Even Gwen had to laugh.

Really, it was most ridiculous!

How had they not considered it might be a gentleman arriving for the card party who might fall victim to Sylvia's trap?

Percy shook his head and flicked water across the wallpaper. 'I do not suppose there is somewhere I can change?'

Rilla was laughing too much to be of any help. Sylvia appeared unable to replicate human speech, and the other wallflowers had all looked away in astonished embarrassment. That left...*her*.

'Here,' Gwen said quietly, rising. 'I can show you somewhere you can remove those wet things.'

Why did her cheeks have to flush at such a statement? It was hardly as if she had offered her own bedchamber, which certainly would have been outrageous.

Yet even though she knew she was doing nothing wrong, Gwen could not help but feel disgraceful as she approached the dripping wet Duke.

'Thank you. That would be most welcome,' said Percy, brushing the water out of his eyes and grinning at Sylvia. 'And you and I, Miss Bryant, will talk about this another time. For now, I would suggest you remove the bucket. Anything to avoid awkward questions from the Pike, I am sure.'

He strode out of the room, squelching on the carpet, and Gwen followed him, trying not to laugh.

'You are laughing at me, Gwen,' Percy said ruefully as he walked soggily beside her up the stairs.

Gwen giggled. 'Serves you right after the way you sent me away.'

She had not intended to speak so directly, but her words did not appear to upset him. Quite to the contrary.

Percy smiled ruefully. 'I deserved that,' he said, shaking his hands. Water scattered about him. 'Well, not this, but your reprimand. My…my mother was visiting me, and she is quite…well.'

Gwen nodded. That was all that needed to be said. His mother would certainly have got the wrong impression if she had walked in—after all, there was no future between herself and Percy. Not unless his brother came back from the grave and changed his mind.

'I… I understand. You are here for the card party, I suppose? I shall enjoy watching you explain the damp patch on your seat to Miss Pike.'

'Perhaps you will,' he countered, although there was no anger in his voice. 'Dear me, what am I going to wear?'

'The only thing I can think of is something from the footmen's store,' said Gwen, thinking quickly.

It took her but a moment to retrieve a footman's outfit from the cupboard at the end of the corridor, though Percy frowned rather doubtfully at the breeches, shirt, waistcoat and jacket she handed him.

'So I can be footman and bar the door to all other gentlemen?'

Gwen grinned. 'Do you want to?'

She should not have spoken so boldly. Percy affixed her with such a serious look that Gwen was forced to look away and walk down the corridor.

How did he do that? Look at her with such intensity her whole body reacted?

'Here,' she said, hardly aware of what she was thinking, led by instinct. 'You can change in here.'

She had opened the door before she could stop herself and Percy had walked in.

The Duke looked around the small room, It was her bedchamber, with its large bed and bay window.

'A pleasant aspect in the daytime, I am sure,' Percy said quietly, placing the footman's clothes on a chair in the corner. 'Whose chamber is it?'

Gwen swallowed, her lungs tight in her chest. 'Mine.'

Silence fell between them. A silence Gwen desperately wanted to break, but could not think how. What had she done? She had invited a duke—Percy, the man she wished to be kissing right at this moment—into her bedchamber.

Percy smiled. 'Well, I thank you. And now, if you do not mind…?'

He glanced at the clothes and, cheeks flushed, Gwen nodded.

Leaving the room without saying another word, she reached out to close the door behind her—but something outrageous within her slowed her movements, until the door was only almost closed, leaving a small crack through which she could see.

It was a perfect view. Percy had already ripped off his jacket, waistcoat and shirt—all sodden, all dropped to the floor. Gwen tried not to gasp, but it was difficult. Even in this small sliver of a view, she could see that Percy was a handsome man down to his skin. Broad shoulders, a strength in his arms she had felt but never seen, a smattering of hair trailing down his chest towards his breeches…

Gwen swallowed. Something was stirring within her— something she did not quite understand. But she wanted more.

Oh, so much more.

There was a twist, a change, a gasp—and Percy looked up and caught her gaze.

Gwen gasped too. At the sudden shock of being caught out. Caught staring at a half-naked duke.

It was quite clear from the look on Gwen's face that she was horrified at being caught—but Percy could not think of anything better.

There it was. The desire he knew was inside her, just waiting to come out. He'd seen it once and was desperate to see it again. First the temper, then the tension, now the temptation.

Excitement rushed through Percy as he saw Gwen's wide eyes. So she had been watching him, had she? And had she liked what she had seen?

After weeks of restraint, after stolen kisses in alleyways and in carriages, after being desperate to know her—all of her—this was his chance.

His chance to...talk.

Striding over to the door and opening it fully, Percy leaned against the doorframe and gave the woman before him a lopsided grin. 'Was there more you wanted to say, Miss Knox?'

'I shouldn't have—I should go. I should return downstairs,' Gwen babbled.

Percy caught her hand in his as she turned and started to walk away. There was a tension in that hand...a fierce passion held back. He shivered. Dear Lord, if there was such desire in her now, just from looking at him, just from knowing what he could do when he kissed her...what more could she promise?

'Come on,' he muttered in a low voice.

Gwen did not need encouragement. She slipped into the room with soft footsteps, and when Percy closed the door and leaned against it he saw a woman who knew both what she wanted, and the fact that it was forbidden.

Percy swallowed. He would have to tread carefully here. Just because he knew Gwen Knox had been won over almost from the first moment he had met her, that did not mean Gwen knew herself what she was craving.

Or just how far she was willing to go to get it.

It was time to be a little more direct. A little more obvious about his own desires, Percy mused. And James be damned. Oh, his brother had meant well, certainly—but with Gwen constantly on his mind Percy had to admit that perhaps his brother, in a very small and insignificant way, had been wrong about women such as her. About ladies in general.

He did not have to seek someone who fitted the perfect list of criteria.

He had found Gwen.

'Does it give you pleasure?' he said quietly. 'To look at me?'

To his great surprise, he heard his own heart thumping wildly and loudly in his ears. Percy looked carefully at the woman before him, at the delicate elegance, the shyness that had swiftly returned to Gwen's features the moment she'd realised she had been caught.

Yes, she was a wallflower. But there was something far more here than just a wallflower. Gwen was more than a simple label that diminished her.

Gwen was a wallflower and a warrior. A scandalous woman in some ways, and a most proper one in others. Percy was not sure he would ever get tired of trying to understand the layers of this woman. But he certainly wished to become better acquainted with some of the layers she was wearing!

Though Gwen was clearly scandalised by his question, and Percy knew she had every right to be, he could not help himself. She was a woman so lovely, so interesting—far more interesting than any of the insipid chits his mother had attempted to introduce him to.

Gwen remained silent, though unusually she had not looked away. So Percy decided to attempt a different tack: honesty.

'It gives me pleasure to look at you,' he said quietly. 'Though I admit not as much pleasure as touching you would.'

Gwen's lips parted, almost unconsciously, but she said nothing. Yet still she did not look away, her gaze affixed on his.

Her desires had won, Percy realised, excitement growing in his stomach and descending to his manhood, which was even now trying to stand to attention. She wanted him to speak like this to her…to tease her, perhaps even to touch her. To caress her.

'What do you want, Gwen?' Percy asked as he took a few steps towards her. When she said nothing, he said softly, 'I can tell you what *I* want. I want to kiss you. Touch you. Hold your hands—hold you close to me. Closer than you could possibly imagine.'

'Why are you doing this?' Gwen's voice held no reproach, just confusion and desire.

Percy smiled as he took another step closer. 'Because I… I was wrong.'

She stared. 'Wrong?'

It was as unnatural for him to say it as it was for her to hear it, Percy realised with a twist in his chest. But then, gentlemen of his breeding were rarely ever told they were wrong, were they?

And since he had inherited the title… Well, since then he could not recall ever being told he was wrong!

'I… There isn't a perfect list for what a woman is, Gwen,' Percy found himself saying. 'My brother was wrong in this one regard, I think, and it is a most important thing for me to realise. Oh, Gwen, I cannot stay away from you! I think no one has ever told you how winning you are, Gwen. How desirable you are. I want more than I think you can give me—certainly more than you should…'

He watched her swallow, watched her pupils dilate as he came closer. By God, she wanted him.

'I knew it when I sent you away,' he said quietly. 'I knew it as I bitterly regretted watching you get back into that carriage—that I never wanted you to do that again. And James…'

Percy hesitated. It was difficult to articulate, even to himself, but he had to try. Gwen deserved that. *He* deserved that.

'James would not want me to be unhappy,' he said, his voice breaking. 'My brother…he created the criteria, made me promise because he thought it would make me happy. But you do, Gwen. It's you.'

He saw the flicker of astonishment in her eyes, the amazement at his revelation—and the excitement at what might come next.

'I would like to kiss you, taste you…know precisely how you moan when I give you pleasure,' said Percy softly. He was standing before her now, probably too close—or perhaps not close enough.

Gwen took a small step forward. They were mere inches away from each other now. 'And…and what then?' she asked.

It was all Percy could do not to crush her to him, desperate as he was to end this tension, this dance they had been doing around each other. But not yet. *Not yet.*

'Then…' he said, in half a voice, half a growl. 'Then I would like to take off your gown and kiss every inch of you.'

'I like the sound of that,' whispered Gwen, her mouth

curling into a smile. A tantalising smile which made Percy wish he had the restraint he should have—*any* restraint. For the words in his heart were threatening to spill out, to shock both of them, in a rush of certainty he had never known before.

Marry me, Gwen. Make me happy. Let me make you happy.

If he'd had restraint, he would not have said the words that would take them past a turning point: once they'd passed it, there would be no turning back.

What was it she had once said? *'Least likely to win a duke.'*

'Why don't I show you just how likely you are to win me?' he asked.

Chapter Thirteen

Gwen stared at the man who had asked her such a dangerous and delicious question.

She knew what it was now—this strange sensation in her chest, this anticipatory tingling across her body, the warmth between her legs.

Arousal.

She wanted Percy to make love to her, to kiss her and touch her and do all the delectable things he had said.

'I would like to kiss you, taste you...know precisely how you moan when I give you pleasure.'

But something held Gwen back, despite all the memories of tantalising pleasure, despite her imaginings of forbidden pleasure to come. Something that confused her.

It took a moment to understand what it was.

Fear.

As Gwen looked into Percy's eyes, his honest face, she knew it was not enough.

It was not sufficient to merely want another, to desire their touch. She cared for Percy deeply, and only now could she admit what those feelings amounted to.

Love.

She loved him.

It was a strange, new, imperfect love, to be sure—one that if she had been a titled lady might have grown into something precious and beautiful.

But she was not. She was a murderess—someone with no beauty nor wealth nor position in Society. And they were all precisely what Percy needed. She knew it; he knew it.

So when he offered her such things, such wonderful delights, it was as a mistress.

Gwen's stomach twisted painfully at the thought, but she could not ignore it.

While she might want to be his wife, marry him, spend the rest of her days falling more and more in love with the man before her... He did not want that. Percy needed to marry as a duke married, and those marital limitations pained her more than she could say.

It was too much. Too painful. Too excruciating.

Gwen knew she should step away...remove herself from such temptation.

But Percy's intoxicating presence was too much. His words were too much. His admission that his brother had been wrong, that he chose instead to be happy...

Although they were not even touching, Gwen was dazzled by the prospect of such intimacy. His naked chest was before her, crying out for her touch.

'Then I would like to take off your gown and kiss every inch of you.'

Something warm and aching slipped from her heart to between her legs. Gwen knew what she wanted: Percy. All of him. Not just his kisses, nor even his lovemaking, but his heart.

Something she knew he simply could not give her.

Besides, it would be scandalous to give in to such hedonistic desires! She was supposed to be a wallflower, not a wanton! No lady could permit herself to simply take the pleasures offered by dukes—even if they were as handsome and alluring as Percy.

'Gwen?' Percy said quietly. 'Are you quite well?'

Gwen opened her mouth, but nothing came out.

How could she speak? What could she say? It was impossible to conceive of any words that would make any sense to a man like him.

Surely he had experience in such matters?

At that very thought Gwen's gaze dropped, unbidden images of Percy with other women cutting through her thoughts.

The movement of her gaze did not help, however. Before it had been affixed to his eyes, something Gwen had thought far too intense, but now she was looking at the trail of hair disappearing into his breeches, under which there appeared to be a rather prominent bulge...

Ah.

Gwen's cheeks seared with heat as she realised what it was. Percy's manhood. He wanted her. His desire was obvious. This was no teasing trick.

But no duke should desire her in this way. Gwen was sure of that.

'I know why you are hesitating.'

Gwen could not help but laugh dryly at Percy's words. 'I do not think you do.'

How could he? Could a duke, or any gentleman, understand what it was to be so utterly overwhelmed? To be on the one hand overcome with desire for a gentleman— a desire Gwen knew she should not be feeling—and on the other hand believe that even if that gentleman made love to her it would not be meaningful unless it came with certain promises?

Promises Gwen knew Percy could not make.

She should never have shown him to any bedchamber,

let alone her own. She should not have watched while he removed his clothing.

She certainly should not have permitted such sensual conversation.

'I think I do,' said Percy. 'You want this to mean something. To be deeper than just physicality, I mean. A connection not just of bodies, but of hearts, minds, souls.'

Gwen looked up. Percy was not teasing her. 'You…you are right.'

How could she put it into words—or did she need to if he already understood?

Tempting as it was to reach out and touch that handsome chest, Gwen took a deep breath and tried to concentrate. It was important, explaining to him how she felt. He needed to know. There might never be anyone else she could explain this to.

'The…the act of lovemaking…' said Gwen. Her cheeks were flushing, but there was nothing she could do about it. 'Kissing, touching, c-caressing…any of that. All of it. I believe it should be…well, between two people who truly care for each other. Who are committed to each other.'

Had she said too much? Gwen's heart was pattering lightly but rapidly in her chest, making it difficult to think, to breathe, to know whether she had spoken too brashly.

There was a rather too knowing smile dancing across Percy's lips. 'You did not say that when you were kissing me in that alley, nor when I pushed you up against that tree.'

Gwen laughed weakly as he lifted a hand to push back one of the curls that had fallen over her forehead. Every inch of her skin came alive when he brushed it, as though for the first time. As though she would die if he did not touch her again.

'I did think it,' Gwen admitted in a breathless voice.

'It was just… I wanted you to keep kissing me so much I did not say anything.'

A flash of something she did not recognise seared across Percy's face. Was it desire? Desperation? Glory? A sense of achievement—or something else?

'I wish you had said,' Percy said. 'It… Gwen, it matters to me that you are comfortable with me kissing you. Touching you.'

Gwen's heart rose. He was a good man. She had known it before but had not been able to put it into words, nor had it demonstrated so clearly.

Gwen said quietly, 'I know. I… I truly care for you, Percy.'

Percy took a step backwards, widening the gap between them as he examined her. Gwen could almost feel the change in the air, the change in temperature as he retreated.

She should not have spoken so openly. Nothing good came of her voicing her opinions or letting loose her temper—Gwen knew that. And just at the moment when it was most important for her to be near him, to feel the reassuring presence of him being close, he had stepped away.

Of course he had, Gwen thought dully.

Dukes did not want wallflowers admitting they had feelings for them. They looked for quick and meaningless relief—pleasure, not partnership.

'Forget my words,' Gwen said hastily, turning away. 'I should not have said—'

'I will never forget them.'

Gwen's heart stopped, skipping a beat almost painfully. She turned back to look at Percy.

'I am relieved to hear you say those words,' he said softly, 'because…because I have known for too long that I care too much for you. Too long and too much.'

It took a moment for Gwen to take in what he had said.

It could not be.

Did the handsome man before her really care for her? It must be a trick of her hearing, even with those words about ignoring his promise to his brother ringing in her ears. Yet Gwen could not imagine what words she must have mistaken for such a declaration of affection.

'Could…could you say that again?'

Percy chuckled softly as he stepped forward. 'You wish me to make another declaration of my fondness for you?'

'Are…are you in love with me?' Gwen asked shyly, stepping into his arms and almost crying out as Percy's arms curled around her and pulled her close.

This was where she was supposed to be. After all this time, wondering why her mother had seen fit to send her to such a joyless place, now Gwen knew why she had been sent to the Wallflower Academy.

To meet him. Percy. To know him. To stand here, in his arms, as his smile became bashful upon hearing her words.

'Oh, I don't think I said that aloud,' Percy said, his gaze slipping from hers.

Gwen smiled, joy flooding her heart. Everything she might attempt to say now could be communicated in a much more delicious way.

This time when Gwen lifted up her lips to be kissed Percy did not start gently. No, he possessed her mouth as a thirsty man reached for water…as though without it he would surely die.

Gwen gasped into his mouth, heady sensations overwhelming her rapidly as Percy's naked chest pressed against her clothed one.

Just a few layers of silk, she could not help thinking, as her hands returned to the nape of his neck, as they had done when they had kissed in that alleyway. Just one gown, easily moved aside as it had been when he'd touched her by that tree. Just a few inches of silk and their skin would touch, would meet with the same passion and reverence they had enjoyed then.

The kiss ended, and still Percy looked bashful.

'You did not say it aloud,' said Gwen hesitantly, certain she should not speak these words, but knowing she would never forgive herself if she did not. 'But do…do you feel it? In your heart?'

At first it appeared as though Percy would avoid the question. But he certainly did not avoid another chance to kiss her lips, and Gwen shivered as his tongue teased greater pleasure from her than ever before.

But when he pulled away, eyes blazing and mouth clearly hungry for more, he murmured, 'Yes. Oh, yes, Gwen—I love you. I did not know it until it was too late to do anything about it, and even then…even then I did not want to. I love you, Gwen.'

It was everything Gwen had ever hoped the moment would be and more. Nestled in Percy's arms, with his strong hands on her waist, slipping towards her buttocks, her hands around his neck, keeping his mouth close, was precisely where she wanted to be, his words ringing in her ears…

He loved her.

Happiness was searing her heart, branding it and branding this moment in her mind as one she would never forget.

He loved her.

'I love you, Percy,' Gwen said shyly, growing in confidence with every syllable. 'I love you even if you are a duke.'

Percy laughed. 'Is that a problem?'

'No! No, I just meant…' Gwen tried to explain, then laughed when she saw his teasing smile. 'You are a most irritating man, Percy Devereux.'

'And you are a most tantalising woman, Gwen Knox,'

said Percy with a groan, his fingers finally reaching her buttocks, cupping them and pulling her towards him. 'I don't know how you've done it, but you've won me over.'

Gwen smiled, delight almost overwhelming her. She loved him. She loved Percy, and he loved her.

'Does this mean,' asked Percy, 'that you will permit me to do what I want?'

Her smile quickly disappearing, Gwen swallowed and tried to think calmly—something that would be far easier if she was not in the warm embrace of a half-naked duke.

What he wanted?

What he wanted was everything, as far as Gwen could tell. She was hardly well versed in the art of making love, but touching, caressing, touching every part of her skin…?

It would be a line crossed that she could never uncross. A departure from her life of good manners and well-behaved solitude. It would mean giving up any chance of keeping that part of herself for her wedding night.

The thought scorched her mind, but Gwen pushed it aside. She loved Percy and he loved her. To all intents and purposes this *was* her wedding night. Their wedding night.

'They'll come looking for us…' she breathed. 'The Pike. The card party—'

'I did not return my invitation, and I'm sure she'll be far too distracted by Sylvia to think of anything else,' Percy said, his gaze hungry.

Gwen nodded, easily convinced by his words. Yes, they were alone, and they would be left alone. And if she could not give herself to the man she loved, what was the point of all this growing love and affection within her?

'I want you,' said Gwen softly, 'to kiss me…everywhere.'

Percy's eyes widened.

She laughed. 'Ladies have desires too, you know.'

'Yes, well, that's all very well… But…everywhere?' Percy said in a half-whisper.

It was as though he could not quite believe his ears.

Gwen could hardly believe she had spoken the words herself, except she knew they had sprung from her own heart, her own desires.

If she could not be open and honest now, with the man she loved, when could she?

'I love you,' said Gwen quietly. 'And I want you.'

Percy did not need greater encouragement. Returning his lips to hers in an ardent yet reverential kiss, he moved his fingers from her buttocks—to Gwen's regret—and started to untie the delicate ribbons along the side of her gown.

Lost in the heady sensations of nibbling lips and searing hot tongues, Gwen was so lost in the pleasure of the moment she barely noticed when Percy had finished his work. It was only when her gown slipped to the floor, leaving her in naught but her stays and under-shift, that Gwen gasped.

'There,' Percy said, kissing just below Gwen's ear, making her shiver. 'And now…'

It was all Gwen could do not to moan as Percy's lips moved across her bare shoulder. Every inch of contact branded her as his and Percy claimed her…all the parts of her no one else had touched.

Now, no one else ever would.

'Percy!' Gwen gasped as his swift and knowledgeable fingers removed her stays and under-shift in but a moment, leaving her utterly naked.

It was a strange sensation. Gwen had never been so vulnerable before another person—had never had a gentleman see any part of her, let alone all of her.

Moving her hands to hide herself, she glanced nervously at Percy. There was such potent desire in his gaze that

Gwen found all her nerves melting away. It was not a disapproving look…

'I never imagined… You are so beautiful, Gwen. I can't stop myself—tell me if you want me to stop.'

There was no sense of demand in his voice, and Gwen could not think what he meant—until he stepped forward and gently pulled her across the room and against the door.

'Percy…?' Gwen whispered, conscious of only this narrow block of wood keeping them from the corridor.

But he did not reply—at least, not in words. Kissing her lips with a passionate moan, Percy left her mouth and kissed down her neck towards her breasts.

Barely able to stand, Gwen grasped the door handle and quickly turned the key in the lock. Her entire body quivered as pleasure soared between each kiss, peaking to an unimaginable height as Percy captured one of her nipples in his mouth, arching his tongue slowly around it.

'Oh, Percy!'

Gwen tried to stay quiet, she really did, but it was impossible once Percy descended to his knees, his kisses moving down her stomach and suddenly to her secret place. Through her curls, his tongue entered her, and Gwen arched her back against the door at the sudden rush of ecstasy consuming her body.

'Percy!' she gasped, hardly aware of what she was saying.

This was too much. When he had said he wanted to kiss her everywhere…

Percy seemed to take her quivering, twisting pleasure as encouragement to continue, and Gwen moaned and sobbed, clutching desperately at the door handle as his tongue twisted within her, sucked and then built a rhythm, bringing her closer and closer to a peak she remembered and ached for, until eventually Gwen cried out his name, with no thought to who might hear her, as her climax shook her entire body.

'Percy!'

His hands reached her hips, holding her there, preventing her from collapsing. Stars appeared in her eyes, and for a moment she was not entirely sure where she was.

After blinking several times, Gwen looked down to see Percy looking up, a desperate hunger on his face.

'I wanted to hear you come,' he whispered, 'and now I need to feel it. Get on the bed.'

Gwen obeyed—not because there was any threat in his request, but because she wished to please him. Oh, she wanted to please the man who could make her feel like that…

Percy had stripped off his boots and breeches by the time he joined her on the bed, and Gwen tried not to stare at that part of him she had never expected to see.

His manhood. Large, hard, stiff as Percy settled himself between her legs and into her welcoming embrace.

'I will go slowly,' Percy promised, kissing her lightly on the corner of her mouth.

Slowly? Gwen did not want to go slowly. She wanted the fast, desperate, hungry pace Percy had given her with his tongue, deep inside her. She was wet with desire as he slipped into her and started to build a rhythm she now recognised—the same rhythm which had taken her body to such heights only moments before—and Gwen's heart quickly rose in excitement at the thought of feeling that again.

At feeling everything again.

Everything he could give her.

'Damn, Gwen, you feel so good,' moaned Percy as he plunged himself into her once more, causing twinges of pleasure to ripple through Gwen's body.

She clung to his shoulders, unsure whether she should say something but actually unable to speak a word. Not when she was experiencing such pleasure—a pleasure that was building and building, as it had done before, and she wanted it, craved it, craved him, Percy, the man she loved—

'Percy…oh, yes!'

Gwen could not help it. She cried out for a second time as ecstasy overwhelmed her, and it appeared Percy had reached the same peak, for he thrust into her rapidly and then collapsed.

Clutching him, pulling him into her arms, Gwen tried to think, tried to concentrate on the breathing that felt difficult in this moment.

To think such things were possible…such sensation was just at arm's reach. How did anyone, once knowing the pleasure such desire could bring, manage to stay away from it?

'I could never have imagined it…' Gwen breathed, unable to help herself. 'Losing my innocence in such a way. In such a…a heated, delicious encounter that fulfilled all my wildest dreams.'

And more, she wanted to say, for she could never have dreamt of such sensuality.

Percy chuckled as he moved onto the bed beside her, pulling her into his arms. 'Good,' he said sleepily, his eyelashes fluttering shut. 'And now I have you right where I want you…'

Gwen snuggled into him, placing her face on his chest. His heartbeat was just as frantic as her own.

'Oh? And where is that?'

'Right in my arms,' said Percy quietly. 'And in my heart.'

Chapter Fourteen

It was cruel that he had to depart.

Percy told himself another few minutes would not matter.
Why not stay here, in the comforting warmth of Gwen's bed,
with her naked form beside him, lost in slumber?

He had awoken early—so early the sun was still not
up. Birdsong drifted through the bay window, its curtains
open. They had been so lost in their lovemaking, then
fallen asleep swiftly.

Gwen's gentle breathing moved the blanket Percy had
drawn over her and he watched, marvelling at her beauty.
To think that he had seen, touched, those delicate fingers,
those sensual breasts…had taken and given pleasure of all
kinds with such a woman.

It was more than he had ever expected. Perhaps more
than he deserved. Certainly more than he should have done.
He had thrown out all decorum, Society's expectations,
his brother's precepts, and his own knowledge of what he
needed to do to cement his title's reputation.

But Percy knew there was little he could keep from Gwen
now, even if he wanted to, now he had given her his heart.

His heart contracted, then relaxed, expanding with his
devotion. She was a wallflower, yes, but a passionate one.

A woman who understood him, who cared for him—who loved him.

Joy blossomed through him. Love—something he had not expected and yet had found with this precious, beautiful woman. If only he could stay. If only this moment, these early hours, with the Wallflower Academy silent and their secret still their own, could continue for ever.

Percy sighed, his breath ruffling Gwen's long dark hair, draped over her shoulders and the pillow.

But it could not be. He had to leave—and quickly, if he was not to be spotted. And that meant leaving Gwen. His stomach rebelled, aching both from hunger and agitation at the thought of leaving her.

There was no other choice.

Percy reached out a hand and softly brushed away the hair from Gwen's shoulder. She stirred, her head twisting, and murmured gently, though her eyes stayed closed.

He smiled.

So, Gwen was not a morning person.

There was still so much to learn about her…so much to discover. He would never grow bored with this tempestuous wallflower.

'Gwen…' Percy whispered.

That seemed to be enough to draw the drowsy woman from sleep. Gently, Gwen's eyelashes fluttered, and she looked up. For a moment there was stillness, and then a broad smile crept across her face.

'Percy…' she breathed.

'Hello, my love,' said Percy.

It was instinct leading him to speak in such a way. Why not speak words of love to the woman to whom he had given his heart? And he had been offered hers so openly in return.

Difficult though it was to accept that they must now be apart, Percy clenched his jaw and forced himself to say the words he knew must be said—even if they pained him. 'I must go.'

Gwen blinked, and then a sharpness appeared in her pupils and a line appeared between her eyes. 'Go? Now? Why?'

Percy jerked his head towards the window. 'Day breaks, and if I am to leave the Academy without anyone seeing it must be now.'

For a moment it appeared Gwen would disagree, debate the fact, but then a look of sorrowful resignation covered her face.

'I suppose so,' she said, but then a mischievous smile crept across her lips. 'Although if you stayed here I could always make it worth your while.'

Her fingers crept towards him, pulling him closer, and Percy groaned.

What had he unleashed within this woman?

Heavens, if he was not careful, he would make love to her again, and doubtless wake the whole household with her cries of pleasure.

His manhood jerked. It was not the worst idea he'd ever had…

'No—no, Gwen,' Percy said regretfully as he captured her fingers in his and held them tight. 'I really must go.'

Gwen's mischievous smile softened. 'I will miss you.'

'I know,' said Percy heavily, wishing he could remain here for ever, in the safety and sanctuary of her affections. 'I will miss you too.'

He allowed himself one kiss, one dipped moment of connection, and his whole body quivered as his lips touched hers. This was more than love, more than affection. It was an intimacy he could never have conceived of…beautiful, perfect.

It was with great regret that Percy broke the kiss. Gwen

appeared to feel the same, leaning up in an attempt to prolong the connection for as long as possible.

'Gwen…' said Percy quietly.

'Percy…' said Gwen, leaning up for another kiss.

He leaned back. This was important, and it could not be said in the middle of sleep, nor while affectionate kisses were addling their minds. He had to make sure she understood—or there would be consequences, and not ones he could control.

Percy took a deep breath. 'Gwen, we will need to keep this…what's between us…between us. Do you understand?'

Perhaps he should explain more clearly, he thought wryly. It was, after all, very early in the morning, and Gwen had given him no sign of being particularly awake yet.

She frowned. 'Keep what's between us, between us?'

Percy swallowed. 'I mean…our lovemaking…the fact we love each other—'

'I do love you,' said Gwen with a sleepy smile.

Percy's stomach twisted. James's list of conditions for a wife—to be elegant, refined, distant, wealthy—had always seemed right, naturally. It was James's list. Only now could Percy see just how cold and isolating a woman like that would have been.

A woman James would have approved of…

He could not imagine her now. Not with Gwen before him.

She was everything he wanted: gentle and loving, passionate and wild. So ready to accept his touch, All the things he had never expected to find in one woman—let alone one so beautiful.

'Gwen,' Percy said firmly, half to get her attention, half to focus his own. 'No one can know—do you understand? It's not the right time. Not yet. This must stay between us.

Our lovemaking, our declarations of love…they must stay a secret. For the moment.'

Because, Percy thought darkly as he watched the words sink into Gwen's sleepy mind, *he had no idea as yet just how to broach this with his mother.*

The idea of telling her that her son, her only remaining son, had given himself away to a chit of a wallflower with no connections nor refinements…

He would find a way, Percy told himself, and then he would declare his passion and affections for Gwen and they would be married. It would all come right, eventually. They just needed to be patient.

'I suppose that makes sense,' said Gwen quietly, yawning. 'We will need to think about how to tell my mother, and Miss Pike—goodness, and *your* mother, I suppose.'

The knot of tension which had been building in Percy's stomach had not consciously been noticed by him before— not until Gwen spoke those words and the knot started to fade away. She understood.

'Precisely,' he said with a sigh of relief. 'Thank you, Gwen.'

Percy kissed her again, unable to resist the allure of those soft, inviting lips, and groaned as Gwen placed her hands around his neck to pull him closer.

'No—no, Gwen. I must away,' Percy said regretfully.

Gwen sighed as she nestled herself into the pillows. 'I suppose you are right.'

'I am not so sure,' Percy said ruefully as he entwined his fingers with hers. 'The very last thing I wish is to leave you here, but I… I have no choice.'

And that was the truth, Percy thought as he looked at the most beautiful woman he had ever seen. *No choice.* No choice but to love her…no choice but to be devoted.

Even if his mother would never have made this choice.

Even if it was going to be one of the most difficult conversations he had ever had, trying to convince his mother to accept Gwen as her daughter-in-law.

And if she did not? If she refused to give her permission? Refused to accept that Percy was going to invest his marital prospects—the prospects of a duke, no less!—in a woman with no dowry, family or prestige?

What if—heaven forbid—he received the Cut from Society? And his mother, in similar fashion, was cut from her friends, her connections, her very reason for living?

The knot of tension had returned, but Percy could do naught about it. He had no idea how he would solve that problem, and a problem it was.

He swallowed, then kissed Gwen lightly on the nose. 'We'll see each other again soon. Last night…you won my devotion, Gwen.'

'I already had it,' Gwen said sleepily, her eyes closing as she drifted back to sleep.

Percy's heart fluttered painfully before continuing in a regular beat.

He might not have started this with…well, with the best of intentions. When everything within him had told him being near Gwen was both terribly wrong and painfully right. But there was nothing he could do now to prevent the loss of his heart.

He would have her. No matter what happened.

Gwen had almost fallen asleep by the time Percy slipped out of the bed into the cold morning air. It took him but a few moments to put on the footman's outfit, finding the breeches a little short but otherwise sufficient. It was a pain, truly, that his clothes were still damp.

But then, Percy thought, *I did not exactly spend much time last night worrying about drying them.*

He had been far too interested in removing Gwen's clothes than looking to his own.

Percy almost made it to the stall where his mare had been lodged overnight without discovery, but as he opened the door to the stables a young voice shouted after him.

'Hi, there!'

Percy sighed. It had been too much, it appeared, to expect to be able to leave without detection.

Turning on his heel, he saw Tom, the stable boy, approaching him with a frown.

'You're not a footman here,' the boy said in an accusatory tone. 'Who are you? A thief come to steal from the house using your trickery?'

Percy stared. It was incomprehensible that the boy should not recognise him—but then he was dressed very differently from the way he had been in their previous encounters.

Oh, the shame...to be taken not even for a footman but for a thief!

''Tis I, Tom,' Percy said in a low voice.

The stable boy frowned, evidently recognising the voice but unable to place it. 'You? Who *are* you?'

Swallowing heavily, Percy saw there was nothing for it. He would have to reveal himself and hope for Tom's natural deference.

'The Duke of Knaresby,' Percy said softly, as though a lower volume would make it less scandalous. 'I had to— My clothes were ruined. I needed to borrow... Just let me get to my horse!'

Striding past the astonished stable boy, Percy reached for the tack and quickly saddled his horse. Tom appeared to be so utterly astonished he was unable to speak. Only when Percy had mounted the mare, wincing slightly as the footman's breeches stretched painfully, did Tom finally say something.

'But...but why are you dressed like a footman?'

Percy sighed. How on earth was he to explain the series of events which had led him to be dressed like this?

Well, he should probably start at the beginning.

'Sylvia—'

'Say no more, Your Grace,' said Tom hastily, cheeks flushing. 'I quite understand.'

That was remarkably simple, Percy thought as he nudged his horse forward.

'Marvellous,' he said in a low voice. 'And no word to Miss Pike, if you please.'

Tom nodded, and was rewarded with a smile—Percy, of course had no coin to give him. Everything was still in his waistcoat, tucked under his arm. He would have to remember on his next visit.

The ride back to London was unpleasant, to say the least. Percy made a variety of discoveries while on his horse in the freezing cold morning air. Firstly, he knew that he would never criticise his tailor again, for he now knew the value of well-fitting clothes. Secondly, footmen had rather a difficult lot, being forced to wear these ridiculous clothes. And thirdly, he could manage to trot down the streets of London to his home and pass the reins to his astonished stable master so early almost no one would be up.

His good fortune, however, did not last. Percy ought to have expected something to go wrong, but his confidence peaked as he slipped into his London townhouse by the back door, closed it as quietly as he could manage, and leaned, exhausted, against the wall.

Well, he was home.

In less than half an hour he could be in a hot bath, left to think only of his delightfully disreputable encounter with Gwen Knox. And he had managed it all without his mother—

'Percival William Devereux—what are you wearing?'

Percy straightened hastily, pulling the ill-fitting jacket down, and smiled weakly at his mother, who was striding down the corridor towards him.

Ah. Now there was a morning person—more was the pity. It would be difficult to explain this away to her as easily as to Tom, the stable boy.

'Good morning, Mother,' Percy said brightly, as though cheerfulness might prevent his mother from seeing the state he was in. 'It is very early, is it not?'

'You are wearing the clothes of a servant, Percy—and not a servant of this house,' said Lady Devereux severely, stopping before him and frowning. 'Dear me, this is a livery I admit I do not recognise. What interesting piping on the sleeves.'

Percy's smile froze on his face. 'Ah. Yes, well, the thing is—'

'Dear Lord, is that the livery of the Wallflower Academy?' The frown on his mother's face deepened as Percy's stomach twisted. 'Percival William Devereux—what on earth were you doing there? I thought you were attending the Kenceysham ball last night?'

'Well…' said Percy awkwardly. 'The thing is—'

'And returning in a servant's outfit!' Lady Devereux shook her head. 'Percy, what am I to do with you? You spend far too much time at that place. If I have said it before, I have said it a thousand times!'

'You have indeed,' said Percy heavily.

'And with all this threat of scandal in the newspapers, your brother's death still unexplained, I would have thought you would take your responsibilities as the new Duke of Knaresby more seriously!'

'I am,' said Percy urgently. Did she think he did not care? 'Which reminds me… I thought I would go to the inn where James was killed—the Golden Hind, I think it was called—and ask—'

'No,' said his mother firmly. 'No. I forbid it.'

Frustration stirred in his chest. Did she not wish to know more? Questions about his brother's last moments had always whirled through his mind. 'I have never understood why you have no wish to know—'

'Is this what you call taking your requirement to marry well *seriously*? Wearing the clothes of a servant? Percy, really!'

Blast. It was too much to hope that his mother would understand the hilarious circumstances in which the wearing of the outfit had occurred.

Explaining about Gwen, he thought darkly, *was not a good idea—not now.*

He would shelve that for another time.

'You see, the thing was,' he said, with what he hoped was a light-hearted smile, 'one of the wallflowers—a Miss Sylvia Bryant—played a trick involving—'

'I do not want to hear it,' his mother said sharply. 'I hardly need further proof that you should not be visiting the Academy—if one could even call it that. You are better than that, Percy. Always were. And especially now. You have your title to think of!'

Percy swallowed, but said nothing. He well knew his mother's opinion, and could only guess the response he would receive if he revealed that he had fallen for one of the Academy's occupants.

Fallen and fallen hard.

Love is a powerful force, Percy thought. *Oh, yes, Gwen— I love you. I did not know it until it was too late to do any-*

thing about it, and even then...even then I would not have wanted to. I love you, Gwen.

Something stirred within his heart—something bold, brash—and he determined to make a clean breast of it to his mother. He loved Gwen. That was not going to change. And the sooner his mother could start reconciling herself to that truth, the better.

'Mother,' Percy said firmly. 'I must tell you. I have decided I will marry—'

'Yes, yes, I know. And all we have to do is find the right lady,' said Lady Devereux, waving a hand. 'That is precisely why you need to hurry.'

Percy smiled. 'Well, actually, there is no need to hurry. I have already found—'

'When I say you need to hurry, I say it advisedly,' said his mother sharply. 'Go now, upstairs, and get changed. They'll be here in less than an hour, and I cannot have you wandering around looking like a servant.'

Percy blinked. 'Who will be here in an hour?'

'*Now,* Percy!'

Kissing his mother on the cheek, he nodded. Well, what else was there to do? Arguing with his mother was rather like shouting at a mountain: one might feel better afterwards, but the mountain would be unchanged.

A bath, however, would be welcome.

Sinking into its almost scalding embrace, Percy sighed heavily and leaned back. It was strange to think how far he had come in only the last few hours. This time yesterday he'd had no thought of revealing his feelings to Gwen.

In truth, he'd had no idea how deeply they went until he had seen her watching him undress.

There is such an attraction, he mused, *in seeing attraction in another.*

Now he had shared his affections, and Gwen hers, and

they had shared in delightful lovemaking, all he had to do was find the right time to speak to his mother.

With guests arriving in less than an hour, now was certainly not the right time…

After a quick shave from his valet, and the relief of getting dressed in his own clothes, Percy felt a little more human again. He descended the stairs hastily as he looked at his pocket watch. Almost eleven o'clock—an early visit, indeed. But then his mother had never seen the point in wasting the day away.

'Well, Mother,' Percy said as he entered the morning room. 'I hope you will find this outfit more accept…'

Eyes wide, he stared at the scene before him and wondered whether he had entered the wrong room—the wrong house. This appeared to be far more like a scene from the Wallflower Academy than his own home.

His mother was seated in an armchair by a small table, where a tea tray had been laid, and was smiling broadly. Opposite her, standing in a line, were three young ladies, all dressed in their finest gowns. One had even put a flower in her hair. They were staring as though they had been waiting for hours. One was flushed. Another fluttered her eyelashes coquettishly.

'Ah, there you are, Knaresby,' said Lady Devereux smartly, using his title name as they were in company. 'See—I have three very eligible young ladies for your viewing.'

Percy opened his mouth, but no words came out. How could he speak? What could he say to such nonsense? To such a way of shoving him towards an appropriate marriage?

What on earth was his mother doing, speaking about these ladies as though they were not here?

'Now, the Honourable Miss Maynard—that's the one on

the left—she comes from a very good family, with sufficient dowry but nothing too impressive,' began his mother, pointing at the first young lady.

Percy saw Miss Maynard's cheeks flush as his mother spoke of her so callously.

'Whereas Lady Rose has a very impressive dowry, but rather unimpressive brothers,' continued Lady Devereux, with a knowing look at her son. 'If you chose her, you would have to do something about their behaviour, I declare. For one of them would soon bring us down in Society if left unchecked. And Miss Middlesborough—'

'Mother!' Percy said, mortified, as he shut the door behind him and strode towards the seated women. 'Really!'

This was awful—worse than the way the Wallflower Academy treated its inhabitants. Why, what was she thinking, having them standing there, listening to her nonsense, lining them up as though at a cattle market!

'Oh, you care too much,' said his mother, tapping him lightly on the shoulder. 'These young ladies knew what to expect when they received my invitation—did you not, ladies?'

'Yes, m'lady,' came the murmured replies.

Percy's stomach clenched. 'Nonetheless—'

'Nonetheless, nothing,' said his mother sharply, her eyes affixed on her son. 'Mark my words, Percy—Knaresby. When a duke marries, he must consider all these things. He marries not for himself but for the betterment of the family and the title. There is a great weight of responsibility upon him. 'Tis not as though you will have a love match. We seek a marriage to benefit both parties.'

Percy opened his mouth, but his typically eloquent tongue failed him. How could he speak when his mind was clouded not with reasonable arguments against the

nonsense before him, but instead on how each of these ladies was nothing compared to Gwen?

He found them wanting, despite their superior breeding
and their dowries. He felt nothing for them. There was no
comparison to Gwen.

'And besides,' his mother said, her gaze still fierce, 'it
is what your father would have wanted. Would have *expected*.'

Percy closed his mouth as his heart sank. He would?

In his vague recollections of his father he had never
spoken to him of such things. Why would he? Percy had
been nothing but a child when his father had died.

'What would James have wanted?' he blurted out.

His mother's eyebrows rose. 'James? What on earth
does your brother have to do with this?'

Percy hesitated. He knew he could never express to her
the tumultuous emotions turbulent in his heart. How was
he ever to explain them to his mother, who surely would
never accept a mere wallflower?

Chapter Fifteen

'We are going out for afternoon tea,' Miss Pike announced grandly, as though she had just given the wallflowers a precious gift as they sat around the luncheon table. 'With members of the aristocracy.'

Sylvia's eyes widened.

Miss Pike nodded approvingly. 'Indeed, you may look impressed, Miss Bryant,' she said grandly. 'I have worked especially hard for this afternoon tea to be a perfect opportunity for you ladies to make an impression on a gentleman with a title—take a leaf, perhaps, out of Miss Knox's book.'

Gwen flushed as the owner of the Wallflower Academy nodded impressively in her direction. Her hands twisted in her lap, her plate of cured ham and potatoes abandoned.

How could she eat? How could she act as though everything was normal, as though her life was perfectly ordinary, when she knew it was not?

Worse, the one thing Miss Pike was apt to praise her for—attracting the attentions of a duke—made her heart so unsure of the future?

The remembrance of Percy's heated touches, his clever fingers, crowded Gwen's mind and made it impossible for her to follow the conversation now circling around the table.

'Gentlemen of note do not all need to have titles, surely?' Sylvia was saying.

Rilla laughed. 'Are you honestly telling me you would decline the advances of a gentleman merely because he had a title?'

'That is not what I am saying at all...'

Titles, Gwen thought wryly. True, when she had been a little younger, a little more foolish, she had daydreamed about being taken away by a gentleman with more riches and titles than he knew what to do with.

Until that fateful night.

Until the whole of her world had fallen around her because of what she had done.

Until her mother had discovered her.

Since then, it had been easiest to keep her head down and be silent. A wallflower, indeed, even if it was merely because she was afraid of being found out.

But Percy was that imagined perfect gentleman, was he not? Wealthy, with a title, but kind, too. With something deeper in him she had never discovered in any other man.

Of course they would not wish to announce their engagement before he had spoken with his mother—so did his absence mean Percy's mother had taken against her? It had, after all, been almost a week.

Seven days without him. Without a word. After giving herself to him so willingly...

Perhaps she had been foolish to consider herself worthy of him, to think their union would not be endangered by the truth of the past. But she loved him. Oh, how she loved him. And a very real pain twisted in her stomach at the idea of never seeing him again.

From the moment Gwen had seen Percy—admittedly

she had been on the gravel of the drive—she had been unable to resist him. Resist his presence. Resist the growing attraction budding inside her...

Even when he had acted so haughtily against any union between them at the start.

And after giving herself to Percy it was a cruel separation.

'Many members of the aristocracy—at least ten—have confirmed their attendance at tea, and there are more I hope will attend,' Miss Pike was saying. 'We will enter the carriages half an hour after luncheon.'

Something stirred in Gwen's memory.

'We'll see each other again soon.'

Was this what he had meant? Gwen's heart fluttered at the hopeful thought which now invaded her mind. Had he been thinking of this afternoon tea?

A smile graced Gwen's lips, if only for a moment.

Oh, if only he would be in attendance today.

She had not paid attention to the place where they were going, only taking in the fact that it was a lady's home in London. A chance, Miss Pike had said, to practise their manners.

And if Percy was there...

They would have the opportunity to talk, to laugh. Perhaps he would move his fingers across hers. A sense of anticipation rushed through her. Perhaps, if they were very careful, they would be able to slip away together.

Gwen swallowed the scandalous thought, but now it had occurred there was no way to ignore it.

Picking up her knife and fork in the hope that the other wallflowers and Miss Pike would not notice anything amiss, Gwen lost herself for a few minutes in delightful imaginings of Percy pulling her aside while no one was looking, the two of them running up the stairs hand in hand, slipping into a bedchamber and making love, hastily and passionately, trying desperately to muffle their moans of joy...

And then, Gwen thought wistfully, *they would talk— properly talk.*

Talk of when their wedding would be, and where they would live, and how happy they would be. For they would be happy, wouldn't they? It would be glorious to be together for the rest of their lives.

A prickle of guilt interrupted these pleasant thoughts. *As long as the truth of her past could remain hidden.*

That was vital, of course—but what was the point in waiting? They had given themselves to each other, Gwen thought with a smile. What was left but their marriage?

'Gwendoline Knox!'

Gwen started. 'What?'

Miss Pike was shaking her head. 'You really are lost in the clouds at the moment, aren't you? I asked how was your visit with your mother and your...gentleman friend? You never did tell me, but I have not forgotten.'

Gwen swallowed. So far she had been able to relate the details of her excursion without lying. Only Rilla knew the truth of her intentions, and even she did not know the awkward reality of her journey.

'It was without incident,' Gwen said quietly, looking to the expectant face of Miss Pike, who now nodded approvingly.

'That is what I like to hear. Take notice, ladies! "Without incident" is a great accomplishment for any wallflower. Next, I would appreciate a little announcement, Miss Knox...you know the sort I mean. After all, you know whose home we are visiting today...'

Cringing inwardly at this pointed reference to a wallflower's inability to navigate social situations without embarrassing herself, and still utterly at a loss as to where they were going, Gwen held her tongue rather than add to the Pike's irritation.

Thirty minutes did not feel adequate to prepare herself for returning once more to London—to the place where she had danced with Percy, had been kissed by him for the first time.

But this would be different, wouldn't it?

Gwen tried to convince herself of that as she and the other wallflowers gathered outside the Academy, taking turns to step into the carriages waiting to take them to Town.

As it happened, the first carriage was full, so she stepped towards the second, where Rilla stood waiting.

'There you are, Gwen,' she said.

'How did you know?'

Rilla snorted. 'You think I cannot hear someone coming? I often don't know who they are until they speak, but Miss Pike said you'd be in my carriage. Here, help me up.'

It was a relief to be settled in the carriage with Rilla and no questioning Miss Pike or Sylvia, Gwen thought ruefully.

With a sudden jerk, the carriage moved forward.

'Well, then—are you ready to talk?' asked Rilla.

Gwen swallowed. 'I don't know what you mean…'

Rilla snorted. 'Wallflowers usually hide in their bedchambers before this sort of thing, but I think you need someone to talk to. Something's changed, hasn't it?'

Gwen flushed at the very idea of someone as innocent as Rilla knowing that she had lost her own innocence. Why, it was wild indeed just to have done it—but for it to be *known*!

'Look,' said Rilla quietly as the carriage rattled on, 'I am blind. And that does not mean I become a savant in the other senses—that is just a story told to children. But

I do have other senses, and, Gwen, I smelt the Duke's cigars on you the day after he was soaked by Sylvia's jest. I am not mistaken, am I?'

It had been delicately done, but that did not mean Gwen was not mortified. Rilla had smelt Percy's cigars on her... Well, of course she had—he had been pressed up against her! Even now she could remember his heady scent.

'And you did not come downstairs to the card party after you showed the Duke upstairs,' Rilla continued in a low voice—so low that Gwen could only just hear her. 'The following morning you said you'd had a headache, and no one questioned you, but...'

Her voice trailed away delicately, and Gwen's heart thumped so painfully it echoed in her ears.

'You...you won't tell anyone?' she managed. 'Please, Rilla—'

'I will not betray you, I promise—'tis not my secret to tell,' said the blind woman with a smile. 'And I do not believe anyone else has noticed. At least, they have said nothing to me, and I am sure if Sylvia even suspected it would be all she could speak of.'

Gwen laughed weakly. Yes, that was a fair comment. If Sylvia had any inkling that the newest arrival at the Wallflower Academy was now no longer an innocent it would be her primary—perhaps only—topic of conversation.

Streets were starting to appear through the carriage windows, and the clouds of the wintry day were heavy in the sky.

'The question is, what are you going to do about it?'

'Do about it?' repeated Gwen. The idea of *her* doing anything, when Percy was a duke... 'I... I don't know.'

What was a wallflower—a murderess wallflower, no less—supposed to do after such an encounter? When they had shared their mutual love not only in words but in ecstasy?

The carriage was drawing to a stop. They were here, and that meant she might only be a few minutes away from seeing—

'Wallflowers!'

Gwen winced as Miss Pike's cry echoed up the street. Surely it was bad enough that they had been brought here under the inauspicious description of a wallflower. Did Miss Pike really have to shout out such a moniker right in front of the row of impressive townhouses they had halted by?

'Well, I suppose it's time...' murmured Rilla.

The carriage door was opened by the driver, and Gwen helped Rilla out. The other wallflowers had collected by the front door, nervously standing close to each other. She could see the fear on their faces.

Another day...another set of forced encounters with eligible gentlemen.

Another expectation of gaining a proposal.

Gwen's heart pounded painfully in her chest.

Another hope of seeing Percy.

'Here we go again,' said Sylvia with a dry laugh, stepping over to them. 'Will we be seeing your duke, Gwen?'

'He is not my duke,' Gwen said, with the strange sensation that she had said that phrase too many times.

It was not as though she did not want him to be her duke.

She did. Desperately.

But it was all so complicated, and she'd had no word from Percy as to what they would do next.

Gwen squared her shoulders. 'Let us see what type of gentlemen Miss Pike has managed to accumulate for us.'

Sylvia laughed as Miss Pike led the wallflowers towards the door and rang the bell. 'If there *are* any gentlemen.'

Rilla frowned. 'What do you mean?'

'Well, did you notice Miss Pike used her words very carefully?' Sylvia said as they walked forward, entering an impressive hall. A chandelier tinkled above them as the door was shut. '"Aristocracy", not gentlemen. We could be about to attend a gathering of ladies, not men.'

It appeared Sylvia's suspicions were well founded.

When they were ushered into a drawing room there were elegant piles of cakes and sweets on platters around the room, along with steaming teapots and many cups.

There was also a plethora of ladies.

'Hmm...' said Sylvia knowingly, glancing at Rilla and Gwen.

Gwen's shoulders slumped. From what she could see there were a number of older women seated around the room, their conversation halting, clearly talking about the wallflowers as they entered.

But no gentlemen.

More importantly, no Percy.

He was nowhere to be seen and Gwen's heart sank.

Well, she would merely have to enjoy this opportunity to escape the Academy—and the room where they stood was certainly elegant and refined. The latest in printed paper adorned the walls—a delicate blue with a flower motif. A console table made of marble hosted several teapots, cups and saucers, and the rug by the fire looked to be antique, from what Gwen could make out.

Yes, here were all the trappings of respectability and wealth.

So, whose home were they in?

'There's our hostess,' Miss Pike hissed, her cheeks slightly flushed and her hands waving in the general direction of at least four finely dressed ladies. 'Gwen will introduce you, I am sure. Won't you, Gwen? Go and thank her, ladies, for she is doing you an eminent service by—No, Sylvia, absolutely not!'

Miss Pike strode off to pull Sylvia away from the window, where she was waving at the passers-by, before clarifying who precisely it was who had invited them. Gwen was mystified. Why on earth would *she* be able to introduce their hostess to the wallflowers? She knew no one in London.

Besides, every moment was pointless if Percy was not in it with her.

Would this feeling ever pass? she wondered as she took up a position by another of the large windows overlooking the bustling street. Or would it fade over time as they became more accustomed to each other?

As we live happily together, Gwen thought with a brief smile, *how will that happiness change?*

The door opened and she turned eagerly towards it—but a gentleman she did not recognise, with large teeth and a haughty laugh, entered. After two successive entrances by gentlemen, she was still disappointed.

It appeared the Duke of Knaresby would not be attending this particular gathering.

It was only when she had reconciled herself to the fact that he would not be attending, and she would simply have to learn to be patient, that Gwen was finally rewarded.

'Ah, Knaresby!' The large-toothed gentleman strode forward to clap Percy's shoulder as he came in and Gwen's heart leapt. 'Never expected to receive an invitation from your mother. What an honour!'

Curiosity overcome her shyness, and Gwen peered across the room at the woman who would soon be her mother-in-law.

Impressive. That was the only word Gwen could think of when looking at the woman who stood beside Percy wearing a conceited expression. She was dressed in the most fabulous gown, with more ruffles and delicate embroidery than Gwen had ever seen on a single skirt. There was a string of pearls around her neck, and she looked around the room as if she was rather displeased.

'Yes, I should think it *is* an honour,' said Lady Devereux imperiously. 'But then I am always doing what I can for the unfortunate. Inviting these poor wallflowers to Mayfair House is nothing at all. Percy, bring me some tea.'

No one appeared astonished at the lady of the house ordering her son about, rather than calling a footman. Perhaps that was just how it was with nobility.

Delight tempered with astonishment curled at the edges of Gwen's heart as she watched the man she loved step across the room to pour his mother some tea.

Mayfair House...this was Lady Devereux's home? Oh, now there could be no mistaking it. This tea party was a kindness for her, surely! Percy must have told her, quietly, and the two of them had cooked up this excuse to meet her.

Gwen's stomach lurched at the very idea.

He was here.

With his mother, admittedly, which Gwen had not foreseen.

Miss Pike had surely not mentioned it was Lady Devereux who had invited them for afternoon tea—but that was no matter...not now.

It would certainly be a discomforting sort of encounter, this first time—and in public too. And she had not prepared herself emotionally for meeting the mother of the man she loved—but still... It was a start.

After all, Percy had had ample time to acquaint his mother with the truth of their affection.

Although, Gwen thought hastily, *not perhaps the whole truth.*

Just enough for Lady Devereux to know she would soon be acquiring a daughter-in-law.

And that meant eventually Percy would have to meet her own mother.

The thought caused a shudder to rush through Gwen, which she forced aside. She would not enjoy that.

Perhaps Percy was uncomfortable—perhaps that explained why he had not looked over at her, or taken the chance to introduce them immediately.

Gwen took a deep breath, smoothed her skirts, and tried to ready herself for what was to come.

Her first meeting with Lady Devereux.

All she could hope was that it would go well.

It was about as bad as Percy could imagine—and he had imagined some rather awful scenarios. But this was the worst, and it was all his doing. His dishonesty. His idiocy.

He had not even mentioned Gwen by name to his mother, nor referred to her in any way.

This whole afternoon was a mistake—and he had been unable to convince his mother to call it off when she had first revealed what she had done not an hour ago.

'But you cannot! Mother, you must send a messenger to the Wallflower Academy immediately and rescind the invitation,' Percy had argued vehemently.

His mother had only raised an eyebrow. 'What a thing to say, my boy. Rescind my invitation? I have never done such a thing in my life and see no reason to start now.'

Now Percy swallowed, his heart thumping, as he saw the wallflowers in his mother's drawing room. This was a mistake—and now there was no opportunity to stop Gwen as she meandered her way towards them.

If Gwen was about to do what he thought she was—introduce herself to his mother, on the assumption that the introduction would be welcome—everything would fall apart.

Tension crept across his neck, and Percy's heart pounded painfully in his chest, but nothing could stir him to move. His mother sat on the sofa beside Lady Windsor, and just as Gwen reached them Percy spoke, words he could not hold back spilling out of his mouth.

'Are you quite comfortable, Mother?'

Lady Devereux looked up. 'Comfortable? Well, as comfortable as I could hope to be, I suppose, surrounded by such people.'

The tension around his neck increased. Percy could almost feel the indignation rising in Gwen, but could neither acknowledge her nor comfort her.

This had to go well—but how could it be anything but a disaster?

'Indeed, I reconsidered whether this was something I wished to do. After all, the parks in London are teeming with the very best of people,' Lady Devereux continued, even as Percy winced at her disdain for those around her. 'But then, you are a duke now, and must do your best for the unfortunate.'

Out of the corner of his eye Percy saw Sylvia bristle at those words. He stepped to the right, to prevent his mother from seeing the ire she was creating in the wallflowers of the Academy, but unfortunately that took him further away from Gwen. From the one person in the room who could give him any sense of peace. If only they could be alone…

'All these unwanted daughters,' his mother said loudly, taking a sip of tea.

'Mother,' said Percy hastily, trying not to look at Gwen. 'Really!'

'Do not attempt to say they are otherwise, Knaresby. It does you no benefit to pretend they are other than what they are,' said his mother impressively. She nudged her companion on the sofa. 'Some poor gentlemen will eventually be trapped by them, I suppose…'

If only the ground would swallow him up here and now, thought Percy desperately, preferably taking Gwen with him—or, better, if only it would swallow up his mother!

The room was starting to quieten as people listened to the harsh words his mother was saying, and Percy tried to laugh loudly as a way to distract them. That was the trouble with hosting an afternoon tea; people were wont to actually pay heed to your words.

If she could just stop there, he thought frantically, glancing at Gwen and seeing the rising anger he knew dwelled within her. *If his mother could just hold her impertinent opinions—*

'What did you say, Your Ladyship ?' asked Miss Sylvia Bryant sweetly, stepping around Percy despite his best efforts to get in her way. 'I am sorry, Your Ladyship, did you say we are here to entrap gentlemen? We came on *your* invitation.'

Now everyone in the room was listening. Percy felt the pressure of their gazes, and the discomfort of his stomach stirred as he tried not to notice the whispers of the gentlemen.

This was precisely what he had not wished for.

'I am sure that is not what you meant, Mother, is it?' Percy said pointedly, conscious that his mother had not replied. 'There are many ladies of quality here, and—'

Percy was not sure how, but his mother managed to cut him off with a sniff.

'Well,' she said coldly. 'I am not so sure, my dear. This is an occasion for charity, not matchmaking. I doubt very much that a wallflower could entrap a duke, even if she wished to. A wallflower is not an appropriate wife for a duke, and I should not have to be the one to tell you that.'

A movement just out of the corner of his eye made Percy turn and he saw that Gwen had taken a step back, as though retreat was the only option when facing such an onslaught.

Perhaps she's right, Percy thought wildly. Perhaps he and Gwen should just leave, abandon his mother to her terrible opinions and—and run away together!

But he did not move. Despite knowing what his mother had said was rude, arrogant and hurtful, he said nothing. James would have agreed with his mother, likely as not, and the idea of forming a contrary opinion to his brother was painful in a way Percy had not expected.

Lips clamped shut, mouth dry, heart pounding, he found he could not contradict his mother in public. Not in her own home. Could not bring shame upon her when all she had done ever since he had ascended to his title was attempt to calm the rumours about his brother.

'Wallflowers,' Lady Devereux said then, 'can be very pretty things—and a few are, I see. But they are decoration, Knaresby. One plants wallflowers for a season, and then one grows tired of them and they are replaced. They are not what one has a garden *for*. They are not roses.'

Percy's pulse was ringing in his ears, and his gaze was pulled inexorably to the one person he did not wish to hear such things: Gwen.

She was pale—far paler than he had ever seen her. Her eyes were wide, flickering between him and his mother as though she was expecting him to do something.

Yes, do something, Percy's mind craved, and yet he stood motionless.

Perhaps this was his punishment. If he had just been brave enough to speak to his mother before the wallflowers had arrived, at any point in the last few days, he would not be suffering the agony of bringing Gwen this hurt.

But he had not spoken to her. Years of obedience... years of following James and never having to make a stand against his mother... Only now did he realise what that had bred into him.

Inaction.

Well, no longer.

Percy swallowed. No. He would not allow it. 'Mother, I must say—'

'Lady Devereux, these cakes are delicious,' Miss Pike said hastily, rushing over to their hostess, cheeks crimson. 'Your cook must tell mine precisely how the delicate sponge is able to—'

Percy could wait no longer. His mother's attention was diverted, if only for a moment, and this was his best and perhaps only chance to speak to Gwen. He took her hand, pulled her away. Ignoring Sylvia's gasp and questioning look, he opened the nearest door, stepped through it, and took Gwen with him.

It was the dining room.

Percy shut the door heavily and did what he had wanted to do the moment he had seen Gwen by the window. Cupping her face with his hands, he kissed her desperately, as though everything could be wiped away as long as they were together. As long as their love was at the centre.

But the kiss did not last long.

Gwen pushed him away violently, cheeks now scarlet. 'How can you kiss me?' Gwen hissed, even as murmurs of the conversation in the next room flowed under the door. 'How can you kiss me after permitting your mother to... to speak about me like that?'

Percy shrugged helplessly, his hand rubbing absentmindedly at where she had shoved him. Quite forcefully, as it happened.

Respect, honour, love, affection… They were at war within him. He could not respect and honour his mother while also loving Gwen.

She waited for him to say something, a quizzical eyebrow raised, and then her expression changed. Her fury hardened into something more akin to coldness.

'I am wanted back in the drawing room, I am sure,' she said icily as she strode past.

'You are wanted here!' Percy said desperately.

How could he make her see how impossible this was? Make her understand that it was difficult, and would take time. Time he knew he didn't deserve, but so very desperately hoped she would give him.

Gwen examined his face for a moment, then shook her head. 'I am not so sure. After all the things you said…after what we shared… I am wanted, you say? I am accustomed to being the least likely to win your true affections, Percy. Be sure, next time I see you. Be sure of what you want. I would hate for that meeting to be our last.'

The door snapped shut.

Percy leaned against the wall, his chest tight, as uninvited emotions swirled within him. This didn't feel like winning the heart of his future wife…

Chapter Sixteen

'*Wallflowers can be very pretty things, and a few are, I see. But they are decoration, Knaresby. One plants wallflowers for a season, and then one grows tired of them and they are replaced. They are not what one has a garden for. They are not roses.*'

No matter what she did, Gwen could not prevent Lady Devereux's cruel words ringing in her ears.

Over and over again, even as the days slipped by, the words would not leave her alone. They were relentless, appearing in her dreams, preventing her from rest and paining her heart as she saw the completely insurmountable pressure that was on their love.

She cleared her throat, as though that would clear the painful remembrances from her mind, but it was no use. They plagued her.

It was as if the library echoed with the sound, then the book-lined walls absorbed the noise and left Gwen once again in silence.

Silence and solitude. That was what she craved.

Ever since the afternoon tea party Gwen had attracted the great ire of Miss Pike—for her impertinence and her stubbornness.

'You have refused to attend even one of my evening parties for five days now!' Miss Pike had snapped at dinner the evening before. 'Really! It is most unbecoming of you to be so rebellious, Miss Knox. I never would have expected this from a wallflower! I should write to your mother!'

Gwen had clenched her jaw, tightened her grip on her fork, but said nothing.

What could she say?

That she had never been a wallflower to begin with, but had been sent here because her mother knew her to be a murderess?

That she had no intention of ever attending another of the Pike's foolish events, for if there was even one single chance she could see Percy again…

Gwen snapped shut the book in her hands. She was barely taking in a word anyway—and besides, the library had been stocked with severely dull books that Miss Pike evidently thought wallflowers should be interested in.

There was nothing more Gwen needed to learn about how lace was made in the French style, or the way roses needed to be arranged, and everything else was dull, dull, dull.

Standing and meandering down the shelves, Gwen gently brushed the spines of the books with her fingertips. There must be *something* interesting in this library that would capture her attention for at least half an hour. Distract her from the thoughts that were swiftly overpowering her.

Gwen swallowed. It was not enough, it appeared, that Percy's mother had spoken so harshly—words that could have come from her own mother's mouth…a feat remarkable in itself. No. The encounter had also reinforced all her fears about Percy and their love for each other—a love fragmented as soon as it had formed. He wanted her, yes. But not for marriage. For a tup.

She would not see him again.

Gwen knew that deep within herself, and although it pained her to be away from him it was surely a lesser agony than what she would suffer if she was in his presence again.

Whatever they had, it could not be love. Lust, perhaps. Desire, certainly. But nothing that could last, or surmount the growing pressures of parents and prestige. Her past would not permit it.

Gwen sat heavily in an armchair by the bay window and looked listlessly at the gardens. Winter had arrived with a vengeance, and the trees were now almost bare. The wind rattled them, shaking the last few leaves which had managed to cling on.

Her parents had never been particularly demonstrative in their affection for each other. She had hoped, foolishly, for a match of happiness. That would bring her something…*more.*

'This is the library, isn't it?'

Rilla was standing in the doorway, the cane she used to feel her way around the corridors when alone in her right hand.

'It is,' said Gwen with a wry smile.

Even when she wanted to be alone it was impossible. Discovered by a blind woman—who would have thought it?

'Ah, there you are, Gwen,' said Rilla with a laugh as she stepped into the library. 'Any possibility of helping me to the sofa?'

Gwen rose. 'Of course.'

When Rilla was seated, she patted the space beside her. 'Come, join me.'

Gwen hesitated, not immediately accepting the invitation. It was solitude she sought, not company—rather ironic, now she came to think about it, as she would likely be spending the rest of her life alone.

Still, it would be rude not to join Rilla.

Gwen sat slowly on the sofa and folded her hands in her lap. She knew sometimes Rilla merely wished to have the sense of someone's presence around her. It did not necessarily mean she wished to talk about anything, let alone—

'Your duke is by the front door, you know,' Rilla said conversationally.

Gwen sighed heavily, her shoulders slumping as she fell back into the sofa. 'He is not my duke.'

'So you keep saying,' said Rilla. 'I am astonished that you keep protesting, you know. No one believes you.'

Gwen took advantage of the woman's blindness to glare at her.

'Don't give me that look.'

It was impossible not to splutter at Rilla's retort. 'How did you—?'

'You think I need to see to know precisely how you will react?' Rilla laughed. 'I'm blind, not mute. You are, if you will forgive me for saying so, Gwen, a rather predictable character. Now you're going to tell me that you do not want to see him.'

'But I don't want to—'

'Protesting again?' cut in Rilla with a smile.

Gwen frowned, a growing knot of irritation twisting her stomach. 'So if I say I do not want to see him, and that he is not my duke, that merely means I do want to see him because he is?'

Her companion smiled. 'I know… It is rather a contradiction in terms.'

Gwen had never considered the matter much but, if asked, she would have said it would be easier to lie to a blind person than someone with sight. So many clues in one's body language, one's face, would be missed. It did not appear that mattered to Rilla.

'I truly have no wish to see the Duke of Knaresby,' she said finally, as aloofly as she could.

'I do not need to see to know you are lying.'

'You heard what his mother said!' Gwen could not help her outburst, and they were alone in the library. 'You heard her! All that talk about wallflowers trapping men, and being useless, a-and—'

'And a lot of other things we wallflowers have heard our entire lives,' Rilla completed.

'You heard what Lady Devereux said,' Gwen repeated, her heart contracting painfully at the memory.

Rilla was quiet for a moment. 'Yes. But I did not hear her son say it.'

Gwen stared. Although Percy had never said anything of the kind, his silence had cut deeper than any blade.

'He has almost knocked down the front door, you know,' Rilla said quietly. 'The footman says he demands to speak to you. The Pike is furious that you won't see him.'

Gwen almost smiled. Oh, if only that passion, that desire, could have come from *Mister* Percy Devereux—the same man, but without all the challenges that came with a title, without a reputation to maintain, a dead brother to honour, a mother to please. Just a man who could love her. A man without the need to protect his nobility.

'He has brought you a letter. I have it here.'

Startled, Gwen looked around. 'What does it say? I mean—' She had to laugh. 'I do apologise, Rilla.'

But her friend merely smiled. 'Oh, it does not matter—but I too am intrigued by the contents. Will you do me the honour of reading it?'

Gwen tried not to think about what the letter might contain as she took the small envelope from Rilla. It was sealed with a wax dollop formed into the shape of a very elegant K intertwined with a D.

Knaresby. Devereux.

Gwen swallowed. It was disgraceful, receiving a letter from a gentleman to whom one was not formally engaged—but then, their…entanglement, for want of a better word, was far more intimate than many engagements.

It could not be wrong, could it, to receive and read such a letter?

'I don't hear any opening of a letter.'

Gwen sighed and shook her head. 'You are a menace, you know.'

'I know,' said Rilla cheerfully. 'Perennially underestimated—that's me.'

When Gwen had pulled apart the seal and removed the letter from the envelope her first emotion was disappointment. The letter was short—a scrawl, really—clearly written in haste and with terrible penmanship.

Gwen—
>*You must let me explain.*
>*Let me apologise.*
>*I know not how to convince you that nothing my mother said was…*
>*I am still navigating my responsibilities as a duke, and the expectations placed upon me, but one thing I do know, and that is I have always been forbidden from contradicting either of my parents in public. It is a hard habit to break.*
>*But I am not a child now, I am a man, and I should have defended you. If I could take back her words—*
>*Perhaps that would not be enough.*
>*Meet with me, and I will show you just how devoted I am,*

Your humble servant,
Percy

Gwen's throat constricted.

How could she believe a single thing he had written? How could she countenance the idea of meeting with a gentleman who gave her so little respect?

No, Percy had been pained by her parting words when he had written this, but that did not mean he could make any change within his circumstances to make this…this love…this marriage…a possibility.

Pain seared Gwen's heart, but she knew she could do nothing about it. She had given her heart, entirely, to a gentleman who could not keep it.

Percy was a duke.

She was a false wallflower with a secret in her past that would risk not only her reputation in Society but his own. The wife he needed was one with wealth and connections, and she had none.

Worse, her secret…what she had done that fateful night…it was too much. She would ruin not only Percy, but the Knaresby name. There were too many obstacles. Too many walls to breach if they even attempted to seriously consider a future together.

Something strange tugged at her memory and Gwen glanced at the letter again. Although Percy had only written a short amount, almost all of it was taken up with his mother. There was no declaration of love, no formal offer of marriage, no commitment of any kind.

Worse, his request to see her was surely only an attempt to seduce her once again!

Matrimony was a topic never mentioned by either of them, Gwen thought, and wondered, her heart pattering painfully, that she had never noticed before.

How had she permitted herself to be so undone, so vulnerable—giving away her innocence, the most precious thing she could bring into a marriage—without any sort of promise?

Yes, he had spoken of love, Gwen thought wildly, and of wanting, of desire…but not anything more tangible.

She was a fool. A fool easily taken in by a handsome face and a dream of marriage to a man so delicious as the Duke.

'Miss Gwendoline Knox!'

Gwen rose hurriedly from the sofa, heart racing, to see an irate Miss Pike glaring from the doorway.

'Miss Pike…?' she ventured.

What could she have possibly done this time?

'There is a duke at my front door,' said Miss Pike, her eyebrows raised.

Gwen fought the desire to snap that it was not her fault. 'I am aware, Miss Pike.'

'What I am aware of is the fact that you have not seen him!'

Of course, Gwen thought darkly. No one would understand why she was not falling over herself to secure a duke.

'He is damaging my front door!' Miss Pike glared at Gwen. 'I command you to speak to him. He is a *duke*, for goodness' sake!'

'That is no reason why I should speak to him,' Gwen said, as calmly as she could.

Rilla moved her head from side to side, following the sound of the conversation.

But Miss Pike was not finished. Affixing Gwen with a glare, she hissed, 'This is the entire reason you, Miss Knox, were sent to the Wallflower Academy in the first place! To find a husband! Do you not think a duke might be a suitable option?'

Gwen opened her mouth, hesitated, and closed it again. What could she say? It was true—any lady would consider herself lucky to receive the attentions of a duke—any duke—and Percy was a very likeable gentleman.

If only it was not so complicated.

Gwen was not sure she could even explain it fully to herself.

Still, that left her with but one option.

'Fine,' she said testily, returning Miss Pike's glare with her own. 'I will see him.'

Miss Pike breathed out slowly, as though she had been fighting a great beast, and placed a hand on Rilla's shoulder. 'Come away, Miss Newell.'

Rilla said nothing, but rose and followed Miss Pike's guidance out of the library. Gwen beseeched her with her expression to stay, but there was nothing she could say in Miss Pike's presence and the door was shut behind them.

It did not remain shut for long. Given hardly a minute to compose herself, Gwen gasped as the door slammed open and Percy appeared.

'Gwen,' he said, shutting the door behind him and stepping forward.

Gwen curtsied low. 'Your Grace.'

'Don't give me that. We have never treated each other—'

'Perhaps that was our first mistake,' interrupted Gwen, hating herself for doing so, but knowing it was the only way. She had to show him how impossible this was. 'Perhaps if I had treated you as a duke and you had treated me as a wallflower—'

'I no more think all men should be treated one way than that all wallflowers should either,' Percy said, with a grin that unfortunately made him incredibly handsome. 'Come on, Gwen, you know I am not like that.'

Gwen glared, but said nothing for a moment. This conversation had to be brief, to the point, and above all without tears. If that was possible.

'Your Grace,' she began stiffly, 'when your mother—'

'Forget my mother.'

'You think I can so easily do such a thing?' Gwen snapped, her temper rising. 'You think it is easy for me to brush aside the indignities spoken to me? To all of us?'

It was clear Percy regretted his words. Biting the corner of his lip, he said, 'I have already apologised for her. I regret to tell you I think it unlikely she will offer an apology herself.'

'It is not your mother I am…upset with,' said Gwen, heat whirling in her throat, making it difficult for her to speak. 'It is you.' Gwen's temper flared. 'You should have defended me, Percy—Your Grace—and I don't buy your story of always obeying your mother as a child, because you are not a child, you are a grown man, and your mother was rude!'

'I should have said something…'

Gwen waited for more, her heart desperate, willing him to share something that would convince her, that would put the entire situation in a different light.

But nothing came.

'You are the sort of gentleman who always gets what he wants,' Gwen said with a dry laugh, her bitter temper finally unleashed. 'But in this situation you should have known better. Another duke would have known better—hell, any gentleman would have known better.'

It was as though she had physically slapped him.

Percy's mouth fell open, his eyes went wide with pain, and he took a staggering step back.

'I had not known your temper was so violent,' Percy said quietly.

Gwen blanched. That he would say such a thing—and to her! But then he did not know, did he? No one did. She had been sure, when she came to the Wallflower Academy, that no one knew of her terrible past.

'Dear God,' said Percy, a puzzled expression on his face. 'Why do you react so?'

'Because…' Gwen knew she should not answer, knew she should keep her counsel, but it was too much. Her heart was breaking, and her head hurt, and the tirade she knew she should not let loose came pouring from her lips. 'Because earlier this year I killed a man!'

She clasped her hands over her mouth in horror, but it was too late. The words were said.

Percy stared at her as though unseeing for several seconds in silence, then said, 'Killed a man?'

'I did not mean to, but he…he had stolen from us… my family…'

Gwen knew not from where these words came—knew she should laugh, pretend it was all a jest, make Percy love her again. But he could not love her. He could not love a murderess.

'My family's inn…the Golden Hind. My mother said she saw the body…she knows I did it! He stole from us and then he tried to kiss me, to force me to—I told you before. I fought him off.'

'The Golden Hind?'

Gwen stared. Of all the things she had said, the admissions she had made, the confession that she was a murderess… And Percy was more interested in the location of where her crime had taken place?

She nodded. 'My parents' inn—my mother's now, I suppose—'

'The Golden Hind in Sussex?' Percy said urgently, stepping away.

Gwen nodded again. What did it matter? The deed was done, the man was dead—not because she'd wished to do it, but to protect herself.

'You killed my brother.'

Gwen blinked. She could not have heard those words. She had imagined them.

'You killed James,' said Percy dully. 'Oh, God… To think for all these months we have wondered… He was found outside the Golden Hind inn…dead from a blow to the head. Murdered by a common harlot.'

'It was not like that,' whispered Gwen, feeling stinging tears enter her eyes. 'The man would not pay…and he grabbed me…he tried to kiss me. His hands were all over me—I told you before—and I pushed him. And when he fell—'

'I have heard enough.'

Percy's gaze had slipped away, was now focused on a point just above her shoulder. He straightened his jacket.

'Dear God, I never would have expected… Thank you for this information, Miss Knox, it will finally put my mother's heart at rest. We will not meet again. Good day.'

Chapter Seventeen

Well, he should have guessed he would end up here, Percy thought hazily as he hiccupped for a second time in a row.

Did not all dukes end up this way eventually?

Was it not the one direction every duke took: towards drink?

The glass in his hand was resting upon his stomach as Percy sat lazily in his armchair by the fire. It was seemingly empty. That could not be. He had filled it with brandy but five minutes ago… Was it five minutes ago?

Percy glanced at the grandfather clock in the corner and was astonished to find the clock was moving.

No—no, wait. That was him. He was moving.

After reaching to clutch at the arm of the chair, Percy was struck by the unfortunate realisation that neither himself nor the clock were moving. But his room was.

How many brandies had he had?

Percy reached to the floor, where he had left the brandy bottle, and was surprised at the ease with which he could lift it up to his eyeline.

That was because it was empty.

'Dear God…' Percy groaned into the silence of his study,

and wondered whether his hangover would be as bad as he was already imagining.

Probably. Perhaps worse.

Perhaps then his body would feel as awful as his heart, with that twisting pain, the agony and the heaviness he could not shift from his soul. Perhaps then it would all align and he would feel as appalling as he knew he should.

Rising in a swift movement, then staggering forward, Percy sighed and sat down again. Maybe retrieving another bottle of brandy was not a good idea. Perhaps it was safer to merely sit here, alone, watching the dying embers of the fire disappear, taking the warmth with them.

When so much was wrong with the world, why not sit and experience the simple things?

'Because earlier this year I killed a man!'

Percy's jaw tightened. He should have known. He should have known the minute he had walked into Gwen and received her tirade for knocking her down.

It was all too good to be true.

A wallflower with that sort of temper…the way Gwen's eyes brightened when she became passionate…the way she became more beautiful when aroused…

All too good to be true.

And just when he'd thought he was close to happiness—finding that Gwen desired him just as much as he desired her, and that their mutual attraction sparked into a pleasure that was riveting—his inability to stop his mother talking had led to a revelation he could hardly ignore.

Percy dropped his head into his hands. He had thought the most difficult challenge to surmount would be his mother and Gwen never seeing eye to eye—but to find himself face to face with the woman he loved, who was also his brother's murderess!

It was too much. No one would blame him for finding a little liquid solace.

Not when the woman he wanted to hold on to for dear life…the woman he knew, loved, had bedded…was not just a wallflower with a temper…

No. Gwen was so much more.

Percy would never have been lumbered with this title and all the rules and restrictions that came with it if it had not been for Gwen.

It couldn't be.

There had been times, in the five days since Gwen had made her startling revelation, when Percy had believed himself confused. He must have misheard her, he had tried to convince himself in the dead of night, with sleep eluding him.

What word sounded like murderess?

Countess?

Actress?

No. No, it was no good. Percy knew himself to be a fool, certainly, but not that kind of fool. He had not misheard. He just did not wish to believe, as well he might not, that the woman who was still overtaking his thoughts at every moment was the woman who had taken the life of his brother.

That temper of hers.

That fiery blaze, always just underneath the surface.

Percy laughed bitterly as he sat up and shook his head, looking into the fire. He had seen it—it had been there the whole time. Not always visible, but when one knew where to look—there it was.

He had known she was no wallflower from the very beginning. He should have trusted his instincts. But instead of doing so he had fallen in love. There was this pain in his heart, this twisted devotion, this desire to see her even now…even after knowing she had murdered James…

What else could it be, if not love?

Percy sighed and wondered what the time was. Glancing at the grandfather clock, he saw to his relief that it had stopped its merry dance and was now showing near eleven o'clock.

He had given his heart to a woman who could hate as strongly as she could love, whom he certainly should not love, and he was late.

Percy chuckled in the darkness, the only light the amber flickering of the fire.

Late? He was far more than late. Terminally late.

Lady Rose would surely have put the card tables away by now...disappointed, he was sure, at missing her chance of hooking the Duke of Knaresby.

Well, he was in no mood to be accepting pretty compliments or agreeable charms. Not when he wanted to see the delicately frustrated expression of Gwen, when debating with him about the right way to drive a horse, or laughing at the way Miss Pike attempted to orchestrate impossible matches.

His stomach twisted and he placed a hand upon it. He would never recover. Gwen had a piece of his heart now, even if he did wish to have it back.

'More brandy, I think,' Percy muttered.

The door to his study opened behind him.

'Do not disturb me,' he snapped at whatever servant had entered the room.

'There is no need to speak to me like that,' said Lady Devereux curtly as she stepped around him to glare into the eyes of her son.

Percy swallowed. There was an unwritten rule in the townhouse that he would not enter the parlour without his mother's permission and she would not enter the study without his. Having Mayfair House made that easier. Most of the time his mother stayed there.

It was entirely different at the estate in the country, of course. Percy was still learning his way around the place, more in need of a map than mere directions, and his mother had an entire wing to herself. Apparently the Dower House was insufficient.

But here, in Town, it was important to have different spaces.

It avoided awkward scenarios like this, for example, he thought darkly as he placed his empty glass hastily down beside the empty brandy bottle and hoped his mother would not notice.

'Ah,' he said aloud, as though that would clarify things.

Lady Devereux raised an eyebrow. 'Ah, indeed.'

Well, it was his own fault for being the worse for wear, Percy thought awkwardly as his mother settled herself in a chair opposite him.

'Well, you were greatly missed at Lady Alice's, of course—but then you know that,' said his mother impressively, her gaze still affixed to his own.

Percy swallowed. 'I do.'

'You do,' said Lady Devereux pointedly, 'because you were not there.'

Blast and damn it. He should have known better than to think his absence would go unnoticed. He should have attended for half an hour or so and then slipped away, convincing his mother later that he had merely been in a different room.

As it was…

'What is wrong, then?' asked his mother curtly. 'Come on—out with it.'

Percy knew what the correct answer was, of course. 'Nothing is wrong. I merely felt tired and wished to—'

'Poppycock.'

Percy's eyes widened but his mother said nothing, waiting for him to continue.

As though he could continue.

What was Percy supposed to do? Admit to his own mother that he had fallen in love not merely with a wallflower—a type of person she clearly disliked—and not only with a woman with no title, no connections, nor anything to offer the Knaresby title, but with the murderess of her eldest son?

No. Percy was not a cruel man, and he saw no reason to inflict this pain upon her. Lady Devereux had buried her brother-in-law and her son in the last year. He would not force her to bury all her hopes for his marriage.

''Tis as I say,' Percy said stiffly. 'Nothing.'

Lady Devereux examined him for a moment, and when she spoke again it was in a far softer voice than he had expected. 'I am your mother, you know.'

It was such a different line of attack—one Percy had not been expecting—that he found he had once again dropped his head into his hands.

'Nothing is wrong,' he said, his voice muffled, knowing how ridiculous it was. His mother was no fool.

She snorted. 'I raised you, Percy Devereux, long before you were ever destined to become a duke. I know when you are lying. Now, I demand to know what the problem is. It surely cannot be any worse than my imaginings.'

Percy lifted his face and looked straight into the eyes of his mother. Could she understand? Would he ever be able to make her see just how awful the whole thing was?

Lady Devereux blanched. 'Perhaps it *is* worse than my imaginings.'

'I…' Percy hesitated, but he knew the truth had to come out eventually.

She would need to know why he wanted to shut up the London townhouses and disappear to their country estate. There would be questions. Society would talk…wonder why. At least this way his mother would have answers.

Unless she decided to stay, of course, and face them.

Percy took a deep breath. 'I… I have broken things off with a woman I… I truly cared about. There. Now you know.'

Lady Devereux gasped, a hand moving to her chest. 'A woman you—? Percy Devereux, had you offered marriage to this woman?'

'Yes—No,' corrected Percy quickly, his mind whirling.

How had that never occurred to him before? He had never noticed till now, but in truth he had never mentioned matrimony to Gwen. It had seemed so obvious, so clear that he wished for it. Had she expected him to offer directly? Had she been pained, perhaps, that he had not spoken the words?

He pushed aside his concerns. What did it matter? She'd killed his brother. Gwen did not deserve such loyalty, such consideration.

'But I did not know you were even courting anyone!' Lady Devereux looked most put out. 'There I was, parading ladies before you for your choice, when you had already made it!'

'Well, I have unmade it,' said Percy hastily, and felt a wrench pulling through his heart. 'Which should make you happy.'

His mother was silent for a moment. 'And the young lady in question was…?'

Percy did not know what made him do it. He only knew he must keep the truth of Gwen's identity to himself. What good would it do now, to name her to his mother, when she was not only no longer to be her daughter-in-law, but was confirmed as her son's killer?

Still, it was impossible to withstand the glare his mother was subjecting him to for long, and Percy found himself saying, in some sort of defence, 'One of Miss Pike's ladies.'

Percy waited for the onslaught of criticism. He should never have gone in the first place...should never have talked to those ladies...should never have compromised his affections...

He could well imagine the criticism his mother was about to level at him.

As he'd expected, Lady Devereux groaned. What was unexpected, however, was her words.

'Oh, Percy, I wish you had said something at the time! I must have offended her so deeply—I do hope the breach between you is not on my account!'

Percy blinked. He waited for the words to realign themselves and mean something different, with more clarity, more like what he'd been expecting.

But they did not. And now he came to look more closely Percy realised there was a flush of something that might be shame upon his mother's cheeks.

What on earth was going on?

'Oh, I have deeply regretted my words since that afternoon tea ended,' said his mother, shifting uncomfortably in her seat. 'I wish I had spoken differently, to be sure, and that was even before I knew I could be doing you such harm.'

'What—? Harm?' Percy could not help himself; he was bewildered. 'What do you...? Mother, I have never known you to regret speaking in your life!'

'When you have lived as long as I have, my boy,' said his mother sharply, 'you will find there are more than sufficient ways to embarrass yourself. But I had hoped I was past the worst.'

Percy could not understand it. Perhaps it was the brandy, but he was certain that in living memory his mother had never apologised for anything she had said or done.

And this was to be the first time?

'The truth is, I always feel a little awkward around wall-flowers,' his mother said with a heavy sigh. 'They never do or say anything, do they?'

Memories of Gwen flashed before Percy's eyes: Gwen laughing, Gwen challenging him to a game of cards, Gwen teasing him at the dinner table or in the carriage, telling him how much she cared for him…

'Well,' he said dully, 'you do not have to worry on that score any longer. As I said, I have broken things off with her.'

'And why, precisely, is that?'

Percy tried not to laugh, but it was difficult not to. It was not a laugh of joy, but one of desperation. How could his life have descended into this…this pit of despair?

'Because she has no dowry, no title of any kind, no family, no connections and no prestige in Society. She does not fit any of the criteria James would have wanted, and she also,' Percy said quietly, unsure if he was brave enough to speak these words, 'has guilt on her hands.'

Lady Devereux frowned. 'Guilt on her hands?'

Percy nodded.

His dear Gwen…the woman he had given his heart to…

'She is a murderess.'

His mother's mouth fell open. She sat for almost a full minute, then managed, 'I—I beg your pardon?'

Nodding again, Percy found he could say nothing else. There was nothing more to be said. The woman he loved— a woman he could never have imagined doing such a terrible thing—had committed one of the most heinous acts a person could.

She had taken a life—and not just any life. The life of his brother.

'And who, precisely,' asked Lady Devereux icily, 'was the woman in question?'

Percy swallowed. 'Miss Gwendoline Knox.'

He had no real expectation of what his mother would do with this information—which was why it was most alarming when his mother's cheeks turned pale and she rose so hastily that her gloves fell to the floor.

She strode across the room, opened the drinks cabinet, and pulled out a bottle of whisky and a glass.

'Hang on, there,' protested Percy, 'that is my whisky you are—'

'It is for both of us,' interrupted Lady Devereux calmly, returning to her seat and opening the bottle. 'Pass me your glass.'

Percy obeyed wordlessly. His mother drank alcohol, of course, just like any lady with taste. But it was usually a delicate sweet wine in a small glass, on a Sunday evening after supper.

He watched in silence as his mother poured a generous helping of the amber liquid into each of their glasses, drank hers in one, then replenished it.

'Steady on, Mother,' Percy said quietly. 'I do not think there is any need for—'

'You have just told me you've fallen in love with a woman you believe has killed,' said Lady Devereux succinctly. 'Killed, as I suspect you know, your brother. I believe there is every need.'

Percy blinked. He was dreaming. That was it. He had fallen asleep on the sofa after his brandy. Though even he would never have expected his mind to concoct such nonsense.

How on earth did his mother know?

'Oh, Percy, you were always such an innocent,' said his mother heavily.

Percy straightened up on the sofa. 'I would not say I was—'

'I am your mother. I shall decide,' Lady Devereux said smartly. 'And you always did idolise your brother, no matter the… Well, the rather unsavoury habits he developed as he grew up. He was so much older than you, wasn't he? Eleven years… What a difference that can make.'

Percy swallowed. James had been quite a bit older than him, it was true. It had felt like an insurmountable distance when they were boys, but as they had both grown Percy had hoped to spend more time with him.

Then it had been too late.

'James was away so often—at Cambridge, then the Inns of Court as a lawyer,' Percy said hoarsely. 'There was never much time to—'

'He was not at Cambridge,' interrupted Lady Devereux, a painful note in her voice. 'Not for long, anyway. Nor at the Inns of Court, I am afraid. All lies. All untrue.'

Percy stared. It was not possible. 'But James said—'

'He was not a good man, Percy. It pains me to say it, but there it is,' said his mother. 'Sometimes one has to accept that the boy one has borne and raised is not the man one would have hoped he'd be. He got himself into… difficulties.'

Percy leaned forward. He had believed Gwen's revelation to be the greatest shock of his life, but clearly he had been wrong. 'Difficulties?'

A nerve twitched in Lady Devereux's jaw. 'With money. With ladies. He was…disrespectful. He attempted to… Well, the less said about that the better. But I was forced to give quite large sums of money to ladies who had suffered his attentions being pressed just a little too hard.'

Nausea rose in Percy's stomach and mixed with the brandy, making his head spin. No. No, it was not possible, James would never—

'He was not a good man, Percy,' Lady Devereux said again. 'Lord knows, I should have spoken to you about this earlier. His behaviour… I would not call it merely bad. Criminal, perhaps.'

Percy could not speak—he could barely breathe. James had never thought much of obeying the rules, to be sure. And there had been that streak in him… Not cruelty. Not exactly…

'When his body was discovered outside an inn, a gash across his head and a rock—an immovable rock, mark you—stained with his blood,' said Lady Devereux calmly, 'with the daughter of the house hysterical and shouting about how she would not permit him to touch her… Well. That was an end to it.'

Silence fell in the study, although Percy was sure he could hear the pumping of his heart, the twisting of his lungs as they worked hard to keep him alive.

Gwen.

Gwen and James.

He had tried to…

'It was her,' Percy mumbled. 'Gwen. He tried—'

'The important thing is that he did not,' said his mother curtly. 'I looked into the matter, of course. The Knox family—mother and daughter. The daughter was well spoken of, well liked, though very shy and quiet, and withdrawn after the…the incident. I had thought her kept quietly at home…'

'But she was sent to the Wallflower Academy,' said Percy, his eyes wide. 'And that is where she met—'

'You.' Lady Devereux sighed. 'Oh, Percy, I hope I did not

offend her. I wish you had told me of her before you went bumbling in and got the wrong end of the stick.'

Percy stared at his mother.

She could not be serious.

How was this his fault? All he had done was fall in love. Was that his doing? How could he have prevented such a thing from occurring?

'You are a fool,' said his mother.

'Me a fool?' Percy spluttered. 'Why on earth do you say—?'

'I have heard about your Miss Knox, and from a very reputable source,' said his mother with a dry laugh. 'Yes, Miss Pike cannot stop singing her praises. Rather unusual for that woman. I now see why. She obviously believed I knew of your feelings. You would be lucky to have her, Percy.'

He was definitely dreaming. Percy could well remember all the lectures he had endured from his mother about how to find a wife who would further the Knaresby name, a woman who had the elegant breeding of the very best of Society, with money to boot.

'But all the gossip...the newspaper reports and the questions about whether I am a suitable heir to the line,' Percy continued wildly. 'Do you think marrying a woman with nothing to recommend her will help?'

'No, but—'

'You were the one who said I needed to marry for the Knaresby line,' Percy reminded his mother. 'For money and prestige all the things Gwen does not have!'

Lady Devereux fixed him with a beady eye. 'Yes, I did, didn't I? But I married for love...and it brought me nothing but happiness with your father.'

Percy smiled ruefully. His father. Gone these seven and ten years now. His memories of his parents together had faded, yes, but the colour had not gone from them. Neither had the sense of happiness.

'That was different,' he said weakly.

His mother raised an eyebrow. 'You are right. You are a duke now. You have responsibilities and you currently have no heir. I have seen arranged marriages blossom into love, and I have seen arranged marriages wither with no children, for they could barely stand the sight of each other. Answer me this, Percy. How will the Knaresby line continue if you do not marry someone you truly love?'

Chapter Eighteen

Gwen had never looked at the ceiling of the orangery before. It was not the sort of thing one paid a huge amount of attention to, not really, but as she lay there on the cold, calming floor, she was remarkably impressed by the intricacy of the lattice work.

'You are overreacting.'

'I am not overreacting,' said Gwen firmly from the comfort of the floor. If anything, she was underreacting. She had just admitted to murder, to a duke—the duke she had fallen in love with, no less—only to discover that the killed man in question had been his own brother.

What a disaster.

She could not have imagined a more devastating blow to the growing love they had been desperately trying to keep alive—and it was too late now. It was over.

Movement.

Her gaze flickered away from the orangery ceiling to see the face of Sylvia.

'You don't have to lie there, you know,' she pointed out as she looked down.

Gwen shrugged from her prone position on the floor. 'I

don't have to lie anywhere. I don't have to do anything. Nothing changes anything. Nothing matters.'

The dull ache in her heart had settled there the moment Percy had turned his back on her, refusing to hear her explanation—as though it would have made any difference—and disappearing from her life.

After holding him at arm's length for days, for fear of him not being able to love her, and fear of his mother's disapproval, Gwen thought it was poetic justice that it was her own actions which had finally torn them apart.

And she hadn't cried. No matter how much she had attempted it, alone in bed at night, upstairs in her lonely bedchamber, Gwen had not been able to force a single tear to fall.

Perhaps that was why she felt so adrift in the sea of life. What did it matter whether gentlemen came to the Wallflower Academy to view them, take tea with them, dine with them?

None was Percy.

None would ever accept a murderess for a wife.

She was going to be here, at the Wallflower Academy, for the rest of her life.

A foot nudged her—not painfully, but enough for Gwen to wince. 'Ouch!'

'Didn't see you there,' said Rilla placidly, from her seat beside Gwen on the floor. 'And I don't know what you're so upset about.'

Gwen glared, though she knew it had little effect. 'You don't?'

'It is not as though you would ever have been able to convince Lady Devereux of your suitability for her son,' Rilla said plainly, her face expressionless. 'Even if you hadn't revealed whatever it was that made the Duke leave so suddenly.'

A heavy weight settled in Gwen's stomach. 'You are not very comforting, you know.'

'I am doing my best,' countered Rilla. 'You've not given me much to go on.'

Gwen sighed and turned back to look at the ceiling of the orangery. That was certainly true, but nothing any of the wallflowers said would convince her to reveal precisely why Percy, after banging on the front door for nearly an hour and demanding to see her, had spent less than ten minutes with her before storming out.

He had not returned to the Wallflower Academy.

He never would, Gwen was sure.

'Perhaps it was best to break things off,' said Rilla, her voice softer now. 'I mean…before things became too serious.'

A tear welled up in Gwen's eye and slowly trickled into her hair.

Too serious.

Rilla had only guessed at what she and Percy had shared in her bedchamber—and she had clearly underestimated just how intimate they had been.

Too serious.

Gwen could not imagine anything more serious than her feelings for Percy, complicated as they were, tinged with sadness and confusion after his mother's words, affection and desire after their conversations and kisses, pain at his brother's death, frustration and hurt…

'I am doing all I can,' muttered Rilla above her. She was speaking to Sylvia, who was whispering rapidly into her ear. 'No, I will not tell her to buck up!'

Gwen sighed. No matter how hard the other wallflowers tried, she knew it was not possible to restore her spirits.

'Well, does she *look* comforted?' Rilla's voice was irritable. Evidently she was exasperated by the harassment Sylvia was subjecting her to.

'You should have a good cry,' said Sylvia, matter-of-factly, as though she had survived several heartbreaks and lived to tell the tale. 'A good cry will do you the world of good. Then eat cake. All the cake we can find.'

Gwen blinked. It was not the worst idea she had ever heard. Truth be told, of all the wallflowers at the Academy at the moment, Sylvia was the last one she had expected to be so...so understanding.

She looked up at the concerned face of the woman.

Sylvia smiled wryly, her black eyes glittering with what might have been tears. 'You are not the only one of us to have had her heart broken. It happens to all of us eventually.'

Gwen opened her mouth to ask the question. Had she had her own heart broken?

But approaching footsteps, smart and purposeful, halted her tongue. There was only one person who walked like that at the Wallflower Academy.

'Miss Gwendoline Knox,' said Miss Pike sternly, leaning over her wallflower. 'What are you doing?'

Gwen's heart sank. It was not enough that she was to be heartbroken, left here to fester as a wallflower until the end of her days. No, she had to be criticised for it into the bargain.

'When can we expect the pleasure of His Grace's company again?'

Gwen swallowed, tasting bitterness on her tongue. It was all over. It was too cruel, too harsh to make her say it again, but she would. She would say it until the rest of them believed her. Percy was never coming back, and in a way she could not blame him.

She had no siblings, no one to protect or feel protective of. But Percy had adored his brother.

There was no possibility that Percy would find it in his heart to forgive her—none at all. The more she hoped for it, the less likely it would be.

She needed to come to peace with it, Gwen thought as she drew in a deep breath, *and that meant being frank.*

Until she could speak openly about it without tears, without fear of overwhelming emotion, she would be a captive to this pain.

'I am sorry to inform you, Miss Pike,' said Gwen quietly, still lying on the floor—well, she had not been instructed to rise, had she?—'that I have broken things off with the Duke of Knaresby. I do not believe he will be visiting the Academy again. He will wed another.'

The thought cracked her heart in two.

She had not considered it until the words had tripped out of her mouth, but that was likely, wasn't it? Whether he found her here at the Wallflower Academy, or at Almack's, or in someone's dining room, or at a card party, Percy would meet someone else. Another lady he would learn to love, who would not have the ignominious past of having murdered someone he loved.

'B-But…if an invitation was sent to him—'

Gwen sighed. 'Miss Pike, I regret it, but there it is. I do not believe an invitation even from your own hand would be sufficient to entice the Duke of Knaresby back to the Wallflower Academy. That is my opinion, of course, but I share it advisedly.'

Not after revealing my terrible secret, she thought wretchedly, tears threatening and prickling at the corners of her eyes again. Not after she had finally answered the question which had clearly plagued Percy for many a month: who, precisely, had murdered his brother?

If only it had never happened. But Gwen had known, deep down, that the moment would one day come back to haunt her. She could not be let off with merely the fear of being discovered; she would be punished, somehow, and now she knew how.

In a strange way, it was a relief. Now at least she would not have to concern herself with the fear of being found out. The worst had already happened. Percy would be protected from her and her terrible temper. She would never have to fear that one day she would lash out and hurt him, too.

Who knew what scandal might have occurred if she had married him? The Duchess of Knaresby…murdering the heir to the Knaresby line. It would have been terrible.

'Miss Knox, I am ashamed of you!'

Gwen's gaze focused on Miss Pike as her words echoed around the orangery like a death knell. 'A-Ashamed?'

Miss Pike rose to her full height, which from the floor of the orangery was a great deal, and affixed a most malignant stare to the unfortunate wallflower. 'Miss Knox, I cannot prevent myself from berating you, you shameless woman! Losing the affections of a duke…perhaps the best marriage offer you could ever have had!'

Out of the corner of her eye, Gwen noticed that Sylvia had taken Rilla's hand and quietly begun leading her out of the orangery.

Evidently they had no wish to be witnesses to another scene of Gwen's shame. She could not blame them. She did not particularly wish to witness it herself.

'And to think the only reason you are here is because your mother wishes you to find a husband!' continued Miss Pike, eyes blazing. 'What ingratitude to show her…when you were on the brink of securing for yourself the finest husband any wallflower here has ever attained!'

Gwen bristled and sat up to glare directly at Miss Pike. *Well, really!*

Her mother had only wished to be rid of her, and if Miss Pike had ever taken the time to get to know her she would have known that her mother would be mortified if her daughter had married someone as impressive as a duke! Her daughter? Outrank her? It was not to be borne!

Besides, it was scandalous, the way Miss Pike was talking. She spoke of husbands like—like fish! Specimens to be caught—to be mesmerised into falling onto hooks, scooped up out of the water and displayed like prizes!

Percy—if she had been fortunate enough to become his wife—would have been far more! Far more than just a trophy…a prize to crow over with other women!

'You may have lost,' said Miss Pike, lowering her voice but losing none of her intensity, 'the one and only chance you will ever have at happiness.'

And that was it.

Gwen could take no more.

Her heart had been bruised, battered, squeezed beyond belief, then broken. She had tried desperately to cry tears of agony, had railed against the darkness of her life, had wished she had never even been there that night at the Golden Hind.

But this was too far. How dared Miss Pike criticise her for her own heartbreak?

Though her heart had been ripped from her chest, while it was still beating, Gwen was still certain she had done the right thing.

Her confession had spared Percy from a lifetime of misery as her husband—and through it all she loved him. She loved him too much to condemn him to a lifetime of defending himself against a scandal he had never been informed of.

Percy deserved better. That was her gift to him.

'I am very disappointed in you,' said Miss Pike, with feeling.

Gwen rose to her feet. Every inch of her body was humming with rage, a rage she could barely keep inside, but she would do her utmost to make sure she was calm and collected.

She had a certain few things to say to Miss Pike, and as they were alone this was the perfect opportunity.

A small smile crept across Gwen's face. She was going to enjoy this. Her temper rarely had an opportunity to be released, particularly since the incident at the inn, and it had been fizzing inside her for far too long.

She would relish the chance to tell Miss Pike a few home truths.

'The trouble with you, Miss Pike,' Gwen said quietly, 'is that you think there is nothing more important in the world than mere marriage.'

Miss Pike blinked, startled. She had evidently never heard such a measured, yet forceful statement. 'I—I... I beg your pardon?'

'The Wallflower Academy is not the be-all and end-all of the world, Miss Pike,' said Gwen triumphantly, warming to her theme.

Oh, it felt wonderful to finally stand up for herself. She could not recall doing so since first arriving at the Academy, when...when Percy had knocked her down.

Speaking her mind, her true opinions, with no malice but merely honesty, was a balm for her broken heart.

'Yes, I have lost the affection of the Duke of Knaresby, and arguably for good reason,' Gwen said calmly, hoping beyond hope that Miss Pike would not enquire just what that reason was. 'And, yes, I loved him—still love him, in fact, far too much to tie him to me when he is unwilling. But he is not my last chance of happiness!'

Miss Pike's mouth was opening and shutting in the same fashion as her namesake, but no words came out.

Gwen took a step forward. Power crackled in her bones, as though she had been given the gift of speech after being forced to be mute for decades.

It was wonderful to say these things—but it was even more wonderful to mean them.

'One's happiness is not merely tied to a husband. One should not be defined by one's connection to a man! They do not own us—we are not possessions! I admit I would have loved to be Percy's wife,' said Gwen, a little emotion tremoring in her voice. Miss Pike's eyes had widened at her use of the Duke's first name, but Gwen continued onward before the owner of the Wallflower Academy could interrupt her. 'Perhaps I may not marry, and I will find a different kind of happiness then, but there is every chance someone else will want me. They will. Because I am a fine match for—for anyone. Duke or not! I may be the least likely to win a duke, but perhaps a duke is least likely to win me!'

Her last words echoed around the orangery, and Gwen could not help but feel victorious as she spoke them. Because she was only now starting to believe it. Someone, one day, would recognise her worth, her value. See that she was a good person, and could be an excellent wife. For someone.

'I am worth winning,' Gwen said, smiling at Miss Pike. 'And I would never wish you to forget that, Miss Pike.'

'I could not agree more,' came Percy's voice. 'Well said, Gwen.'

Chapter Nineteen

The shock and surprise on Gwen's face was palpable, and Percy regretted for a moment that he had allowed his tongue to be so unguarded.

If only he had thought—had stopped himself from speaking so quickly. If only he had pulled Gwen aside after her conversation—or rather, altercation—with Miss Pike. He could have taken her into a quiet corner, gained a moment to remember his words, and had the pleasure of her presence alone.

But it was too late. The astonishment on both ladies' faces was a picture of surprise that anyone had overheard their rather stern words, and Percy's stomach twisted.

He had not expected Miss Pike to be a potential audience to his declarations…had intended to make them private, not public.

But as his pulse sounded a hasty drum beat in his ears, Percy found he was starting to care less and less about the way people looked at him. As long as Gwen looked at him. Her startled eyes were wide, her pupils fixed on his, and Percy's heart soared to see the connection there. However faint. However much it had almost been destroyed.

A glimmer of hope fractured his heart.

Yes, Gwen was a fine match. Far more than she could possibly understand, and far more than he had understood until yesterday.

Percy was not going to make the same mistake again. He had lost her twice. He was never going to lose her again. Not if he had anything to do with it.

'Gwen...' he said, rather weakly.

It was not what he had intended to say. During the un-endingly long ride Percy had prepared a speech so impressive, so wonderful, Gwen would have no choice but to accept him. To believe him. To love him. To understand that his heart had been bruised, but so had hers. And, while he had been dishonest, foolish, idiotic to the extreme, she had done nothing but defend herself against a man who, Percy had to accept, was not what he had thought.

It had not consisted of the single word 'Gwen'.

Miss Pike's eyes were flickering between them. 'I—I... I don't... Y-Your Grace!'

Percy smiled awkwardly. How long would it take him to truly become accustomed to hearing 'Your Grace' instead of Devereux? A lifetime, perhaps.

If he was fortunate, a lifetime with Gwen.

The orangery was starting to chill as he stood there in the doorway to the garden, so Percy stepped inside and closed the door behind him.

There was another doorway, open into the main house, and just beyond it appeared the faces of Miss Sylvia Bryant and Miss Marilla Newell, not to mention every other wallflower in the place. They were all listening carefully.

'My word...' said Sylvia, not attempting to keep her voice down.

Gwen whirled around and coloured. 'Sylvia!'

'Sorry, Gwen,' said Sylvia, with absolutely no hint of

actual remorse on her face. 'We wanted to hear what the Pike—what Miss Pike had to say.'

'Sylvia!'

'Sorry, Miss Pike,' came the uncontrite words.

'Gwen,' said Percy again, wishing beyond anything to be alone with her. This was not exactly the reunion he had expected.

'Ah,' said Rilla with a knowing smile. 'Your duke's back.'

Gwen coloured, her cheeks flushed pink, but she said nothing.

Percy grinned.

So he was her duke, was he?

Well, if fortune was with him, by the time he finished this conversation with Gwen he would be.

Though it could all go so wrong, even now.

Percy clenched his jaw. He must make it work. He was not sure how he would be able to go through life without her.

'Good,' said Rilla with apparent relish. 'Is he here to make an honest woman of you?'

'Rilla!'

Percy took a hesitant half-step back, almost against his will.

Now, that was unexpected.

Gwen had told the wallflowers, then, precisely what they had shared together—*well, hopefully not precisely.*

It was a disconcerting thought.

Making sure not to catch anyone's eye at all, Percy swallowed, and discovered to his surprise that he did not care.

Let them know.

Let the world know.

He had nothing to hide except the fact that he had been such a fool. Before knowing that Gwen had been in any way mixed up with James's death, Percy had been foolish enough to permit his mother to sow seeds of doubt in

Gwen's heart—seeds which should never been permitted to take root.

But he was here to change that. He needed her. More than Society and reason should dictate.

And, seeing her here, Percy knew just how deeply he cared.

Gwen did not belong in the Wallflower Academy, being berated by Miss Pike for being true to her own heart. She was no wallflower—not really. She had been forced to be here…forced into silence for an accident that had not been her fault…

Percy's stomach clenched. A dark deed had been committed that night, but it had not been by Gwen's hand.

'Gwen…' he said softly.

As though she had been waiting for his very breath, Gwen turned to him, eyes wide and brimming with tears, though he could not tell whether it was because he was here or because he had stayed away.

Oh, to think he had risked not having Gwen in his life. It was intolerable. He would regret these few days he had been without her for the rest of his life.

'Percy…' Gwen whispered, a single tear trickling down her cheek.

Without a word, without invitation, Percy stepped forward and brushed away that tear, cupping her cheek and lifting her chin.

Oh, when she looked at him… He could have melted right there and then.

There was something about the woman he loved… something more important than he was, than the promise he had made.

His life was only complete with her. His body craved hers, yes, but it was his heart, his very soul, that demanded she be his. He could not be without her—would not permit anyone to separate them.

There was only one person who could make him miserable now, and that was Gwen herself.

If she was still resolutely against him...

Gwen was stammering. 'B-But you cannot be here—Wh-What are you doing here?'

He glanced around them. Miss Pike looked triumphant, as though she had somehow managed to orchestrate the entire thing, Sylvia was gawping, mouth open, and Rilla had inched closer, in the clear hope of hearing more.

They could not stay here.

There were things he had to say to Gwen Knox, Percy thought darkly. *Things not for the hearing of the general public.*

'Come on,' he said, offering his hand with a twist of a smile.

Without hesitation Gwen took it, and Percy's heart soared.

She would not be so trusting, would she, he thought wildly as he pulled her out of the orangery and into the garden, *if she had entirely decided against him?*

After several minutes of striding through the freezing garden, with Percy feeling Gwen's hand in his but refusing the instinct to look at her, knowing he would do nothing but kiss her if he succumbed to that temptation, he finally found somewhere he was certain they could speak without being overheard.

Though he would not put it past Sylvia or a few of the other wallflowers to creep out into the garden and attempt to overhear them, Percy thought with a wry smile.

He could hardly blame them.

'Gwen,' he said quietly.

Gwen pulled her hand away as they stopped in the rose garden. Most of the roses were over now; only the rose

Gwen had admired so much the last time they'd been there still had a flower remaining.

'Percy,' she said, just as quietly. 'I mean, Your Grace.'

Percy waved it aside. 'Oh, Gwen, do you not think we are far beyond that?'

A rueful smile crept across Gwen's face as she stared at the lawn. 'I... I thought we were. But then we went further still, and seemed to circle back to civility. And now...'

'Now?' Percy had tried not to speak too eagerly, but he had not succeeded.

Gwen swallowed. 'Now...'

After waiting for a moment Percy became certain she was unable to speak, so took matters into his own hands. It had been by his brother that Gwen had been so injured in the first place, forced to bear the burden of a murderous misunderstanding, and he and his mother had merely compounded the injury.

It was time for him to make amends.

'I am sorry.'

Gwen looked up, her sparkling eyes meeting his. 'Why on earth would you say that? After what I have done—'

'You have done nothing,' interrupted Percy, taking a step towards her, but halting as Gwen took a step back.

She was not ready—not yet.

'Gwen, I assumed the worst in you when you told me of your...your difficulty with my brother. I was wrong. I knew you. I should have known better.'

Gwen appeared overpowered by emotion. A mere nod of her head seemed all she could manage, and Percy knew why. She still believed herself a murderess...someone who had taken a life. And that could no longer continue.

No matter how complicated his emotions towards James were—and he would undoubtedly spend the rest of his life

unpicking them—Gwen should not have to live with unnecessary guilt.

Not if he could do anything about it.

Percy swallowed hard before he tried to speak. It was
still painful. One did not lose a brother in mysterious circumstances, and then discover one's beloved was mixed
up in the sordid detail, without taking time to heal.

'Your mother would not wish you to be here.'

Percy almost laughed at Gwen's words, and saw surprise
in her eyes as he said, 'It was actually my mother's idea for
me to ride out here at once. But do not mistake me. I would
have been here by luncheon regardless of her advice.'

Because he couldn't hide from the truth for ever. No
matter his rose-tinted memories, Percy knew Gwen's
words had rung true. It had not been easy to accept his
brother had not been as he believed. But now, although it
had taken time, the path that lay ahead of him was clear.

It went to Gwen.

'But—but I do not understand,' said Gwen, a crease across
her forehead. 'Percy, you should not be here!'

'I could not stay away!'

The words echoed around the garden. Percy had not
intended to speak so loudly, so vigorously, but it was too
late. He simply had to speak. Had to show her what he felt.

'Gwen, do you think I could live life without you?'

Percy stepped forward and this time Gwen did not step
away.

'Life without you…painful and lonely…with the greatest absence of my heart dragging me down to misery? You
think I could live like that?'

'But I am no good for you!' Gwen's voice was taut with
emotion, pain etched across her face. 'No good for you at all!
Do you not think marrying your brother's murderess would
be a mistake? My mother has made it perfectly plain—'

Percy took a shuddering breath and tried to collect his wits. She was in pain, and so was he, but together could they be healed. He was sure of it.

The question was, how could he convince her?

Percy turned away, desperately trying to think, and then turned back to the woman he loved. 'I assumed the worst of you, and that was wrong.'

'I am rather good at assuming the worst of myself,' admitted Gwen with a dry laugh. 'But…oh, Percy…do you think I would permit you to bind yourself to me? In every possible way, I am the very last person you should be considering as a wife!'

'No!' said Percy, stepping towards her, panic filling his heart. He would not let her escape him again—he had to be with her. 'No, Gwen, you don't understand—'

'I think you are the one who does not understand!' Gwen said, her voice sharp. 'You say you wish to spend your life with me, but I would bring shame upon you, upon your family, even if we…even if you offered me…'

Percy saw her hesitancy, knew it would be painful for her to speak the word which had rested on his heart for so long. 'Marriage?'

A flush darkened her cheeks as a cool wind rushed by. 'You said it—not me.'

'I know I said it,' said Percy with a smile. 'Do you think the word has not been nestled in my heart since the first moment I kissed you?'

Gwen's flush deepened, and it was enough to give Percy hope.

She has not walked away.

She had not cut him off, told him icily that it was impossible and left. She was still here. Gwen was still here, wanting him, wanting this to work.

He would make it work.

Percy stepped forward, only about a foot from her, and Gwen did not retreat. 'You…you apologised to me once, and I told you that if I ever gave you a reason to apologise, you would need to mean it.'

Gwen laughed—a coarse laugh with as much joy within it as pain. 'At the Wallflower Academy dinner. I remember.'

'Since that moment you have never given me cause to hear an apology from your lips,' said Percy seriously, his gaze affixed to hers. 'Even…even for my brother.'

A look of agonising pain flashed across Gwen's face and she made to move, but Percy was too quick this time. He grabbed her hands, keeping her close, desperate to make her see.

'Let me go!'

'You were not the cause of James's death,' Percy said quietly.

Gwen ceased her struggling, though tears had once again pierced her eyes. 'You don't know that. You did not even know I was there. It was my family's inn—'

'It appears there are quite a few things about my brother I did not know,' Percy said bitterly.

To think he had revered the man…a blackguard who had attempted to force himself upon unsuspecting young ladies.

If James had been any other man Percy would have wanted him shot. Perhaps it was a good thing he had never known.

'My mother told me… Well, she told me quite a bit about my brother of which I was previously unaware,' Percy revealed, hating that he had to sully his own brother's name, but knowing it was vital for Gwen to hear this. 'You were defending yourself, and it was by sheer chance that James hit his head on a rock. Chance, Gwen. You did not want him dead, and it was chance that killed him, *not you*.'

He spoke the final two words with feeling, seeing relief yet disbelief on Gwen's face.

She had never known.

Of course she hadn't, Percy thought bitterly.

A young woman fighting off a titled gentleman in the dark, a struggle, a fall, cries of murder, and she would have been bundled off, away from it all, to the Wallflower Academy, without any explanation.

She was due that explanation now.

'It…it was not my fault?' Gwen whispered.

Percy shook his head. No words were necessary now. He could see that the truth was starting to wipe away some of the pain, the confusion. Gwen's shoulders slackened, all the strength of her hands disappeared and she stood there, as if in shock, as though it had just happened.

'My mother…' Gwen swallowed. 'My mother said I had killed him. That I was a murderess—no one would ever want me.'

Repressing the desire to call the wrath of the heavens down upon Gwen's mother, Percy pulled her close into his welcoming arms.

'Just because your mother thought you least likely to win a man's heart,' he said gently, 'it does not mean you have not done so. Gwen, you are someone who is worthy of love. Worthy of protection. Worthy of a life without scandal.'

Gwen laughed, wiping her eyes. 'I am not so sure…' Then her eyes widened, as though she was surprised at something. 'Did—did you say your mother sent you here? But you would come regardless?'

Percy nodded. Joy was starting to creep into his heart— his bruised and rather battered heart. But it was still whole, and still hers, nonetheless.

He knew what he had to do. It was a surprise it had taken him this long.

Still holding Gwen's hands, Percy lowered himself onto one knee.

'Percy...' said Gwen warningly, an eyebrow raised. 'What are you doing?'

Percy grinned. Everything was going to be perfect. They were even in a rose garden—albeit one that had died away for the winter. He could not have wished for a better moment to propose matrimony to the woman he wanted so much.

'I may have been the one to knock you down when we first met,' Percy said seriously, looking up into Gwen's wondrous face, 'but I am the one who has been bowled over again and again by—by your beauty and your brilliance... Oh, Gwen. All I want is for you to be my wife.'

For a heart-stopping moment, one which Percy certainly did not enjoy, he was not entirely sure what Gwen was going to say. She looked hesitant, passionate emotions flickering across her face, as if each of them was attempting to overwhelm her.

Then she was on her own knees—Gwen, his Gwen—in his arms, her lips on his own, and she was kissing him, clinging to him as though she would never let go.

'Yes,' Gwen murmured, her kisses intertwined with her words. 'Yes, Percy. I will marry you. Yes, with all my heart.'

Percy's arms wrapped around her, pulling her closer.

Least likely to win a duke—that was what she had said. Well, she'd won him, and his heart—though, in truth, he rather thought he was the true victor.

Epilogue

The sunlight that flickered through the large bay window could not be real.

She must be dreaming—must have been dreaming for a long time. Weeks, in fact.

For it could not be her wedding day.

Could it?

The day of her wedding to Percy Devereux, Duke of Knaresby.

A slow smile spread across Gwen's face as she examined her reflection carefully in the tall, full-length looking glass Miss Pike had deigned to have moved into her bedchamber just the day before.

A rather startled and disbelieving woman looked back. She had Gwen's eyes, Gwen's dark hair... Gwen's face, in fact. But it could not be her.

She had never seen herself wearing a gown so elegant. It was of a periwinkle-blue satin, with scalloped edging around the hem, and little embroidered forget-me-nots within the bodice. It was a gown she could never have dreamed of purchasing in all her life.

A tutting sound came from behind her, and Gwen turned with a smile. 'Well?'

Sylvia sighed. 'It is a beautiful gown.'

Gwen glowed. Why shouldn't she, on this day when she was allowed to be the happiest person in the world?

Today she would become Percy's wife. After wanting him so much, and fearing that such a want was wrong... after waiting weeks and weeks, for ever...the day was finally here.

Her wedding day.

'The embroidery is delicately done,' said Rilla quietly. She was holding a matching ribbon in her hand, rubbing her fingers against it slowly. 'I do not believe I have ever felt such small stitching.'

'And the Dowager Duchess purchased it for you herself?' Sylvia said, in amazement.

'Lady Devereux,' corrected Gwen quickly. 'Yes. She said it was both something new and blue.'

Her stomach twisted at those words. She had not yet spoken with her future mother-in-law—at least, not properly. Not alone. She had always been accompanied by Miss Pike, by Percy, or by any number of the wallflowers who had agreed to protect her.

But she could not put it off for ever. After such a generous gift, along with the purchase of gowns for her bridesmaids, Gwen knew she could not ignore Lady Devereux for ever.

Even if she might wish to.

'I never thought this day would come,' Gwen admitted shyly, looking back to the looking glass and marvelling at the transformation one single gown had made. 'But it has.'

And after today she would never need to worry about being apart from Percy. They would be spending the rest of their lives with each other.

'I must thank you,' came Rilla's voice from behind her, 'for including us in your day.'

Gwen's heart contracted painfully. There was no bitterness in her friend's words…no envy. Rilla did not blame her for having found happiness—no more than she blamed anyone for having found joy in the arms of another. But it still hurt her. Gwen could see it in the way Rilla was quieter today than she could ever remember. See it in the way she held herself, shoulders slumped, her usually questing fingers slow and unmoving in her lap.

'I am the one who is grateful to you—and to you, Sylvia,' said Gwen with a bright smile, hoping Rilla would hear it in her words. 'I could not have hoped for two more excellent bridesmaids to steady my nerves in the past few weeks.'

Sylvia grinned as she stepped across the room, a plethora of hairpins in her hands. 'Well, I could not agree more—though it's a shame no other wallflower wished to see the spectacle. Stay still!'

Sylvia was attempting to pin Rilla's hair, one pin now in her mouth, but Rilla twisted away.

'Careful, I may end up scalping you!'

'It doesn't matter,' said Rilla with a sigh. 'No one will be looking at me. They'll be looking at Gwen—quite as they should.'

Gwen swallowed.

She was not going to let this conversation overwhelm her.

'They will look at all three of us.'

'I am just glad of the excuse for a new gown,' said Sylvia with a laugh, pins spilling out of her mouth. 'Blast—sorry, Rilla!'

Rilla shrugged as the hairpins fell to the floor. 'And I am grateful too, even in all my dourness. After all, this might be the closest I get to being a bride myself.'

'Nonsense!' Gwen spoke automatically, hating the defeated tone in Rilla's voice, but there was not much she could say to dissuade her.

After all, she might be right. No gentleman who had ever attended one of Miss Pike's invitations had ever shown a mite of interest in Rilla, despite her beauty and witty conversation. They could not see past her blindness—a sad irony.

Sylvia was chuckling as she helped Rilla put on a pair of earbobs. 'You know, sometimes I think this place is packed to the rafters with rebels, not wallflowers.'

Gwen giggled, sitting on the edge of her bed as she watched her. 'What on earth do you mean?'

'Well, look at us,' said Sylvia, straightening and placing her hands on her hips. 'Me, least likely to actually be a wallflower... Rilla, most likely to become Prime Minister, given half the chance—'

'I still haven't ruled it out,' said Rilla with a wicked laugh.

'And you, managing to bag yourself a duke!' Sylvia finished with a laugh.

The three of them giggled—until a voice cut through their merriment.

'Yes,' said a woman's cold voice. 'Yes, she has.'

Gwen turned in horror, knowing even before her gaze reached the doorway precisely who it would be.

There was something about that family, she told herself miserably, *that made them excellent at standing in doorways and overhearing conversations not intended for them to overhear.*

Lady Devereux was standing there, her arms folded.

Sylvia's laughter stopped abruptly, but Rilla's chuckles continued on for a few heart-stopping moments. Gwen wished she could tell her to be quiet, but her mouth seemed to have frozen and she was unable to say a thing.

Oh, this was it.

Never before had she heard of a wedding being cancelled merely an hour before it was supposed to take place, but she had done it now!

She had offended her future mother-in-law, right before her eyes.

'We…we are not laughing any more,' said Rilla, her joy subsiding. 'Why?'

'Because,' said Gwen in a strangled voice, 'Lady Devereux is here.'

There was a moment of silence, then Rilla broke it. 'Ah.'

'We will wait for you downstairs,' said Sylvia hurriedly, rising even as Gwen turned around to beseech her with her eyes to stay—not to abandon her to her fate. 'Come on, Rilla.'

Rilla rose without a word, and Gwen knew that if she was not to be abandoned by them both she would have to speak.

'I am sure Lady Devereux can have nothing to say to me you cannot hear,' Gwen said desperately, looking at Sylvia with wide eyes.

'I would not be so sure,' said Lady Devereux in clipped tones as Sylvia and Rilla passed her.

Gwen swallowed as the door shut behind her two friends, leaving her alone with her future mother-in-law who had once described her as a flower unremarkable compared to a rose.

It would not be a pleasant meeting, but then, it had had to come. She could not avoid her future mother-in-law for ever. Perhaps it was better to have it out now, here, on her own terms. She was in her own bedchamber, at least.

Still, somehow Gwen wished it had been after the wedding, not before. There was a strange sense of foreboding in her stomach telling her that if she was not careful there would not be a wedding at all.

Oh, if only they had not been laughing about her 'bagging' Percy!

'Miss Knox,' said Lady Devereux in clipped tones.

Gwen smiled weakly. All she had to do was get through this conversation without embarrassing herself. How difficult could it be, really?

Lady Devereux stared at her without smiling. 'A pleasant day.'

Gwen waited, sure the older woman would say something else, but no more words seemed forthcoming.

It was down to her, then, to provide the rest of the conversation. Easier said than done.

'Yes. Very pleasant.'

Very pleasant? Were they talking about the weather?

Gwen had laughed at Miss Pike once when she had tried to teach them about small talk, had considered it ridiculous that resorting to talking about the weather would be a reasonable response in a conversation with someone in Society. But now she could see just how desperately those topics of conversation might be needed in discomforting situations.

Speak. She needed to speak—needed to say something… anything! This was her chance, Gwen knew, to say something to her before the wedding and without an audience.

It was not as though they were going to have any other mother in attendance, after all. Gwen could still remember the sickening sensation that had settled in her lungs as she had read the letter from her mother that had come in response to hers about her impending marriage.

She was to marry Percy Devereux, Duke of Knaresby. Gwen had foolishly believed her mother would be happy—

would be pleased that her daughter had managed to find such a wonderful match.

She should not have been so naïve.

What had that paragraph said?

I think it absolutely disgraceful that a daughter of mine should have decided not only to marry above her station, but above the rank of her own mother's husband. You can forget any hopes of us hosting your wedding reception, let Miss Pike do so if you are so ready to take her advice. How dare you show me up? How dare you?

Gwen had burnt the letter. There was no point keeping anything that dripped such hatred.

Lady Devereux cleared her throat. 'So. You are marrying my son.'

Gwen nodded, and felt a little spark of the boldness she had always been told to force down rising within her. 'Yes. And I am glad to be. And grateful.'

Was that too sycophantic? Gwen could hardly tell. But she knew it was important that Percy's mother knew just how much she loved her son—how grateful she was to have him.

After such confusion, after discovering a tangled past which neither of them had known about until it was too late, Gwen was certainly grateful that they had managed to make their way here, to happiness.

Happiness that, Lady Devereux permitting, would last for ever.

'You are grateful?' Lady Devereux raised an eyebrow. 'I am afraid I do not approve.'

Tension bubbled in Gwen's stomach, bitter bile threatening to rise up her throat, but she managed to swallow it. 'Really?'

'Yes, really,' said Lady Devereux calmly. 'I do not know why you are so grateful. 'Tis my son whom I believe is the lucky one.'

It took Gwen a few moments to realise she had not mis-heard the woman. Percy the lucky one? Percy, fortunate to be marrying her?

There was some mistake, surely. Perhaps Percy had informed his mother that Gwen had a large dowry, or a connection to an impressive family—which she certainly did not. It made no sense! Why, after such harsh words only a month ago, was Lady Devereux so taken with her now?

But despite Gwen's silence a slow smile had crept over Lady Devereux's face. 'I did not raise him to be a duke, you know. My brother-in-law was married, had two sons... Even when they died it never crossed my mind that Percy would inherit the title. In a way, I think that has made him a better man.'

Gwen swallowed, forced herself to speak. 'I would agree, my lady.'

'And now he can continue to be a better man by marrying someone who is not interested in his title, but in him. In Percy. The man,' said Lady Devereux with a small twinkle in her eye. 'You have endeared yourself to me, Miss Knox, for that. You have won his heart. That wins my loyalty.'

It was all Gwen could do not to sink weakly to her knees onto the floor. Only now did she recognise the tension in her bones for what it was: fear. Fear that Lady Devereux, Percy's mother, the only other important woman in Percy's life, would reject her—as she so nearly had done at that terrible afternoon tea.

'And I believe I owe you an apology.'

Gwen blinked.

Had those words truly come from Lady Devereux's mouth?

The older woman looked uncomfortable, her hands twisting. 'I... I should not have spoken to you so that day, nor the other wallflowers. It was wrong of me. I beg your forgiveness.'

If anyone else had said those words Gwen would have been hard pressed to believe them. No one apologised to a wallflower without significant cause, and Lady Devereux certainly had not been put under pressure by anyone.

Save perhaps Percy, Gwen thought hastily. But even then she could not imagine Lady Devereux would be easily swayed by her son.

But there was a strange look on the woman's face...one that Gwen could not understand.

Regret?

Fear, perhaps?

Lady Devereux walked towards the large bay window, looking out onto the garden. Her eyes were misted, and there was a strange smile on her face.

'I never liked these curtains,' she said quietly. 'But I liked the window. I liked feeling as though I was close to nature...as though, if I wished to, I could escape and disappear out into the wilderness and not return.'

Gwen stared.

No. It could not be—

'I was surprised when Miss Markham sold the place to Miss Pike,' said Lady Devereux with a sigh. 'I had hoped it would close... But there it is.'

She turned to face Gwen, who spluttered, far more rudely than she had intended, 'Y-You were a wallflower here? You cannot have been!'

Lady Devereux raised an eyebrow. 'Why? Do you think

you are the only woman placed here because she is far more trouble than she's worth?'

Gwen laughed, hardly able to believe what she was hearing. It was wild…it was nonsensical…it was…

Believable.

What was it Sylvia had said? Those words she herself had thought numerous times after coming to the Wallflower Academy?

'You know, sometimes I think this place is packed to the rafters with rebels, not wallflowers.'

Gwen swallowed. 'I… I do not know what to say.'

Lady Devereux took a deep breath. 'Quite right too. You'll have plenty of time to think about it later—and then, Your Grace, I hope we will get to know each other better.'

It took a moment for Gwen to realise what Lady Devereux meant, and this time she really did reach out for the side of her bed to sit down upon.

'Your Grace…' she whispered.

Her future mother-in-law chuckled. 'You'll be the Duchess of Knaresby in just under an hour, so you had better get accustomed to it. Here.'

Lady Devereux stepped across the room and pulled from her reticule a box covered in blue velvet. She placed it in Gwen's hands.

'Open it,' she whispered.

Gwen did as she was bade, her head spinning.

Inside the jewellery box was a sapphire tiara.

'You already have your something new and blue,' said Lady Devereux softly. 'I thought you would appreciate something old and borrowed. Blue as well, I suppose. The Devereux sapphires.'

Gwen stared in wonder at the beautiful tiara. It was more fabulous than anything she had ever seen—and only now did her stomach squirm as she wondered, with a jolt, just how many other jewels might be waiting for her in her new life.

Her new married life…as a Devereux.

'Th-Thank you.'

'Oh, you don't need to thank me,' said Lady Devereux with a crisp smile. 'I never had a daughter, and it's high time I spoiled someone. Now… Haven't we got a wedding to go to?'

The day sped by so quickly Gwen could hardly remember it.

A rush of colour, of laughter, of joy. Solemn music and solemn vows, and then smiles all around her.

She saw Miss Pike seated in the front row on her side of the aisle, with a rapturous look at having married off one of her wallflowers so well.

There was a squeeze of her hand. Gwen looked down to see Percy's hand had taken hers, and he smiled as he squeezed it again.

'Ready?' he whispered.

Gwen took a deep breath and nodded. And as they swept down the aisle hand in hand, husband and wife, she could not understand how her heart could withstand such joy, such eager happiness.

She had everything she wanted.

Almost.

'Percy,' Gwen said suddenly, halting in her steps as soon as they'd stepped outside the church. 'We have forgotten something.'

Percy's beaming face was transformed into one full of panic. 'We have?'

Gwen leaned forward and kissed him delicately on the side of the mouth. 'We have forgotten to make any plans for our honeymoon!'

'Oh, you can leave that to me,' he said with a laugh. 'I have some ideas...'

Gwen was not given a chance to ask what they were—his lips had already captured hers, his hands were tight on her waist, and Gwen lost herself to his kiss, to the tantalising, tingling sensation Percy always sparked in her.

'Well, really!'

Gwen and Percy broke apart with wry smiles as Miss Pike's words reached them.

'You have done that before,' Gwen said in a smiling whisper.

Percy grinned as their wedding guests poured out of the church. 'Yes, and I intend to do it again—and again—with increasing frequency.'

'Your Ladyship!' Miss Pike was bustling past them straight to Lady Devereux, with a respectful yet eager look on her face. 'Now you are in a way indebted to the Wallflower Academy. You have your daughter-in-law, and what a fine woman she is. I wonder whether you could see yourself...?'

Percy groaned, and Gwen could not help but laugh. 'It appears your mother is about to be roped into improving the Wallflower Academy! Or at the very least, heaven help us, hosting more afternoon teas...'

Percy sighed and pulled her closer. Gwen's heart was beating so quickly she was certain the whole congregation could hear it. 'Well, perhaps you and she can do an exchange. You can come and live with me, and we can send Mother to the Wallflower Academy.'

He laughed at his jest, but Gwen merely smiled. It was clear Lady Devereux's son had no idea that she herself had once been a wallflower. Fascinating...the secrets one kept from one's family.

'And now, my Duchess?' said Percy with a grin. 'What shall we do now?'

Gwen took a deep breath and felt all the tension and stress and worry—all the things she had believed would hold her back from happiness—fall away.

'Be happy,' she said simply. 'For the rest of our lives.'

'Miss Pike, what an outrage!'

'And try to keep your mother happy,' said Gwen hastily, with a laugh as Percy groaned.

Lady Devereux was staring at Miss Pike in horror.

'Come on. We had better go back to the Academy. The wedding reception will begin soon, and I do not believe it safe to leave Miss Pike and your mother together.'

Percy shook his head with a smile. 'I love you, Gwen—and you have won my affections so utterly I am afraid I am quite in your power.'

Gwen's heart almost burst with joy.

'Good. Just as you should be.'

* * * * *

MORE THAN A
MATCH FOR
THE EARL

For my bridesmaids. GB, SB, BC and SP.

And to PB, PB, BB and BB.

Chapter One

The room was busy, far busier than Marilla Newell could ever remember in all the three years she had lived at the Wallflower Academy. The heady noises were bouncing off the walls, mingling with each other, worsening the weary headache after such a long day, making it difficult for her to pick out individual voices as she sat quietly in an armchair by the fire.

'Wonderful wedding, charming girl...'

'And who is her family, precisely? I have met neither mother nor father, yet Lady Devereux was telling me...'

'Never been inside the Wallflower Academy, though I have heard plenty about it! I once heard there was a blind woman here...'

The soft satin of the gown Lady Devereux had been so kind to gift her, and Sylvia, too, had small embroidered flowers upon it. They were a different style and shape to those on the bride's dress: Gwen's were forget-me-nots, Sylvia had told her, and these were daisies.

There were differences. Longer petals, a different kind of stitch. As Rilla sat silently in the melee of noise, she allowed her fingers to gently move across them. Daisies. One here... and here. A space of around two inches between them. Very delicate work.

'Is *that* her?'

'No, that's Miss Daphne Smith, nice girl, too quiet for my taste…'

Rilla sighed when the words became clearer as the speakers grew closer, then farther away, hoping that the ache in her feet would soon settle.

It would have been too much to hope that they intended to approach her. She was not the sort of woman, she knew, that any gentlemen bothered to speak to. It had not taken her the full three years at the Wallflower Academy to know that.

Why, Rilla could not recall a single gentleman actually speaking just to her since she had arrived here, which was a great disappointment to her father. What was the point in learning how to attract a gentleman, he mentioned in his latest letter, if she never put her learnings into practice?

Well, the service was over. Gwendoline Knox, newest wallflower to enter the Academy, was married—and to a duke.

Rilla permitted herself a small smile. No one would have predicted that the most recent wallflower to join the Academy would be the next to wed. But then, just because Gwen had been least likely to win a duke, that did not mean that it was impossible.

And she had.

With no father to host the wedding reception, Gwen had graciously accepted the offer to hold it at the Wallflower Academy. Which had its advantages, Rilla thought dispassionately as she sat quietly in her chair, out of the way. And its disadvantages.

Someone approached her, someone who spent far too much time with the carbolic soap and not enough time considering her words.

The smile became wry on Rilla's lips before Miss Pike spoke. It would be the same old topic, of course. The owner of the Wallflower Academy did not appear to have any other.

'Miss Newell,' said Miss Pike sharply. 'It is I.'

Rilla nodded. 'I know, Miss Pike. Please, sit down.'

She was accustomed to uttering the phrase, even though she had no idea whether there was another seat close by that would be convenient. In the murky, shadowy vision she had, it was impossible to tell.

In Rilla's experience, it did not really matter. Either her conversational partner would sit, or they would not. The only difference was the height from which the next words came.

'Miss Newell, I have something of great import to discuss with you.'

Rilla nodded but said nothing. What was there to say? Miss Pike had evidently found a chair, for her voice came from lower and to her left, but nothing Rilla could advance would prevent Miss Pike from her conversation.

It would be the same tired old conversation they had been having for above a year now. It was too much to hope, Rilla thought with a sinking feeling nestling in her stomach, that the woman would actually say something original.

And after such a day, too. Whispers in the church, the half-heard mutters wondering why on earth she was still unmarried, the desperate attempts to continuously plaster a smile on her face…

'I have spoken with your family once more, and they quite agree with me,' came the terse tone of Miss Pike above the hubbub of the wedding reception. 'You would be a marvellous tutor here at the Wallflower Academy. And with the additional help, I could open up the west corridor, welcome even more wallflowers here!'

Rilla nodded, boredom slipping into her soul as she forced herself to remain silent. An ever more frequent habit, now she came to think about it.

It was the same argument over and over, and though the Pike was not rude enough to say it aloud, her meaning was clear.

No one would marry Rilla. No one would offer for her hand. No one wanted a blind wife.

It rankled deep in Rilla's soul that Miss Pike could even think such a thing, but it was so obvious. Why else would she continuously attempt to persuade her to give up her position as a wallflower, and instead become a tutor to others?

'I think that would be a little premature, do not you?' said Rilla quietly. 'I mean, I am still young, not yet thirty. There is still a chance that I could become a wife. Have…have a child.'

She did not need to be able to see to know Miss Pike was scoffing. Rilla could hear it in her shifting movement on the chair, the way she clicked her tongue most offensively.

'Really, Rilla,' said Miss Pike dismissively. 'I am not so sure.'

'But if you were actually attempting to help me wed, to find someone to marry,' said Rilla hotly, trying to keep her voice down as she was unsure who else was around her but was unable to prevent ire from slipping onto her tongue, 'then you would know!'

There was a moment of silence. Rilla tried to hold her tongue.

'You are—'

Someone shouted across the room, blotting out Miss Pike's word. 'I beg your pardon?'

'You are ungrateful, Miss Newell.'

Perhaps she should not have asked. 'I do not ask for special treatment,' said Rilla, trying to keep her voice level. 'Just the same opportunities as the others. You see what Gwen could do, if merely left to her own devices and not prevented from success?'

Well. Gwen had perhaps not entirely been perfect in the odd courtship she and the Duke of Knaresby had entertained.

Not that Rilla was about to reveal that to the Pike.

'Here I am, running the Wallflower Academy, which is solely designed to help ladies such as yourself find husbands,' Miss Pike almost shouted over the hubbub. 'And prices go up every month, and do I ask for more funds from your family?'

A prickle of pain. 'No, Miss—'

'Five miles from London,' the proprietress was saying, though Rilla could barely hear her now. 'And close to Brighton, and as you can imagine it costs a pretty penny to…more than half…a chicken!'

Rilla frowned. A chicken? What on earth was she talking about?

'And another thing—'

The room was becoming rowdier, the noise almost deafening, Miss Pike's words were getting lost in the kerfuffle. A card table had been set up in the Orangery, Sylvia Bryant had told her earlier, and there were real fears from the servants that blows would be had over some of the hands being dealt.

'Have to sort out—'

'Miss Pike?'

Rilla received no reply. It was infuriating, not knowing whether one's conversational partner was merely thinking, hesitating, or had wished her well under the cacophony and departed, thinking that Rilla had heard her goodbye.

Though she had lived her life without sight, Rilla had a vague view of light and dark. It was not enough, however, in the chaos of this room to see whether Miss Pike had walked away.

A hand rested on her shoulder. Rilla did not jump; she was too accustomed to it. It was one of the ways the wallflowers announced their presence.

'It is me. Gwen,' said the bride. Her hand was soft on Rilla's shoulder, and disappeared though the voice continued. 'What were you talking about with Miss Pike?'

Rilla's shoulders sagged. 'She is gone, then? 'tis so noisy in here, I could not hear.'

'I believe she was distracted by Sylvia attempting to run away again.' There was just a hint of mirth in Gwen's words, enough to make Rilla believe Miss Pike had no choice but to dash after the miscreant. Typical Sylvia.

'No.'

'It…it did not appear to be a pleasant conversation between the two of you,' came Gwen's soft voice.

Rilla almost laughed. The woman married a duke not two hours ago, yet was still hesitant to speak her mind. Gwen was part empress, part wallflower. A very strange mix.

'It was not,' she said aloud. 'You may as well know—all the other wallflowers do—though I suppose you are not a wallflower now.'

Rilla heard Gwen laugh.

'Once a wallflower, always a wallflower, I think,' Gwen's voice said, merriment in her tones. 'But you were going to tell me what you and Miss Pike were speaking of. I am sorry it was not pleasant.'

It was not, and it was surprisingly painful for Rilla to admit, but there should be no shame in it. It was not her decision, after all.

'My family and Miss Pike wish for me to give up any idea of marriage,' Rilla said quietly. A hand touched hers—Gwen's, she had to assume. It clasped hers. Somehow, it made it easier to speak. 'They wish for me to settle instead as a tutor here, at the Academy.'

Why did it pain her so much? Not only to say it aloud, but to say it to such a person: a woman she had only met a few months ago, who had already managed to find a match within that time.

And to a duke, too. No wonder Miss Pike was delighted.

'I am sorry,' said Rilla hastily. 'I should not speak of such things on such a wonderful day for you. This wedding reception, it is marvellous.'

'It is altogether too noisy, and has too many people,' Gwen said dryly. 'Over one hundred people, I don't know what Percy— Miss Pike was forced to hire two men to act as additional footmen, you know.'

Well, that explained the noise pounding on Rilla's eardrums, taking away another one of her senses, making it a challenge to navigate the rooms she knew so well.

'Still. You are married now. I hope— I am sure you will be very happy.'

Gwen's hands squeezed hers. 'Thank you, but you do not need to apologize. And I certainly do not agree with Miss Pike.'

'I do not want to be a tutor at the Wallflower Academy,' Rilla said slowly, greater strength entering her voice with every word. 'I have no wish for this to be my life forever.'

The Wallflower Academy was not the worst place to live, to be sure, but to dwell in the monotony of the place for the rest of her life? To be entrapped here through a tutor position?

No. No, Rilla would not permit it.

A gentle squeeze again from Gwen, then she released Rilla's hand. 'You can do whatever you put your mind to, if you ask me. Why, you are the cleverest among us wallflowers, and without your advice and rather sarcastic comments—'

'I did not always intend sarcasm!' protested Rilla.

Gwen laughed. 'I know. And I do wonder sometimes whether...well. Not everyone understands your sense of humour.'

Rilla's stomach churned. Yes, she knew that. Had known it the moment the Earl—

'But I stand by my comment,' continued Gwen happily. 'You can do whatever you put your mind to, Rilla.'

A slow and determined sigh rushed through her lungs as she took a deep breath. 'I know. And I will.'

'Gwen? Gwen, come over here and meet—'

'I'm talking with—'

'—the Marquess of—'

'Oh. Oh, Rilla,' came Gwen's nervous voice with a touch of tension which had not been there before. 'I know you do not like being left alone, but you do not mind if I...'

'Go—meet a marquess,' said Rilla, not unkindly, as her heart sank.

'I'll come straight back,' promised her newly wedded friend. 'It's just, Percy wants to introduce me, and I…well, I'll be back.'

A quick squeeze of the hand, a rush of skirts, and Rilla was almost certain she was alone.

Alone. The word sank into her stomach like a stone. Alone, as she had ever been.

Not that she wished to be introduced in turn to the marquess, whoever he was. No, there was a special sort of awkwardness in standing before a gentleman, knowing that you were being judged, unable to see whether he approved or disapproved of what he saw.

It was intolerable.

Unless he fell head over heels in love with you, a small part of her whispered—the part of her she had tried to ignore for the last three years. And then he would marry you, and—

And then what? Rilla forced aside the thought, even as the longing for love and marriage and companionship and adventure rose in her heart.

That was not her lot in life. Though admittedly, perhaps if she took a leaf out of Sylvia's book and flirted a little…

Fear gripped her at the very thought.

Flirt? Her? She barely knew how. Just being surrounded by all these people that she couldn't see struck discomfort down her spine.

Well, she'd remained downstairs in the drawing room for long enough. Her dues had been paid, she had been perfectly polite, and now Rilla could do what she had wished to do almost the minute she had entered the church.

Retreat to her bedchamber and concoct her next defence against Miss Pike's constant demands that she become a tutor.

Rilla felt the soft heaviness of her skirts shift as she rose and grasped her cane, the reassuring warmth of the wood under her fingers. She had been placed, thanks to some manoeuvring from Sylvia, in the armchair closest to the door to the hall. Six steps—eight, in these formal shoes.

She reached out for the door as she approached it, felt the roughness of the wallpaper, the cooler wood of the door frame. It was open.

Of course it was, Rilla told herself as she carefully stepped through, listening intently for anyone stepping across the marble-floored hall, her cane making a different noise on the different floor. She had not heard the subtle click of the door, had she?

Four steps, and she would need to lean slightly to the right to avoid the plinth upon which, she had been told, sat a planter with a large overgrown something within. Rilla had felt the luscious leaves once, when she had been left alone in the hall waiting for Gwen. Springy, and warm to the touch, like the leaves of the plants in the Orangery.

Another six steps, and she would reach the bottom of the staircase. Almost free. Almost—

'Goodness gracious,' came a male voice as Rilla's cane tapped into something solid, her free hand wandering ahead of her and finding something warm.

She recoiled, drawing her hand back towards her after the sudden contact.

The memory of the touch remained. A strength, a broad-ness, muscles defined even through a linen shirt and soft wool jacket. A warmth, a presence, something that heated her fingers even through the gloves.

Rilla rocked for a moment on her heels. This was a contact she would not swiftly forget.

'I do beg your pardon,' she said stiffly.

Mortification poured through her chest. Dear God, she would be grateful when the pack of them left and gave her back her Academy.

'I apologize myself. I have never been here before, and I was taking some drinks over to—'

'Ah, one of the footmen the Pike hired,' Rilla said with a nod. 'It is of no matter.'

'One of the—'

'Yes, Gwen mentioned there were a couple of you,' she said, steadying herself now even as her mind whirled with the scent of the man.

Sandalwood, and salt, and lemon. A freshness and a newness that made Rilla tilt forward, just for a moment, to take another breath.

Oh, he smelt delicious.

Heat flushed Rilla's cheeks. She couldn't go around sniffing footmen!

Flirting. Well, it wouldn't hurt, would it, to flirt a little with a footman? He was only at the Wallflower Academy temporarily, after all. And no one would know.

Her whole body was reacting to the man in a way it had never done before. Heat was rising, tendrils of desire curling around her heart, warmth in her chest, an aching need to lean toward him—

Rilla caught herself from falling into his presumably outstretched arms just in time.

Get hold of yourself, woman!

'I suppose you've been traipsing about after these idiots all afternoon,' Rilla said in a low voice.

It was most indecorous to speak so, but then, he was a footman, and a temporary one at that. He'd be gone by the morning, taking his delicious scent with him, more's the pity.

There would be no consequences to this conversation.

'Idiots?' said the man lightly.

Even his voice was delectable. Rilla had never heard anything like it—like honey trickled over a spoon that coated one's lips.

She forced down the thought, and the accompanying warmth that fluttered in her chest.

'The nobility, the guests,' Rilla said softly so that only he could hear her. 'I imagine they've been ordering you about like no one's business.'

Perhaps she ought not to speak in such a manner. Perhaps the footman would be offended. She had no idea.

The noise of the drawing room was echoing around the hall, making it a challenge to concentrate on the hurried and awkward voices before her.

Half of conversation, Daphne had once read in a book and announced in hushed horror to the other wallflowers, was silent. In other words, half was not actually the conversation at all: how people looked, the sparkle in their eyes, the tilt of a head, the warmth in an expression.

All elements Rilla could not see.

She had other senses. The man standing before her had a presence that she could sense despite her lack of sight. He was mere inches from her, and though Rilla wrestled against it, she could not help but lean closer. The man was…attractive. There was no other word for it.

Yet it told her nothing about the man himself.

She was typically so wary of meeting new people. So much of who they were was invisible to her. Their opinion of her, assumed rather than known. The unspoken part of the conversation lost to her.

'You are right, these people have been absolutely outrageous,' said the man in a conspiratorial whisper. 'But don't tell anyone I said that.'

A curl of a smile tilted her lips. It was almost a flirtation! And with a servant!

It should have felt wrong, utterly unconscionable. Somehow the spark of attraction between them overrode any sense of decorum, any typical reticence with the opposite sex.

The last time she had enjoyed such a thing… Well, she could hardly recall.

Miss Pike would be horrified—a flirtation, with a servant?

But this did not matter. He would not matter in a few hours. And so she didn't even introduce herself with her proper title.

'Miss Marilla Newell,' she said lightly.

'Finlay Jellicoe,' the man said beside her in a low, sultry voice. 'And I must say, you are beautiful, Miss Newell.'

A voice, now she came to think about it, that was…warm. Amused, perhaps. A low voice, but coming from a few inches higher than her head. He was tall, then. Whoever he was.

'You flatter me, sir,' Rilla countered, her heart skipping a beat.

'Hard not to flatter a woman so elegant and so refined,' said Mr Jellicoe, his voice quiet, private, as though they were the only two in the world and were not surrounded by a cacophony of unknown voices. 'Beauty will always reveal itself, and I have to say, I am delighted it has revealed itself to me.'

And she giggled.

Giggled! What on earth?

But Rilla felt surprisingly comfortable with Mr Jellicoe; there was no other word for it. There was no tension in her shoulders, and her laugh was natural and light.

Perhaps it was because he was a servant, perhaps because he would be gone. Rilla could not explain it—but he drew something from her that no man ever had.

A longing…to know him better.

The odd thing was, she felt an overwhelming sense that he knew her already. As though this meeting was…fated. Designed.

As though she could be herself with him, as with no other.

The attraction did not hurt, of course, but it was more than that. More than anything she had ever known.

'Is there any chance that you will be retained by Miss Pike? As a footman, I mean,' she heard herself saying.

Which was a ridiculous question to ask. Her, wed a footman? The very idea!

Though a footman that spoke like this and smelt like this and who had a chest that felt like that...

Mr Jellicoe was chuckling gently, and Rilla longed to reach out and feel the movement of his joy. 'I very much doubt it. I, ah, I am not a footman, Miss Newell.'

Rilla stiffened. A half step back was easily taken as a cold chill fluttered through her lungs. 'Not...not a footman?'

'In fact, I am afraid I am one of those idiots being served,' admitted the man. He was still laughing. 'I was actually taking glasses over to my friend, Lord—'

'You rogue,' said Rilla darkly.

'You— I beg your pardon?'

A year ago—perhaps even less—Rilla would have stopped there. She would have demurred, attempted to pass off her rudeness as a jest, and hoped that the conversation would move on.

But she was tired. Tired of always being left out, tired of the Pike's assumptions about her, tired of listening to the wedding vows of other wallflowers as they stepped—or stumbled—up the aisle.

No. No longer.

Rilla was not going to put up with it any longer.

The heat of embarrassment that Rilla always attempted to avoid, and never managed to, seeped into her cheeks.

'I must say, you make a pretty poor wallflower,' said Mr Jellicoe conversationally, as though the whole thing was entertainment for his own amusement. 'Your conversation is magnificent—I'm rather disappointed.'

Rilla's mouth opened, but she was so stunned by the man's ease, she could think of nothing to say.

How dare he just come here and...and speak to her thus!

'Miss Pike tells me you'll be a tutor here before long,' Mr Jellicoe said, utterly oblivious apparently to the fact that she had ceased contributing to the conversation. 'Good for you. I suppose.'

And his nonchalance, his complete inability to understand her obvious chagrin, poured through Rilla's body like the fine brandy the wallflowers had been permitted upon the announcement of Gwen's engagement.

In the mere moments they had spent together, Rilla had felt...well, a kinship, of a sort.

Which was ridiculous, she told herself. How she could have got such an idea she did not know. It was ridiculous, foolish to the extreme.

She was feeling betrayed by a man she hardly knew...but that was rather the point, wasn't it? So swiftly into their encounter, he had presumed to know her, to speak so blandly of her future as though it did not matter...

And she had liked him. Been attracted to him.

It had been a trying day. That was what Rilla told herself later, when she looked back on what she did next.

A long day, and a trying one. She had been pushed beyond all endurance by the whispers in the church, the hushed pity of everyone she passed, the Pike's insistence she would never marry, Gwen's well-meaning but misplaced compassion...

And that was why she finally gave up all attempt at civility.

'You, sir, are a man of the lowest order and I have no wish to speak to you,' Rilla said, glaring in the direction of where the man's voice had last come from, and desperately hoping he had not stepped to the side—or worse, gone entirely. 'I am sick and tired of the boorish behaviour of men like you, and I don't care if you know it!'

And there was no response.

No spluttering. No outraged gasp. No retort that she was wrong, or rude, or disrespectful.

Instead, his voice came low, and soft, and quiet. 'Lowest order? I'll have you know I'm an earl. The Earl of—'

Rilla snorted, relishing the freedom of saying precisely what she wanted. Well, it wasn't as though she would ever encounter this earl again, would she?

'An earl? Of course. I should have guessed by your rudeness,' she said, speaking over the man. 'No manners to even introduce yourself properly. Why am I not surprised!'

'I am surprised,' said the Earl of… Rilla couldn't recall. 'As an earl—'

'I have no wish to hear it,' Rilla said curtly, fire blossoming through her lungs.

She would regret this. She knew she would; she always did when she allowed her frustrations to overcome her tongue. It was a rare occurrence, but when her temper burned, it burned bright.

To think she had believed him a footman! Had allowed herself to relax, to accept his pretty compliments!

An earl! After all she had suffered at the hands of an earl… but Miss Pike did not know that, did she? No, her father had gone to great pains to keep that within the family…

'No wish to hear it?' The earl sounded…not amused, but something else. Intrigued? 'Miss Newell, I admit I am captivated. Tell me…'

'I have no wish to tell you anything,' Rilla said, exhaustion starting to creep into her mind, demanding payment for the debts made earlier that day. 'I wish to go upstairs—alone, sir!'

The last words were spoken as a hand touched hers—a hand that was unexpected, sudden, and unwelcome.

Rilla wrenched her hand away. There was nothing more disorientating, more alarming, than being touched by a stranger when one was not expecting it.

He had probably attempted to help her, Rilla thought darkly, but naturally he didn't know. She'd lived in the Tudor manor that was the Wallflower Academy for over three years. She knew every inch: the wide hallway, the corridors, the drawing room with its sofas and armchairs that the servants and wallflowers knew better than to move, the dining room with Rilla's chair always near one end, two in from the left.

This was her world—her domain. She could, she thought with a wry smile, navigate around it with her eyes shut.

Not that it would make much difference.

'Go away, Earl of wherever you are,' Rilla said dismissively, stepping forward and reaching out for what she knew she would find.

The cool wood of the banister was a relief to her fingertips.

'But—'

'I don't want to hear it,' she said quietly. 'Tell Miss Pike I've retired upstairs. I'm not some entertainment for you, whoever you are. I'm just Rilla.'

Chapter Two

It had been, all things considered, a very long day. And now a woman was shouting at him.

Finlay stood still, as though a strong wind had just passed him and he'd had to lean into it to prevent himself from falling.

Well. That was…different.

Certainly different from Miss Isabelle Carr.

'My lord, I must apologize,' came a voice behind him. 'I had no idea you were speaking with Miss Newell!'

Finlay turned and shrugged languidly, seeing with some relief that he still appeared to have an effect on the ladies.

Miss Pike giggled. 'She is an incorrigible bluestocking that woman, my lord. You must not pay attention to a single word she says.'

Almost against his will, Finlay found his attention drifting to the stairs which Miss Newell had so recently ascended.

Not pay attention to a single word she says?

'Yes, not a single word,' he said softly.

I have no wish to tell you anything. I wish to go upstairs— alone, sir!

A bluestocking. Well, that certainly did not explain why Miss Newell had been so obviously disgruntled to discover that he was an earl. Strange. Finlay had always discovered that it aided people's opinion of him, rather than diminished it.

Most strange.

Finlay blinked. Only then did he realize that the proprietress of the Wallflower Academy was still watching him closely, evidently curious to know what he was thinking.

Not that he was thinking about much. Definitely not.

'Fear not, Miss Pike,' Finlay said, giving a broad smile which made Miss Pike flush. 'I shall not give her a second thought.'

And he truly did not. Well, he did, but it was swiftly followed by a third thought, a fourth thought and a fifth. By the time the following day had dawned and Finlay had suffered through an awkward ride with his betrothed, Miss Isabelle Carr, a monotonous conversation with his mother about the guest list for the wedding, and a dinner which he had agreed to host as a favour to his mother, he had thought about Miss Marilla Newell at least four hundred and thirty-two times.

Which was not, Finlay told himself silently as he nodded along to his friend's words as they entered his own home, technically a second thought.

'That ball was absolute rot,' Lord George Bartlett was saying with a laugh as they entered Staromchor House.

Finlay snorted. 'You always think that when they hand out subpar cigars.'

'And so I should! Outrageous behaviour,' said his friend with another snort as he strode, without invitation, into the drawing room. 'I suppose you have better here?'

It had always been their habit to finish up an evening's entertainment at Staromchor House. Finlay moved almost without thinking to the drinks cabinet, pulling out three cigars and picking up a bottle of brandy.

'A nightcap?'

'Please,' said Bartlett, throwing himself bodily onto a sofa with a groan. 'And a large one. I still have Lady Lindham's conversation ringing in my ears.'

Finlay grinned as he poured a hearty measure into three glasses and then...

'What's wrong, Fin?' came his friend's voice from behind him.

Jaw tight, stomach twisted into a knot of pain, the childhood nickname helped Finlay to speak calmly. 'Damn. I poured three glasses.'

When he turned around, there was a glittering in Bartlett's eyes that Finlay recognized. 'Damn. I thought of him again tonight, you know.'

'It's hard to go a day without thinking of him,' said Finlay heavily, picking up two of the cigars and popping them in his waistcoat pocket before lifting up two of the three glasses. 'Cecil would have hated that ball.'

'He would have loved hating it,' Bartlett countered with a wry smile, accepting the glass offered to him with a nod of thanks. 'The blackguard.'

The two men fell into silence for a moment, then wordlessly toasted their absent friend before taking a sip of the burning liquid.

'Sit, man,' Bartlett said eventually. 'And tell me how these wedding plans are going.'

Finlay groaned as he dropped into an armchair opposite the sofa, hoping the heavy movement could disguise his disinterest with said wedding plans.

Wedding plans.

It had always been this way. With his father gone for so many years, it had been Finlay's responsibility to uphold the Staromchor title in Society's eyes. That meant dinners, card parties, attending the right balls.

And now it meant ensuring that his wedding would be suitable for the Jellicoe name.

'The plans are going,' Finlay said, waving a hand. 'My mother and Isabelle are doing most of it.'

'Isabelle,' mused Bartlett. 'It's been weeks since I've seen her.'

Isabelle Carr. Finlay forced a smile back on his face. Since their engagement had been announced, he could not avoid her.

Not that he had wanted to—at least, not at first.

'How did she seem to you?' he asked quietly. 'The last time you saw her, I mean.'

'She…she looked fine.' Bartlett's voice was low, but his eyes did not waver as he spoke. 'It's strange, isn't it? She and him were so similar. When we were young, that time Isabelle cut off her hair, do you remember?'

'I remember I was blamed for it,' Finlay said dryly.

'You couldn't tell them apart from a distance,' his friend continued, a faraway look in his eyes. 'And she's grown, obviously, a woman now. And yet sometimes, in some lights, I can see Cecil in her. It's like…like a part of him is still here.'

Finlay swallowed, hard.

Bravado—that was what Cecil had always called it. Finlay's ability to move through the world with a smile and seemingly no care in the world.

Cecil had always seen right through it.

Pain.

Finlay blinked. There was pain, inexplicable pain, in his hand. He looked down.

His hands were clenched, both of them. One of them appeared to be— Dear God, he wasn't bleeding?

But he was. The pressure of his forefinger pressing deep into his palm had been far fiercer than he had expected, and a small cut, almost like a papercut, was beading blood.

Without altering his expression, Finlay casually wiped his hand on his breeches, thanking fate that his valet had chosen a dark pair for that evening.

He was not going to think of Cecil Carr again. Not tonight.

It had been his own fault for relaxing, Finlay knew. No, the illusion of laughing bravado always had to remain on his face. To admit that he felt any different, to allow himself to feel for a single second the overwhelming pain of—

'And when I last saw her, she looked…different,' said a voice.

Finlay blinked. Bartlett, one of his oldest friends in the world, appeared again before him. 'Different?'

Bartlett nodded. 'Different. I mean, I knew she wouldn't be exactly the same. I hadn't seen her for three years, not since she'd gone to Switzerland.'

'The Trinderhaus Menagerie for Young Ladies,' said Finlay with a grin.

'The Trinderhaus *School* for Young Ladies,' corrected Bartlett with a corresponding grin. 'You teased her something terrible when the Carrs told her she'd be going.'

'She didn't mind overly much,' he said defensively, pulling out the two cigars he had deposited in his pocket. 'Want one?'

His friend nodded, and it took a few minutes to cut and light them. And his mind meandered not to the Trinderhaus School, but to another place where young ladies gathered. To one young lady in particular. One with a sharp tongue and a wit that had intrigued…

When they were both blowing smoke into the room, Bartlett continued as though there had been no interruption.

'I hadn't supposed that finishing school would alter her overly. I mean, it was Isabelle. Spirited, loud, nonsensical…'

'She's changed,' said Finlay quietly.

He had not intended his words to be so harsh. But it was true. The woman who returned had not been the fourth musketeer to their little group. No longer was she the sister who had hung around the three boys something dreadful, the person who had been pretty as a child but nothing to spark desire in a man's chest.

And now…

'She has taken the death of her brother hard, Fin,' said Bartlett softly.

Finlay's stomach lurched. 'We all have.'

And somehow the tether that had kept them all together had been cut. He hadn't realized, not until Cecil's death, just how much they had all relied on him.

'She looks like her,' he found himself saying. 'She looks like Isabelle but all the warmth has gone, the joy. The mischief. She just…sits there, and lets my mother talk.'

'In fairness, no one can stop your mother talking.'

'And this whole arranged marriage…' Finlay's voice trailed away.

He was not going to think about her. Miss Newell. Most definitely not.

When he glanced up at his friend, there was a knowing look in those eyes that told him Bartlett was holding back. Which wasn't like him.

'Come on, out with it, man,' Finlay said easily, or at least as easily as he could manage while his hand stung. 'I won't be offended.'

He had meant the last few words as a quip, but he saw with a sudden dart of the man's eyes that it was apparently a real consideration.

Interesting. What was going on?

'You…you are not in love with Isabelle, are you.'

It was not a question. Bartlett spoke conversationally, as though they discussed whether or not they had fallen in love with their friend's sister all the time.

Finlay's smile held as he said, 'In love? With Isabelle Carr? Of course not.'

It was an admissionn freely made. No shame rushed through Finlay's chest as he made it, though there was a slight tension in his shoulders.

Bartlett was frowning.

'Well, I am happy to say such a thing,' Finlay said, ensuring no trace of defensiveness could be heard in his voice. 'Men of our status are not expected to fall in love, are they? And it's Isabelle, for goodness' sake. We've known her for…forever!'

He and Isabelle had been perfectly clear in their negotiation. A marriage of convenience—that was all this was. Cecil would have…well, maybe not approved. Finlay had nightmares sometimes, that Cecil would not have approved.

But Cecil was not here. Not here to go riding in Hyde Park, or play cards at White's, or—Finlay's stomach lurched—pay off his family's debts. Substantial debts.

The agreement had been made two months ago, and everything was going to plan. Someone needed to marry Isabelle, provide her with a home, protection. Pay off her family's debts—and with no dowry…

He wasn't about to reveal to Bartlett that despite his best efforts, no feelings of warmth had surfaced. None at all.

'Marriage,' Finlay said aloud into the silence, 'for people of our station, it is rarely for love. If love comes at all, that is unusual.'

'You didn't have to offer for her.'

'What, and you were about to?' he scoffed with a grin. 'Come on now—I'm the earl. I've got the income. It made sense for me to offer her my hand.'

'Out of the blue,' his friend pointed out. 'Carr…he died, and then you were gone. I didn't know where you were, couldn't find you…'

Bartlett continued as Finlay took a puff of his cigar and tried not to think about it. That time when he had desperately tried to lose himself in sorrow, certain that he could get out all the emotions and then would feel better.

As he was before. As though nothing had happened.

'And here you are, engaged to her,' said Bartlett with a snort. 'Though I noticed that Knaresby's experience of matrimony has been quite different. You must think him strange.'

Finlay leaned forward. 'No, not at all! My good man, think it through. He found love, which is all to the good. But he would have married without it, would he not?'

They all did, eventually.

And of all women in Society, Isabelle was one he actually

liked. At least, he had before the engagement, but now it was all formality and rules and never being able to actually speak to each other. And the Isabelle Carr he had known, the joyful, smiling sister of his best friend, had disappeared.

A crackle of pain shot up his side. Though he was hardly the same. Not after they had all lost Cecil.

'Before this, I would have ventured to say that Isabelle was one of the most charming women of my acquaintance.'

Finlay shrugged, placing his cigar on an ashtray. He'd lost the taste of it. 'To be sure.'

Most charming. And most changed. And nothing in comparison to—

Don't think about her, he told himself firmly. Miss Newell should not be clouding his thoughts. Should not be distracting him. Should not be tempting him to return to the Wallflower Academy and—

'I worry about you,' Bartlett said, sitting up now and leaning towards him with a serious expression. 'You... We've both lost a dear friend. The three of us, I always thought... I thought we'd grow old together. Be wittering on at White's in fifty years about the youth of today.'

Finlay snorted, mostly to cover up the stinging in his eyes.

'And I don't think you're happy offering matrimony to Isabelle,' continued Bartlett seriously. 'You...dammit Fin, you don't smile anymore.'

He was doing the right thing, wasn't he? Doing what Cecil would have asked him.

There was no way of knowing, but that certainty, though it wavered at times, was the only thing which had kept Finlay together when...when it had first happened.

His jaw tightened. His heart may be unaffected by Isabelle, but he was doing the right thing.

'And she deserves—'

'I know what she deserves, and I know what I'm doing,' said Finlay shortly. 'You don't have to mother us, Bartlett.'

His friend sighed. 'I suppose not.'

Finlay did not reply. He intended to, but at that precise moment, his mind was overcome with the memory— No, the sharp words of a woman worlds apart from Miss Carr.

I'm not some entertainment for you, whoever you are. I'm just Rilla.

His lips lifted in a rueful smile. He was thinking about Miss Newell again. Most inconvenient. What did that make it, four hundred and thirty-four?

By God, he was losing count.

'Besides, what else is a man in my position to do?' Finlay said, ensuring his voice was a mite stronger now. 'I am an earl, I have responsibilities.'

'You should flirt more.'

Finlay laughed. 'With Isabelle?'

'Well, maybe not,' Bartlett said with a shrug. 'If you don't love her…'

'I have respect for her. Great respect. Just because I have not fallen in love with her yet does not mean I shall not do so. In time.'

Perhaps. It did not matter, after all. They had agreed: it was the only way.

'But a flirtation would cheer you up,' his friend said, gesturing around the room as though there were a plethora of ladies just waiting to be flirted with. 'I'm not saying have an assignation.'

'Definitely not,' Finlay said darkly.

'But a flirtation, someone to make you smile, dust off those skills.'

'You think I've forgotten how to charm a woman?'

The very idea! He was known for it, after all. Finlay Jellicoe, the Earl of Staromchor, was one of the most charming men in the *ton*. He had been careful, even in the depths of grief—especially then—to maintain such a reputation.

'I think it's more likely that you'll realize you don't care for Isabelle enough,' Bartlett responded quietly.

Finlay bristled. Not care about her enough? He was marrying her, wasn't he? He was doing his duty—far more than old Bartlett here.

'She won't make you happy.'

'Oh, stuff and nonsense,' Finlay said sharply to the calm face of his friend. 'Don't—'

'You think the marriage will make you happy? Prove it. Flirt with another, and find them dull in comparison,' Bartlett shot back, though with none of Finlay's animosity.

It was difficult not to be a little suspicious. 'You're awfully concerned that I don't marry her—and I made a promise to her. Even if I…well, even if I did meet a woman who I liked better…'

'Now that's an interesting thought,' said Bartlett with a dry laugh as he extinguished his cigar and sipped his brandy. 'I'll throw down a wager for you, Fin.'

'A wager?'

'A wager, a bet, whatever you want to call it,' Bartlett said easily, peering above his glass.

Finlay frowned. 'Look, these wagers of ours, they never end.'

'Oh, it's not going to be as dramatic as all that,' his friend said with a wave of his hand. 'It isn't going to be like last time.'

'It had better not.' Last time had involved a bag of lemons, a dark alley, and a most inconvenient conversation with a peeler. Never again.

'My point is this,' said Bartlett with a grin. 'You need to cheer yourself up, and Isabelle… Well, you have made a commitment to her, and that's admirable. But before you launch yourself into spousal servitude—'

'You really have a way with words, you know that?' Finlay interrupted conversationally.

Bartlett threw a cushion. 'Are you going to let me finish?'

Finlay had caught the cushion. 'Your aim is getting worse.'

The second cushion caught him in the face.

'You think love is inconsequential, immaterial for marriage. I think you are hiding that fact behind your pretence of—'

'The wager, sir,' Finlay teased.

'I wager you'll feel infinitely better for a flirtation,' Bartlett said, a twinkle in his eye. 'I think it'll bring you joy, and won't betray Isabelle in any way, and you'll enter the married state far happier. If I'm wrong, you can…oh, I don't know…choose your punishment.'

Perhaps if Finlay had not been attempting to ignore the throbbing ache in his hand…perhaps if the brandy had not been so potent…perhaps if he had not been looking for an excuse to return to the Wallflower Academy and converse once again with Miss Newell…

She had been so beautiful.

The thought intruded, as it had so often since meeting the wallflower. She had been beautiful. The dark black hair that shimmered almost like starlight. The way her gown had slipped past her curves, allowing one's gaze to meander leisurely. The purse of her lips, full and shell pink, when she argued with him.

Finlay swallowed.

He was being a damned fool, he knew. Tempting flirtation or not, he had made a promise to Isabelle, and regret it he may, but that did not undo it.

He needed to think rationally. Holding Bartlett's gaze, Finlay threw out his hands and shrugged with a laugh which showed the world just how little he cared.

'A wager it is, then,' he said with a laugh. 'A flirtation—what harm can it do? And what do I win, once I win it?'

'Win?' Bartlett grinned. 'You're not going to win.'

Finlay leaned forward. 'When I win?'

His friend examined him for a moment, and a strange emotion flickered over his face. If Finlay had not been concentrating at that very moment, he would have missed it.

'You… I'll buy you and Isabelle a painfully expensive wedding present,' he said quietly. 'With my best wishes.'

Finlay's heart skipped a beat. Wedding present. His wedding, to Isabelle. The woman he had considered more a sister than a woman for most of his life. But he was doing it for—

Agony, bitter agony twisted in his heart. A pressing on his chest. Lungs constricting.

Finlay forced the grief back where it belonged, deep, dark down within his chest. Where it should not be permitted to escape.

It did not matter. He was not going to lose this bet.

Finlay rose from his seat, stepped over to the sofa, took the man's hand, and shook it hard, once, twice, thrice.

'Excellent. We have a wager.'

Chapter Three

Rilla took in a deep breath. It did not help.

'Well, it's only an afternoon tea,' came the happy voice of Sylvia, just to Rilla's left. 'We're hardly being fed to the lions.'

'Speak for yourself,' said Daphne, her tone soft. 'I think I'd rather take the lions.'

Forcing down a smile that Rilla was almost sure her friends would not appreciate, she sat quietly as the two of them chattered away.

'Never heard anything so ridiculous! Go on, wear them.'

'But I can't! They're your only pretty pair of earbobs. You'll have nothing to—'

'How long has it been since he's visited? That's what I thought, you can't remember. Here you go, let me help you.'

A gentle breeze fluttered through the open window beside where Rilla sat. She'd been placed there by Sylvia's gentle hands the moment she'd entered her friend's bedchamber. Rilla did not need to be able to see to know that this kindness was twofold. Firstly, because although she could find a seat with her cane, it was more pleasant to be guided to one without effort. Secondly, because Sylvia's habit of untidiness meant it was quite likely an unknowing foot could easily stumble.

It had only happened…what, five times before?

Rilla brushed her fingertips across the skirt of her gown. It was striped. She hadn't needed Daphne's awkward praise to tell. The contrapoint weave, lines going this way and then that, was more than enough to tell.

Her thumb stroked the weave as a sudden weight beside Rilla told her that one of her friends had sat beside her.

'You know, you don't look the least excited,' Sylvia said from close to her left. 'I thought you'd be jumping at the bit for a change.'

Rilla shrugged. 'It's not so different from any other day, really.'

And any day at the Wallflower Academy was just like any other. Day after day, trickling by like a stream. Unchanging, always the same.

It might all still be new and exciting for Sylvia and Daphne. Try getting excited about an afternoon tea after three years, she wanted to say.

And didn't. What would be the point?

Rilla was perhaps the only wallflower who truly knew what it was to feel alone here.

It had taken her a little while to grow accustomed to the monotony. After all, it was against nature for nothing to change, for the seasons to pass by without much alteration. Other than temperature and a slight difference in scents in the gardens, Rilla could not have known that time was even passing.

Not like at home. The bleats of the newborn lambs, the lowing of the cows as their calves came. The sharpness of the growing barley, the delicate scent of ale as the brewing houses began their work. The rushing of the wind through the wheat, supple then brittle as the changing—

'Rilla,' came Sylvia's voice, with just a tinge of censure. 'You're being most dull, you know.'

Rilla could not help but chuckle. 'I suppose I am right where I belong, then.'

A sudden intake of breath was all the hint she was given. For a moment, just a moment, Rilla's heart skipped a beat.

It was impossible, at times, to guess at the reactions of her fellow wallflowers. Even after a year of friendship, there were nuances she was certain she missed. Oh, they said this and that, but did they truly mean it? Were the expressions on their faces matching those in their hearts?

She could never tell.

Rilla supposed that there were liars even amongst those who were able to organize their features into pleasing shapes. She could not tell from experience. It was impossible to know.

The subtle signs that were her only clues could be so disagreeably similar. A sudden intake of breath from Daphne could mean shock. Or shame. Or embarrassment. Or just her shyness, something that Rilla had discovered swiftly in the hesitations before each of her speeches.

But in Sylvia? The same action could mean something entirely different. The precursor to laughter, a mock shock that sounded precisely the same as the genuine article.

Or something else. Of all her friends, and Rilla had few, Sylvia was the most unpredictable.

'Where you belong?' Sylvia repeated, and Rilla's shoulders relaxed as she heard the teasing tone. 'By God, are you suggesting my bedchamber is the dullest place in the world?'

'Nothing should be happening here, certainly,' Rilla teased back, her heart settling into its old rhythm. 'The Pike will have your head!'

'I... I am sure Rilla did not mean—'

'Well, even if she didn't, I choose to take offence,' came Sylvia's mischievous reply to Daphne's delicate suggestion.

Rilla could not help but smile.

The Wallflower Academy existed to take ladies like Daphne, true wallflowers, ladies who found it impossible to even look at a gentleman without collapsing into fits of nerves, and make them...

Well. Rilla's stomach lurched. Acceptable.

It was an infuriating thought, but there it was.

The trouble was—for the Pike, at least—that as far as Rilla could make out, the Wallflower Academy was packed not with wallflowers, but with troublemakers. Those who did not obey Society's rules, or fit neatly into the boxes it provided.

Daughter. Wife. Mother.

With only six wallflowers currently in residence, Rilla was almost certain that Daphne was the only true wallflower here. And that meant that when the Pike organized these ridiculous events...

Something which had been spoken some minutes ago suddenly crept forward in Rilla's mind. 'Daphne?'

She felt the warmth and pressure of a hand on her shoulder. 'Yes?'

It was a relief to have her friends approach as she preferred. A sudden voice before her was always most discombobulating. 'Did I— Did you say that your father was attending?'

There it was—that hesitation. And because Daphne had left her hand on Rilla's shoulder, she could feel her friend turning slightly. Turning in the direction of Sylvia, who was still seated beside her on the window seat.

Rilla swallowed into the silence. They were doing it again. Well, she supposed they couldn't help it. She almost thought they did not even realize they were doing it.

They were...pausing.

Being born without sight meant Rilla had nothing to explain the strange pauses which littered conversations like sudden gusts of wind across a sunny afternoon. What were they doing? How could a conversation be continued without words? What if one misunderstood what the other was saying—would you ever know?

And then the moment was over.

'Yes, my father... He...he said he would attend the afternoon tea,' Daphne explained, her throat thick with repressed emotion. 'He said he had a...a lady friend.'

Precisely what the emotion was, Rilla was not sure. The youngest of the wallflowers had never spoken much about her parents, and her father had only visited the girl once in the last six months.

One of the Society afternoon teas that the Pike insisted on hosting, however, was hardly an intimate family affair. But it was something.

'Which means,' came Sylvia's triumphant voice, 'we will finally have something to talk about at one of these tedious affairs. Lord, why do these ladies of Society bother coming other than to gawp at us?'

Rilla's smile was humourless. 'I think that is precisely why they come.'

'Miss Pike hosts them to improve our social skills,' Daphne said quietly as a gong rang downstairs. They were required below.

Sylvia's snort was close to Rilla's ear as she helped her to her feet. 'Social skills, social skills... I have more social skills in my little finger than the Pike does in her entire—'

'You know full well that until we are married, the Pike considers us in desperate need of socializing,' Rilla said quietly, her equilibrium shifting as Sylvia led her around what must be the bed on her right. 'Gwen always said—'

'Gwen had the right idea,' interrupted Sylvia happily.

The air changed; their voices echoed louder, and the carpet changed to a thicker rug. They were on the landing.

'What, marry a duke?' Rilla asked sceptically, slipping her hand into her friend's arm.

She did not need to. If it were not for the afternoon tea, she could make her own way to the drawing room without a fuss, with the cane which was almost a part of her body in her hand.

But with guests milling about, and servants rushing back and forth with pelisses and coats and hats…

No. Much safer this way.

'Marry anyone,' came Sylvia's voice with a tinkling laugh.

Rilla heard the gasp on her other side.

'Sylvia! You wouldn't just marry—'

'To escape this place?'

'It's hardly a prison,' Rilla pointed out.

There was a hearty sniff from Sylvia. 'It's a prison! Don't you want to leave?'

'And do what? Go where?' It was not a pleasant line of conversation. 'I have been offered neither a home nor a husband, so what options do I have? What could be better than here?'

It was a damning thought.

'B-but Sylvia, you wouldn't—'

'Daphne, I'd marry old Matthews if I thought he'd take me away from this place,' came Sylvia's voice as they stepped down the wide, sweeping staircase. 'But don't you be getting any ideas, Matthews.'

'Wouldn't dream of it, Miss Bryant.'

Rilla chuckled. They were on the second-to-last step, and Matthews always kept his position just to the right, by the front door. He never had to announce himself to her as the other servants did. He was always there.

Besides, she could smell his dank, oily boot polish. He was the only footman not to use the same as the others. She could sense him a mile off.

'Now then, the drawing room,' said Sylvia, as though she informed footmen that she would not marry them every day of the week. Which, Rilla had to admit, may well be the case. 'Let's see who today's victims are.'

The victims, if such a term could be used, were surely the wallflowers themselves, though Rilla did not have time to point this out. By the shift in the rug under her feet—softer, more luxurious—she could tell they were now in the draw-ing room.

In the midst of Society.

The babble of voices suggested that there were perhaps twenty people in there, milling around. Just less than half were the wallflowers and Miss Pike, Rilla presumed, which left ten or twelve of London's Society who had been dragged the half an hour's carriage ride away from London to the Wall-flower Academy.

'So,' she said pleasantly, as Sylvia pulled up and halted them. 'Who do we have here?'

It had become their custom since… Now Rilla came to think about it, she could hardly recall when. Attempting to speak to those who came to gawp at the wallflowers was never a very pleasant experience, and so Sylvia and Rilla had grown the habit of standing by the side of the room and care-fully cataloguing those who bothered to come all this way out of London.

They were to be treated like they were in a zoo, were they? Well, two could play at that game.

'There are a few peacocks, as always,' Sylvia began.

Rilla smiled despite herself. Peacocks referred to ladies who wore outrageous outfits to ensure they were looked at. There were always a few of those.

'A tiger, but we'll ensure to avoid him.'

A tiger was a gentleman on the prowl, typically one who had got himself into a bit of bother in London and needed a swift marriage to distract from the scandal.

'A pair of sheep following a fox. Male, all of them.'

A trio of men, then. Rilla nodded. A fox was a gentle-man who should not be trusted, and two of his followers who thoughtlessly agreed with anything he said were sheep.

Perhaps a year ago she would have replied to Sylvia. Cer-tainly two years ago. But three years at the Wallflower Academy had worn her down, like waves upon a rock, and so much of herself had faded away. Been crushed.

'And my goodness, but he is handsome.'

Rilla nudged her friend. 'No animal this time?'

'You know, I'm not sure what sort of animal this one would be,' breathed Sylvia, her interest palpable. 'Very handsome, though. I wouldn't mind a little conversational practice with him—dragged here by his mother, from what I can see. A demure peacock, almost stylish.'

'You really are terrible, you know?' Rilla said lightly.

Her arm was squeezed. 'You know, I don't recognize the very handsome gentleman, but he rings a sort of bell. Attended Gwen's wedding, maybe?'

Rilla tilted her head on one side. Now that was a tone she did not often hear in Sylvia's voice. Not desire. No, it was curiosity…but something more than that. Something almost startled.

'By Jove, he's coming this way,' Sylvia breathed.

Rilla shifted uncomfortably on her feet. It was disarming, the thought that a stranger was marching towards you, with no sense at all who he was or why he may be doing such a ridiculous thing.

'Not actually towards us, though,' Rilla said quietly. 'There's no reason he—'

'You know, it does almost look as though he is making straight for us, in all honesty.' Sylvia's voice had lowered in volume, surely because the gentleman was coming closer. 'Oh, Daphne! Daphne, it's your father, and who's that with—Daphne, let go of me!'

'Wait,' was all Rilla managed to say.

And then she was gone. Sylvia's exuberance was well known by the wallflowers, which was undoubtedly why Daphne had pulled her away—as a buffer to whatever conversation Daphne did not wish to have. Sylvia did tend to act first and think later; they would both feel guilty, Rilla knew, at abandoning her here.

Because it left her...exposed.

Not exposed, Rilla thought sternly as she ensured her head did not droop with the sudden loss of her companion. She was hardly helpless, and her cane gave her the comfort she needed. Just...alone. That was all.

And besides, she was accustomed to being alone. Alone was what she did best.

A slow smile crept across her face, and Rilla saw no reason to hide it. Yes, perhaps her father was right all along. Perhaps she would be better suited—

'What are you smiling about?' asked a curious, quiet voice.

Rilla's foot hit the wall as she instinctively attempted to put more distance between her and the speaker. Pain throbbed in her ankle and up her shin, but there was no possibility of reaching down and rubbing it. Not when she could precisely tell where the mysterious gentleman who had just spoken was. Too close.

Lord, the idea of accidentally leaning down and headbutting—

'You look very well, Miss Newell,' came the strange voice.

Then the memory slipped into her mind and threw up a name.

'Very well,' he repeated.

Rilla swallowed and ensured that no hint of a grin approached the corners of her lips. She was not amused.

She recognized the scent now. Sandalwood and lemon. She had only encountered one person who smelt like that.

'The earl, isn't it?' she said as airily as possible. 'From the wedding a few days ago.'

'Impressive,' came the reply, confident, calm, collected.

Rilla snorted. 'Not so impressive. I may be blind, but I am hardly a fool. I am more than a match for you. Why, you—'

She bit down on the words just in time to prevent them spilling out. For what could she say? *You have a particular scent that marks you out?*

'Blind,' said the man quietly. Strangely. As though he were not afraid of the word, which was a most strange occurrence indeed. 'You see absolutely nothing, then?'

'I can see right through you,' Rilla muttered before raising her voice. 'Not that it's any business of yours.'

'Of course.' The man sounded...apologetic. And yet unruffled. 'You must forgive my curiosity.'

Rilla often found herself forgiving many things, and in the grand scheme of things, the man's enquiry about her sight was at least spoken with a modicum of respect.

Still. That did not mean she had to suffer his presence. Though her body was hardly suffering—it was leaning. Leaning!

Ridiculous. She was annoyed at this man, she reminded herself sternly. He had made her feel a fool. There she had been, trusting him, flirting with him...

Which admittedly, had been her fault.

Oh, God, she was still leaning!

Rilla straightened up and ensured her voice was cold and distant. 'How odd that you are here again.'

'Oh, not so odd, I assure you,' the earl said, louder now. Too loud. Would not others be turning to look? 'My mother dragged me here as part of her, and I quote, "charitable efforts." She has this ridiculous idea about the unfortunate and the lesser... Well, I saw very little point in putting up a fight.'

Rilla blinked.

Very handsome, though. I wouldn't mind a little conversational practice with him—dragged here by his mother, from what I can see...

Dragged by his mother... Well, that would account for him being here again.

An earl. Here.

Embarrassment bubbled in Rilla's chest, but she did not

permit herself to display the heated emotions firing through her body.

This man, this stranger—he was an outsider. He did not deserve to know what she was thinking. He'd already made her look the fool.

'How are you, Miss Newell?' came the earl's voice gently.

Rilla attempted again to take a step back, forgetting momentarily that her back was almost already up against the wall. It was most alarming. The man had somehow grown closer to her, far closer than was acceptable.

And they were in public, too! What on earth did the man think he was doing?

'Your name is…?' she said stiffly.

The chuckle blew warm breath across her upper arm—a fact she was most definitely not thinking about. Hardly noticing. Not at all. Not in the slightest.

'I told you I was an earl, and I was not lying,' came the cheerful voice. 'I am Finlay Jellicoe, Earl of Staromchor. For my sins.'

'And I suppose they are numerous,' Rilla said tightly.

Really, it was most unfair of Sylvia to abandon her like this. Even if the man was handsome, it was not like Rilla could tell. Or care.

Attractiveness—now that was different. There was a warmth to some people, a strange magnetic quality she could not describe but had felt once or twice. A need to be near. A pull, a tug under her navel that had caused her once to accidentally fall into that gentleman's lap and—

The Earl of Staromchor's chuckle was low, as though they were sharing a secret. Heat flushed across Rilla's cheeks, and she hoped to goodness no one would notice.

The very idea of an earl and Miss Newell, giggling together in a corner!

'I suppose they are,' said the Earl of Staromchor easily. 'But they aren't nearly so numerous as those of my mother. She's accosted a gentleman and appears to be berating him.'

'Berating him?' Rilla said, unable to help herself.

Well. She couldn't be blamed for her curiosity. She had lost Sylvia's eyes…it was only fair that she use this earl's. For the moment. Not that she wanted to.

There came a movement, the slightest of movements. It could have been a wool jacket against her skin, the very tip of her arm. Rilla's lips parted at the sudden sensation, and then it was gone. Like a whisper she had imagined.

'I think that is Lord Norbury,' came Earl of Staromchor's voice. 'He's standing with a wallflower, as far as I can make out. She looks…terrified. My mother isn't that bad.'

Even with the slightest of descriptions, Rilla could not help but identify the wallflower. 'That is Miss Daphne Smith—with her father, I think.'

'Her father,' the Earl of Staromchor mused. 'That would explain, at least in part, my mother's critique.'

'Critique?'

Rilla had not meant to say it. She certainly should not be conversing with this man, this interloper—this earl!—and most definitely not exchanging gossip. Gossip about one of her friends, no less. It was most indelicate.

Unfortunately, her wonder overcame her.

'Yes, it appears Lord Norbury has not been visiting his daughter enough,' said the Earl of Staromchor softly. 'The gossip is all over Town, as you— Oh, I suppose you may not know. I'd heard it myself, but never thought…the differences in name… My mother won't stop talking about him.'

Rilla swallowed. And that was what came of opening her mouth and allowing herself, just for a moment, to be swept up in a conversation.

Daphne's parentage was not something discussed. Not openly. And certainly not with strangers.

'Go away,' she said sharply.

There was a low chuckle just to her left, then it moved to before her. Cutting her off from the rest of the room.

'Here I am, volunteering to come to the Wallflower Academy to aid you in practising your conversation,' the Earl of Staromchor said with a teasing, lilting voice, 'and you wish me to go away?'

'I did not ask for your help, my lord,' Rilla said, pouring as much disdain as she could manage in the last two words.

'Miss Pike did.'

'Miss Pike does not speak for me,' she retorted, though immediately she regretted the sharpness of her words.

She felt heat rise from her stomach and up her chest. It did no good to critique the Pike in public, either. Good grief, she must be tired. She was not usually this…this lax.

'Nevertheless, I am happy to provide the service.'

'I do not need servicing by you,' Rilla snapped. Then the heat in her chest spread across her face. 'I… I mean— You know what I mean!'

'I certainly do. Or at least, I think I do,' came the obviously amused voice of the Earl of Staromchor.

It was an interesting voice. Oh, Rilla did not experience much variety in the way of male voices at the Wallflower Academy. There was Matthews, of course, and John, the other footman. Sometimes Cook, a man with a voice that sounded like fruit cake and spiced currants when he came into the dining room and asked opinions on a new recipe.

But this earl…his voice was different. There was a confidence there, almost no hesitation in his speech. A lilting lightness, a confidence. A warmth, like a summer breeze wafting through a forest, picking up the little scents of growth and life.

It was doing that thing to her stomach again.

It was all Rilla could do not to push past the man and storm to the door. She knew the way; it was but eight or nine steps from here, and other people would simply have to move out of the way, that was what.

But she wouldn't allow this earl to win. She just wouldn't.

'Besides, if anyone needs practice for their conversation, it is you,' she said sharply. 'You are the one who failed to introduce himself when we first met. Allowed me to make a fool of myself with Miss Pike gone. And you...'

You're an earl, she wanted to say. *You're not to be trusted. I know your sort.*

She detected a soft noise, perhaps the shifting from one boot to another.

'You are the one with the exemplary conversation skills, are you?'

Rilla held her head high. At least on this ground, she was stable. 'I don't depend on titles or good looks. I may not be exemplary, but I'm a damned sight better than you.'

She had expected an almost immediate reply. Strange, in a way, she was a tad disappointed to stand in the silence after her bold comment.

It wasn't that she was starved for conversation. Far from it. Sylvia and Daphne were perhaps her closest friends, but there was not a person in the Wallflower Academy that Rilla did not have a passable friendship with.

And that was the trouble, wasn't it? Three years in the same situation, the same place, with the same people. Oh, a few arrived but they left just as swiftly. Look at Gwen, married within months.

'I... You don't... I... I didn't...'

And then Rilla smiled. She had ruffled him. She had ruffled an earl. 'I'm sorry, is this your example of excellent conversation?'

The Earl of Staromchor cleared his throat, and he was close, far closer than she thought possible. 'How did you get here, Miss Newell?'

'Why, through the door after descending the stairs,' Rilla said sweetly, joy twisting around her heart as she imagined how irritated she could make this man.

Well, serve him right. Coming here to help wallflowers practise their conversation, indeed!

'No, I meant—well, before the Wallflower Academy. Where do you come from, who are your people?'

Immediately the joy started to melt away. She was not going to tell him—no. He didn't know her title, he didn't know her father, and it had to stay that way.

If he caught whiff of that scandal...

She had her sisters to think of, Rilla thought sternly, pressing her hands together as though that would prevent her from spilling any secrets. Any details. Or any information whatsoever.

No, this man may jolt her off balance, make it completely impossible to think clearly, and smell absolutely divine...

She was not thinking that an earl smelt divine!

'Your people are, Miss Newell?'

'My people,' Rilla said stiffly, 'are the Newells.'

'And where are they?'

'I don't actually have to tell you, you know,' she said as calmly as she could manage. Where on earth was Sylvia? 'Besides, I have no time for earls.'

'No time for earls? Why the devil not?'

Rilla silently cursed her inability to keep her mouth shut. Just when she had decided that she was not going to reveal any of herself to this stranger—this earl!—she had to go and make a comment like that. It was infuriating.

Most upsettingly, it was herself that she was annoyed at.

'Good day, my lord,' she said curtly.

She made it almost six steps. That brought her within touching distance of the door frame that led back into the hall, and she would have made it, too.

If it wasn't for the most maddening hand on her wrist. A hand whose touch should not have burned, should not have sparked a tingling heat that travelled up her arm.

'Let me help.'

'I know the way,' Rilla said, attempting to step around him.

The trouble was, the Earl of Staromchor had the advantage of her, quite literally. Just as she moved left, she could hear him, feel him mirroring her, stepping in her way. A step to the right and there he was again, her hands outstretched and brushing up against the silk of a waistcoat, the cold metal chain of a pocket watch.

She halted, cheeks burning. What must the rest of the room think!

'All I asked was—'

'Are you here to choose a bride?' Rilla interrupted, hoping to God that her deflection would be sufficient. 'The Duke of Knaresby did, but you know that, since you attended the wedding. So, here to pick a wallflower bride?'

Apparently, it was an excellent deflection. The Earl of Staromchor hesitated just a moment too long before he said, 'I have no need to come to the Wallflower Academy to choose a bride.'

Rilla swallowed, and remembered what Sylvia had said.

And my goodness, but he is handsome.

If this Earl of Staromchor was as pleasing to look at as Sylvia said, then evidently he knew it. Knew that any lady in the *ton* would be pleased to receive his attentions.

All earls were the same. They were interested in what they could get, not what they could give.

'I have no desire to plan a wedding at present,' the Earl of Staromchor continued, his voice low as though they were sharing a private conversation. 'Or, in truth, to be married. In fact—'

'Fascinating as that is,' Rilla said curtly, 'I—'

'Staromchor, come on, we'll be late back to London!'

The woman's voice was loud and rich, sounding like how plums tasted. Rilla turned her head just for a moment to the left where the voice came from, but as she did so, a voice replied.

'Coming, Mother.'

It was the Earl of Staromchor. Footsteps, shifting away.

Rilla swallowed. So. He was gone.

And she was glad, she told herself firmly. No good could ever come out of speaking with an earl.

Chapter Four

Good weather drew Londoners out like bees, and like bees, they swarmed.

The place they swarmed to, Finlay always thought, was Hyde Park, which was as central as one could be to the fashionable part of London. The tall, towering trees shone green light down on everyone who passed beneath them.

And today, that was a great many people.

Safe atop Ceres, the mare he'd brought to Town, Finlay looked out at the crowds of people.

Ladies, as far as the eye could see. Farther. Ladies with tall bonnets that demanded to be seen from a distance, some bearing feathers, some bearing lace. Ladies with gowns that swept along the bone-dry paths, scattering fallen leaves and dust in their path. Ladies wearing blues and greens and yellows, pastels and prints, stripes and even in some cases, spots.

Finlay was not exactly an expert in the world of fashion—quite proudly not so—but even he thought the spots were a bit much.

Though the gentlemen were hardly any better. Some of them were following what he considered to be the Beau Brummell line of things, dark colours, little velvet or lace. Others appeared to be wishing to gather as much attention as the ladies, if not more. They sported gloves lined with fur, top hats that were creeping up to the heavens, canes for those who really wished to make a statement.

And children. Governesses. A few people exercised their dogs, others wandered with their pets in their arms, as though their little feet could not make the ground. Carriages rolled past, trimmed with silk and with golden paint across their wheels. Horses whinnied as they clopped through the place.

Hyde Park was a veritable sea of colour, ever changing, swiftly moving. The streams of people constantly shifted, their colours intermingling then clashing then separating. It was enough to give even the rainbow enthusiast a headache.

Yet despite all those before him, his thoughts did not tend to those he could see, but rather to one of the few ladies who did not appear to be taking the air in Hyde Park today.

Miss Isabelle Carr.

Finlay's stomach twisted painfully at the thought, and not because Ceres had stepped awkwardly across the path to get out of the way of another man who was galloping as though he were late for an appointment.

Isabelle. The shell of the woman she had been before. She had to stop hiding away from the world. It wouldn't— Nothing could bring him back.

She was slipping far from his thoughts. The space in his mind, in his heart, was unfathomably being replaced by a fiery gaze and a delicate figure.

Miss Newell.

He was dragged away from pleasant musings—such as the exact tilt of Miss Newell's head as she castigated him—only by the most important of topics.

Like the Carr debts.

Just that morning when he had stepped downstairs to break his fast, he had been halted from entering the morning room by a dour Turner.

'Turner?' Finlay had asked the butler curiously. 'Don't tell me my mother has given you a wild instruction again. Demands for strawberries?'

'I wish it were that simple,' replied the loyal butler quietly. 'Here.'

From a pocket in his livery, Turner removed a small bundle of letters, tied together with what looked like garden string.

And Finlay's heart had sank.

He had known precisely what they were. He had not needed to take them to the study—the one room that was his own in his mother's townhouse—and break the seals and read them.

'To the sum of fifteen pounds,' Finlay had read aloud, keeping his voice low just in case his mother did what she so often did, and barged into his study to see what he was up to. 'A debt of three pounds, but with interest...six pounds four shillings. Another one, yes...eighteen pounds and thruppence, though as unpaid for several months, rising to...'

It had been all he could do, when Cecil had died so suddenly, to track down the bulk of the debts.

Oh, every gentleman lived right to the edge of his means; that was expected. When Finlay had first met Cecil, up at Cambridge, the two of them had never exceeded their income but often danced right along the edge.

But Cecil and Isabelle's father had been a famous spendthrift, and Cecil's untimely loss came barely a month after their father had died. Finlay's friend was only halfway to understanding how the estate had got into such a mess, and Isabelle was left alone. Penniless.

The trouble was, as Finlay's friend had always said when he had lived, there was always so much more expense when it came to living in London than one expected—and his father had never known when to cut back and economise.

The upkeep of the house, yes—servants, and food. But also clothing. Keeping the horses, stabling the carriage. Keeping it running. And there were dinners to host; one had to host dinners. And parties to attend, and card parties included their own awful debts. Art to buy. Wallpaper to import. Statues to commission.

And then there were all those costs one did not expect. Lawyers and accountants and tradespeople—more tradespeople, Cecil had always said, than could reasonably be expected to even be found in London.

Finlay's smile was pained as Ceres turned a corner in Hyde Park.

Cecil has a way with words.

Had. Had a way with words.

And that was the trouble. For as soon as Finlay was certain that he had paid off the debts of the Carr family, more seemed to turn up. And the worst of it was, Isabelle had no dowry. All had been spent by her father, without her knowledge.

A flash of dark, almost black hair, a laugh.

Finlay's head turned so suddenly he actually cricked his neck. Lifting a hand from his reins to rub at the offending sore spot, he blinked after the woman who had so suddenly caught his attention.

And his stomach settled. It was not Rilla Newell.

Not that he should be thinking of Rilla Newell, he told himself most firmly as he took his reins back in hand and nudged his steed forward. He was engaged—though he'd realized how foolhardy offering a marriage of convenience to Isabelle was about five minutes after the matter had been concluded.

If only words could be taken back…

Though now he came to think of it, Finlay thought ruefully, he hadn't learned. Now there was that ridiculous bet with Bartlett.

And still his mind meandered to Marilla. Miss Newell. Though after such a damning conversation at the Wallflower Academy only a week ago, he supposed he should give up thinking about her altogether.

I don't actually have to tell you, you know. Besides, I have no time for earls.

The trouble was, she intrigued him. Finlay had never encountered a woman with such a visceral reaction to his title.

Well, perhaps a few—but those ladies had smiled, simpered, shot him looks that told him in no uncertain terms that they would be rather pleased to accept his advances.

Meeting with a woman who heard the title and baulked… it was unheard of.

What was even stranger was how the pain in his chest had wavered, no longer pressing on his lungs like…

Finlay blinked. That had only happened when he had been speaking with Miss Rilla Newell.

Now that was worth thinking about.

'…plenty of pleasant ladies to converse with here in Hyde Park,' a man was saying to his companion as they walked past. 'Just don't bother heading towards the Serpentine, the Wallflower Academy chits are there.'

Finlay swiftly turned in his saddle towards the ornamental lake and his eyes widened.

By Jove.

A line of ladies was meandering with purpose through Hyde Park. At the front was quite clearly Miss Pike, pointing up and around them as they went. The wallflowers followed her in pairs, arm in arm, heads down, evidently not enjoying the public outing.

And at the back…

It was Miss Newell. Finlay blinked, hardly able to believe it.

But a flirtation would cheer you up. I'm not saying have an assignation but a flirtation, someone to make you smile, dust off those skills—

He had an opportunity to charm Miss Newell. Just the thought of it made his body hum, his loins spark with heat.

Because charm he would. True, Finlay had not had much

of a positive start with the wallflower, but all that was about to change. He was well dressed, and they were in public but had been introduced so it was perfectly acceptable, wasn't it, to approach her…

And this time, he was going to turn up the charm so high, she wouldn't know what had hit her.

Metaphorically speaking. Of course.

The main trouble was Miss Pike.

Dismounting from Ceres as nonchalantly as he could manage, Finlay followed the trail of wallflowers as they snaked through the Hyde Park crowds.

'Great architecture to be seen throughout London, but today we are focusing instead on nature,' came Miss Pike's voice from the front of the crocodile. 'Over here, if you look up, you'll see a huge oak tree, one of the finest…'

Miss Newell was right at the back of the line of wallflowers, a cane in one hand and the other tucked in with that of a Black wallflower Finlay could not recall the name of. Cynthia? Simon? No, that couldn't be right.

Following them so close that he was almost surprised that they did not turn to berate him for his ill manners, Finlay considered what his next move should be. The blind wallflower was being led by her companion, and would instantly notice any approach by a strange gentleman.

As would everyone else in Hyde Park.

Perhaps this was a mistake. Perhaps he should just retreat home, admit to George that he didn't care for Isabelle as he should but he had no choice but to go through with the marriage now he had offered it, and…

'Ridiculous idea to leave my cane in the carriage. You know I hate being without it when away from the Wallflower Academy. And to bring me on this nature walk, honestly!' Miss Newell was saying.

Her friend snorted. 'What, you have no other senses?'

'Oh, I can hear the wind through the trees and smell the flowers,' said Miss Newell, breathing in deeply. 'And—goodness. The Earl of Staromchor. Sylvia, why didn't you say?'

Finlay stiffened as the two wallflowers turned their heads. Sylvia, that was her name, looked startled, and Miss Newell...

Miss Newell looked remarkably pleased with herself. As well she might.

'Rilla, I had no idea he was there, but you're right,' said Sylvia, a curious gaze raking over Finlay's features. 'How did you know?'

It was an important question. Finlay would not have described himself as an expert, but by God, he hunted. It should have been easy for him, in the melee of Hyde Park on this sunny Sunday afternoon, to follow the wallflowers with ease without being detected.

And for some reason, pink was blossoming across Miss Newell's cheeks. Most prettily, pairing with the soft, inviting pink of her lips in a way, Finlay was certain, she could not know.

'I... I just knew,' Miss Newell said lamely.

Finlay wasn't convinced, and neither, it appeared, was Sylvia. 'Knew? Poppycock, you must have—I don't know, smelled him or something.'

Sylvia continued chattering away and so she did not, unlike Finlay, spot the sudden dark red that splotched across Miss Newell's face—nor how she turned away from them.

Dear God, was that truly it? She had...smelt him?

Attempting surreptitiously to sniff the lapel of his collar, Finlay was startled by the ladies' sudden movement. They were continuing on with their walk, rejoining the gaggle of wallflowers.

Irritation sparked in his stomach. What, they were just going to walk away from him?

But it appeared Miss Newell had no compunction in brushing off the attentions, however slight, of an earl. By the time Finlay had caught up with them again, leading Ceres by the reins, he heard her say, 'No need to talk to him, that's all.'

'No need to—he's an earl!' Sylvia hissed.

'I am, you know,' Finlay said helpfully, casting an eye over Miss Newell.

She was beautiful. Strange, in a way, that he had not noticed before. Oh, he'd noticed the pleasing shape of her mouth, the delicate way her hair swept across in its pins, inviting hands to—

Dear God. Get a grip of yourself, man!

'Here, you take her,' Sylvia said suddenly, removing Miss Newell's hand from her own arm and placing it unceremoniously onto Finlay's. She met his eye with a grin, and gave him such a theatrical wink, he was astonished he wasn't seated at the Adelphi Theatre. 'I'll distract the Pike with a question about aqueducts. Miss Pike—'

'Wait!' cried both Finlay and Miss Newell together.

His heart skipped a beat as he glanced at her, now walking stonily by his side in silence, refusing to turn to him.

Sylvia evidently believed the two of them to be in cahoots, though to what end, he struggled to imagine. Surely she did not think…?

Finlay swallowed hard and ensured he kept his head high, ignoring the curious glances that were being shot his way by other pedestrians in the park. He was walking in public with a woman. It was perhaps a little unusual, but not entirely scandalous…was it?

This was what he had wanted, wasn't it? The chance to charm Miss Newell.

To win a wager, Finlay reminded himself. He was engaged to be married to Miss Carr. Not a love match, certainly not, but one he was going to see through to the bitter end.

So. Charming. He could be charming. The bet depended on it.

'May I fetch you a drink, Miss Newell?' Finlay attempted with a laugh. 'I am afraid I am a poor footman, but...'

'Spare me your pleasant nonsense,' came the curt reply.

His laugh died on the wind. Ah. Well, perhaps that was not the best idea. It wasn't as though they had parted on the best terms the last time he had the pleasure of her company.

So. Where to begin?

'Miss Newell, you look radiant today, did you know that?' Finlay said with a wide grin.

Only when the words were out of his mouth did his face fall. *Oh, hell...*

Miss Newell's twisted expression contained no mirth. 'You know, funny you should say that, but no, I can't say I've had much use for my looking glass of late.'

Finlay swallowed. Well, that perhaps wasn't the best opener. But that was of no matter. He had others.

'And what a splendid day it is,' he said cheerfully, waving his free hand about to gesture at...

At what she could not see. Hell on earth, but he was going to have to think harder than that.

Miss Newell's face was a picture of restrained mirth. 'You're not very bright, are you, my lord?'

'I just... I forgot... Well, it is pleasant to be walking with you in Hyde Park, Miss Newell,' Finlay said, pretending to be utterly undone by her wit.

It wasn't particularly hard to pretend, in truth. Not that he would have ever admitted it.

Yet still she kept him at a distance, as she appeared to do with the whole world, as far as Finlay could tell. It wasn't the cane. It was her very demeanour.

Silence. It appeared Miss Newell had no interest in responding to his words, no matter how polite they were.

'And are you enjoying your time in London?' Finlay continued as he steered her gently along the path, which curved to the left.

There was a slight pressure on his arm, and then it returned to the light touch it had been before. A tingling feeling crept up to his shoulder, something warming and unknown, unusual and unfamiliar.

Finlay swallowed. It was a feeling he could dismiss. It meant nothing, obviously.

'Yes,' said Miss Newell dismissively.

He waited for a moment, expecting her to continue, but when she did not he found himself unreasonably lost. Well, how did one make conversation with a woman who evidently had no interest in said conversation whatsoever?

Well, he'd told old Bartlett that he had the charm. Time to butter her up.

'You are clearly a very intelligent woman, Miss Newell,' Finlay said firmly as he followed the wallflowers, wishing to goodness he could sit Miss Newell at a bench where he could accidentally on purpose brush his leg against hers. That always worked. 'In fact, I—'

'I'm not that easily impressed, you know,' Miss Newell interrupted with a blank look that she cast his way. 'I'm not like Sylvia. I don't desire to be admired everywhere I go. Nor am I like Juliet, who accepts compliments so prettily.'

A twisting discomfort was making itself at home in Finlay's stomach, precisely where he did not wish it to be. Though he attempted to distract himself by looking at the plethora of beautiful ladies around them in Hyde Park, he was most bewildered to discover that none of them held the simple elegance that the woman on his arm did.

'I don't want you to be like any of those other ladies,' Finlay said, hardly certain which one Juliet was, and not particularly caring. 'I just—'

'What?' Miss Newell shot back, causing tingles of anticipation, warm and alluring, to shoot up his spine. 'You just what?'

It would be a great deal easier to converse if he were not so damned attracted to her.

She was…unlike anyone else he had ever met. Oh, Finlay had met a great number of people; as a member of Society, it was impossible not to.

And none of them glared like Miss Newell, spoke to him so cuttingly as Miss Newell, made him feel as though speaking to her was a privilege he had not yet earned.

In anyone else, it would be off putting.

But there was a warmth to her, one she evidently could not fully contain. Finlay could no longer ignore the desire she sparked in him, the need to know her better.

To touch—

Steady on there, he told himself firmly. *You're in public. And you don't go around touching young ladies against their will!*

'You're very quiet,' Miss Newell said.

There was a look almost of disappointment on her face.

Warmth crept across Finlay's face. Try as she might to argue the opposite, she wanted to talk to him.

The knowledge buoyed him as nothing else had, and the shot of excitement and joy was unparalleled.

I wager you'll feel infinitely better for a flirtation. I think it'll bring you joy, and won't betray Isabelle in any way, and you'll enter the married state far happier.

Or not at all.

Dammit. He may have to tell Bartlett he was right and lose the bet. What was the penalty for losing, again?

'And it's not like I care,' Miss Newell continued stiffly. 'Your conversation leaves much to be desired at the best of times, when you're not lying about who you are or making a fool of yourself at afternoon tea. But you are preventing me from conversing with Sylvia, and—'

'Look, I'm trying to butter you up here,' said Finlay before he could stop himself, the foolish admission slipping out. 'The least you could do is—'

'Enjoy it?' Miss Newell said, tilting her head towards him. Something blazed in her expression, something he could not fathom. 'And why are you buttering me up, pray? Not exactly the charming opening I thought earls were supposed to have.'

Finlay took a deep breath and attempted to regather himself.

Well. It was exasperating in the extreme, not to be immediately liked. Worse, it was most unpleasant to discover within yourself an expectation of being liked.

If only she could see the amiable tilt of his jaw, his dazzling smile, the way he carried himself. He was even wearing one of his newest waistcoats and jackets, elegant and cut remarkably close to his figure. A figure that, Finlay would previously have boasted, had got more than one woman in a tizzy.

But none of that mattered. Not to Miss Newell, anyway.

Fine. Charm hadn't worked. Time for direct questioning. 'Why don't you like me, Miss Newell?'

Evidently she had not been expecting that. She almost tripped over her own gown, and Finlay reached out and placed a hand on her waist to steady her.

And unsteady himself.

Rapid thoughts of molten desire that were most unsuitable to be thinking and feeling while standing in the middle of Hyde Park rushed through Finlay's body. Unbidden, uncontrolled, all inspired by the merest contact with a woman who pulled herself free of him the moment she had regained her balance.

Finlay almost stepped back, but he managed to keep his presence of mind and retain hold of Miss Newell's arm. For her benefit, he told himself, mind whirling as he attempted to understand what precisely he had just experienced.

'It's not you,' Miss Newell said curtly. 'It's the fact that you're an earl.'

'An earl?' Finlay repeated blankly.

They were standing still now, the train of wallflowers disappearing off along the path. But Finlay didn't care. How could he, when such a beautiful enigma was staring up at him?

Miss Newell's eyes were a startling grey. It was the first time he'd noticed that. No wonder he hadn't realized she could not see the world as it was when they had first met. One could almost be forgiven for not noticing, such was her beauty.

And she hated earls?

'Forget I said anything,' said Miss Newell awkwardly. 'And return me to Sylvia. The Pike will soon notice.'

'I'll return you to Sylvia safe and sound once you've answered me,' Finlay stated far stronger than he intended.

He was not, after all, a cad. They weren't that far behind another pair of wallflowers. He wasn't alone with her. Not really.

What, a small voice muttered in the back of his head, *would Isabelle say about that?*

Miss Newell bit her lip, her head turning, her cane moving as they started again slowly along the path. Was she listening for Sylvia, for the other wallflowers? Was she wondering just how far from them she was?

Evidently she would not risk it. Dropping her head and speaking so quietly that Finlay could hardly hear her, she said softly, 'I'm not actually Miss Newell. Well, I am.'

Finlay blinked. 'Well, that sorts that out.'

There was brief flash of a smile, then it was gone. 'I'm actually the Honourable Miss Marilla Newell and I was... I was once engaged to the Earl of Porthaethwy.'

This time Finlay did let her hand slip from his arm.

Engaged before? Honourable Earl of Porthaethwy?

He blinked, the sunlight of the day suddenly dazzling—or was that her? Miss Newell was a woman far above the station he had assumed for her. What was a woman of that breeding doing in a place like the Wallflower Academy?

'Was once engaged?' Finlay repeated the one part of Miss Newell's statement that gave him the most pause.

Once engaged? A scandal, then?

Miss Newell shrugged, though there was evidently more pain in that expression than she knew she was revealing. 'He broke off the arranged marriage the day he met me. I was sent to the Wallflower Academy the following week. There. Now, will you return me to my friends?'

But Finlay could think of nothing but the outrage that was curdling around his heart.

Broke off the arranged marriage? The cad, the lout, the—

'The very idea!' he said hotly, words breaking out against his will. 'I don't see what— I mean, why should he care about... about...?'

Finlay swallowed.

Rilla was glaring just past his ear. 'He didn't care that I was blind. He knew that—everyone knew that. I was born that way. No, he broke it off for quite a different reason. Only earls know how to end a match.'

And he understood that, didn't he?

It was that annoying voice again, and this time, Finlay swallowed hard and was unable to ignore it.

Because it wasn't entirely wrong. There had been moments, hadn't there—more frequently with every day that passed— that he considered breaking off his arranged marriage with Isabelle?

Not because there was anything wrong with her, no, but because...

Well, he didn't have a good reason. Something in him just rebelled at the idea of wedding a childhood friend. Particularly when she was so...so altered. So lost.

'Are you going to return me to Sylvia or abandon me here?' Miss Newell said darkly, cutting through Finlay's thoughts.

'Though you are an earl, I wouldn't be surprised if you chose the latter.'

And that did it. Finlay pulled himself together, puffed out his chest, smoothed back his hair...then realized that every single one of those motions was lost on the woman before him.

Blast.

'I shall return you to Miss Pike now,' Finlay said quietly, deflating. 'And I hope I shall soon—'

'Oh, no,' said Miss Newell firmly, reaching out and deliberately placing her hand on his arm without a hesitation. 'No, Your Lordship. I wouldn't bother to hope.'

Chapter Five

'And she will be here any moment!' declared Miss Pike, a froth of excitement in her tone. 'A duchess visiting the Wall-flower Academy is hardly a run-of-the-mill event, and some of you—yes, you, Daphne—are dreadfully unprepared. So please, for goodness' sake, be on your best— Sylvia Bryant, put that footman down!'

Hurried footsteps grew louder then fainter as the Pike traversed the drawing room, moving from the polished floorboards to the rug then out to the hall. Muffled laughter. A muttering in a low voice, embarrassed, contrite.

Rilla smiled.

Well, as there was no telling what mischief Sylvia would get into next, she had ceased attempting to predict it around four weeks after the woman's arrival.

After all, had she not orchestrated a most unpleasant encounter with *that earl*?

Try as she might, she could not conceive why the blackguard had sought her again.

It was irritating. He was irritating. And much against her wishes, the true vexation was that he had not appeared the last five days at the Wallflower Academy.

And why would he? Rilla asked herself darkly.

Besides, she didn't want him to. The delectable-smelling man, the one whose presence raised her hackles and made it impossible to concentrate, why would she want him here?

Dragging herself away from remembrances of strong hands on her arm and the sense of danger, of being separated from the other wallflowers, Rilla returned to the conversation in the room.

And immediately regretted it.

'Duchess here,' Daphne's voice whispered, sotto voce and filled with terror. 'Why she would want to come here—'

'No need for that, now!' Sylvia's voice was half mirth, half frustration. A sudden weight dropped onto the sofa beside Rilla. 'I don't see what was so bad about—'

'I think you know precisely what the problem was here,' came the Pike's stern yet steady tone. 'Leave the poor footmen alone, you know they can't— Ah, here she is. Now, let me go and greet our honoured guest.'

Rilla's nerves prickled as chatter rose up once more about the arrival of a duchess.

A duchess.

What on earth was she coming here for? She certainly couldn't be meeting with a friend, and they were just too far out of London for this to be a coincidence. Besides, the Pike had been informed in advance. That meant planning.

Another one of the nobility coming here to peer at us to see what a wallflower looks like, Rilla thought darkly. *And they wonder why the London Tower menagerie is so popular...*

New footsteps. Light, measured, definitely coming from the hall.

Rilla's spine stiffened, her stomach tightening into a knot. Could she avoid notice? It was always a challenge, being the one who could see naught but a vague sense of light and dark. Avoiding unwelcome conversation was just that much more difficult.

And there was no time now to retire to her room. That would require crossing the hall, and there was no possibility she could avoid—

'Her Grace,' intoned Matthews's voice from about ten feet from Rilla, 'the Duchess of—'

Her heart sank.

And then it rose.

'Gwen,' Rilla breathed.

She was nudged none too gently in the side.

'Now how on earth,' muttered Sylvia as the footman droned on, 'did you know that?'

There was only one person in the world, Rilla was certain, who still scrubbed the back of their neck with carbolic soap out of habit, but also now wore the delicate rose scent her husband had presented her on their wedding day.

It was a jarring medley, and it was altogether Gwen.

'Gwendolyn Devereux, wife of the Duke of Knaresby.'

'Yes, yes, we don't need any of that nonsense,' came the ruffled voice of Gwen. 'I only came to see Rilla and Sylvia. We don't need all this.'

'But Your Grace!' The Pike was obviously rattled, though Rilla could hardly comprehend why. She'd managed to get a duchess to cross the threshold, hadn't she? 'Visiting all the wallflowers, it would do a great deal for their reputations, elevate them.'

'I'm here, and you are fortunate I came at all,' shot back the determined voice of the duchess.

That was Gwen. She may have been sent to the Wallflower Academy, but she was no shrinking violet.

'Yes, move a chair here.'

A scraping noise jarred Rilla's nerves and a hint of worry fluttered around her mind. It was always so much more difficult to navigate a space like the drawing room once something had been moved.

'Don't you worry, Rilla, I'll ask him to put it back,' came Gwen's voice, closer now, and lower. She was seated on the chair opposite her. 'I know you like sitting in the sunshine there.'

Despite herself, Rilla smiled. 'Thank you.'

It was a kindness not everyone offered, and as chatter erupted around the drawing room, she surmised most of the wallflowers had returned to their conversations, embroidery, and reading.

Still. That did not mean they could speak freely.

'The Pike's gone,' came Sylvia's carefree tone with a laugh. 'Lord, Gwen, when she was banging on about a duchess, I never conceived that it could be you.'

'I sometimes get surprised myself when I'm announced into a room.' Gwen's words spoke of shyness and surprise, but Rilla was not fooled. She could hear the pride, the delight, the joy.

Did anyone else hear it? Was she perhaps the only one who could tell, who was concentrating on the slight shake in the vowels, the hesitation of the consonants?

Sylvia snorted. 'Don't be daft, you love it!'

'I certainly do not.'

Rilla allowed the words to wash over and around her. It was like bathing in a pool of warm light. Or at least, what she presumed it would feel like.

She was so…so lonely.

Perhaps it was only when surrounded by chattering ladies, like now, that she noticed it. Alone with her thoughts, never truly sharing them, never wanting to share them. Lost in a sea of wallflowers.

Though she had hardly noticed it before, she had missed her friend. Gwen had been a part of the Wallflower Academy for a mere matter of months, but Rilla could not deny that she had grown to truly like the woman.

The woman who was now, apparently, the toast of the *ton*.

'So kind, so affectionate,' Gwen was saying in that lilting, carefree tone. 'And he is just…'

Wonderful, by all accounts. Try as she might, Rilla could not entirely attend to the words of her friend. No, she was altogether distracted by a thought which, once made, could not be unmade.

Gwen had made love to her husband.

Heat sparked in her cheeks, but Rilla could not dislodge the revelation from her head. What was it, to be touched by a gentleman? To have him love you, to connect to that most intimate place? To bear oneself and never worry again that you would be alone?

Shifting awkwardly in her seat, she tried not to consider it. It was not as though she would ever be blessed with such knowledge.

One night, one encounter would surely be enough to satiate her appetite. One—

'But you've hardly spoken, Rilla.'

Rilla allowed herself to nod. 'I suppose not. I suppose I have nothing new to offer because…'

Because she could not see.

Those were the words Rilla did not say aloud, but they hung in the air, heavy in their unspokenness. All three of them knew what it was she had not said. She had never feared being open with them, her friends.

The way people spoke to her, or did not speak to her. The way they presumed she was helpless, useless, ignorant! The assumption that no one would wish to marry her.

Why were they treated as prospective brides, and she treated like a dried-up old spinster of a teacher? The very idea of staying here at the Wallflower Academy, helping others to marry when no one wished to wed her…

How she longed to find someone who knew her, truly knew her…and loved her.

Rilla had hinted at as much when she had spoken briefly to

Gwen at her wedding, but this was the first time she had admitted to so much in front of Sylvia.

The sudden intake of breath to her right proved her expectation correct.

'But she can't do that!'

'She can do whatever she likes, she's the Pike,' Rilla opined wryly.

She was nudged in the shoulder.

'Don't be ridiculous,' Sylvia said, and the merriment and teasing had left her voice now. 'You can't actually be considering— she can't force you to leave!'

Rilla sighed, reached into her corset—an excellent place for keeping things, it was a misery that true pockets were not the province of the lady—and pulled out the letter that had arrived that morning. The paper was expensive; she could feel the delicacy of the grain. 'Here. You can read it. I don't mind. Sylvia already has.'

The hand that took the paper approached as a waft of rose water confirmed it was Gwen who had taken it.

'Keep it,' said Rilla with as airy a manner as possible. 'I know it by heart.'

It had surprised people, when she had first arrived at the Wallflower Academy. Her ability to memorize things once spoken to her was astonishing, apparently.

Rilla could not think why. How else was she supposed to enjoy things? She was hardly going to always find someone to read her letters to her, over and over again.

Under the genteel chatter around the drawing room about the right thread for this next portion of embroidery, and where someone's missing book was, and just how precisely Sylvia thought she was going to get away with her next adventure, Rilla heard the unfolding of the paper.

Her fingertips unconsciously moved to the seat of the sofa. The velvet underneath was soft, comforting, warm, a balm compared to the words shortly read aloud by the newest member of the aristocracy.

"'My dear Marilla,'" Gwen began to read softly. 'Oh, it's from your father.'

She must have glanced to the end, or perhaps there was a difference in the handwriting between men and women. Rilla did not know.

'Yes. My papa.'

"'My dear Marilla,'" Gwen repeated. "'Thank you for your last letter. Do consider speaking to Miss Pike about opportunities to better yourself.'"

'Better yourself?' Sylvia's voice dripped in resentment. 'I hate that he wrote that. I thought you were rather splendid already.'

Rilla reached out, lifting a hand, and her friend knew to take it and squeeze it. A lump came to her throat and though she had intended to say something witty and amusing, nothing came.

Sylvia squeezed her hand back and held on to hers, dropping their clasped fingers onto the sofa.

She must have nodded at Gwen, or indicated somehow to keep going, for the duchess continued.

"'I will admit, my child, that it would be a relief to us if you did consider leaving the Wallflower Academy and taking up a position somewhere that indicated that you had resolved not to marry.'"

'Not to marry?' Gwen's voice was startled as she repeated the words, but then she continued reading. "'Your two younger sisters—'"

'I don't want to hear this again,' Sylvia cut in. 'It was bad enough reading it the first time.'

'Keep going, Gwen,' Rilla said, her heart contracting painfully. 'Or I can recite it, if you wish? "Your two younger sisters are unable to attend Society events, not with an elder sister out and unmarried. If you wish them to ever find suitors of their own, then you will need to take a step of kindness and move out of their way. You know the estate is entailed, and you know I have to marry off as many of you as I can. And if you are so fortunate as to meet an earl again, do us all a favour and steer clear. Yours faithfully, your ever-loving Papa.'"

Silence fell after this pronouncement. At least, silence between the three of them. Daphne and Juliet appeared to be bickering good-naturedly over a skein of red thread in another corner.

Sylvia's hand squeezed hers. 'It's outrageous.'

'It's certainly not a letter I'd wish to receive,' said Gwen quietly. 'Though I must admit, marriage to Percy has put paid to the unpleasant missives my mother was sending.'

'Another benefit of winning a duke, I suppose?' Sylvia quipped.

Rilla sensed Gwen's smile, imagined the tilt of her head which had once been described to her, the flush upon her cheeks.

Whether she was correct or not, of course, was quite another matter.

'Oh, I cannot imagine not being Percy's wife,' Gwen said, happiness radiating from every syllable. 'Being loved, being adored in the way that he loves me—one reads about such things, but you never expect it to happen to you. Why, the other day...'

Rilla did not attempt to reach out for the return of her letter. She did not need the paper back to have the awkward words of her father ringing through her mind.

And it was hardly her place to interrupt the happy words of a newly wedded wife.

Envy was an unpleasant emotion. It prickled and stung as it meandered through the chest and into the heart, poisoning everything as it went.

It was not as if two people could not be happy at one time,

or that Gwen's happiness marked or prevented her own. It was simply that Rilla could not help but feel sad. There was something unpleasant about the idea that she herself would never—

'And have you met Rilla's earl?' Sylvia's voice said, cutting through her thoughts.

Rilla opened her mouth immediately. 'He is not my—'

'He approached you right in this room,' said Sylvia, with a triumphant air that was most disconcerting. 'And at Hyde Park—the cheek of the man! He must admire you greatly to do such a thing.'

'An earl?' Gwen's voice was all curiosity. 'Who is your earl, Rilla?'

'He is not my—'

'Well, he's certainly not mine,' chortled Sylvia. 'I think you've made quite an impression there.'

Nausea blossomed up in Rilla's chest.

I think you've made quite an impression there. Her father's words echoed through time. *And His Lordship wishes to end the engagement. What in God's name did you do?*

'Rilla? Rilla, are you quite well?'

Try as she might, Rilla could not force down the sickening feeling sweeping over her chest. Her fingers gripped Sylvia's tightly, a mooring stilling her in a storm.

'Rilla? Should we send for a doctor? She's awfully pale, and she's not responding…'

'I am quite well,' lied Rilla, hoping she had injected sufficient warmth into her voice. 'Quite well.'

End the engagement. Well, the Earl of Porthaethwy was perfectly entitled to walk away, since they had not yet wed. It was just a betrothal. Just the sum of her hopes and dreams. Just an insult to herself and her family when he walked away, right there, at the altar. Just—

'Oh, bother, there's my coachman,' Gwen declared. Rilla

heard a trace of anger in her voice. 'And I had hoped to tell you— Blast. I'll have to go.'

'Go?'

'Do not ever marry a man without meeting his mother. That's all I'll say, Sylvia,' Gwen said in a dark tone as her voice shifted. She had stood up. 'I'm expected back for dinner, and I'll need to change and—'

Rilla allowed her friends' chatter to wash over her. The moment had passed. Their attention was no longer fixed on her.

Which was all to the good, she attempted to tell herself a few hours later, as she was putting the final touches to her toilette before one of the Pike's official dinners. Attention on her was never good.

Especially when offered by arrogant earls who thought they could merely walk up to a woman and have her swoon into his arms...

Look, I'm trying to butter you up here. The least you could do is—

Enjoy it?

'Another Wallflower Academy dinner,' Rilla said with a sigh as she gently lifted a long string of jade beads over her head, arranging them over the bodice of her gown. 'Another chance for the wallflowers to impress. Or, as the case may be...'

It was a good idea in the main, she supposed. The Pike had instituted six official dinners with members of the *ton* during the Season, hosting them at the Academy itself.

All in the attempt to marry off her charges.

Rilla did not wait for Sylvia this time. She knew the way well enough, and Matthews, judging by the scent of boot polish, was holding his usual station at the bottom of the staircase. The chatter in the drawing room was loud, but Rilla did not bother to approach.

Why should she? There would be naught but awkward conversation, loud chatter masking the sound of her footsteps, and the chance that some fool had moved a chair.

That was the last thing she needed—to fall flat on her face. No, the dining room was safer.

Only twice did Rilla wonder, as she stepped across the hall and made her way to the dining room, whether Finlay was in the room filled with all the noise.

Only twice. Which was impressive, Rilla decided as she opened the door and stepped forward, hands reaching for the chair at the end of the table. The warm wood met her fingertips. Because she had thought about Finlay almost constantly while dressing for dinner.

One, two, three...

Rilla counted the chairs as she moved down the left-hand side of the table. Ten—a large dinner then, at least twenty-two.

Pulling out the chair right at the end of the table, so as to keep out of the way as best as possible, she sat and waited for the gong.

It was not long. The sonorous noise echoed around the house and the door opened. Footsteps, many and heavy, laughter and hands clapping on backs, mutterings and noise...it was overwhelming.

Rilla was relieved she had chosen to seat herself before the racket assaulted her ears. It was so much harder to concentrate on navigating, on finding her way around—

'Miss Newell,' said a voice that was far too familiar. 'We meet again.'

Rilla's stomach dropped out of her chest, through the chair, and into the floor. 'Sylvia.'

The word had slipped from her mouth before she could stop it.

The Earl of Staromchor cleared his throat. 'N-no, it's not— it's Finlay.'

Trying her best not to panic, sheer irritation driving her forward, Rilla snapped, 'Where is Sylvia?'

'Don't get your bloomers all knotted up,' came a clear voice across the hubbub, causing gasps from some and mutters of, 'My word!' from others. 'I'm coming!'

Rilla suppressed a smile. Well, no matter what else happened in the world, there was always Sylvia. Always the same.

'Get out of my— I live here, you know. If you don't move—'

'What on earth is she doing?' breathed the gentleman now seated beside her.

Rilla stiffened, a cold wash of terror flowing over her again. *Had he not taken the hint? Had he truly seated himself beside her?*

'Sylvia is my…my…'

The words were impossible to say as shame poured into her chest.

All she had to do was squash down all feeling, she told herself sternly. Force away all hints of desire, pretend she didn't want to converse with him…

But it was no use. The man intrigued her, most annoyingly, though she would be mistress of herself. She would focus on the dinner, and not the dinner guest.

Oh, how she hated these dinners. She had asked the Pike again and again if she could be excused from them, yet the woman had not accepted her more than reasonable request. And so she had made a bargain—an agreement, with Sylvia.

A Sylvia who was panting as she sat on Rilla's other side. 'Honestly, the state of some of these men. I would hardly call them gentlemen!'

'Neither would I,' Rilla said pointedly to Finlay—to the Earl of Staromchor, she corrected herself—before turning back to Sylvia. 'You…you will assist me?'

'Always,' came Sylvia's prompt response without any hint of embarrassment.

Some of the tension that had crept into Rilla's shoulders melted away. There was no one she could depend on quite like Sylvia.

And besides, she could feed herself, and dress herself, and walk confidently with a cane; she was no child! It was, however, helpful if someone arranged the food on her plate in a set way, so she could easily find it, and then place the cutlery in her hands. Sylvia had sat beside her for every meal at the Wallflower Academy for just such a purpose.

'I actually wished to speak to you privately,' came Finlay's voice on her right.

Rilla ensured that her expression remained perfectly still. 'And yet you cannot.'

'But I—'

'We are at dinner,' she pointed out coldly, hoping the man would take the hint.

Honestly, were all earls this dim-witted?

'Privacy is impossible.'

Thank goodness.

In the quiet of her own mind, Rilla knew how deeply she was tempted. There was something about this man. Not merely his persistence, which made no sense before one even started.

No, it was something else. When she had first spoken to him, believing he was nothing more than a footman...

Well, it had been like talking to Matthews. And yet nothing like talking to Matthews. There had been warmth, and ease, and comfort.

And now she would have to forget all that, push it away most decidedly, and concentrate on what was before her.

What was before her?

'Some sort of meat and vegetables,' said Sylvia's voice, as though she had heard the silent question. 'Smells good, if you ask me.'

'Chicken,' said Rilla nonchalantly. 'Seasoned with dill, sprigs of rosemary from the garden to garnish. Honey-roasted parsnips, burnt slightly, I believe, along with winter peas and what I believe are boiled potatoes. Yes, definitely boiled.'

Well, it was hardly difficult. They all had noses, didn't they?

She reached out for the napkin she knew would be just to the left of her plate.

It was not there.

'Allow me,' came a quiet voice she was attempting to ignore.

Rilla's fingers splayed out in a futile attempt to stop the inevitable. Finlay merely moved around her. The sudden sensation of her napkin on her lap was intrusive, but so much more was the sense that he had leaned forward, invading her personal space…

Bringing a scent of sandalwood and lemons. A warmth, his breathing fluttering on her skin. The sense that if she just leaned forward, just an inch, she would touch—

'I just wish to talk with you,' came Finlay's soft voice. He must have leaned back, for the sound was not as loud as she had expected. 'There is no crime in that, Miss Newell.'

Rilla snorted. *No crime, indeed.*

'I have no interest in talking to an earl.'

'If I could take off the title to please you, I would,' came the sardonic reply. 'But as that isn't possible, do you think you could remove your prejudice?'

It was most difficult to glare at someone you could not see, but Rilla attempted it nonetheless.

The whole dining room was filled with chatter now—mostly the gentlemen to each other, as far as she could hear. The wallflowers of the Academy were not known for their comfort in the presence of so many people.

Hoping to goodness her words would be hidden under the noise, Rilla said darkly, 'I don't want to talk to you, my lord.'

'Finlay.'

'My lord,' Rilla repeated, gripping her hands tightly together in her lap. 'And I'm hungry. Sylvia?'

Feeling exposed as she always did when it came to mealtimes, but a thousand times more now that she had such a brigand to her right, she parted her lips.

And waited.

'She's talking to the gentleman on her left,' came Finlay's voice. 'M-may I?'

The hesitation in his voice sounded genuine, but Rilla's stomach lurched. How could one tell? How could any gentleman be trusted when she could not look into their eyes and know, for certain, their intentions?

Her stomach growled.

Oh, this was ridiculous. It was only food, wasn't it?

'You may cut up the chicken,' Rilla said stiffly. 'And…and then place the fork in my hand.'

There was a noise on her plate. Then the scraping noise on the crockery ended, and Rilla waited.

The arrival of the fork in her hand was gentle. Then came the brush of a thumb over her palm, and a rush of heat poured up her arm.

Don't think about it.

She speared a piece of chicken and lifted the fork to her mouth, chewed, and swallowed her mouthful in silence, relieved yet slightly surprised that the earl had not spoken. Her heart thundered, her stomach churned—because of the chicken, Rilla tried to convince herself—and she forced her breathing to remain regular.

'More?' His voice was soft, intimate, his breath warm on her neck.

He must be leaning close to her, Rilla thought as her head spun. Oh, God, but it was so sensual. So intimate.

'Y-yes, please,' she breathed.

This time she waited expectantly as he cut more chicken and returned the fork to her. Waited for his fingers brushing against hers. Her breath caught in her throat. And then his fingers returned, lingering this time, sliding against hers.

Rilla knew she shouldn't be enjoying this, shouldn't be permitting a man, any man, to do this.

And in public!

So why did this feel so…so…?

Good grief.

She wasn't starting to…to trust him, was she?

'I've never gained so much enjoyment,' came Finlay's quiet voice, 'from food. Not ever before.'

Rilla hastily swallowed as her fingers tightened around her fork. 'If you think I'm going to let you—'

'Don't you enjoy this?'

Damn and blast, the man was incorrigible.

'If you don't want to be thrown out by the—by Miss Pike,' she amended swiftly, 'I would recommend stopping.'

'You don't like it when we touch?'

Heat blossomed in her chest and Rilla knew it was too much to hope that the colour, whatever it was, had not reached her décolletage. The man was…was flirting with her.

Flirting! With her!

'If you can't behave, I shall have to ask Sylvia to—'

'I can behave,' came Finlay's quiet voice, and Rilla felt the loss of his presence as he moved back, a sense of emptiness around her. 'I can behave.'

Very much doubting that, yet unable to stop herself, Rilla sighed. 'Then…then you may help me.'

'And…?'

'Don't talk to me,' Rilla said darkly, wondering what on earth she thought she was doing. 'Consider it a compromise.'

Chapter Six

I can behave.

Then...then you may feed me.

And...?

Don't talk to me. Consider it a compromise.

Finlay jerked away as the half dream, half memory faded into immediately obscurity.

Damn. It had been remarkably pleasant, too.

'And that is why the modiste absolutely has to be a French-woman,' said the Dowager Countess of Staromchor sternly, the carriage rocking the three of them side to side. 'In truth, Miss Carr, I do not see how you can advocate any other.'

Finlay blinked blearily at his mother, seated directly opposite him in the Staromchor carriage, and then his gaze slid to the woman beside her.

Miss Isabelle Carr.

She was not flushing at his mother's rudeness, nor stammering her objection to the woman's demands.

No, she was just looking out of the window as the carriage rattled down the Brighton streets. No expression tinged her face, nothing at all. It was curiously empty.

'Miss Carr?' Finlay's mother said sharply.

Finlay winced as Isabelle turned to his mother with a blank, almost confused expression.

'I beg your pardon,' she said quietly. 'Did you say something?'

He had known it would be a bad idea from the very start.

Of course he had; it had been his mother's. The dowager countess had been absolutely certain that all he and Isabelle needed to spark more romance between them—her words— was time together. Time to enjoy each other's company. Time to fall in love.

Poppycock.

She had insisted, however, and Finlay was hardly in a position to deny her. It appeared that Isabelle had been unable to argue with his mother, either. That, or she simply did not care.

And so a trip to Brighton was decided. A week there, no more. A chance to take the waters, enjoy the sights, see Prinny if they were lucky, and attend the Assembly Rooms. Brighton was a place, his mother had assured both of them, that no one would suspect the engagement. It was easier to keep it quiet, she had said. There had been enough gossip about the Carr family, in the dowager countess's acidic tone, to last a lifetime. So, Brighton it was.

Which was where they were headed now.

'Hard to believe the wedding isn't that far away.' His mother beamed with a knowing look. 'And once your happiness is all tidily sorted, I can see to my own.'

Finlay rolled his eyes at that. As though his mother did not prioritize her own happiness already. Why, from the bills that had arrived from the modiste last week, and that dinner she'd thrown—

'Don't you roll your eyes at me, young man.'

He smiled weakly. 'My apologies, Mother.'

His mother sniffed. 'I should think so. Here I am, a widow.'

Finlay groaned this time, though with a wry smile. It wasn't as though he hadn't heard it all before, after all.

'Losing your father so long ago, and here I am, without the continuation of the line,' the dowager countess continued with a glint of steel in her eye. 'Something you are, at least, going to finally correct in the near future.'

It took all Finlay's self-control not to look at Isabelle, which unfortunately meant that he had little left over to prevent his cheeks from reddening.

Well, really! Talking about such a thing before Isabelle!

'You look troubled, Miss Carr,' said the dowager countess with a raised eyebrow. 'Why, I would almost say that there was something on your mind. Pray, tell.'

Finlay looked again at the woman he would be marrying in just a few short months. Not that the *ton* knew that yet.

His mother was right. Isabelle did look distracted. At least, she did not appear to be attending to those she was seated with in the carriage.

Cheeks flushing, the younger woman reached into her reticule, pulled out what appeared to be two letters, seals broken, and offered them to Finlay with a trembling hand.

He couldn't help but notice the tremble. Dear God, what had happened to her? The Isabelle Carr he had known before she had disappeared off to that godforsaken finishing school had once trounced him so hard in chess, she had crowed all day and been sent to her bedchamber for unsportsmanlike behaviour.

Isabelle had argued that as she was not a sportsman, it did not matter. Then she had climbed out of her window down the wisteria and made faces at him, Cecil, and Bartlett through the dining room windows.

Where was that woman now?

'I… I am afraid… Well, I did not expect any more, but…'

Isabelle pressed the letters into Finlay's hand as he wished to goodness she would just call him Fin, as she'd used to.

The letters were cold against his fingers. He did not need to look to see what they were.

More debts.

'Oh, dear, how frightfully uncomfortable for us all,' said his mother, quite unnecessarily. She whipped out her fan and fluttered it, as though that would make the unpleasant sight of bills disappear. 'Dearie me.'

Finlay quickly pocketed them. 'Thank you, Miss Carr,' he said formally, as was required of him. 'I will pay them the moment we return to London.'

Isabelle did not reply. She had already turned away, hands clasped together in her lap, gaze directed out the window.

It was not as though she could see much. The autumnal evenings had drawn in faster than Finlay had expected and night had fallen early that afternoon. Grey clouds had gathered on the horizon, and though the expected downpour had not yet occurred, he would be surprised if they returned to their lodgings in the dry.

But between now and then...

'Ah, here we are,' announced the dowager countess, all hints of debts and money forgotten. 'The Assembly Rooms. I have heard the food is much improved since we were last here—not that it could be much worse! Indeed, as I told Lady...'

Finlay allowed his mother to witter on as he stepped from the carriage and offered a hand to Isabelle. She took it, descended without meeting his eye, then waited silently on the pavement for the dowager countess to descend.

For a moment, he was tempted to say something.

Do you miss him?

Do you wonder why? Why him? Why us?

Do you ever think...?

'I see they haven't lit the place any better,' sniffed the dowager countess.

Finlay jumped. Evidently he had helped his mother from their carriage without noticing.

'Not nearly enough candles,' his mother continued, striding forward without waiting for either of her two younger charges. 'I shall have to speak to someone about that.'

Finlay had never liked Brighton, and he was reminded of why as he entered the Assembly Rooms with Isabelle on his arm.

The place was crowded. Once again more people had been

admitted than was proper, and they were all paying the price for it. Not a single person appeared comfortable in the crush, and the multitude of candles and smoke from the many cigars heated the room up something terrible.

And worst of all, there was no one of his close acquaintance to be seen. It was to be expected. They were not, after all, in London. And yes, it was mollifying in part to see so many pretty young ladies immediately turning to him and smiling, beaming at his handsome features, the expensive cut of his coat, the way he was immediately at home in any room.

But for some reason, the typical pleasure Finlay gained from being so admired…it felt lacking. Not that there was an absence of it, but it lacked the potency of the past.

Don't talk to me. Consider it a compromise.

An unbidden smile crept across his face as warmth flickered through his chest. A teasing remark from Rilla was suddenly far more pleasurable than the sycophantic expressions of a dozen women. Which did not make sense.

Fawning was already occurring ahead of him. Evidently someone had realized that a dowager countess had entered the place, for there were two gentlemen already offering his mother food, drinks, and likely as not the chance to redesign the decor of the place.

Finlay glanced at Isabelle. Her eyes were downcast. Her lips were pressed together, not pursed in an attitude of judgement or thought. They were merely closed, with no expectation that they would open.

When had it suddenly become so difficult to speak to the woman? If he had met Isabelle now, he would have described her as dull.

Dull? The woman who had, at the age of seventeen, smeared her father's telescope with ink and paid off all the servants not to tell him for three whole days!

Dull? The child who had learned to swim by pushing Cecil into a river and been forced to rescue him!

Dull? The woman who, when she had written to her brother upon first arriving at the Trinderhaus School for Young Ladies, had described her companions with such boldness that he had almost split his waistcoat laughing!

Where was that Isabelle?

Finlay's gaze flickered over the woman who would in a short time be his wife, and he felt nothing. What on earth was he doing? This was madness: he'd had doubts about the suitability of this match the instant he'd offered it. Did it really help Isabelle to be tied to a man who could not love her?

Surely there was a way to… Well, end the engagement. Only a few people knew about it, so the scandal would not be overtly disastrous. Did…did she wish to end it?

'Isabelle,' he said awkwardly.

'George,' Isabelle breathed.

Finlay frowned. 'What do you— Oh, thank God.'

Shoulders relaxing the instant he saw a familiar face, he steered them towards a table covered in canapés and slapped the arm of the man with his back to them.

'What the devil are you doing here?'

Lord Bartlett turned, mouth full, and sprayed pastry all down his front. 'Isabelle!'

Chuckling as his friend reddened, trying to put down the canapés he was holding and brush the pastry from his front at the same time, Finlay felt a surge of relief. Well, at least there was one person here he could speak to. And, if he were careful…

'Didn't expect you to be here, Staromchor,' Bartlett was saying, his tone easier now he was no longer covered in flakes of pastry. 'Isabelle—Miss Carr, I mean…'

'I did not know you were in Brighton,' Isabelle said in a rush, voice low and eyes downcast.

And Finlay saw his opportunity.

Well, it wasn't as though they didn't know each other. They had grown up together; they all had! And it would give him a chance not to speak awkwardly to his betrothed for five minutes together. That was a risk he had to take.

'Bartlett, you wouldn't mind taking care of Isabelle for me for a few minutes, would you?' Finlay said, speaking over the two of them.

Both Bartlett and Isabelle were staring.

'Taking care of her?' Bartlett said.

'A few minutes?' repeated Isabelle.

'Excellent,' said Finlay firmly, lifting her hand from his arm and placing it on Bartlett's. 'I just need to— I have to...'

His voice trailed away as he stepped from them, hoping Bartlett would forgive him for abandoning Isabelle in his lap.

There was just a small twinge of guilt as Finlay helped himself to a glass of wine, downed it, then gave it back to the footman who had offered it.

Cecil would not have approved.

It was a painful thought, and one he could not ignore. He had attempted to do what was right by Isabelle, and he was certain Cecil would have approved of that. The marriage, that was.

The abandoning Isabelle because Finlay just didn't know what to do with a woman so changed...

Probably Cecil would not have approved of that part.

He had attempted to be honourable. He was doing the best he could. What else could Finlay do—just watch his best friend's sister fall into penury?

No. No, he had taken steps against that. These thoughts that pained him, that reminded him Isabelle was hurting just as much as he was, that eventually the name of Cecil would have to be mentioned between them, that if he entered into a marriage like this he would be lonely for the rest of his life...

Finlay would certainly have done something about those

thoughts, rattling through his mind like a barouche without any concern for its passengers, except for—

Except for a flash of something in the corner of his eye.

It was just a movement. A moment. If he hadn't spent so much time in the carriage thinking about Marilla, perhaps the genteel movement of a woman ten feet away would not have caught his interest.

But he had been thinking of her, and so Finlay did look around when he saw a woman who looked remarkably like her. The same dark black hair, the same figure, the same bearing. So similar, in fact, that a twinge of guilt crept into his heart as he looked over.

Isabelle deserved better than that—better than him. If he didn't get his act together…

Finlay blinked.

It wasn't a woman who looked like Marilla.

It was Marilla.

'I said,' came an irate voice with the force of a gale, 'are you going to ask Miss Carr to dance?'

Finlay blinked for a second time. This time his view of Marilla—*Marilla! What on earth was she doing here?*—was blocked by a woman of more advanced years and significantly advanced irritation.

'Mother,' he said weakly.

'I have been attempting to speak with you for nigh on five minutes,' said the Dowager Countess of Staromchor with a glare.

An exaggeration, Finlay was sure. Certainly he could not have been so lost in his thoughts that he had… Well, perhaps it was five minutes. It couldn't have been!

'And you're not listening again,' intoned his mother darkly. 'What are you thinking about?'

Finlay swallowed, and knew he could not tell the truth. And so, unusually for him, he told a lie. 'Cecil.'

His mother's face immediately softened. 'You dwell too much on the past, my dear.'

'It is hard not to,' he said honestly.

'And yet you have the future to look forward to, a future with a good woman,' his mother pointed out. 'Honestly, Staromchor, anyone else would hope that you had romance on your mind!'

She fluttered her fan suggestively and waggled her eyebrows over its ribbon.

Finlay's stomach lurched. It wasn't possible, surely, that his mother had guessed… But then, he had acted in a most outrageous way at the latest Wallflower Academy dinner. It had occurred over a week ago, and he had half expected the scandal sheets to mention the disgraceful way that he had been seen feeding Marilla.

It wasn't his stomach that lurched this time, but something a little further down.

Flirt. That was what Bartlett had said. Was there anything more flirtatious than that?

And the man was right. He did feel better for it.

'I must say, I am delighted Isabelle is starting to finally worm her way into your heart,' Finlay's mother said with an approving nod.

Finlay's jaw dropped. Then he cleared his throat and closed his mouth swiftly, as though he had always intended to do that.

His heart—Isabelle?

How could his mother be so wrong?

'And while on the subject of your betrothed,' the dowager countess said with a beady eye, 'I think you have been remiss.'

Finlay frowned. 'Remiss?'

Had he not done everything in his power to sort out the tangled mess Cecil had left? Had not every debt been paid? Had he not offered marriage, the one thing left in his power, to the woman who would otherwise be left alone in the world with no one to—

'You have barely spoken to her since we arrived, you know,' his mother said sternly. 'You palmed her off to that Bartlett boy!'

'That Bartlett boy' had a moustache, was over six feet tall, and had punched a man clean out in the boxing ring last Tuesday.

Finlay said none of this. 'Bartlett knows Isabelle just as well as I.'

'But he is not engaged to be married to her,' his mother pointed out sharply. 'You are.'

He was. And Finlay was going to do precisely what was required of him, as soon as he stopped staring past his mother's shoulder at Miss Newell.

Miss Newell, who was alone. How was that possible? Where was Sylvia, the Pike, others from the Wallflower Academy?

'Outrageous that you aren't dancing with Miss Carr,' the dowager countess was saying, half to him, half it seemed to herself. 'What people will say, I don't know.'

'I don't care what people will say,' Finlay said before he could stop himself.

It was now his mother who was in the corner of his eye; all his attention was taken up with the radiant Miss Newell. A Miss Newell who was wearing a gown of elegant blue silk, a foil to her hair and her colouring, one hand clutching that cane of hers.

'Society will talk,' his mother was saying. 'It's the look of the thing that we have to worry about. If it looks—'

'I don't care how things will look,' Finlay said, ignoring his mother's outrage and incoherent splutters. 'It would be abominably rude of me not to greet an acquaintance.'

His heart almost skipped a beat as he waited for his mother to respond.

The dowager countess was biting her lip. 'I suppose that's true.'

'I wish to speak to Miss Newell.' And before he could

change his mind, before any hesitancy could enter his chest, he pushed past his mother and approached…

Marilla.

She was standing on her own at the side of the Assembly Rooms. Evidently her companions, whoever she had come with, had been asked to dance. Marilla Newell, however, was clasping a dance card utterly unmarked with pencil, her gaze downcast.

Finlay cleared his throat and, fighting the urge to put his hand on her arm, said quietly, 'It is I, Miss Newell. Finlay Jellicoe. Earl of… It's Finlay.'

Why, precisely, he did not wish to speak about his title, he could not fathom. Well. Marilla—Miss Newell—had given him plenty of reasons to cease speaking of such a thing. Her broken engagement, a topic which he dearly wished to speak on, had to play some part of that.

But to despise him so utterly merely because he shared a peerage with a cad?

'Staromchor?' Rilla's eyes widened, her cheeks flushing most prettily.

And she had no idea, Finlay realized with a strange lurch in his chest. No idea how tantalizing she looked to him in that moment. No idea how close he was…

Although apparently she did. Miss Newell took a step back, thankfully missing a footman who was transporting a silver tray of empty glasses, and frowned.

'What…what are you doing here?' she breathed.

Finlay tried to smile, then remembered she could not see the expression, and shrugged.

Damn and blast, but he was a fool.

'It's the Assembly Rooms,' he said feebly. 'In Brighton. Much of the *ton* is here.'

'But this is Brighton,' Miss Newell said, most unnecessarily. Her voice caught.

Did he make her breathless?

'It is indeed,' Finlay said, his smile finally natural. 'I might ask you what you are doing here, far from the safety of the Wallflower Academy.'

Miss Newell scoffed. 'I need no such safety. I am hardly about to be ravished by a passing gentleman.'

Fighting all his instincts to tell her that she was indeed most ravishing, and he would be more than happy to offer his services, Finlay instead accidentally bit his tongue.

God in heaven—he was supposed to be flirting with her! *Say something, man!*

'And what are you doing here?' Miss Newell asked, bearing the conversational burden. 'Not in the Assembly Rooms, I mean. In Brighton.'

Finlay hesitated. There was so much he could tell her. So much. About Cecil, and his death, and how much it hurt. About Isabelle, and the Carr family debts, and how he was trying to do the right thing but it was a millstone around his neck and every moment he thought about it the rope grew tighter.

About how changed Isabelle was, and their marriage of convenience, and Bartlett's words a few weeks ago about a flirtation and joy and a last hurrah before succumbing to the drudgery of the married state.

About how his mother had dragged him here, and there was nothing he could do but allow himself to be swept away by the storm of the decisions he had made. Decisions he had made before he had ever met Miss Marilla Newell.

'S-Staromchor?' Miss Newell's sightless eyes flickered over him, around him, her voice uncertain. 'You...you are still there, aren't you?'

There was a flinty sharpness in the depths of that voice. Here was a woman, Finlay was starting to see, who assumed the worst of people. Did she really think he would just walk away without declaring the conversation at an end?

Or was this merely another method of hers to keep people away?

'I am still here,' he said softly.

Something like a shadow of a smile flickered across Miss Newell's face. 'I thought so.'

'How could you tell?'

'The world is different when you are close.'

Heat evidently blossomed over her cheeks and was mirrored by the heat in his own. Finlay could never have hoped for such a sign of her regard, but—

'I should not have said that.'

'I am glad you did,' returned Finlay, his heart skipping a painful beat. 'And I wish you would call me Finlay.'

He did not have to listen for the shock; he could see it on her face and in the way her breasts rose with the sudden intake of breath. Every part of his notice seemed attuned to Miss Newell.

'Why on earth would you wish that?' she said softly.

Finlay grinned, wishing to goodness she could see him. This whole conversation would be so much easier if he could reply with a mere sparkle in his eyes, a look of wicked mischief.

As it was, he was forced to say aloud, 'Because...because I wish to call you Marilla.'

It was an intimate request—but then, when a man had fed a woman by hand, in public, such things ceased to be so wicked. At least, in his mind.

Evidently not in Miss Newell's. 'And why on earth would I give an earl permission to do that?'

'You know, the least you could do is attempt to see past my title,' Finlay said with just a hint of irritation.

It wasn't until Miss Newell raised a sardonic eyebrow that he realized his error.

'Ah. Erm...figure of speech,' he mumbled.

Damn and blast it, he would have to go and say something

like that! Attempt to see past his title? He had to say that...to a blind woman?

'I know what you meant,' Miss Newell said softly, and there appeared to be real understanding in her voice. 'Lord knows, you aren't the first to fall foul of a slip of the tongue.'

And a roar of anger, unbidden and uncontained and most unexpected, rose in Finlay's throat.

'Who the devil has done that?'

'Oh, most people,' Miss Newell said, seemingly misunderstanding his ire. 'Do not concern yourself, my lord. I do not take offence, not any longer. I am more than a match for them.'

Yet there was a tired lilt to her voice that suggested something else. Some other kind of injury.

'You don't have to push people away all the time.'

'Yes, I do,' she said firmly, a renewed strength in her voice. 'I always do, and I always will. Besides, I like being alone.'

Finlay had not intended to speak the obvious truth, but there it was. 'No, you don't.'

A flicker—just for a moment, it looked like she was about to say something. But she could not deny it, even if the flush in her cheeks suggested she did not appreciate him stating it.

Finlay swallowed. 'I still wish to call you Marilla.'

The words had slipped from his mouth before he could stop them, but Finlay saw to his surprise that Miss Newell did not shy away from his tenderness.

Her lips curled into a smile. 'I suppose you do. But the people I like call me Rilla.'

Oh, hell. What did that mean?

'So,' said Finlay, desperately attempting to calculate precisely what the best approach here was. It would be so much easier if there weren't so much noise in this place, the music and the chatter rising to such a pitch that his ears seemed full. 'So...'

It appeared for a moment that she was not going to put him out of his misery. Then she dipped her gaze to her hands.

'You may call me Marilla, I suppose,' she said airily, as though she had bestowed a great gift. 'I am still not sure about you, Finlay Jellicoe.'

A barb of boiling-hot steel pierced his heart as Finlay grinned like a dolt. Hearing his name on her lips—it was almost as potent as being given permission to speak her name.

Almost.

'Marilla,' he breathed, wishing he were closer to her. 'Marilla…'

'But you must wish to return to your party,' Marilla said, the stiffness which had momentarily melted away now returning to ice over her expression. She turned to look towards the dancers, her face impassive. 'Do not let me detain you.'

Finlay closed the gap between the two of them. Perhaps it was not very politic. Perhaps others would stare, and gossip would arise, and Isabelle would see and break off the engagement.

He stepped back. 'I have no wish to return to my party.'

Marilla raised an eyebrow. 'You…you do not?'

Finlay shook his head, muttered a curse under his breath that was thankfully lost in the thrum of applause and warm laughter as a dance ended and the assembly applauded both dancers and musicians, and knew what he was about to say was a dreadful mistake.

A mistake he wanted to make.

'I would rather spend time with you, Marilla,' Finlay said softly. 'I find that lately, I would always rather spend time with you.'

Chapter Seven

But really, this was a most ridiculous idea. Of all the people who could be chosen for such an idiotic, unthinking, preposterous—

'I know I can rely on you,' said the Pike sternly as a wall of noise hit Rilla in the face.

It was almost unbearable. Like losing another sense. The barrage of noise was heavy like iron, a painful medley of sharp and soft. Sharp like the clack of heels on marble, the slam of a door, the clink of a glass hitting stone, shattering. Soft like the rush of fabrics, the gentle laughter, the susurration of a thousand voices murmuring.

Rilla staggered slightly, putting out her hand to she knew not where, the other grasping her cane. Damned cane. All it did was remind her of her difference.

Oh, God, she had known this would be a mistake. She should have put her foot down, refused point-blank to come. One would think, after all, that her almost complete lack of sight would protect her from such nonsense.

How on earth would she navigate such a situation?

'I've got you,' came Sylvia's quiet voice.

There came a hand on her arm, a steadying sensation, the world righting itself…but the noise was still incredible.

Where had the Pike brought them, a cattle market?

'The Assembly Rooms at Brighton are most impressive,' the Pike's voice continued, as though she had neither noticed nor cared just how unsettled Rilla had become. 'You can see, Miss Smith— Miss Smith, are you attending?'

From the fractious tone of the woman, Rilla presumed Daphne was not.

'I am sorry, Miss Pike.'

'I did not choose the three of you to attend me on this trip to Brighton merely for my own benefit,' snapped the curt voice of the Wallflower Academy proprietress. 'You three have been my charges the longest, and it is time you put what you have learned in my lessons to good use—in public!'

'And yet here I am, and I can't think of a single thing I've learned in that damned lesson of hers,' Sylvia muttered in Rilla's ear.

Rilla attempted to nod. They were no longer moving, which was a great relief, but it was still highly disconcerting.

She did not like leaving the Wallflower Academy. Not because its environs were particularly pleasing. No, it was that once Rilla had grown accustomed to the layout of a place, it was highly unsettling to be dropped somewhere entirely unfamiliar. The corridors of the Wallflower Academy were well known to her, her seat in the drawing room, her place at the pianoforte, her knitting bag. Even the gardens held no surprises for her.

It was all hers, and everything right where she expected it to be.

But this…venturing out to Brighton, of all places, a carriage ride away and with none of the certainty she relied upon…

Rilla's jaw tightened.

To be reduced to a dependent.

Sylvia's hand had remained on her arm. 'Let's find a quiet place near the wall, shall we?'

Rilla attempted to show her gratitude through her lack of complaining, though wasn't sure whether her friend understood the great effort.

Miss Pike chattered on with every step. 'And as chaperone,

I am expecting you, Miss Newell, to provide a careful examination of—'

'Miss Pike,' Rilla said, her tongue loosening as she and Sylvia came to a stop. Yes, she could feel the sense of a wall behind her. Good. That would reduce the approaches that strangers could make. 'What on earth did you think you were doing, bringing me here?'

There was a hesitation, a momentary silence. She presumed the proprietress of the Wallflower Academy was looking, bewildered, at the two other wallflowers.

Rilla had once asked Sylvia to explain what bewildered looked like. Oh, she knew how it felt. That strange dizziness in one's mind, the sense the world was shifting, an inability to understand what on earth had happened.

But what did it look like?

'Why, I brought you to act as chaperone for Miss Bryant and Miss—'

'And how precisely do you expect me to do that,' Rilla interrupted, as sweetly as she could manage. 'Considering I cannot see?'

It was perhaps a tad harsh. Lord knew, Miss Pike had never treated her poorly due to her lack of sight. But still, Rilla had had enough. Wrenched from the one place she felt comfortable, suffering motion sickness all the way along the coastal road, then forced out of their snug lodgings to attend a gathering in which she could not participate?

No. Not without protest.

'Ah,' came the voice of the Pike.

Rilla heard what appeared to be a snort. It came from Sylvia's general direction.

'I suppose it will be difficult for you to—'

'Miss?' said a new voice. A low one, a dark one—a man's voice. 'Though we have not had the pleasure of being introduced, would you do me the honour of dancing with me? Mr Jones is the name.'

Rilla forced down a smile. Well, it was equal odds which of her friends the man had approached. Both Daphne and Sylvia, apparently, were very pretty. Refined. Elegant.

The response of the Pike, on the other hand…

'Not properly introduced!' she was saying, in full flow. 'No, no, I am sorry, young man, this simply won't do. Come on, we'll find the master of ceremonies. You too, Sylvia.'

'But—'

'But me no buts,' uttered the woman grimly. 'Miss Newell, you stay there. You…you just stay there.'

Footsteps sounded, hurried and accompanied by the continued muttering of the Pike, and started to drift away. And then they were gone, and Rilla was left alone.

Letting out a large sigh, she supposed it wasn't the end of the world. She had no difficulty in standing for long periods of time, and all she had to do was wait for the Pike's feet to tire and they would all return to their temporary lodgings.

In fact, it was pleasant to be left alone with her thoughts for five minutes. After that carriage ride and Sylvia's incessant chatter—

And then he was there. Before her. Finlay.

Words slipped from her mouth without much intervention from her mind, and before she knew it, Rilla had blurted out, 'But this is Brighton.'

If only her voice could remain steady and that she was not alone.

Oh, but that isn't true, is it? whispered a voice just in the back of her mind. *You haven't been able to stop thinking about him, have you? Why, in the carriage ride here when Sylvia was enumerating the multiple ways the Wallflower Academy had injured her, you allowed yourself to imagine—*

Their conversation meandered and Rilla found herself struggling to pay attention sufficiently to speak. Words that she was most certainly not going to say continuously threatened to burst from her lips.

I've never gained so much enjoyment from food. Not ever before.

If you think I'm going to let you—

Didn't you enjoy it?

What did he want from her?

None of that was appropriate to say. Admitting such a thing to anyone was shameful indeed, but to disclose to the very object of her desire that she was so conscious of him, so warmed by his presence? For that was what this was, wasn't it? Rilla had never felt anything like it before, and she had run the gamut of emotions in the past.

Fear, anger, joy, bitterness, regret…she had known them all.

But not desire. Not this delight that he was here, Finlay, in Brighton. Not this wish she could step closer to him, feel his skin against hers.

And then she was giving him the opportunity to leave, and he did not take it, and Rilla could not understand why he was being so…so odd. So attentive. So—

'I would rather spend time with you, Marilla.'

Rilla's lips parted.

How could he say such a thing, with calm, and equanimity, and a sense he was telling the absolute complete truth?

'Besides, I want to dance.'

A cold chill rushed across her collarbone. 'I am not stopping you.'

'No, but I'll need your hand,' returned Finlay with alacrity.

This time Rilla really did laugh. 'You are jesting.'

'Not in the slightest.'

'But…' He had to be jesting. Rilla could not see the man,

but honestly, he was being ridiculous! 'I... I don't know how,' she said quietly.

Admitting such a thing was an unpleasant experience. Rilla knew well the limitations the world placed upon her, and it was galling to admit that there was something she could not do.

Dancing was all very well at the Wallflower Academy ballroom, with the Pike shouting out instructions and no one likely to get in her way. That was different.

But here? In public? In the Brighton Assembly Rooms?

'My cane... I cannot possibly...'

'I'll give it to a serving woman. Here...'

It was pulled gently from her hands, her one anchor to time and space, and then she was at sea, utterly lost, ready to be buffeted back and forth in the noise and the clamour.

A hand rested on her arm, then came a tug. Rilla stepped forward, unable to resist the pull.

'Finlay...'

'You know, I do like it when you call me Finlay,' came the low, guttural voice of the man who appeared to be pulling her through a crowd of people. Rilla could feel fabrics brush up against her arms, just past her gloves. 'Though you should probably call me "my lord" now that we are in the line.'

And he was gone and Rilla panicked, flaring dread rising as she stood somewhere in the middle, she presumed, of a room filled with people.

'One step forward, curtsey,' Finlay said quietly.

It was not an order. Not quite.

True, there was a certainty in his speech that brooked no opposition. Here was a man who spoke and was accustomed to being obeyed.

And it wasn't as though she had much choice.

Rilla did not have to think. Her feet obeyed, her knees bending as she curtseyed towards a gentleman she could not see in a rush of other skirts either side of her.

'And back,' came his command.

A shiver of something hot and delicious rushed through Rilla's back. People did not order her about! She had her own thoughts, her own determination, her own—

And wasn't it wicked, being told what to do by such a man as this?

The music continued and for a moment she froze, unsure what to do, conscious of the many eyes now following her.

'Step left, right hand up,' came the now expected instructions. 'And back…'

It was a slow dance, for which Rilla was thankful. A fast dance would have made it impossible for Finlay to give her moment-by-moment directions, but her ear was so attuned to his voice now, she could make out even the slightest hint through the din of the dance.

And what a dance. Each time Finlay's hand touched hers, every time his presence thrummed beside her, Rilla could not deny the sensual attraction that flowed through her.

He was…

And she was…

In danger.

That was the thought that rose to the top of her whirling mind as Finlay promenaded her, slowly, down the set.

Feeling like this was not safe. Feeling like this about anyone was…was a weakness. It was a chance for them to hurt her, to disappoint her. To reduce her to something she was not.

Caring for this earl was only going to bring her pain, and she most certainly should not permit it.

When the dance ended, therefore, Rilla told herself sternly that her heart was thundering in her chest due to the efforts of the dance, and no other reason.

'Some fresh air?' Finlay's hand had taken hers again, placing it on his arm as her cane was pushed into her other palm.

She did not pull away.

Because I require someone to navigate for me, Rilla thought sternly.

For no other reason.

The Brighton Assembly Rooms surely had a balcony. That was her first thought after Finlay had woven their way through the hubbub of people—no sign of the Pike, thank goodness—and opened a door to reveal fresh air.

But when Rilla was guided down steps instead of onto a terrace into the night air, she started to realize they were not stepping outside, but leaving.

Leaving the Assembly Rooms. Alone.

The sharp scent of salt and the crunch of pebbles under her feet revealed a very different story.

'You…you have taken me to the beach!'

'Well, when in Rome. Brighton,' Finlay amended, and she could hear the laughter in his voice. 'Here, sit on my coat.'

It was most disorientating, lowering oneself not to a chair or sofa but to the crunch of pebbles. But there was something intoxicating about the sea breeze tugging at her curls, the smell of the sea and driftwood piercing in her nostrils, the gentle lapping of the sea not too far away.

And the warm presence of Finlay beside her.

'Now, tell me,' he said jovially, as though he frequently escorted wallflowers out of public places to interrogate them on beaches. 'What's next for Miss Marilla Newell?'

Rilla was nonplussed. Well, it was hardly an exciting question. 'The Pike will probably tire in an hour or two, and…'

'I don't mean tonight,' came his quiet voice.

'Oh,' she said, a mite unbalanced. 'Well. We do not intend to stay long in Brighton, and Sylvia—'

'No, I don't mean— I mean the future. Your future,' said Finlay. His voice was gentle, encouraging. 'You cannot intend to stay at the Wallflower Academy forever. Not a woman of your beauty and wit.'

Beauty and wit.

When was the last time someone had described her thus? Rilla could not recall. She could not recall it ever happening.

And perhaps it was the unseasonably warm breeze, or the lull of the tide, or the fact that her heart was still fluttering from the dance. Perhaps it was the rebellious nature of leaving the dance, the scandalous nature of being alone with an earl.

Whatever it was loosened her tongue. Rilla found herself saying, 'Well, whatever I intend to do, I can't... I won't go back home.'

A subtle sound was accompanied by a movement. Finlay appeared to be leaning back on his hands. 'And why is that?'

Rilla wet her lips.

How was it possible to feel so safe with a gentleman, and yet so in danger?

'I... I do not believe they would welcome my return. My sisters—one is married, and I have two younger who are unmarried—are awaiting my marriage or admission into spinsterhood, and then they can enter into Society.'

'I do not see why.'

'You know how it is The elder must marry before the younger enters Society. And in truth, I do not think my parents ever fully recovered from the scandal of my broken engagement,' Rilla said, more harshly than she had intended. 'With no brothers and an entailed estate, something has to be done and I am not the daughter to do it. A Newell wedding would blot all that out. My sister Nina's two babies have already done some of the work, bless her.'

The words had flowed before she could stop them, and she was not surprised at the silence from the gentleman beside her.

Yes, sometimes you just had to speak, and that speech would drive away the only man who had bothered to pay more than five minutes of attention to you. What had she been thinking? There was no reason for—

'That is…that is outrageous!' Finlay spluttered, voice breaking with seemingly suppressed emotion. 'Your broken— I am most certain it was not your fault, so why should you be punished for some brute's…? Damn. Oh, damn. Oh, fiddlesticks.'

Rilla was laughing now.

How could she not be?

'You do not have to fear. Sylvia swears like a sailor. There are few curses I have not heard.'

The almost inaudible chuckle made her heart skip a beat. 'I do apologize. It's just… Well, you are the most interesting woman I have met in…in a long time. And beautiful. The idea of not wishing to— I mean, any man who has eyes in his… damn.'

She did not even have the wherewithal to be offended.

What was Finlay trying to say? Was he…? No. He couldn't be.

'You are trying to seduce me.'

'Can you be seduced?'

'No,' said Rilla, perhaps a mite harsher than she had intended. 'So I wouldn't bother if I were you.'

'But half of the fun is the flirtation,' came Finlay's teasing voice. 'More than half, if the flirtation is of any calibre.'

Despite herself a slow smile crept over her face. 'And you believe you offer flirtation of a high calibre?'

It was a foolish thing to say. What did she know? How could she compare Finlay Jellicoe's flirting to any other man's?

No man had ever bothered.

There was a shifting movement beside her. Even if she had not felt the pebbles move, she would have known Finlay had moved to be closer to her. His scent was stronger, and she could feel the warmth of his chest as his shoulder touched hers.

And even without those two senses, she would have known. How, Rilla could not explain, but she would.

There was something about Finlay that made it impossible not to know when he was close.

'I only offer flirtation of the highest calibre.' His voice was warm, soft, smooth, enticing. It was a voice a woman could grow painfully accustomed to. 'And you may attempt to deny it, Marilla Newell, but you like me.'

She did like him, and she would deny it, if pushed.

This man—any man—was not supposed to charm her so utterly, so quickly. She was not supposed to think about that dance as shivers of heat shot through her body. She should not want to feel his hands on hers once more. To know his touch.

Well, there was only one way to nip that in the bud. Some good old Rilla Newell sarcasm.

'I knew you would be attracted to me,' she said airily, as though she said such things all the time. 'But you do not have to make it so obvious, my lord.'

Rilla expected a laugh. She expected a denial. At the very least, she expected him to rise, brush off the dirt from his breeches, then coldly suggest he return her to the Assembly Rooms.

What she did not expect was for a warm hand to graze her cheek, a thumb to part her lips, and a low voice to say, 'I'm going to kiss you now. Unless you want me to stop.'

Rilla wet her lips, mouth dry, and before she could speak, Finlay Jellicoe, Earl of Staromchor, was kissing her.

And oh, what a kiss. With searing heat and delicate power, his tongue teased her lips apart and lavished pleasure on her mouth such as Rilla could never have imagined.

Every part of her body had come alive. She could sense herself on the beach, kissing Finlay, in a way she had never known herself to feel. The temptation to lean back, pull him against her, feel the crush of his chest, the weight of him—

And then it was over.

Rilla blinked, her eyes dry.

Had she just...? Had he just...?

'Well,' she said with a long, low breath. 'As long as you don't fall in love with me, Your Lordship, I suppose I shall chalk that up to high spirits.'

It was a foolish thing to say. The moment she had said it, Rilla cringed.

She cringed even harder when the man seated beside her chuckled, a low rumble in his chest making her think of heat and the way he seemed to know precisely how she wanted to be kissed.

'I wouldn't worry about that,' came Finlay's low voice. 'I have no intention of falling in love with anyone.'

Chapter Eight

It was not a long walk from the Brighton Assembly Rooms to his lodgings, but after kissing Marilla Newell senseless on the beach, Finlay decided not to take a carriage back. The cool of the evening was required.

His thoughts meandered back to those stolen kisses, causing him to almost slip off the pavement as his footsteps came too close to the edge.

'Watch it!'

Finlay turned, slightly stunned, to see a barouche driver shake a fist in his general direction. He merely grinned.

How could he do anything else? He had shared what was perhaps the most incredible evening with a woman, one he could never have predicted. Just a few short weeks ago, Marilla was nothing to him. He had not even known that she had existed.

Dear God, a world without Miss Marilla Newell. How had he managed to stand it?

It had been a wrench to leave her, but as Miss Pike had started to look for her wayward charge, there had been no choice. Not after being informed by a strangely morose Bartlett that Isabelle and his mother had called the carriage to return to their lodgings an hour ago.

Finlay knew precisely what would happen if he stayed. He would offer to escort the Wallflower Academy party to their lodgings, and before he knew it he would start to declare nonsense about love and affection and marriage.

And he couldn't do that, could he?

Finlay's wandering feet should have taken him straight to the rooms his mother had taken. It was but a five-minute walk.

But in the gloom of the evening, with partygoers dressed in their finery, pie sellers yelling their wares, and a great deal of noise and excitement on every street, Finlay found calm in the midst of them.

And in that calm he knew he had to ask himself one question.

What was he going to do about Marilla?

Finlay passed the building which held his mother and Isabelle but did not turn aside. He could not go up now. He needed to think—and he could not help but feel that the presence of his mother would hardly help matters.

Instead he continued on, passing a lamp lighter, two gentlemen clearly already deep in their cups, and a woman who was attempting to solicit their interest.

I knew you would be attracted to me. But you do not have to make it so obvious, my lord.

Finlay's manhood stiffened at the mere memory of what they had shared together, what he had wanted to share with her. All his thoughts, his feelings, his emotions.

His heart.

For all that this had started out as a bet, a jest between himself and Bartlett, Finlay knew it could go so much further than that.

No, this was getting out of hand. Try as he might to convince himself that his heart was not getting entangled, he could no longer pretend it was something else. That meant he had to act; he had to speak to Isabelle.

Guilt crushed his chest but Finlay could see no other alternative. He had to break off his engagement with Miss Carr, break it to his mother that he had made another choice, and break all Society's expectations by courting Marilla.

Oh, it would hardly be an enjoyable conversation. There

was nothing more that he wanted to avoid, now he came to think about it.

Isabelle would be alone, unprotected, unguarded.

But she will have no debts, Finlay tried to console himself as he stepped across the road and walked around a corner.

Almost all the Carr debts had been paid, had they not? He had done that for her. True, it would be a challenge to find a husband without a dowry, yes, but there were no outstanding arrears to drag her down.

'You did that, at least,' Finlay muttered.

'You talking to me, fine sir?' said a newspaper seller, gazing up at him.

Finlay blinked. 'What? Oh, no. No, my apologies.'

'Least you could do is buy a paper,' sniffed the young man.

Now that he came to look properly, he was nothing more than a child, really. Finlay stuffed a hand in his pockets, pulled out a sixpence, and gave it to him. Then he kept on walking.

'Oi! Oi, doncha want ya paper?'

Finlay ignored him. His mind was already whirling with too many thoughts, too much information. Too many decisions.

And the thing was, there wasn't anyone he could go to for advice.

He knew what his mother would say. He had made an offer to Miss Carr, and he should honour it. A gentleman should have nothing less expected of him—and an earl? His word was law. His word was supposed to be trustworthy.

He couldn't go to Bartlett. Oh, how Bartlett would crow over him, Finlay knew, if he made the mistake of going to his closest friend. After all their talk about a flirtation, Bartlett would find it most amusing that Finlay had managed to lose his heart—and to a wallflower, of all people.

Finlay's stomach lurched.

The trouble was, the one person whose opinion truly mattered to him was…was Cecil.

Brushing away an errant tear that Finlay was not going to permit to fall, he could not deny that it was Cecil's advice he craved. A rush of guilt poured through him every time he considered breaking off his engagement with the man's sister—but then, Cecil had never asked him to offer a marriage of convenience to Isabelle, had he?

Finlay had done so because he had thought it right, but had Isabelle expected such a thing?

He tried desperately to remember her reaction when he had first, awkwardly and stiffly, proposed the match.

Had she appeared in any way excited? Joyful? Relieved, even?

No. No, there had just been a sort of stoic acceptance.

Relief sparked in his chest, removing some of the twisting doubts around his heart. Well, Finlay had to speak to her, break it off. Why, for all he knew, she would be delighted to be free. She hardly cared for him, as far as he could tell.

And she was a pretty sort of woman, he supposed. There would surely be someone else willing to marry her.

Finlay's shoulders lightened immediately as the load bearing down on them melted away.

He was going to marry Marilla.

Well, first he had a little work to do on that front, he supposed. Marilla may welcome his kisses, but marriage—that was quite another thing entirely.

Granted she was a member of the Wallflower Academy. Surely she would accept the hand of any passable man to get out of that place?

And to be sure, he had the slight inconvenience of a fiancée. That was nothing that a quiet and delicate conversation couldn't solve.

And then, Finlay thought as his heart rose, he could start the charm offensive. Show Marilla that earls were not all blackguards—that this earl, at the very least, was not.

The fluttering in his chest was growing, paired now with the warmth he had felt on the beach.

Yes, it was sudden. But when one knew, one knew. That was all there was to it.

All he had to do was break off an engagement a few weeks before the wedding, try to calm his mother from her hysterics—he knew she would have them—then propose to Marilla and convince her to marry an earl.

Finlay sighed as he approached the front door that led to his lodgings. Simple.

Shutting the door behind him and leaning against it heavily, Finlay congratulated himself on his decision. After all, it wasn't as though he had to do anything about it now. He could relax this evening, perhaps have a long bath to soothe his aching muscles, and then tomorrow—

'Ah, Your Lordship,' said Turner politely, stepping into the hall. 'I thought I heard you enter.'

Finlay stifled a smile. It was Turner's pride that he always was there to welcome the Earl of Staromchor back at all hours. It had become a form of competitiveness with the most senior footman, and once again, the older man had triumphed.

'I have placed your guest in the drawing room, and your mother is entertaining her,' said Turner, his frown still lining his forehead.

Finlay's heart skipped a beat.

Guest? Her?

Surely it was not possible. Why on earth his mother would invite Rilla he had no idea. He had never mentioned—

'Miss Carr, I believe, has rung for some supper,' said his butler delicately. 'Apparently the fare at the Brighton Assembly Rooms tonight was insufficient.'

The slight slump of his shoulders was, Finlay hoped, covered by the debonair shrug that he swiftly forced. Oh, of course.

Technically, he supposed, Isabelle was their guest. Foolish of him. 'Oh. Oh, I suppose so?'

'Shall I announce you?'

'Thank you, but I am almost certain my mother and my betrothed know who I am,' said Finlay, frustration seeping out. 'That will be all, Turner.'

Whether or not his servant appreciated the abrupt dismissal, he was not sure. Finlay did not look up when his butler marched away, and dropped his head in his hands when he was certain he was alone.

Oh, God. He had to face her—though perhaps this was for the best. The conversation had to be had, and it was far better to do so in private with his mother in attendance so that she could accept the change in their plans.

Now all he had to do was find the right words.

But as Finlay approached the drawing room, it appeared there were already plenty of words already being spoken in the elegantly apportioned room. The door to the corridor was ajar, and just as Finlay reached out for the door handle, some of those words caught his ears.

And he froze.

'I care deeply about his happiness, of course, but I cannot help but feel—'

'You will make him very happy, I am sure.'

Finlay hesitated, guilt searing through his heart.

It was his mother and Isabelle, talking in quiet voices. Their voices were full of restraint, somehow, as though they were talking around a particular topic for fear of disturbing it.

For fear of what it could reveal.

'His happiness is… It is the most important thing to me,' Isabelle was saying, her voice warm and full of affection. 'There is not a single day that does not go by when I do not think of him.'

Finlay's mouth fell open.

He had never heard Isabelle speak in such a manner. There

was more than warmth and affection in those tones—there was love.

And he knew damned well it was love, because that was how he knew he sounded whenever he thought of Marilla.

Surely...surely he had not been so blind? Surely Isabelle Carr had not fallen in love with him?

'You do not speak with him about it, I suppose?'

That was his mother. Finlay leaned closer to the door, careful not to push it open any farther, desperate to hear more.

'Speak to him about...?'

'About how you feel,' came the dowager countess's voice. It was serious—far more serious than Finlay could recall her ever being.

Well, this was a serious business, he thought darkly. This marriage of convenience was about to become something entirely different.

'Oh, I could never speak to him about the depths of my feelings.' Isabelle's voice almost sounded apologetic. 'Besides, I do not think it would be appropriate. He does not expect it. He would not... I do not think he would wish it.'

And the guilt Finlay had been pushing aside as much as he could all evening, from the moment he had decided to take Marilla to the beach, roared through him like a dam had broken.

How had he been so—well, there was no other way to say it—so blind? All this time, he had been operating under the assumption that Isabelle was as nonchalant about their engagement as he was. She had never shown much interest in him, hardly spoken to him since Cecil had died, had never suggested she felt any joy in becoming his wife...

And now he was to learn that this was merely because of the depths of her feelings?

'Love is a strange thing,' the dowager countess was saying. Even through the door, Finlay could hear the power of her words. His mother was someone who always knew her own mind. 'A person may think they are in love, but in fact all they have is admiration and affection borne from childhood.'

Finlay swallowed. Had Isabelle ever shown any preference for him when they were children? He could not recall…but then, he had hardly been thinking of such a thing, had he?

'Oh, but this is far more than mere preference.' Isabelle's voice was direct, determined; she was absolutely sure of herself. Finlay could not recall ever hearing her speak so—not since she had returned from the Trinderhaus School for Young Ladies. 'I love him, my lady. Everything he says is music to my ears, everything he does is the best thing a man has ever done!'

Finlay's eyes widened. *Oh, hell.*

'Whenever I am with him, I can think of nothing but the pleasure I gain from being in his presence,' continued Isabelle, her voice warming with every word. 'Whenever I am not with him, I am overcome by longing, by counting down the days, the very hours until I can be with him again.'

Hell's bells.

'I do not believe I have ever met a man who has so perfectly attuned himself to my needs, my wishes,' said Isabelle tenderly. 'The kindness he has shown me—'

'He is a very kind man,' the dowager countess agreed lightly. 'I suppose.'

Finlay almost snorted, but managed to stop himself in time. Well, that was hardly high praise from a mother, but as it was his mother, it was rather more than he had expected. She never was one for over-the-top declarations of affection.

Very kind, indeed.

'He is the very pinnacle of manhood,' Isabelle said, her voice lowering. 'I love him, my lady. He is the only person I could ever conceive of marrying. Being his wife—'

'Your wedding is in a few weeks.'

'Y-yes. Yes, I know.'

Finlay allowed a long, slow breath to escape from his lungs

as the two women continued chatting. He did not listen to the words, not any longer. He did not need to.

Well. Isabelle Carr was deeply in love. It could not be denied—he did not need to see her to sense the depth of her feeling.

How she had managed to keep such powerful affections so hidden, he did not know…but then, Finlay was starting to realize that there was a great deal about the feminine psyche that had passed him by.

Perhaps Bartlett knew about all this?

'I am not sure what to do.'

Finlay tried to slow his breathing as Isabelle's words cut through his mind.

'Do? I do not believe there is anything to do. You are getting married.'

'And marriage is a very important thing, yes,' came Isabelle's soft voice. 'I would not wish to—'

'You love him,' said the dowager countess sharply.

Finlay's heart rose to his throat. His fingers were clutching the door handle so tightly that even in the shadowy darkness of the corridor, he could see the whites of his bone pressing through the skin.

'I love him,' came Isabelle's voice, and it was bolder now, sharper. More like the Isabelle he had known.

Was she still in there somewhere?

He heard his mother sigh. 'Well, in that case, there is nothing for it.'

Finlay straightened up, resolve stiffening in his chest.

Yes, there was nothing for it; his mother was completely right. How precisely he had managed to entrap himself like this, in a cage, he did not know, but the point was that he had.

Isabelle Carr loved him.

It was not a love he had wanted. He had not demanded it, nor attempted to gain it. He had not courted or wooed; he had believed the whole thing to be a marriage of convenience that benefited her, yes, but did not touch her heart.

Well, now he knew he was wrong.

Finlay had only tried to do what was right, to care for Cecil's sister. Now he would have to do what was right, even if it kept him from the woman he...he felt something for. What it was, he would not yet name.

Not yet.

Whatever it was, it was hotter and far more tempting than the staid loyalty he felt for Isabelle. But he had to put that aside.

He stepped into the room.

'Finlay!' exclaimed Isabelle, cheeks suddenly splotched with red.

'There you are,' said the dowager countess, a frown on her face but a similar concern in her eyes.

Finlay attempted not to notice. He really should not have been eavesdropping, and he was hardly going to admit he had done so.

Still. There was one way to put Isabelle's mind to rest, and he was going to do that right now. Even if every word would have to be dragged from him. Even if Marilla's face swam in his mind, her laughter, her joy. Even if she was a woman he was now divided from forever.

The two ladies were seated on a sofa together near the fire. The drawing room had, until this moment, been one of his favourite rooms in these lodgings. The place was decorated in the French style—not too French, because Napoleon had made it far too unfashionable thanks to his ridiculous antics. But the paints were that delicate blue that the French so preferred, and the chandelier was designed to the French taste. The paintings on the walls, however, were distinctly British, the pianoforte in the corner Italian.

It had been a room where Finlay had spent a great deal of time. They always came here, whenever it was time to indulge his mother with a trip to Brighton. He had always been happy here. There had never been anything to connect it with sadness.

Now it would always hold the memories of this moment. This disaster. This decision.

'Miss Carr,' Finlay said formally. 'I wish you to know I am completely committed to this marriage. Our marriage.'

Isabelle was blinking furiously.

Dear God, was she blinking away tears of joy? Finlay thought wretchedly.

'That…that is… Well, I—'

'And I want you to be sure of this,' Finlay continued, hating every word but knowing she needed this reassurance. Lord knew he had hardly given her much over the last few weeks. 'There is nothing, nothing that will prevent our marriage from going ahead.'

'Staromchor,' his mother said quietly. 'I would wish to have a small word in your ear.'

Finlay glanced at his mother, almost irritated she was interrupting this very important conversation.

After all that she had just heard from Isabelle, did his mother not understand that this was crucial? That the poor woman evidently needed to be reassured, that she wanted to hear some sort of warmth from him?

The Dowager Countess of Staromchor was frowning. 'Staromchor. I really must speak with you about—'

'This is not the time, Mother,' Finlay snapped, turning away and back to Isabelle.

His future bride, for that was how he must consider her, was a beetroot red. 'Actually, my lord, I—'

'Look, I know you have expected more from me, and I suppose most of that is my own fault,' Finlay said in a rush, forcing the words out now in the hope that if he said them quickly enough, they would not be so painful. 'I have been an inattentive fiancé, I am afraid, but that changes from this moment on.'

Isabelle blinked, evidently confused. 'It…it does?'

'This marriage is important, and it will go ahead,' Finlay said firmly, as though there were nothing he wished for more in all the world. 'You deserve a wedding, Isabelle, and…and affection. I will do my best to give it to you.'

Even if I cannot match the depths of feeling you so clearly have for me, Finlay thought wretchedly. *Good grief, what did a man do when his wife was head over heels in love with him, and he was just…nonplussed?*

Well, he would have to learn. In a month or so, he would have a wife, and he would have to make it work.

Isabelle was still stammering. 'I… Well, I—'

'You can be assured of that,' said Finlay stiffly, walking over to her and bowing low.

Would it be too much to kiss her cheek? Yes, probably.

'You will be my wife, and I will be your husband, and we… we…'

He saw Isabelle swallow hard as she looked at her hands.

'We will live,' she said softly to her fingers, 'happily ever after.'

Nausea rose in Finlay's chest as the enormity of what he had done began to overwhelm him.

He was going to marry Isabelle Carr. He could no longer see Marilla, not in that way. Not as a woman who entranced and inspired him.

And he was instead to be wed to a woman whose insipidity had somehow come from nowhere, despite the fact that she apparently loved him.

'Happily,' Finlay said, his mouth dry. 'Happily ever after.'

Chapter Nine

It was a feeble protest that Rilla had put up. So feeble, in fact, that she had been slightly concerned that the Pike would suspect something.

As it was…

'I knew you would finally come around to my line of thinking,' Miss Pike declared importantly, rustling in the carriage as though she were a leaf in the wind. 'And Miss Smith is grateful, I am sure, for the companionship!'

If she knew Daphne, Rilla thought darkly, and she did, the woman was about as miserable as it was possible to be. She was a true wallflower, one who would have escaped this evening's entertainment if she could.

'So kind of the dowager countess to invite you, Miss Smith, to her card party this evening,' trilled the Pike as the carriage slowed to a jolting stop.

Rilla's wry smile must have gone unnoticed by the proprietress, for there was no reprimand. To the contrary, the Pike was unusually gracious to her, helping her down from the carriage without so much as a complaint that it delayed them from entering wherever it was they were, and placing her cane carefully in her hands.

'Now, this is a big night for Miss Smith,' the Pike hissed in Rilla's ear, as though Daphne was not standing right beside them. 'Heaven knows why she was invited.'

'I do believe she can hear you, Miss Pike,' said Rilla in a calm voice.

Her cane tapped on the ground experimentally. It was most irritating, having to depend on such a thing. The Wallflower Academy grounds were so well known to her now, she did not need a cane. She barely needed an arm to traverse the gardens, or even make her way to the stables. Not that she had much cause to.

A warm and slightly shaking hand took hers and then placed it on an arm. Daphne.

Guilt seared through Rilla as the three ladies moved up a small flight of steps. She was just as ignorant as Miss Pike as to why Daphne—Daphne Smith, of all people!—had been invited to such a thing.

Still, she could hardly complain. The Pike had demanded that Rilla act as chaperone, a ridiculous request yet again, but this time she was hardly going to argue.

She was going to see Finlay again.

Pushing aside the thought as best she could, Rilla submitted to having her pelisse taken off her by an unseen footman, her heart hammering.

The last time she had been with him, he had been kissing her furiously.

What on earth would he say when—

'Ah, Miss Smith, Miss Pike— Oh.'

Heat rushed to Rilla's cheeks. She had presumed she would have at least a few moments at the dowager countess's card party to collect herself before being thrust into the presence of the man she—

Of the man who had kissed her, Rilla attempted to tell herself. Nothing more.

Well. A little more.

Parts of her were unfurling like leaves which had closed during the cold of wintery night, desperate to feel the sun again.

The parts of her which had been subdued by the long sojourn in the Wallflower Academy were awake again.

She was ready to open her heart.

But the expected joy was not accompanied with the heat that was suffusing her lungs, drying out every breath, making it impossible to talk.

Because when Finlay had spoken there was such...such coldness.

'Oh, my lord, such a wonderful evening, I know we shall have a pleasant time,' Miss Pike was trilling in her best fawning voice. 'And to think, Miss Smith has caught your mother's eye! I did speak to her once about her acting as a sort of guide, or sponsor, you know. Almack's is such a wonderful place to find suitors, and I wondered...'

'My mother is in the room to the left,' came the short reply from Finlay. 'Please, Miss Pike, Miss Smith. Do go on in.'

Something settled a little in Rilla's stomach, making it less likely that her luncheon would be making an appearance.

Of course, he had to be stiff and sullen before the Pike. The last thing they wanted was for her to think that they...

They what?

Rilla had been unable to untangle precisely what it was that she felt for the man, and had most studiously avoided interrogating it. What good would that do?

Still. It was pleasing to be here, to be around him. The moment the Pike and Daphne were gone, they could—

'What are you doing here?' Finlay said, voice tinged with shock.

Rilla took a step back, her cane tapping on the ground instinctively to ensure she did not fall down an unsuspecting step.

Even with the cane, her head reeled.

What the—

'I don't know what you—'

'My mother's invitation was for Miss Smith, with Miss Pike as her companion.' Finlay's voice was distant.

Discomfort prickled against her temples. 'Miss Pike said—'

'Trust Miss Pike to take it upon herself to invite another. And you, of all people.'

Of course, came the sinking thought that nestled painfully in her heart, weighing it down like a lump of lead. Of course.

What had Rilla been thinking? She should have known that nothing would be different. That he wouldn't be different. That an earl couldn't be trusted.

All expectations of warmth and connection, of perhaps a repeat of the florid kiss he had poured down on her—all was forgotten.

She had to leave.

'Where do you think you're going?'

'Out,' Rilla snapped, unable to bear it. She had turned to what she recalled was the direction of the door. 'My pelisse, if you please.'

'You cannot think to—'

'Why stay? I am clearly unwanted, though that is hardly a new sensation and so I do not know why it bothers me so,' Rilla said, the words spilling out before she could stop them. 'My pelisse, please.'

Footsteps. The rustle of silk.

And yet no pelisse was placed in her hands or around her shoulders. To the contrary, Finlay spoke in a low voice, and not to her.

'Give it to me, and return to the door, please.'

Irritation sparked in the edges of Rilla's eyes. Trust an earl to order people about and just assume they would follow. What had she been thinking?

'This is why I shouldn't have trusted an earl,' she said in a low voice as presumably the footman returned to the doorway. She'd just have to hope he would follow the precept of most servants and pretend he could not hear a single thing. 'Just when I thought—'

'Thought what?'

Rilla struggled to articulate what was more a sensation than a thought, a feeling not a meaning.

She thought that there had been something between them. Something different. Something that meant her first kiss was going to mean something, go somewhere, though where precisely, she did not know.

Oh, she felt so foolish. How could she have come here, to his mother's house, and expected a welcome!

No, women like her were for kissing on a beach out of sight of the world. Not for actually acknowledging in public.

'You cannot out-argue me, you know,' came the irksome tease.

Her temper once again flared. 'I think you will find I am more than a match for any earl!'

'I will not deny it. Any earl would be lucky to—'

'Forget I said anything. Forget I came.' Rilla moved forward, pelisse or no. The very thought of staying here was unbearable.

'Rilla, wait!'

A hand on her arm. She jerked away violently. 'I told you. I hate it when—'

'And I suppose I should have just let you fall down the stairs and break your neck?' Finlay snapped, pulling her roughly back so that her arm burned. 'You might just have to accept that sometimes people are actually trying to help you!'

'And you might just have to accept that sometimes people don't want your help!' Rilla had attempted to keep her voice down, cognizant that other guests could arrive at any moment. And that blasted footman was still there. Oh, well, at least it would be something to protect her reputation.

Though she was not entirely sure, Rilla thought Finlay swore quietly under his breath.

'You are making this impossible.'

She had to laugh at that. 'I am? You are the untrustworthy one. The last time I saw you, it was kisses and—'

'Keep your voice down!'

But Rilla was fired up now, heat burning through her veins, shame and embarrassment coursing through her. To think she had let this man kiss her! Kiss her, and on a beach, in the dark!

And now he did not even want her here?

'Why is my presence here so odious to you?' she demanded, trying to keep her voice low. 'Why?'

There was a moment of silence. The silence grew longer and longer, and eventually what broke it was Finlay clearing his throat.

'I… I cannot say.'

Rilla snorted. 'What a surprise.'

'I don't like keeping secrets.'

'And I don't like being one!' she retorted, her cheeks burning at the merest hint of a suggestion. 'I mean, it's not like I am… I am not your… I won't be…'

'You do not have to sound so mortified,' came Finlay's quiet voice. 'Nothing happened.'

And just when she did not want them, tears promised to burn in the corners of her eyes.

Nothing happened. Oh, no, to an earl, she supposed nothing had happened. Just a fervent kiss on a beach. Just a sharing of herself in a way she had never done before. Just a connection formed that was heightened by the secrecy, and the smell of the sea, and the knowledge that such an assignation was forbidden.

Just Finlay, a man she had thought…

'I should have known,' Rilla said, her voice thick as she attempted to control her emotions. 'It's always the same. You know, I comforted myself when I was a child, and the maids were teasing me behind my family's back—they denied it when confronted, of course, and were permitted to stay—I comforted myself by telling myself that things would be better when I was older. Better!'

There was an odd sort of noise from Finlay. A sort of— could a grimace make a noise?

'You were teased by…by your family's maids?'

'Oh, yes, the maids, a footman. Once our housekeeper changed all the furniture in our drawing room so that I couldn't navigate by myself. I got a black eye, in the end,' Rilla said, the words pouring from her like water, righteous anger launching them forward. 'A village boy almost drowned me in a pond. Once, our vicar pulled me up to the front of church to demonstrate how the blind would no longer exist in heaven.'

'The bounder!'

'And that's nothing compared to what I endured when I was sent to school!' Now tears were threatening to pour down her face, but Rilla did everything she could to hold them back.

And she was well practised at such an art. Her life had required her to be.

'And yet again, and again, I told myself that when I was a woman, I would at least be respected,' Rilla continued, her fingers gripping the top of her cane as though it were the only thing rooting her to the earth. 'And I was engaged to the Earl of Porthaethwy.'

'I was going to ask you about that.'

'But of course, God forbid that I be happy,' she shot back at him, speaking over the quiet question with a rapid hiss of her own. 'I've never felt wanted, or safe, never known who to trust, and you are the perfect example, Finlay Jellicoe, of why—'

'Rilla…'

'Don't call me that,' Rilla said sharply. 'You haven't earned the right.'

Her words hung in the air, weighty with meaning and caught in the web of tension between them.

It wasn't supposed to be like this. A kiss like that, on the beach, was meant to be the beginning of something. Not the end of something.

Were her desires, her dreams, truly so odious to anyone she encountered? Once again Rilla forced back the tears, holding herself upright and ensuring her head did not drop.

There was no shame in wishing to be married—unless one was a wallflower, she supposed. And it wasn't as though a kiss was just a kiss, to some gentlemen at least. She had not expected, nor demanded, promises of happily-ever-after.

Even if her heart had longed for them.

'I'll call your carriage,' came Finlay's quiet words when the silence was eventually broken.

And the last remnant of hope—that he would fight for her, that he would try to convince her—died in Rilla's heart.

'Thank you,' she said stiffly. 'I'll wait in it.'

'And I will visit you at the Wallflower Academy to…to apologize properly.'

'I won't hold my breath,' Rilla said darkly, as the harsh fabric of a footman's livery brushed against her arm. She was being guided now, and not by Finlay. 'Do not bother to lower yourself, my lord, by coming to the Wallflower Academy unless you are certain—absolutely certain—that you can bear to be seen with me.'

A part of her hoped that Finlay would accompany her out to the carriage. A part of her hoped he would help her into it, and then be overcome with remorse and longing, and enter the carriage after her, and—

But they were foolish hopes. Hopes that were proved wrong.

And as Rilla waited for what felt like hours in the Wallflower Academy carriage, waiting for Miss Pike and Daphne to be finished at the card party, she told herself the same thing again and again.

You are not a match for an earl.

Chapter Ten

The Tudor manor rose beautiful and golden in the afternoon sun. With winter drawing ever closer, the sun was low enough to cast glints of sparkling gold on the windowpanes in the three-storey building.

And as Finlay rode along the drive and glanced at the formal gardens to his left, he saw two women. One he immediately ignored. The other was Marilla Newell.

And that was when he almost fell off his horse.

'Oh, damn!'

The rest of his curse was silenced by the unsettled neighing of Ceres, his horse. The two women turned, both staring curiously in the direction of the man who evidently couldn't control his own steed.

Finlay swallowed the embarrassment.

At least she hadn't seen him make a complete prat of himself, he told himself as he dismounted—shakily—and straightened his riding coat.

'I think your earl has fallen off his horse,' came the murmured whisper of the woman holding on to Marilla's arm.

Oh, for the love—

'I didn't fall,' Finlay called over the ten-yard gap between them. 'I... I dismounted.'

'He's not my earl,' he heard Marilla mutter into her friend's ear.

It wasn't Sylvia. This was a different wallflower: Miss

Smith, if he remembered. Not that he had much interest in her. It was the woman she was guiding around the formal knot garden he wished to see, though he could not have hoped to orchestrate such a perfect meeting as this.

Well. Discounting almost falling from Ceres, that was.

If only he could separate them, Finlay found himself musing as he stepped forward, hands hanging by his sides.

Were hands supposed to hang by your sides? What on earth did hands do, anyway? What had he ever done with his hands before? Had he ever had damned hands in his whole—

'My lord,' gushed the wallflower, dipping in a low curtsey that far exceeded what his rank demanded.

Finlay did not look at her. He looked at Marilla.

She was radiant. A delicate blue gown with a cream spencer jacket matched the bonnet which partially hid her dark rich curls. There was a frown on her forehead, a pained one that should have told him immediately he was not about to be welcomed.

And he did not care.

Staying away from Marilla Newell had proved impossible. So putting aside his guilt, and telling himself most firmly that there was no law against an engaged man talking to another woman, here he was.

Like a fool.

Finlay swallowed. The last time they had been together, he had refused to give any explanation as to his rudeness and aloofness, and she had revealed…well, some rather awful things about her past, and just how deeply he had hurt her.

Could hurt her again.

And yet…

'Would you be so good as to leave us to talk, Miss Smith?' Finlay asked with one of his most charming grins.

Miss Smith. Well, it was an innocent enough name for the illegitimate daughter of Lord Norbury, he supposed. His mother hadn't been able to stop wittering about the man all week. Apparently he—

Miss Smith immediately stammered, in a rush of red cheeks and downcast eyes, 'Oh, b-but that wouldn't do at all, m-my lord, I c-couldn't possibly.'

'Do you want to ruin my reputation?' came the expected hiss of Marilla.

'Just for a few moments, thank you, Miss Smith,' said Finlay smartly, as though the very idea of opposition was preposterous.

Miss Smith had dropped Marilla's arm in apparent shock. 'Oh, that won't be—'

'Excellent,' said Finlay brightly, taking the abandoned arm of Marilla just as swiftly as Miss Smith released it. 'My, there appears to be a very pleasant walk about this knot garden, Miss Newell. Will you favour me with your company?'

Miss Smith had already walked a great distance by the time he had finished his pronouncement, and was not surprised when Marilla instantly wrenched her arm from his.

'No one is impressed by your posturing,' she said tartly, turning away.

There was no real malice in her words. At least, Finlay did not think there was. He was still learning the contours of Marilla's moods, the changes so instant he could barely keep up.

But he wanted to. By God, he wanted to.

'It's not posturing,' Finlay said as he watched her. 'And you were the one who announced me with my title, I didn't— How are you doing that?'

He hadn't intended to actually ask the question, but it was impossible not to.

It was a miracle. Despite the complexity of the garden, the multiple low hedges weaving around in intricate knots, Marilla was walking around them seemingly without a care in the world.

How was she not falling over?

Marilla glanced back over her shoulder. 'Doing what?'

'That!' Finlay knew he should have explained himself better, but he could barely articulate it. Stepping forward, he tried to take her arm. 'Let me help.'

'It may surprise you to learn that I don't need your help,' said Marilla tartly. 'And I don't appreciate people just touching me whenever they feel like it. If I want help, I'll ask!'

Her voice rang clear and sharp across the garden. A pair of ravens squawked unhappily and rose from a nearby oak tree.

Finlay bit his lip.

Well, when she put it like that...

'I am sorry.'

Marilla turned her ear to him as though attempting to take in every facet of every syllable. 'I beg your pardon?'

'I apologize. I shouldn't have touched you. I just—' He caught himself just in time. 'There is no excuse. I am sorry.'

She stared at him, those delectable lips parted in shock.

'And while I'm at it, I suppose I have a few more apologies to offer,' Finlay said quickly, before she could send him away. 'I—'

'If you are going to apologize for that kiss,' Marilla said in a warning tone.

His shoulders slumped, though he was momentarily heartened by a flashing thought.

She wants to be kissed again.

'No,' said Finlay quietly. 'No, I am afraid it is far more serious than that. It's... Well, I should not have been so abrupt with you. At my mother's card party.'

'No, you should not.'

There was a hardness to her words which concealed her true thoughts. Her face, too, was difficult to read.

Finlay swallowed. 'I cannot pretend to share all, Marilla—

Miss Newell, apologies. I am not a perfect man, and I make no claim to be. I would, however, like…like to be a friend to you.'

More than a friend. But he had committed to Isabelle Carr, so a friend was all Marilla could be.

Perhaps the tension and the regret seeped into his voice as Finlay added, 'Lord knows why you would forgive me. I'm not sure I would forgive me. I… My mother has expectations of me.'

Expectations that I will marry a completely different woman.

And quite unexpectedly, a slow smile spread across Marilla's face.

'Well. That's the first time I've heard an earl admit to being unforgiveable. And you are… Well, you are not the only one whose parents have expectations. You are forgiven. This time.'

Continuing to pick her way through the complex knot garden, she did not forbid him from joining her. That was the rationale Finlay offered himself, at least, for moving to walk by her side.

They continued in silence for a few minutes, until Finlay said, 'I still don't know how you're doing it.'

'Doing what?'

'Walking. I mean, without your cane,' he explained. 'Navigating sight unseen.'

Marilla said softly, 'I know this garden well. I helped plant it when I first arrived, three years ago.'

Three years?

Finlay had not realized that the woman—that any wallflower—had been here quite so long. 'And so…so you know it off by heart?'

'Do you learn the corridors of your home "off by heart"?' she chided him gently. 'Just because I cannot see, that does not mean that I cannot recall where I walk. And I walk here often. I like it here.'

Finlay looked about them.

It was a pretty enough garden. Most of the flowers were over by now, and a few weeds were starting to break through the soil at the borders. Precisely why it was so beloved to Marilla, he could not fathom.

'The feel of the box, the scent of the bay and the lavender,' Marilla said, answering his unasked question. Her hand trailed into the border, brushing her fingertips on the plants. '*Buxus sempervirens. Laurus nobilis. Lavandula.* They are beautiful.'

'You are very clever.'

'I have a great deal of time on my hands,' she returned with a laugh. 'And I like learning. It is why the Pike—excuse me, Miss Pike—believes I should be a governess or teacher. Believes no one will ever care enough for me to...to offer for my hand.'

And that was when Finlay knew he was in danger.

In danger of caring, of admiring this woman too much. In danger of allowing the desire he felt for her, the attraction that such a bold and intelligent woman sparked in him, over-whelm him.

In danger of wishing to be here more often, to be beside her more often, to be a part of her life.

'You are very quiet.'

Finlay's gaze jerked up, and he saw a curious expression on Marilla's face. Wasn't that interesting—that a woman who had never seen a curious face could still offer one?

'I was just admiring your knowledge of Latin,' he lied.

Well, there was absolutely no possibility he could reveal the truth.

'A true bluestocking, if ever I saw one,' he continued.

'You say that as though it were an affront,' Marilla said lightly, turning a corner as they crunched onto a gravel path and leading him into what was evidently the rose garden. The bushes had been cut back hard, though a few petals still rested on the cold soil.

'I do not know many ladies who would relish being de-scribed as a bluestocking,' Finlay pointed out.

'But I am not a bluestocking. Not really,' she shot back. 'What, because a woman is not traditionally beautiful and she has a passing understanding of books, she must be a bluestocking?'

Marilla laughed. It was a light laugh, a teasing one, one that rang through the air like music.

Finlay's stomach lurched.

'Don't you project your feelings of inadequacy onto me, Finlay Jellicoe,' Marilla said, nudging him in a way that made Finlay's heart skip a beat.

Swallowing hard and telling himself he had absolutely no desire to kiss her again, no, not at all, Finlay said, 'Look, Marilla…'

'No,' she said softly.

Finlay halted. She had come to a stop beside a climbing rose by the wall, her fingers outstretched, brushing up against the prickly stem as though to see what efforts the gardener had made.

And there was an inscrutable expression on her face.

'What do you mean, no?' Finlay said quietly. 'When I asked— I mean, at Brighton, you said I could call you Marilla.'

Don't think about that kiss don't think about that kiss don't think about—

'I said that my friends called me Rilla,' she said without turning to him. 'I think it…it is time for you to call me Rilla, don't you?'

Finlay swallowed hard. 'And you should call me Finlay.'

'And you'd like that.' Rilla's voice was soft, and they were the only two people in the entire world. 'It would bring you happiness, and that…that is something in short supply in your life, isn't it, Finlay?'

His jaw fell open.

Dear God, how could she possibly spot that? He hadn't told her about Isabelle—not that he was sure how he would explain that—and she was blind. She couldn't see him, couldn't know how often his face fell into melancholy or know how frequently he only appeared to be attending to what was going on around him.

So how the devil did she know?

'I can sense a great sadness in you,' Rilla said, turning around and once again answering his unasked question. 'I can't explain the perception, but I do have it. Even if you do not speak sadly, even if you have no wish to tell me about it—you are not obliged to. But you are sad, aren't you?'

Finlay hesitated. He could tell her. He could attempt to explain about Isabelle, about how the girl he had known had transformed into a stranger, a woman he did not understand.

Finlay had realized that morning, in horrendous clarity, just what his life was going to be.

His married life.

Isabelle, there but not there. And himself. And he was trapped; he couldn't get out. He had made a commitment to her, a promise to care for her. How would he, in all honour, escape it? Escape her?

And now he was here, standing in a dead rose garden, being told by a blind woman who he was starting to truly care about that he was sad.

Finlay brushed away the tear that fell. Thank God no one was here to see it.

'You cannot see me,' he said aloud, awkwardly. 'You cannot possibly know if I am happy or sad.'

'That's where you are wrong,' Rilla said softly. She had turned from the rose now to face him, and took a step forward as she spoke. 'Do not misunderstand me. Those who are blind are not magically able to "read" a room. And yes, I cannot see you. I have only a vague sense of light and dark, and it's not something that has ever changed. But I don't need to see to know.'

'How, then?' Finlay asked quietly.

After all, he'd done his damnedest to keep his gloom away from Society's prying eyes. Grieving Cecil…it was best done in private.

But it appeared there was no private when it came to Miss Marilla Newell.

There was a sad sort of expression on her face as she tilted her head. 'I have learned to pay attention to the unspoken words, as well as the spoken ones.'

A lump formed in Finlay's throat. Somewhere, a robin started to sing.

'Besides, there is so much more to communication than mere speech,' Rilla continued. 'Tone of voice, inflection, hesitancy. The way people move—I cannot see it, but with you…you are a very physical being.'

Finlay was not the only one to flush a dark red.

'You know what I mean,' Rilla said into the silence. 'You… Well, you know what I intended by that.'

He did. It was just a little startling that she could be so perceptive, so understanding of him after just a few encounters. Even if each one had felt intense, and deep, and far more meaningful than anything he had ever shared with anyone else.

Finlay brushed his hair from his eyes as though that could bring him some sort of equilibrium, but it did not. And that was when he found himself opening his mouth and saying something he had not said to anyone.

'My friend died.'

Rilla stepped forward, but then halted, as though she were not sure if her presence would be welcome.

Oh, how he wished she had continued, that her hands had been outstretched and he could have taken them, grounded himself with her touch.

For he was exposed now. Naked, as though he had peeled off all his clothes and bared himself for the world to see.

'What was their name?'

The lump in Finlay's throat made it almost impossible to speak, but he finally managed to say, 'Cecil. Cecil Carr. Well, I suppose he was Lord Carr, but I always knew him as Cecil.'

Speaking his name… Finlay had expected it to be painful. He rarely permitted himself to do such a thing, after all. His heart could only take so much.

Yet speaking it here, in the quiet and the gentleness of the rose garden, with only Rilla as his audience…

The lump in his throat lessened.

'I am sorry for your loss,' Rilla said softly. 'Losing a friend…that is awful.'

Finlay found himself nodding. 'Yes. Yes, sometimes…sometimes I wake in the night. It's dark, and I'm alone, and it's cold, and I wonder why I have woken. Nothing seems to have happened, no noise to startle me, and—'

The words ceased, almost immediately.

There was a pain in his chest, a tightening around his heart he knew all too well. This was the grief, this was the agony that prevented a single syllable being uttered.

He had been a fool to think he could speak of Cecil.

'And then,' Rilla said softly.

She was closer now, just a few feet from him. Almost close enough to touch.

And though he did not feel her contact, Finlay was heartened by her closeness. The sense of peace she brought him was unlike anything he had ever known.

The hand squeezing his heart relented. It began to beat again. His lungs relaxed.

'And then I remember. He is gone, and to a place where I cannot bring him back,' Finlay said quietly, his voice taut. 'And I think, how could I have forgotten? Forgotten Cecil, my closest, my very best friend, how could I forget that he is gone?'

It did not require an observant person like Rilla to hear the self-loathing in his voice. Finlay knew every word was dripping with it.

What sort of a person was he—what sort of a man forgot such a thing?

'I believe it is natural,' Rilla said softly. 'In our dreams, we wish—we long for the things we have lost. The people we have had to say goodbye to.'

Finlay's dark laugh filled the small garden. 'Say goodbye— I didn't have time to say goodbye. I didn't even tell him...there was never any need to tell him how much his friendship meant.' He cleared his throat. 'An accident. A hunting accident, one the fool was too tired to go on but too polite to decline the invitation and... I should have been with him.'

He could have saved him. If he had been there—

'Being there wouldn't be enough,' came Rilla's soft words.

Finlay flinched, the strange sensation of hearing her speak what he had just been thinking hotly jarring in his chest. 'You speak as though you know.'

There was silence, but only for a moment.

'My mother,' Rilla said, in a dry, matter-of-fact tone which quickly cracked as she continued to speak. 'I was with her, and yet you think you would know what to do, you think you can save them, but when it happens...'

Finlay stepped closer to her, needing to feel her presence. It soothed, just as much as it burned. 'My father died when I was small, but so long ago that to be honest, I barely remember him. I have my mother, of course.'

'Who is formidable.'

It was difficult to disagree. Finlay breathed out a laugh, the stinging in his eyes ignored as best he could. 'She means well, and so do I, and so we've got on rather well over the years. But she doesn't understand me like...like Cecil did.'

Rilla brushed the top of a lavender bush with her fingertips, and the scent burst into the chilly air. 'My mother was my champion. Losing her—it was more than losing a parent. Like losing my sight, all over again.'

'Yes, that's exactly it. Like losing a sense, one you could not realize was precious until it was gone.' Finlay tried to take the bitterness from his voice, but it was difficult—though perhaps it was the only thing preventing him from weeping.

There was silence between them, but it was not painful. In fact, now Finlay came to think about it, the tension and unbearable pressure on his chest were fading. Melting.

Bearable, once more.

'I don't know how you do it,' he said with a breathy laugh, desperate to close the gap between them but knowing that if he did so, the warring tears would finally win. 'Speaking with you, it's like…it's like speaking to myself. I haven't…haven't been able to talk about this, with anyone. Not like this.'

Rilla's smile was rueful. 'Loss speaks to loss without the need for manners.'

Finlay snorted. 'I suppose so—another thing I've lost with Cecil's death. There's something special about a friend like that, and not knowing it was coming, no way to tell Cecil how important he was, had always been. We were meant to…'

Oh, God, he was going to cry. And the tears came, just a few, and they were silent and so he hoped to God that Rilla would not notice.

The hearty sniff he was forced to take, however, could not be ignored.

'We were meant to grow old together, reading newspapers and complaining about the youth of today,' Finlay said, trying to laugh but there wasn't enough air in his lungs. 'Talking politics and moaning about the cold of the winters. And now he's just…gone. Just like that? How is that possible?'

He had not expected an answer. There was no answer, as far as he could tell. There never would be a rational explanation for Cecil Carr not existing and the world continuing on without him.

When the answer came, it was as soft and as silent as the tears running down his face.

Rilla took his hand.

How she had done it, he did not know. Finlay did not care. The comfort of her skin against his, the warmth, the knowledge that she was standing with him just letting him feel, letting him say all the things he had not said to anyone else…

They stood there together for a few minutes. Or an age. Finlay wasn't sure. It did not matter. Every second was precious.

Eventually he squeezed her hand, and Rilla squeezed back. When he tried to speak, it was on a breathy laugh as though he could sweep all the true emotion away. 'H-how did you know that I needed comfort?'

'I didn't know,' Rilla admitted softly, her voice thrumming with a warmth he had never heard in her before. 'I just guessed.'

Finlay's chuckle lightened, ever so slightly. 'I suppose I should not presume on your powers of deduction too heavily.'

'No, you shouldn't. I was wrong about something.'

'Which was?' he asked.

Rilla did not speak immediately. She appeared to be considering whether or not to speak. When she did, it was hesitant, unsure. Finlay would almost guess she was…ashamed?

'I thought… Well, you have always sounded very carefree. I admit, I did not think you had such depths to your character.'

Finlay shook his head wryly, then recalled she would not sense such a motion. 'If you don't care, then it can't hurt.'

Rilla's laugh was dark, and it pained him right to his core. 'Perhaps we are not so unlike after all.'

'What do you mean?'

She had already stepped away. 'Nothing.'

'Do not give me that. I know you better than that,' Finlay shot after her.

He had not intended his words to be so aggressive, and now that they had been spoken, he regretted them.

Rilla had halted, however, and she did not continue to move away. 'Yes. Yes, you do, don't you?'

Finlay swallowed.

'And yet we are so different,' she continued, a dark humour in her tones. 'I am a wallflower here only because no one bothers to take much of an interest in me. I have no choices, no power, no options for my future.'

'I know all about no choice and no power,' Finlay said without thinking.

It had been a foolish thing to say, but his marriage had been on his mind and the words had slipped out before he could stop them.

Rilla frowned. 'What on earth would an earl know about a lack of power?'

Finlay hesitated. He was dancing along a dangerous line here now. The flirtation had been wonderful—Bartlett had been right—but they were verging on something else here, weren't they?

More than a kiss stolen on a beach. More than a walk together, fingers slipping by each other, hearts skipping beats.

He had shared with her now, and she had with him. He knew her better than any lady in the *ton*, and somehow all the other ladies of the *ton* were dull in comparison.

He needed to tell her about Isabelle.

The thought was sharp and unpleasant, but he could not deny its veracity. This had gone on too long now. Rilla deserved to know—and Isabelle deserved to have his full attention. They may not care about each other in that way, but she was to be his wife.

And yet he couldn't. How could he utter Isabelle's name when Rilla had returned to him, her fingers reaching out for him, splaying across his chest?

Finlay's heart skipped a painful beat. 'Rilla…'

'Finlay...'

'There you are, Miss Newell, I— Oh, goodness! My lord!'
Finlay did three things in very rapid motion.

Firstly, he released Rilla's hand, though it cost him a great
deal to sever the tie to comfort which he had only just found.

Secondly, he raised his other hand swiftly to brush the remaining tears from his eyes. There could be no evidence that
Finlay Jellicoe, Earl of Staromchor, had done anything so pe-
destrian as crying.

And thirdly, he turned with a charming smile that he knew
always worked and bowed low. 'Miss Pike.'

When he straightened, it was to see the proprietress of the
Wallflower Academy looking aghast.

'Miss Newell—and my lord—speaking privately in the rose
garden? It's outrageous!'

'Miss Pike,' Rilla began stiffly. 'It's only—'

What precisely it was 'only', Finlay was never to discover.
He was too fascinated by the way all Rilla's warmth, her softness, her comfort had disappeared. The chill had fallen and
she was now as reserved and as aloof as she had been when
he had first revealed his true identity.

Lowest order? I'll have you know I'm an earl. The Earl of—

An earl? Of course. I should have guessed by your rudeness.

How did she do that?

'And here I am, attempting to make good matches for all
my wallflowers, and—'

'There is nothing to be concerned about. We have only—'

'I was looking for you, Miss Pike,' Finlay interrupted hastily. 'And then I was walking with Miss Smith and Miss Newell,
and now I am delighted to find you.'

The two women halted their words immediately.

Yes, the mention of Miss Smith had immediately cooled the
proprietress's concern; he could see that.

Miss Pike blinked. 'Me?'

'You,' he said warmly, stepping towards her and ensuring that he added a brilliance to the smile and a glitter to his eye.

That was it, be the roguishly charming man that everyone in the *ton* knew him to be…

'Oh, my lord,' said Miss Pike, a pink flush covering her cheeks.

'I was hoping to gain your permission to take a pair of your wallflowers riding,' Finlay said smoothly, as though nothing would make him happier. He ignored the snort of ridicule behind him. No matter how sensitive Rilla was proving herself to be, there was always an undercurrent of mischief. 'Three days hence—perhaps the Misses Newell and Bryant?'

Chapter Eleven

Nothing else smelt like the local village church. Nothing.

'In the name of the Father, and of the Son…'

Rilla breathed in deeply, finding comfort and solace in the dependability of the little church that sat just outside the Wallflower Academy.

Beeswax candles. Heavy starch in the vicar's vestments. The hardness of the pews, lightly scratched along the seats. The cool of the stones beneath her feet. Snowdrops. It must be the Wallflower Academy's turn to provide flowers, for the place was heady with their scent, and they were the current favourite of their proprietress.

In a world in which Miss Pike attempted to change her fate, and in which gentlemen bared their souls to her without her quite knowing what she had done to receive such intimacies, the building was another one of her anchors.

'Amen.'

Rilla swallowed, attempting to follow the church service rather than get carried away by the memories of two days ago.

But it was a challenge. Finlay had—they had never spoken like…

It was more than she could ever have imagined.

H-how did you know that I needed comfort?

I didn't know. I just guessed.

'The reading today is taken from…'

Rilla heard the rustle of pages as fifty or so of the congregation rustled through the Bibles provided on each pew. She heard the genteel cough of someone just behind her, the shifting of someone who was evidently uncomfortable.

It was just another Sunday morning. One which would surely pass just as all the others had.

Except that she had a man on her mind, and Miss Pike was seated next to her and determined to—

Well. Irritate her.

'I suppose your father has written to you,' breathed the woman on her left.

Rilla did not permit a single inch of her face to alter. What on earth was the woman thinking—and after her etiquette lesson only yesterday! 'We are in church, Miss Pike.'

'It's very important. The moment I read it this morning I knew I had to speak to you about it. I merely wondered—'

'Then Moses said to the people, "Commemorate this day, the day you came out of Egypt…"'

'If you had heard—'

'"The land he swore to your ancestors to give you, a land flowing with milk and honey—you are to observe this ceremony in this month—"'

'The news!'

Try as she might, Rilla could not bring herself to grace the woman with a glare. She had worked on her glare for many years, her sisters assisting her at times, and Sylvia had aided her in perfecting the raised eyebrow.

The trouble was, none of those attitudes seemed particularly appropriate for church.

Even if the vicar was, apparently, almost as short-sighted as she was blind.

'Miss Newell,' murmured Miss Pike, nudging her with her elbow as though that would incentivise her to respond. There was tension in her tone that Rilla had never heard before. 'Have you heard from your father?'

Rilla sighed heavily. She would much prefer to indulge in memories of Finlay nudging her, Finlay taking her arm, Finlay revealing his heart to her in such a manner...that of a friend.

No, not quite a friend. Sylvia and Daphne were perhaps her closest friends at the Wallflower Academy, and neither of them had ever wept on her shoulder.

But it was not as though Finlay had said anything about... affection.

'Miss Newell!'

'I heard from my father two weeks ago,' Rilla murmured under her breath, not bothering to turn her head to the side. The woman had to learn.

No, Finlay had said little of affection—nothing about it, in fact. His attention had been fixed, quite rightly, on the friend he had lost.

Besides, earls could not be trusted.

The little voice at the back of her mind which had sought to keep her safe, protected, isolated all these years finally managed to break through the chattering in her head about charming young earls.

He was an earl. Finlay was of that class of gentlemen who thought not only was the world beneath him, but it was supposed to do his bidding. He was part and parcel of the whole nobility, a part of Society that looked down on mere gentry like herself.

'And he mentioned the end of next month?'

And yes, Finlay appeared different from many of the gentlemen of that set she had encountered, Rilla had to accept. He had a...a depth to him no other man had ever revealed to her. And yet...

'You know, then, about the change of circumstances coming?'

Yet it was all too easy to deceive her.

It had been Rilla's greatest fear, ever since that awful encounter with that boy, years ago. She had known the village pond was closer than that, yet he had still called her forward.

And she had believed him. He had said they were friends. Did not friends trust each other?

The subsequent soak had been terrifying. Pond weed inhaled, water clogging her lungs... If her father had not been there...

Rilla blinked. 'End of next month? Change of circumstances?'

Now that Miss Pike's words had finally caught up with her mind, she had probably spoken too loudly. There was an awkward cough from Sylvia beside her, and Rilla heard with a twist in her stomach that the vicar's sermon had momentarily halted.

'That...that is to say... Where was I? Ah, yes. That is to say, when we examine this passage closely...'

'I was not aware of a change of circumstances,' Rilla said quietly, now desperate for the previously loquacious Pike to speak up. 'Miss Pike?'

'I had presumed your father had informed you.'

Now the older woman's voice sounded unsure, unsteady. Most unlike the woman Rilla had known for the last three years.

Oh, how she wished they were no longer in church. It would be easy, then—or relatively easy—to encourage Miss Pike to reveal what awkwardness was to hand, and then Rilla could acclimatize to it. She always did. Always adapted, always found a way through.

Though it was all too easy to deceive her, Rilla had ceased to be so trusting a long time ago. The worry at the back of her mind that she was being taken advantage of never truly disappeared, but there was little she could accuse the Pike of.

Arguing in favour of her becoming a tutor, yes.

But actual cruelty?

No, the woman didn't have a cruel bone in her body. It wouldn't even occur to the Pike to—

'I refer, most unwillingly, to the fact that your father will cease to pay for your place here at the Wallflower Academy at the end of next month,' Miss Pike said in a soft rush.

Rilla was suddenly very aware of her body. Of her buttocks sitting on the pew, her spine against the back rest, her fingers clasped together in her hands, her lungs tight and painful. Her lips parted in shock. Her breath became ragged.

Cease to pay for your place here.

The idea that she would have to one day leave the Wallflower Academy...

It was home. In a way, it was more home than home had ever been. Oh, her father meant well—she was almost sure of it—but with her mother gone and the estate entailed, Rilla had learnt from a young age not to consider Newell Place as her true home.

No, it was here. The Wallflower Academy. It was the place where she had been permitted freedom, the first friends she had made, her escape from—

And now they were going to make her leave?

'And as we can see from the verses that follow, we notice that...'

'I... Cease to pay?' Rilla breathed.

Miss Pike shuffled awkwardly beside her as she whispered, 'I cannot just keep people forever, Miss Newell, you know that. Your father has paid for my help for three years, and you have never...'

Ah, this old tune.

Rilla allowed it to wash over her. She knew this speech, had heard it many times. It was the standard Miss Pike 'I've done everything I can to help you get wed, and you've done nothing' speech. Sylvia was often treated to a variation. Daphne, too.

But though the repetitive phrases may have comforted her

in the past, perhaps even made her smile, Rilla could not do so now.

What was she to do? Where was she to go?

Surely not back home, back to her father. His latest letter had been most clear. He had no wish for her to return; her sisters needed a chance to enter Society without the mark of her past hanging over them. And besides, Nina was still living close by.

So where did that leave her? Where…where could she go?

'And as you are welcome at home—'

'I am not welcome at home,' Rilla said through gritted teeth. Not after they'd all taken Nina's side.

Another elbow in her ribs from Sylvia. She was being too loud again, but she couldn't help it.

She had nowhere to go.

What was to become of her?

'Sort something out,' Miss Pike finished in a low murmur.

Just then the vicar said, 'Hymn number forty-two.'

The congregation rose and Rilla rose with it, moving on instinct instead of any rational thought.

Her mind was buzzing, attempting to take in what she had just been told—and the infuriating thing was, she noticed as the organ started up and voices rose in song, that she couldn't stop thinking about Finlay.

You are clever.

Here she was, about to lose her home, her sense of place and purpose…and her mind instead decided to meander down the trail that led not to solutions, but to an earl who could not be trusted?

An earl who kissed her like the devil on a beach in Brighton, and then simply did not mention it again, as though it had never happened?

The rest of the church service was a blur. Rilla was certain that it had happened; it would have been most strange if it had not. But if she had been asked about it later, there was not a single detail she could have provided.

When the processional music struck up and the congregation bowed their heads as the vicar and the sexton passed by, Rilla found her heart was thundering along with the heavy bass of the organ.

What was she to do?

'Are you coming, Rilla?'

Sylvia's voice cut through her panic and she jerked her head. Somehow the music had ended. The chatter of the end of church had begun.

Her friend's voice was light and airy. She had evidently not heard the shocking revelation from the Pike, Rilla realized, and so was ignorant of the coming disaster. And she would keep it that way.

There was no need for more people to worry.

'I... I will, presently,' said Rilla quietly. 'Don't worry, I can find my own way home.'

The final word she uttered stuck momentarily in her throat. Home? Where was home? If the place her family lived was not home, and the Wallflower Academy could no longer be home in five weeks, then what on earth was she supposed to call home?

But Sylvia either did not notice or did not care. She was gone, her scent of lavender disappearing as the noise of the church started to dissipate.

Eventually there was just one set of footsteps.

'Miss Newell?' came the voice of Miss Pike.

She sounded nervous. It was strange, to hear her so uncertain, and Rilla almost grinned.

Well, it was good to see that Miss Pike had a heart after all.

'I am quite well,' Rilla said softly from her seat on the pew. 'I just wish for a little reflection time in the quiet of the church. That is all.'

There was silence, no answering response from the Pike, but no footsteps to suggest she had departed. Evidently she was unsure quite whether she should leave her here.

Rilla forced down a snort. It was not appropriate in church, and most of all, the Pike would scold her for it—and she wasn't in the mood for being scolded.

'Nothing is going to happen to me here,' Rilla pointed out dryly. 'This is a church, Miss Pike. I will be alone for a short while, then I will return to the Academy.'

'Yes, well…the reverend is coming to luncheon to instruct the wallflowers, but…but I suppose you have a great deal to think about.'

Rilla's throat tightened. 'I do.'

Only then did the footsteps depart, growing fainter as Miss Pike reached the door. And then there was silence.

Shoulders sagging, Rilla allowed herself to feel the weight of what she had so recently been told.

No more money for the Wallflower Academy—and no warm invitation to return home. So where would that leave her?

She was gifted with nothing more than a few minutes of solitude before footsteps appeared again. A prickle of irritation curled around Rilla's heart. Could she not be trusted to sit quietly in a church? Was the Pike truly about to interrupt her, when all she wished was for silence?

'I want to be alone,' Rilla said harshly as the footsteps grew closer.

They suddenly stopped. And then came a scent of lemon.

'F-Finlay?' she breathed.

It was a foolish thing to say. It could not be him. Why the Earl of Staromchor would have left his own church to drive or ride out of London to see her, she did not know. There was no logical reason.

'I have to work out how you do that,' came the light, cheerful voice of Finlay Jellicoe. 'Budge up, there.'

Hardly able to think as her mind whirled, Rilla obeyed, shifting along the pew what she believed was a sufficient amount. A person sat beside her. A person who smelled of sandalwood, and lemon, and whose warmth was moving powerfully through her.

His arm was pressed against hers. His leg—

Rilla swallowed.

His leg was pressed against hers, their hips connected in a way that even through several layers of clothing, a burning heat spread through her.

There was surely no need for him to sit that close to her... was there?

'What are you doing here?' Rilla asked sharply.

She had not intended the words to become an interrogation, but fear and worry were tinging her blood with every thrum of her pulse, and the anxiety poured into her words.

Besides, what could this man possibly want from this strange friendship? What did he want with her?

Oh, he had kissed her—but they had never spoken of it. Sometimes Rilla wondered whether she had dreamt the entire thing. It would not be the first time she had wished to kiss an earl.

'I came to see the church. My mother asked me to...well, look at churches. No reason why,' came the nonsensical reply.

Rilla snorted. 'You do know that makes no sense, don't you? What does your mother need a church for?'

'What are you doing here?' Finlay returned, seemingly without concern that she had been so rude.

'This is my parish church,' she snapped in return, heat blooming in her chest, rising in temperature quite beyond her control.

And she knew she was being unreasonable, but right now, the whole world was. Why should she be sent away from home, abandoned by her family? Why should she be turned out of the Wallflower Academy—had she not helped countless wallflowers find husbands? Did not Gwen owe some of her happiness to her? And Mary before her? And Sarah before her? And when Elizabeth—

'There's no law against stepping into a church, Rilla,' Finlay said sedately, evidently unruffled by her hostile tone. 'In fact, I rather think they encourage it.'

'I wanted to be alone,' Rilla said hotly, unable to stop herself.

'Then be alone with me,' came the gentle reply.

Rilla had to swallow the retort that he was being ridiculous, for two reasons.

Firstly, because her temper was about to get the better of her, and that was never a pleasant occurrence at the best of times.

And secondly because...because he was right.

She had never noticed that before. But Finlay spoke the truth—she could be alone with him, and quite happily. The heat seeping from his body into hers wasn't fuelling her bitterness; it was calming her, washing away the anxiety and leaving calm in its wake.

His presence soothed her.

'You...you are not offended? By the way I speak to you, I mean,' Rilla said awkwardly.

The chuckle beside her rustled up her arm and into her side. 'I suppose other people placate you, accept whatever you deal out to them, just because you can't see.'

Rilla blanched, but unfortunately had little in the way of retort because it was true. It had always been true. The awkwardness people felt around her as a child had swiftly led to her being treated differently, and one aspect of that was the delicacy with which she was treated.

In some cases it was welcome. A little more grace, a little more patience—who would refuse that?

But Rilla knew, even if she had never admitted it before,

that it also led to people accepting rudeness from her that they would never accept from someone like Sylvia or Daphne.

And Finlay had noticed.

'I don't pity you, you know.'

Rilla started, still staring towards the front of the church. 'You don't?'

'Not because you cannot see, I mean,' came Finlay's soft voice. 'Though I do pity you in a way.'

Already the tension was returning to her shoulders. 'And why, precisely, would you?'

'You have fewer options than me,' Finlay said softly. Despite that, the low pluck of his voice seemed to reverberate in the empty church. 'I…well, I don't have every choice set ahead of me, but I certainly have more choices than you. Your future… what does it contain? You never told me, the other day.'

Rilla swallowed back the hated tears.

She would not cry. She would not.

'You don't have to talk to me about it. But I'd like you to.'

And it was the gentleness that prompted her to speak. She had never met a man, or anyone, who spoke with such gentleness. Such understanding.

'I… I do not have much longer at the Wallflower Academy.'

For some reason, the man sitting beside her stiffened. 'What do you mean?'

'Oh, never fear, no man is about to sweep me off my feet and propose marriage,' Rilla said, forcing herself to laugh. As long as she was the one doing the laughing, then it didn't matter if others laughed, too. 'No, it's… Well…'

It wasn't a lack of money, and even that would be shameful enough to admit. It wasn't a lack of space—the Wallflower Academy was busy at the moment, to be sure, but there was plenty of space in the old Tudor manor for her.

It was a lack of care, she supposed, though wild horses would not get her to admit to such a thing about her father.

Rilla sighed, her head dropping. 'I think if I had just married the Earl of Porthaethwy, none of this would be a problem. My father wouldn't—none of my family would be ashamed. There would be no scandal—'

'It wasn't as much a scandal as you think,' came the interjection of Finlay's voice. 'I mean to say, I had never heard of it.'

'I am not sure whether to be pleased or mortified that my life has had such little impact,' Rilla said dryly.

They sat for a moment in silence, and she could not help but notice just how comfortable it was.

He made her comfortable.

And then Finlay made her distinctively uncomfortable by shifting in his seat and asking in a low voice, 'What happened between you and the Earl of Porthaethwy?'

Rilla trotted out the tried and tested formula instinctively. 'There was naught but a misunderstanding.'

'Which was?'

No one had ever asked her that. A misunderstanding was usually sufficient to ward off even the most nosey of gossips.

But this wasn't a gossip. This was Finlay. A man who absolutely should not matter to her, and by God, he mattered.

'I… He wouldn't accept my explanation, my apology, when…' Rilla swallowed. Old wounds never healed, not entirely. The scars still rested on her heart, and tugging at the injury threatened to cause an ache she was not sure she could accept.

But if she were to tell anyone, it would be him.

Sighing heavily, she tried to keep her voice light. 'It was my own fault. I can admit that now, though it was a most challenging thing to accept when I was younger. But I know now that the blame was my own.'

'Blame?'

'I was not always the paragon of virtue that you see before you,' said Rilla, trying to keep her tone light. 'I was…arrogant,

I suppose. I revelled in the idea that I would be a countess—an earl, did you know, an earl wished to marry me? And the Earl of Porthaethwy, he was coming a week before the wedding. His Lordship arrived, for the first time. A house party before the wedding, to meet me, to meet the whole family. The match had been arranged when we were young, and...'

Her voice trailed away. How could she admit this? How could she reveal just how foolish she had—

Her gasp echoed around the church.

Finlay had taken her hand. No request, no hesitation—he had just reached out and taken it in his. His warm fingers entwined with hers and he pulled her hand into his lap, holding it there as a secure anchor against the storm that was railing in her chest.

Rilla swallowed. And could somehow continue. 'Nina and I were in the drawing room. My sister, my next-youngest sister. This was two...no, maybe three days since Lord Porthaethwy had arrived. She asked me what I thought of him, and I... I was young, you must recall, and I did not know what I was about. Anyway, I... I spoke cuttingly of the man.'

'Ah,' came Finlay's voice. 'I have a sense where this is going.'

'I thought to impress, I suppose. I was almost giddy with excitement. I was getting married, and I was to be a countess, and at that age those sorts of things mattered,' said Rilla bitterly. 'I spoke in a way— Oh, how I blush to even think of it now. It is hateful indeed to look back upon the person you once were, and realize that you were unformed, unfinished.'

'What did you say to him?' came Finlay's curious voice.

Her chest tightened painfully. 'None of your business.'

'It's just, to break off an engagement...'

'I was not... Well, not the person I aim to be now,' Rilla said, heat burning her cheeks. 'It was nothing serious, of course, but he was a proud man, and I injured that pride. The damage was done.'

'Naught but a misunderstanding, I'm sure.'

Rilla laughed ruefully. The pew was cold under her free hand as she clutched it tightly. 'I think perhaps more accurately I should say that the Earl of Porthaethwy did not wish to be understanding. I had offended—nay, mortified him. He would not accept my apology, nor that of my father.'

Strange. She had not permitted herself to think of those days for such a long time now, it was as though the colour had been taken out of the memories she held. They were so distant now, yet they were a part of her. Had made her who she was.

'And so he left me at the altar.'

'He—'

'Yes,' said Rilla as lightly as though she barely cared. She would not permit the man to continue to injure her. 'Yes, he waited until the moment that would hurt me, hurt my family the most. There I was, having just swept up the aisle on my father's arm…'

'The brute!'

'He was hurt.' That was what she had told herself then. 'He wished to punish me, I suppose, and earls can do whatever they like in Society. Why not shame the entire Newell family by thrusting aside my hand when it was offered, declaring to the whole church that he had no wish to align himself to a woman with a sharp tongue and an even sharper heart?'

Finlay was spluttering so dramatically his words were almost entirely incomprehensible. 'I— The cheek— If I had— Your father must—'

'It was an arranged marriage,' she said as lightly as she could. 'He never would have chosen me, not of his own free will. And the whole thing, it should not matter, I should not care.'

'I think we're past the point of "should." You obviously cared, in a way. You must have been mortified.'

Mortification did not adequately cover it.

'And I never spoke to the Earl of Porthaethwy again,' Rilla

continued, pushing past his astonishment. She could not dwell on this story much longer. 'I attempted to apologize, but it did not matter. I had injured, insulted, and I was not to be forgiven. He married my sister Nina in the end. My father was insistent that the connection still be made, and after all, he had four daughters.'

She could well imagine the look of astonishment on Finlay's face.

'I am sorry—he merely exchanged one sister for another?'

'What did the substitution for one over the other matter? I did not attend the wedding.'

'And your sister?'

'We have not spoken since. I suppose she feels a duty, a responsibility to honour her husband, and I suppose, rightly so,' Rilla said, attempting to keep her voice level. 'I know I have not visited. No invitations have been forthcoming.'

Some things broken never mended. And it was her fault. Her pride, her arrogance, her determination to be adored, admired. To finally be the fortunate Newell sister.

It was her fault, all her fault—and by the time she'd concocted a way to make it right, it was too late. Too much time, too much silence, too much distance for too long. Too much pain, too many tears. Too many nightmares of standing there, the scent of the church candles, the shocked gasps echoing…

Finlay's hand squeezed hers. 'I am sorry.'

'Don't be,' Rilla said briskly.

'Just take my kindness, will you, and don't brush it away?' Finlay's voice was level, and there was concern, and what could be considered affection if one were seeking it. 'You don't have to always push people away, Rilla.'

Rilla blinked back tears.

Perhaps she did not—but she certainly should have done when it came to Finlay Jellicoe, Earl of Staromchor.

Because here she was, falling in love with him.

Oh, it was a disaster. After guarding her heart so well, for so long, she had managed to allow him in—and he was an earl, too.

Try as she might, Rilla could not deny the intensely emotional tie between the two of them. That connection, the soft and gentle comfort that they shared, belied the undercurrent of attraction.

And it was the thought of attraction that led Rilla to pull her hand away and rise abruptly.

'I should return to the Wallflower Academy,' she said firmly. 'The reverend is having luncheon with us.'

'Yes, I should return, too,' Finlay said. The rustle of his greatcoat suggested he too had risen. 'Would you like a hand?'

It was the first time he had offered, and Rilla knew it would be churlish to push him aside. Besides, she wanted the contact.

Desperately.

His arm was steady as he led her out of the pew and into the aisle.

'I hope you still intend to come riding with me tomorrow.'

'With you and Sylvia,' Rilla corrected, heat flushing through her chest.

But she wouldn't. Her, riding? It was the most ridiculous thing she had ever heard.

'I greatly wish to take you riding,' came Finlay's soft voice. 'Will you not give me the chance to show you?'

Give him a chance.

Had she not been giving him chances every moment she was with him? Did he not know how much she had already compromised for him? Was he unaware that she had undermined her resolve to stay away from earls, her determination never to open herself to a man like that again?

Rilla swallowed. 'I suppose I can walk with you to the stables.'

'Good,' said Finlay, his voice low and warm. It vibrated through her, promising possibilities that were simply not possible.

Their footsteps echoed on the stone-flagged church aisle.

'I suppose it is a good thing we did not meet at the altar,' Rilla attempted to jest. 'It's something neither of us will be doing anytime soon.'

The silence from Finlay suggested, much to her horror, that she had gone too far. But as he stepped towards the church door, his hand over hers on his arm, she could have sworn that he had spoken softly. So softly she could barely hear the words.

'I wouldn't bet on that.'

Chapter Twelve

'Ah, there you are,' said the disapproving voice of Miss Pike. 'We were beginning to believe you had forgotten.'

Forgotten?

Finlay could not comprehend doing such a thing. Forgetting would mean that Rilla was out of his thoughts for more than a minute, which was not something he had managed to achieve since he had deposited her on the doorstep of the Wallflower Academy yesterday.

'I was momentarily delayed in London,' Finlay said smoothly as he stepped into the Wallflower Academy hallway and bowed low to Miss Pike. 'I regret it most sincerely.'

Which was true, though perhaps not in the manner the proprietress of the Wallflower Academy believed.

Yes, he was sorry for the accidental rudeness. But he was more sorry that he had missed even a moment of Rilla's company.

She was standing just behind Miss Pike and was wearing the most splendid riding habit that he had ever seen. It was dark green, and swept down to the floor with elegant brass buttons in the military style along the shoulders and cuffs. She wore a jockey bonnet of last year's style upon her head, and there was a glare in her expression.

Finlay swallowed, his mouth dry. He should have expected it. There were times when he forgot that Rilla was also the

Honourable Miss Newell. Her family must have some wealth, with a title like that. It was entirely appropriate for her to be well dressed.

And entirely inappropriate for him to be staring with his mouth open.

Closing his jaw with a snap and hoping to goodness only Sylvia, similarly attired and clearly stifling a giggle, had noticed, Finlay cleared his throat.

'And what a lovely day you have for your ride, too,' Miss Pike was saying, though whether to himself or to the two wall-flowers, Finlay was not sure. 'I trust you will be able to assist Miss Newell in any way necessary.'

'Miss Newell has no intention of riding whatsoever,' said Rilla sharply, pushing past the older woman and striding confidently towards the Academy door. 'But I'll indulge this nonsense and accompany you to the stables. Come, Sylvia.'

Disappointment twisted in Finlay's chest. Well, it wasn't as though he could have expected anything different. Rilla had never made any declarations of her feelings. Of course, neither had he. But surely she had noticed? Surely she had guessed, after he had kissed her on the beach in Brighton, that he felt something for her.

'And how is Miss Carr, my lord?' asked Miss Pike sweetly from behind him.

Finlay whirled around, his tails flapping in the sudden breeze he had created. Sylvia had departed, racing after the swiftly disappearing back of Rilla. They were alone.

He tried to smile. 'Miss Carr?'

'Your betrothed, Miss Carr,' said Miss Pike, a slight frown puckering her forehead. 'How many other Miss Carrs do you know?'

Cursing himself for not considering this, Finlay attempted to gather his thoughts. Right. He should have expected the announcement to have been read by all. 'She...she is well, thank you.'

What else was he supposed to say?

'I must say, I think it very gracious of you to take time away from your betrothed to help some of our wallflowers practise their conversation and riding,' Miss Pike was saying lightly, as though this occurred every day. 'Marilla and Sylvia will chaperone each other, naturally, and as you are already engaged, there can be no thought of impropriety.'

Finlay's smile weakened. 'Yes. Yes, I quite agree. Now, if you will excuse me, Miss Pike...'

The Wallflower Academy stables were just to the left of the house. Finlay had stabled one of his own steeds there once, when he had come to that dinner.

That dinner when he had fed Rilla. Oh, that sensuous delight, nothing could compare to—

Well. He supposed that something could.

He would have to tell Rilla, of course. There was nothing else for it, not now Miss Pike knew about the engagement. The engagement he had thought was not public knowledge.

Swallowing hard and thanking his stars—and his valet— that his riding breeches were a little loose at the front, Finlay stepped into the stable yard.

Rilla was standing in the middle of it. She had her arms crossed. Rilla's moods were changeable, and passion ran deep in all of them. What had irritated her?

Apprehension and anticipation warred in Finlay's chest as he moved forward. Oh, but one more afternoon surely would not hurt. He would tell her tomorrow. Four and twenty hours, what difference would it make?

'I said you were being ridiculous, and this proves it,' Rilla was saying smartly to Sylvia. 'You cannot think he would believe—'

'Ah, there you are, my lord,' Sylvia said, interrupting her friend. To Finlay's surprise, she gave him a huge theatrical wink he was certain he would have seen from fifty feet. 'I find to my sadness that I have a stone in my shoe.'

Finlay blinked. 'A…a stone.'

Rilla snorted. 'Sylvia, the man wasn't born yesterday.'

'And as such, I will have to spend a great deal of time sitting here, on a mounting block, attending to my boots,' said Sylvia proudly, sticking out her leather boot from her long skirts. 'I fear it will take me most of the afternoon to—'

'Sylvia,' growled Rilla.

Finlay looked bemusedly back and forth between the two women. Evidently there was a scheme afoot.

'So I think the two of you should start on riding without me,' Sylvia said, winking again most ostentatiously. 'I'll catch up when I can, my lord, but it would be a true shame if Rilla were to miss out on a ride merely because I was improperly shod.'

Finlay grinned. It was an excellent excuse—he would have to remember to thank Miss Sylvia Bryant at a later date. For the present, however…

'Miss Pike will be furious,' Rilla said sharply as Finlay stepped to her side.

'Miss Pike believes you are being chaperoned,' he pointed out. 'May I take your hand?'

The beautiful woman shook her black curls back, but evidently did not have the heart to decline. 'You…you may.'

Heat shot through Finlay's body, as it always did when it came into contact with Rilla. Oh, these were the warning signs he should heed, and yet he did not seem able. All he wanted to do was be with her—touch her. Be touched by her.

Finlay almost tripped over a perfectly flat cobble as he led Rilla to his horse Ceres.

'And what precisely are we going to do together?' Rilla asked sarcastically as Sylvia disappeared off into the stables. 'You must know that I cannot ride. Me, sitting alone on a horse, guiding the reins? Preposterous—and in truth, I don't think you will be able to teach me.'

His heart stirred as the delightful idea of an afternoon spent with Rilla, alone—with a ready-made excuse—filled his chest.

This was far better than he could have hoped. Pushing aside the discomfort of keeping his secret from Rilla could be done for a little while longer. His feelings for Rilla, after all, were far stronger.

'That indeed would be a great challenge, and I agree that I would not be up to such a task,' he said seriously, ignoring her sarcasm and looking through it to the pain and the embarrassment beneath. 'But I do not intend to.'

There it was—the flicker of uncertainty, the nervousness Rilla was feeling momentarily expressed on her face.

And Finlay's chest ached. What must it be, to never quite know who to trust? To always be wondering when the next embarrassment would come? When someone would take advantage of your lack of sight, never knowing if one was about to be tricked?

His temper burned against her sister, the earl, the pair of them—but that was not something he could do anything about, not today.

Today, he was about to do something quite different.

They halted before Ceres.

Rilla frowned. 'So…so if we are not going riding, why am I wearing this ridiculous get-up?'

'I don't think you look ridiculous,' said Finlay without thinking. 'I think you look beautiful.'

No amount of silence could prevent him from noticing the flush on Rilla's cheeks—nor could he avoid the fact that it suited her complexion well.

So did the slow smile that tilted her lips. 'You…you do?'

'I do,' Finlay said softly, his own cheeks burning now at the intimacy of their words, matched only by the soft, private tone of their conversation.

'I… I don't know what you mean, then,' Rilla said, the sarcasm and protective anger melting away. 'What will we be doing this afternoon?'

'We'll be riding,' Finlay said promptly.

'But you said— Finlay Jellicoe, put me down!'

And he did…though perhaps not precisely where Rilla was expecting.

'Hold on here, and here,' he said, guiding her hands to the reins.

Though surprising her was a delightful achievement in itself, Finlay congratulated himself for his brilliant idea, too. It wasn't just the execution which had to be just right; it was the inspiration itself.

And seeing Rilla in that dark green riding habit, astride his mare with her head held high and an imperious look on her face?

Finlay's manhood stirred.

That was inspiration.

'You have to be jesting,' Rilla said faintly. 'You cannot—'

'You wish me to take you down?' Finlay asked seriously.

For he would, if she asked. He was no cad, would not force Rilla to do things she had no wish to merely because he could exert his will on her.

And besides, there would be a benefit to lifting her down. The movement had offered closeness and a tantalizing opportunity— which he did not capitalize on—to kiss her again. Rilla in his arms had been something he had thought about far too often. He would not be averse to doing it again.

Rilla hesitated, and Finlay grinned. There was a woman who was bold, and brilliant, and who held herself back just as often as others held her back. 'I just do not comprehend what you could possibly think is going to help. I cannot see, Finlay!'

It took a great deal for Rilla to say that, he knew. And that was why he did not explain, but merely acted on the next part of his plan.

'Finlay!'

Finlay had mounted Ceres in one easy stride. He'd been mounting horses without a block since he had come of age, even before then, and it was not exactly hard.

It was most definitely not a hardship to mount just behind Rilla, pulling her into his arms and taking the reins from her, breathing in the scent of her body, feeling the warmth of her in his chest, her head resting against his neck.

'Finlay Jellicoe!' Rilla said, her breath warm against his cheek. 'This is most scandalous!'

'Perhaps so,' said Finlay, nudging Ceres forward and speaking calmly as they left the stable yard and started to trot gently along the path towards the greater park. 'Do you want to be taken back to the Wallflower Academy?'

He knew the answer; he did not need to hear it. He could feel it in the soft languidness of her body, the comfort she was drawing from him, that they were drawing from each other.

Oh, there was nothing like this. Nothing like being with the woman you—

Finlay swallowed as he slowed his steed to a walk now that they were out of sight of the Wallflower Academy.

That had been a close one. He had almost thought there, for a moment, about love.

It was not a feeling he was going to permit himself to even think about. Not in the slightest. Not even consider. He could not love Miss Marilla Newell. He certainly did not love Miss Isabelle Carr, but that did not mean that he could go around offering his heart to others.

He was going to be married in less than three weeks.

Finlay swallowed hard, pushing all thoughts of Isabelle out of his mind. Surely it was not a betrayal if he had never promised love and affection to begin with. No one could expect anything else from him. He had done everything that had been expected—more, perhaps.

Somewhere deep inside Isabelle Carr was the woman she had once been.

Perhaps, Finlay tried to convince himself, *after they were married...*

The revulsion that stirred at the mere thought was not a good sign.

'You are very quiet,' said Rilla softly.

Finlay tried not to shrug. 'I suppose I am.'

It was not as though he could share his thoughts with her. Why he had kept the truth of Miss Isabelle Carr—the very existence of Miss Isabelle Carr—from Rilla, he did not know.

Well. He had a vague guess.

Bringing those two worlds together, those two women together, even in conversation, would mean having to face up to the fact that he wanted one but could only have the other.

That he was going to be miserable with one, and miserable without the other.

That one of them he respected, and the other he...

Finlay cleared his throat as he nudged Ceres along a left-hand fork in the path. Perhaps...well. Men had mistresses all the time, didn't they? He was in fact unusual in his circle of friends, *not* having one. He had considered it an offence to Isabelle once their engagement had been decided upon, but even before then, Finlay had never wished to engage in such a thing without...well, without his emotions involved.

But now that they were...

'You know, I feel like I can tell you anything,' he said before he could stop himself.

Rilla was silent for a moment. Then she asked, 'Where did that come from?'

'I, uh...'

'You say nothing at all, and then you say you can tell me anything?' She turned slightly in his arms. 'Do you have something to tell me, Finlay?'

His stomach lurched.

Only that I'm lying. That I'm keeping from you information that you would almost certainly want. That I'm being torn in two directions, between who I should be and who I am.

Finlay swallowed. 'No. No, nothing.'

Hell's bells, man, this can't continue.

Trying not to think about the delicate woman curled into his chest, exclaiming with delight at the strange sensation that riding provided, Finlay prodded at his conscience.

Would he, in turn, be content if Isabelle took a lover?

After a moment of introspection, he believed that he would. Well, their marriage had begun as one of convenience only, had it not? Though now he'd overheard her declarations of love, perhaps it was unlikely that Isabelle would wish to look elsewhere…

'And this is riding?'

Finlay's focus snapped back to the woman in his arms. 'I beg your pardon?'

'Well, is this…it?' Rilla said, a slight tension in her voice.

It was a bizarre question. After all, the rolling hills, the frost-tipped branches of the forest of their left, the way the sunlight glittered…

And then Finlay felt very foolish indeed.

When was he going to learn that so much of his experience was different to Rilla's? That he could not simply amaze and dazzle her with new sights, as though that would make her care for him?

Not that he was attempting to do that. Obviously.

Finlay fought the instinct to press a kiss into her hair and instead said softly, 'We are riding along a path covered with leaves. Most of them have decayed, with the winter approaching, but there are toadstools and mushrooms pushing up through the foliage, striving to reach the sun.'

Rilla's breathing changed. Unless he had been acutely attuned to it, he would not have noticed.

He took that as encouragement to continue. 'On our left is the forest—or woodland, I suppose. I never knew the difference. Trees stand tall against the sky, their branches bare. I can see the remnants of nests, the evidence of a summer well lived. There are several ravens, or crows, sitting in one tree and they examine us as we pass.'

'A family?' Rilla breathed.

Finlay chuckled, his chest pressing against her back. 'Perhaps. And on our right are the fields, soaring out into the distance, kissing the horizon. The hedgerows are brimming with berries, and birds flicker in and out, guzzling themselves full for the winter ahead. There'll be squirrels in there, I suppose, and mice perhaps. I can't see.'

'Neither can I.'

He stiffened for a moment, then softened as Rilla's laughter rippled through his chest.

'Tell me more,' she said, a giggle in her voice.

More? How could he possibly think about the countryside around them when Rilla was in his arms?

'There are clouds in the sky,' he said, his Town upbringing starting to betray him. 'Erm…big clouds. Fluffy clouds.'

Rilla snorted. 'Snow clouds.'

'Now how could you possibly know?'

'Can you not smell it?' She took in a deep lungful of air, while Finlay did his absolute best not to notice the most tantalizing swell of her breasts. 'That's snow on the air. I could smell it a mile off.'

'It's not going to snow.'

'Have it your way,' Rilla said with a grin, nestling into him. 'But I'll be proved right, you'll see.'

'You are not too uncomfortable?' Finlay said aloud, concern twisting in his chest. 'I do apologize, I have barely asked.'

'It is a most strange sensation, I will admit,' said Rilla, a laugh lilting in the air. 'I imagine it is like being at sea. The undulation, not knowing what is going to happen…it's a loss of control.'

'Not something you enjoy, then,' said Finlay ruefully.

She had never told him that she needed to be in control, but it was obvious, was it not? Anyone who spent more than five minutes in the same room with Rilla would surely know that.

Rilla shrugged. The movement tightened her in his arms and Finlay revelled in it. 'I thought I would not, in truth—though I admit, I did not think you would actually get me on a horse.'

'And I am sorry for not asking your permission,' Finlay said, regret pouring into the joy, tainting it. 'I know how much you dislike being touched without your permission.'

'You…you remember that?'

Rilla's voice sounded surprised, which was a surprise in itself to Finlay.

'Of course I remember that,' he said, startled. 'I remember everything you say.'

They continued to ride in silence for a few minutes. Finlay was not certain if the silence was awkward for Rilla, but in himself he felt nothing but contentment and satisfaction.

After all his hopes and planning for such an afternoon, he could not have conceived of such a pleasant day. Rilla in his arms, Rilla happy—what else could he want?

'I love to hear you describe what's around me. What's around us.'

The sudden lurch in his chest was most definitely not something he should pay attention to, Finlay told himself. Nor the rising affection, the warmth in his chest, the way he wanted to nuzzle and kiss that delicate neck…

'There's not much else to tell,' Finlay said aloud, partly to redirect himself from his most distracting thoughts. 'Though there's you, I suppose.'

Rilla snorted. 'I know what I look like.'

'Do you?' he could not help but ask. She was warm in his arms. They had never felt empty before, but now he knew he would be bereft once she had left him. 'Do you know how you shine, Rilla?'

She turned at that, her gaze flickering over him as though attempting to discern whether he was chiding her. 'I don't know what you mean.'

'I think you do,' Finlay said softly, trying not to think of that spectacular kiss they had shared. 'I think you know what I think about you. What…what I feel for you.'

Whether it was him who moved first, or Rilla, he was not sure. All Finlay knew was that the woman he cared about deeply had turned in his arms, lifting up her lips to him in a silent plea for his attention, and he had given it most willingly.

Oh, God, it was a challenge to stay on the horse. Rilla's lips had parted almost instantly, inviting him in, and Finlay's grip around her tightened as every part of him longed to pour himself into her.

He made do with his tongue, desperately tasting the sweetness of her mouth, the delicacy of her affection, and tried not to moan too loudly.

But Finlay could barely stand it. Rilla had somehow woven her fingers in his hair, and he had never felt so close, so intimate with a woman before.

This was it; she was it. He adored her. He—

I wager you'll feel infinitely better for a flirtation. I think it'll bring you joy, and won't betray Isabelle in any way, and you'll enter the married state far happier. If I'm wrong, you can…oh, I don't know…choose your punishment.

The memory of Bartlett's words caused Finlay to break the kiss, to lean back, panting, to look at the woman with whom he had intended to enjoy nothing more than a flirtation.

The pang in his chest suggested otherwise.

No, this had gone much further than he had intended. This had gone beyond mere appreciation, beyond respect and admiration, beyond like.

Despite having no intention to create an entanglement before his wedding to another, Finlay had fallen completely in love with Rilla Newell.

Soft flakes of snow started to fall from the sky.

Chapter Thirteen

By the time Finlay whispered in her ear that they were about to enter the stable yard, Rilla knew two things.

Firstly, she knew that Finlay had never mentioned matrimony. He had probably never even considered it—the thought would never have passed through his mind. He was an earl, a man who would marry a beautiful heiress without any hint of stain upon her character.

It was surely no coincidence that Finlay had never spoken of his marital prospects.

Her own reputation was not so marred as it could be, but the fact that she had been sent to the Wallflower Academy and never visited by her family would surely cause eyebrows to rise. And that would be before anyone discovered her shameful history with the Earl of Porthaethwy.

No, Finlay would not marry her. The idea would never occur to him; Rilla was certain. Earls with egos like that did not marry women like her.

Secondly, she knew that when Finlay kissed her, every inch of her came alive in a way that she was certain would never be sparked again.

He knew her, truly knew her, and he desired her. That much was undeniable. Rilla did not care how carefully constructed the man's persona was in Society—he may be charming and light-hearted in company, and more serious and grieving in private, but no man could pretend that sort of desire.

Which made her just like…just like any other woman.

And so with these two facts in her mind, Rilla came to a most astonishing conclusion as Ceres's shod shoes clattered on the cobbles of the stable yard: seducing Finlay Jellicoe, Earl of Staromchor, would be her best opportunity in her life to know what it was to make love.

Rilla knew she could not just suggest such a thing bluntly and without careful consideration. The trouble was, her time was running out. In a few short weeks, her sojourn at the Wallflower Academy would be over, and she would be seeking her fortune elsewhere.

Perhaps, Rilla could not help but think ruefully as the horse was brought to a stop and she lost the sensation of Finlay sitting behind her, she would end up as a governess after all, just as Miss Pike had wished.

But how precisely she made her way in the world after the Wallflower Academy was immaterial. She had this time, this moment now, to create a memory she would never forget.

And besides. She wanted him. A dull, throbbing ache between her legs told her that there was more pleasure to come, if that could be believed. More joy, more sensuality, more decadence—more of Finlay.

She wanted that.

So when Finlay said softly, 'May I help you down?' and Rilla offered her hands out into the unknown, she knew what she must do. What she had to do, if she wanted to continue without adding a regret to the list she bore in her heart.

Finlay's hands were warm, and strong, and gentle. He lifted her down carefully, almost reverently, and as her boots touched the cobbled stones beneath her, Rilla found her lungs were tight and breathless.

Oh, Lord, she was a walking cliché. He made her breathless!

Despite having her full balance now, Finlay's hands did not leave her sides. When Rilla took a step forward, pressing her breasts against him and feeling the rapid rise and fall of his chest, she knew he was just as breathless as she was.

'Is…is there anyone else here?' Rilla asked, her mouth dry.

After all, it would never do for the conversation she intended to have with the man to be overheard. Miss Pike would be the least of her problems.

She felt the brush of air as Finlay turned one way, then the other.

'Strangely, no,' he said quietly, hands still around her waist. 'I think I can see— Yes, they are all inside the servants' hall. An early dinner, perhaps? It appears that we are alone.'

Alone.

Well, thought Rilla, steeling herself for what was about to be a very bold declaration, *there is no time like the present.*

'I like you, Finlay,' she blurted out.

And immediately cast her face down.

She liked him?

Was that truly what she had managed to say, after carefully constructing a logical argument for why they should make love at the swiftest opportunity?

That she *liked* him?

Rilla felt, as well as heard, his chuckle.

'Goodness, I thought you hated earls.'

'I do not generally hold them in particularly high regard, no,' she said as heat suffused her cheeks. 'In my experience, earls are insufferably proud, indeterminately arrogant, and unable to listen to a woman for five minutes together.'

Finlay's second chuckle was deeper. 'And yet you like me?'

I don't like you, Rilla wanted to say. *I… I think—*

'My dislike of earls in general has been tempered somewhat, yes, by…by getting to know you better,' she said aloud, forcing down the declaration of affection she knew would not be returned. 'And I… I trust you.'

Why it was so difficult to admit to such a thing, she did not know—but Rilla knew it mattered.

Trusting Finlay, not only to respect her but to treat her kindly, learning to expect kindness from a man whose position and station in life suggested she would receive naught but pain...

'I am grateful for your trust.' Finlay's voice was low, his breath warm, and she could feel his fingers momentarily tighten on her waist. Then they relaxed—though they did not release her. 'Earning your trust is something I think very... very precious.'

Here they were, Rilla thought. Right on the precipice of what they wanted to say, and yet neither of them willing to be the first to admit it.

They wanted each other.

Desire was not the domain of a respectable young woman. Oh, she knew the basics—the physical mechanics of lovemaking. It had been rather a surprise to learn that that was what happened, but since meeting Finlay, Rilla had come to understand that the stirrings within her whenever he touched her were the first steps on a journey she wished to take...with him.

And now, here, standing in Finlay's arms, knowing him to be a man of passion and caring, desire and understanding, grief and love, as well as joy and jesting...

He was far more than she had presumed.

Rilla took a deep breath. And if she didn't speak now, she would always wonder, *What if...?*

'Finlay,' she said firmly.

'Rilla,' he returned with a gentle chuckle.

Deploying the intense glare Sylvia had helped her to perfect, Rilla said, 'I am attempting to be serious here.'

'I wouldn't dare stop you,' Finlay said quietly. 'Though that doesn't mean that I have to be serious in turn.'

Rilla raised a hand and splayed it against his chest—and

gasped. She had meant it as a censure, but all thoughts of that had melted the instant she had felt his heart.

Thump-thump-thump-thump...

It was racing. In fact, Finlay's pulse seemed to be just as frantic, perhaps more so, as her own.

'Rilla?'

She swallowed. Perhaps she was not about to request something that would be denied, then. Perhaps he wanted this just as much, or perhaps even more, than she did. But she knew what she wanted. Just one encounter, she was certain, would be enough. Wouldn't it?

Well, she would never know if she never asked. 'Would you make love to me?'

Shame soared through her chest at the inelegant—and painfully direct—question. What had possessed her to speak so frankly? Dear God, he would think her a harlot, a strumpet, a woman utterly devoid of—

'I beg your pardon?' came a strained voice from Finlay.

Rilla twisted in his arms, attempting to get away. She would find the wall of the Tudor manor and from there she could make her way around to the front door—and then never leave it again.

How on earth could she be so—

But Finlay had tightened his grip, making it impossible to escape. 'Rilla!'

'Forget I said anything,' she said hastily, her words almost tripping over themselves as she struggled to free herself. 'And let me go, damn you!'

And then she was released.

The sudden space around her, the sudden lack of Finlay, took her quite by surprise. Rilla almost stumbled, her head spinning.

'But just so you know, before you march off,' said the Earl of Staromchor quietly. 'Yes.'

Rilla froze after a single step.

Yes?

He couldn't mean— Surely he did not mean…?

Turning slowly on the spot to where Finlay's voice had last been, Rilla breathed, 'Yes?'

'Yes,' said Finlay matter-of-factly, as though they were discussing something no more important than the expected change in the weather. 'Yes, I… I would very much like to make love to you. Now, in fact. Damn, Rilla, I have done for quite some time.'

Heat was stirring across Rilla's décolletage, but it was not shame, or guilt, or embarrassment, but—eagerness.

For quite some time?

'I know you have no wish to marry. That is, a marriage between us would be impossible,' Rilla said, straightening herself and attempting to approach this as a simple conversation.

Simple conversation? Had anything ever been less simple?

'That is not what I am asking for,' she said, her voice stronger. 'I just… Before I leave the Wallflower Academy, I need to know…know what it is to be loved.'

A hand took hers, and Rilla could tell it was Finlay. Her body was attuned to him in a way she could never have predicted.

'Leave the Wallflower Academy?'

Rilla hesitated—but this was not the time for that conversation. She would tell him tomorrow. What harm would it do, keeping a little truth from him?

'One day,' she said, a little awkwardly. 'I ask this of you, Finlay as…as a favour.'

'I cannot offer marriage to you today,' said Finlay softly. 'And I would still very much like to…to make love to you.'

Make love. Was this what Gwen had experienced, rushed Rilla's wild thoughts? Was she finally about to experience something that she had longed for?

How long they stood there in silence, hands clasped, luxuriating in the knowledge that they were going to enjoy one of life's most delicate pleasures, Rilla did not know. A minute? An hour? She could have remained there all day, she was certain, and as long as she had the certainty of Finlay's presence, she could have endured anything.

As it was, the very worst she had to endure was the uncertainty of what happened next.

Well, it wasn't as though she proposed lovemaking frequently. What did one do, once two people had agreed that they would quite like to take all their clothes off and...?

'Is there a side door?'

Rilla blinked. 'I beg your pardon?'

'A side door,' Finlay repeated. His voice was low, molten, teasing tendrils of desire across her skin. 'I don't think Miss Pike would appreciate seeing me ascend the staircase and enter your bedchamber, do you?'

A jolt of shock rocked Rilla's body. 'But you can't mean now?'

'Why not now?' His voice was urgent, his fingers tightening around hers. 'I don't want to wait for you, Rilla. I want you now, right now. I need you right now.'

And he was kissing her, and his other hand was tangled in her hair, and pins were cascading to the cobbles but Rilla did not care.

How could she when he was kissing her like that, his lips pressing hard hot desire into her, his tongue causing ripples of pleasure that thrummed through her body and settled in that aching spot between her legs?

When he finally released her, Rilla was once again breathless, but far more decisive. 'There's a side door just here. Wait, where is the entrance to the stables?'

Finlay took her hand, made a point with her finger, and moved it. 'There.'

Getting her bearings, a miracle considering how her head was spinning, Rilla took a step forward. 'This way.'

The side door by the stables was unlocked, as it always was before night fell. And Rilla would have known that, unequivocally, if they had managed to reach it.

Unfortunately their need for each other swiftly scuppered their plan to enter the house. The side door was at least, as far as Rilla could make out, ten yards from them.

Not that it mattered. Not with Finlay's arms around her, his lips trailing kisses down her neck.

'We…we shouldn't.'

'No one is here—they are at dinner. I told you,' Finlay said, his voice somehow raw and eager at the same time. 'And I want you, Rilla.'

How was any woman supposed to defend herself against such unashamed desire? How could woman prevent herself from succumbing to such words, spoken in such a tone, by such a man?

'Here, then,' Rilla found herself saying, pulling him in the opposite direction.

'Where are we—'

'You'll see,' she said breathlessly, stepping forward confidently.

Riding may have been a diversion previously unavailable to her in the past, but Rilla had spent a great deal of time around the stables as she waited for the other wallflowers to mount and dismount their horses. She knew the cobbles well, knew that when she reached the stable door, they would become slabs of stone rather than the small, uneven cobbles that typified the stable yard itself.

And so when she reached out in confidence, she was rewarded. The door to the stables opened to her, and with Finlay's hand in hers, she pulled him through.

'You will have to tell me,' Rilla said, her breath short and her cheeks burning as she spoke so directly, 'which of the stalls is empty.'

Finlay's breath caught in his throat. That was the only indication that he had responded at all to her words.

When he finally spoke, it was with an incredulous—and impressed—tone. 'You cannot mean to—'

'You want to wait until we creep down a corridor, pause for the servants' corridor to be empty, go up three flights of stairs, ensure there are no wallflowers on the bedchamber corridor, hope we are not seen, then—'

Rilla's mouth was hushed by a passionate kiss. It spoke of eagerness, and surprise, and delight in her equal hunger.

And when Finlay finally released her, his breathing was quick and his hands warm. 'Dear God, you are magnificent.'

'I don't know about that,' said Rilla, trying to force away the shyness she felt.

She wanted this. She wanted him. There would be no time, no space in her mind for regrets.

'The stall at the end is empty,' said Finlay, his voice low. 'This way.'

Rilla allowed herself to be led along the corridor that ran between the four stalls on either side. The sound of creaking hinges rippled into the air, and she stepped forward with Finlay's hand on the small of her back.

Well, perhaps slightly lower than the small of her back.

Her lungs tight and her heart thundering, Rilla heard the squeak of the hinges as the door to the stall closed. Then she felt the warmth of Finlay's breath on her face. He was standing right opposite her.

What was his expression? Not for the first time, Rilla wished she had that additional insight into the people around her—but this time, there was no painful tinge to her wish.

Finlay Jellicoe had never hidden himself. Not since those ridiculous footman antics at their first meeting, anyway. He would tell her, show her, reveal in his movements and the shortness of his breath precisely what he was thinking.

And he was probably thinking, Rilla thought ruefully, what on earth they should do next. After all, it was not typical to make love to a wallflower in a stable.

'May I take off your jockey bonnet?'

'Yes.'

His hands were gentle. As the jockey bonnet came down, so did the final pins that had been barely containing her curls. Both pins and curls fell down her shoulders, and the appreciative sound she heard told Rilla that the effect must be pleasant.

'May I take off your riding habit?'

Rilla's chest tightened, just for a moment. 'Y-yes.'

'We can stop at any time,' Finlay's voice said, soft yet unshaking. 'Any moment you wish to—'

'I want you,' Rilla said.

Did he know just what she meant by that? Of course not—how could he? She barely knew what she meant by it, by all these feelings and emotions rushing through her, making it impossible to decipher just what she felt for Finlay.

Except love.

As her riding habit slipped from her shoulders, Rilla shivered. 'What about you?'

'What about me?'

She smiled. 'I cannot help but notice that you are still wearing all your clothes.'

'So are you. Mostly. Something I would like to rectify immediately,' came the seductive murmur of Finlay as he pressed a kiss into the base of Rilla's throat.

Unable to help herself, Rilla's head tipped back as she welcomed the intimacy. How did he make her melt under every kiss? He had a way with him that she could never have imagined—and would never forget.

'But I understand,' Finlay added. 'Here.'

Rilla frowned as her fingers were clasped in his own and brought forward. Then her brow unfurled.

'Undress me,' he whispered.

He had guided her hands to his coat—somehow his riding frock coat had obviously been cast aside—and his own hands had dropped to his sides.

She was in complete control.

'Kiss me,' Rilla breathed as her nervous hands undid the first button of his waistcoat.

There was strength under these clothes; she could feel it, and she could sense the strength of restraint as Finlay kissed her. His chest tensed as each button was undone, and Rilla tried to concentrate as his meandering lips teased that delicate spot beneath her ear, her neck, the curve of her collarbone and the swell of her décolletage.

'You're not making this easy,' she gasped, her fingers slipping on a button as his lips danced across the top of her breasts.

'Good,' growled Finlay, his hands cupping her buttocks with a groan. 'Neither are you.'

The idea that anyone, let alone an earl, would find her so enticing was unfathomable to Rilla, but she did not have the concentration to consider that. Not now she had finally managed to undo all the buttons before her.

Well. Not all the buttons. Tempting as it had been to allow her fingers to drift down to his breeches, she was not brave enough for that. Not yet.

'Take them off,' she breathed.

Finlay's hands left her body, just for a moment, as coat, waistcoat, and shirt fell to the stall floor. Rilla had sensed the straw beneath it, knew it would be soft when he...when Finlay...

Rilla swallowed. 'Now me.'

Turning on the spot and hoping to goodness they would not be discovered, she pulled her hair to one side to reveal to Finlay the ties at the back of her gown.

This undressing was not nearly so laboured. In a few quick heartbeats, Finlay had pulled loose all the ties keeping her gown upon her person. It pooled swiftly to her feet, leaving her in naught but—

'Dear God.' Finlay's breath blossomed out onto her now bare shoulder.

Rilla turned hurriedly, fear flooding through her chest. 'If you have changed your mind…'

'Changed my— I'm only regretting not suggesting this to you weeks ago,' Finlay said, his voice thick with desire.

Heat burned her cheeks as her secret place throbbed. 'You only met me weeks ago.'

'Exactly,' Finlay said darkly. 'May I lay you down? I've moved some blankets—you'll be quite comfortable.'

It was an entirely new exercise of trust, allowing Finlay to slowly guide her to the blankets that he had placed on the straw. With any other man she would have felt exposed, in danger—at every moment fearing that this had been a trick merely to make her ridiculous, or destroy her reputation completely.

But this was Finlay. She could trust Finlay.

She was not alone on the straw and the blanket for long. Heat seared along her skin as Finlay joined her, the rough, wiry hair of his thighs brushing up against hers.

Rilla gasped.

This was really happening. The pleasure of his presence, his touch, was about to take on a new meaning.

Fingertips trailed seductively along her hip. 'I… I don't want to hurt you.'

Rilla reached out without hesitation. Her hand cupped a cheek. 'Then don't.'

The answering kiss was slow, and passionate, and seemed to pour all the words neither of them could say between them. Rilla clutched at him, needing to know he was there, needing to know just how greatly he desired her.

And he showed her. As Finlay tilted her head back and worshipped her mouth, his hands were not idle.

Rilla whimpered as his thumb brushed across her secret place. 'Oh, Finlay—'

She was unable to say any more. Not merely because the kiss deepened, taking all breath away—but because Finlay had gently slipped his thumb into her slick folds, causing a spark of unimaginable pleasure through her body.

Oh, God—this was lovemaking?

How did anyone stop?

Finlay did not. As his tongue ravaged her mouth, teasing pleasure she had never known from it, his thumb and finger were stroking a rhythm in her secret core that was throwing fuel on the fiery ache that needed…needed—

Unable to help herself, Rilla tilted her head back. 'Oh, God, Finlay…'

The explosion was exquisite. Her whole body rippled with ecstasy, her limbs quivering at the pleasure which tightened her core and made every part of her glow with fiery heat.

His unrelenting fingers finally slowed. Rilla's panting breaths seemed to echo around the stall.

'That was…'

'I know.' Finlay's voice was thick with emotion, the words breathed not spoken into her ear. 'I've never seen anything more beautiful, Rilla. You're…you're so beautiful.'

Rilla blinked, as though that would steady her whirling mind. To think that such delicious sensuality was mere inches away from any pair, just under their clothes…

How would she ever be in Finlay's presence again without wanting this?

'God, I want you,' he groaned, sinking a kiss into her neck that fluttered longing once more through Rilla's chest. 'You can't know— But if you don't want—'

'I want you,' Rilla said quietly, knowing with a new sense of certainty that whatever followed was precisely what she wanted. What she needed. 'Take me, Finlay. Take whatever you need to.'

Her breath hitched as Finlay's lips brushed over one of her nipples, then tightened as his tongue laved, swirling around the delicate skin.

The ache was back.

'Take me,' Rilla breathed, and there was a pleading note there that she had not intended but could not, would not deny. 'Please.'

He did not appear to need convincing. Finlay's presence shifted, moving from her side to above her. The delicate nudge at her knees was enough. Rilla parted them, welcoming him in. Welcoming the intrusion, yet knowing it was precisely what she wanted.

There was a shift in the straw on either side of her head. Finlay was…leaning on it, perhaps?

'You can stop me at any point,' Finlay said hurriedly, pausing between words to snatch kisses from her willing lips. 'Rilla, you have to know—'

'I know,' she panted, the ache between her thighs desperate now for whatever satisfaction he could give her.

'You have to know how I feel about you.'

'I know,' Rilla said, blinking up into the vague darkness above her.

And there was a pause, and then Finlay was crushing his mouth on hers.

It was the perfect kiss. Rushed, a little raw, but perfect because of that, not despite it. It was a kiss that said they were equals in desire, equals in need—equals in all the ways that mattered.

And it was during that kiss that he—

'Finlay!' Rilla moaned in surprise as something thick and long pushed into her most intimate spot.

Her body knew what to do, far more than her mind. Swelling, shifting, welcoming him in, the stretch was uncomfortable but only for a moment. Rilla gasped, the ripples of pleasure now startlingly familiar.

Oh, this was—

Finlay blew out a sudden breath. 'God, Rilla, you feel so good.'

Good? A much too insufficient word.

'You feel perfect,' she managed, hands fisting into the straw as her back unconsciously arched, drawing him deeper. 'You are perfect, Finlay, perfect for me, perfect for— Oh, God!'

Rilla had not intended to cry out, but the gentle shift Finlay made, out and then spearing into her once more, was too much.

Pleasure roared through her, a fire she could never have predicted but now wished to light all over her body.

Burn.

'Rilla,' Finlay moaned, pulling out almost completely then thrusting back into her with a groan that suggested he was experiencing at least part of the sublime sensuality that she was. 'Yes, yes, yes…'

What words were spoken between them after that, Rilla could not recall. Words and kisses and moans intermingled as Finlay's gentle rhythm became harsher, harder, until she was floating on waves of pleasure that suddenly launched into ecstasy and it was no longer possible to hold it in.

'Finlay!' she sobbed.

The peak of her climax muffled all sound, removed all sense of place, and it was only thanks to her hands, which had somewhere released the straw and instead clutched his shoulders, that she knew Finlay was there.

With her. Beside her, within her through all this.

And then she heard him. 'Rilla, God, yes,' came the muffled grunt as he thrust, shuddering, into her.

The sudden pressure was quickly understood. Rilla felt the pressure of his shoulders on hers, the rough hair of his chest upon her breasts, his arms sinking around her as Finlay collapsed into her arms.

She held him. Held the man who had shown her so much. Held the man she loved.

And was complete. Complete and truly happy for perhaps the first time in her life.

Chapter Fourteen

Happiness was not something Rilla was particularly accustomed to. She had learned not to grow attached to it, and so now that it was here, it was rather a shock.

Sylvia and Daphne had both noticed the following morning and made sure to inform her in their own very different ways.

'You…you seem less morose,' Daphne said hesitantly as they all sat in the drawing room attending to their needlework.

Well. The other wallflowers attended to their needlework. Miss Pike had recently given them a lesson on the correct way to sit while embroidering, to best show off one's natural assets and to entice a gentleman to approach and ask what they were working on.

It sounded like hogwash to Rilla, but then it did not matter much to her. It wasn't as though she could do needlework.

'Less morose?' Rilla repeated sardonically.

It was Sylvia's laugh that filled the room. 'Less miserable, more like! You've been wandering around with a smile on your face all evening. What has got into you?'

And Rilla had flushed, for her friend could not know precisely how her words had been most suggestive.

I cannot help but notice that you are still wearing all your clothes.

So are you. Mostly. Something I would like to rectify immediately.

'Into me?' she said, trying not to laugh. 'I don't know what you mean.'

'It's that earl, if you ask me,' Sylvia said conversationally. 'Oh, would you like a glass of water, Rilla?'

'No. No, I'm fine,' Rilla said, her eyes watering as she attempted to slow her coughing fit. 'Perfectly fine. How is your father?'

It was a low blow, but desperate times called for something truly desperate. Besides, the gossip was all over the Academy: he had been seen, in Almack's, dancing with a woman. And not in a genteel, aloof manner, either.

'I haven't seen the Earl of Staromchor for a while,' said Daphne softly, her gentle voice even quieter. She must be concentrating. Rilla knew Daphne was always quieter when she was concentrating.

'But wasn't that him today?' came Sylvia's disinterested voice. 'I thought it looked like him, in the grounds, just ten minutes ago.'

Rilla stood up immediately. Then she wished she hadn't.

Sylvia's chortling laugh filled her ears as Rilla made her way to the hall. 'I knew it! You tell me all about it when you get back, Rilla. I want to know how you plan to seduce him!'

Little did her friend know, of course, that she had already most decidedly seduced the man, Rilla thought with a grin as she reached for a shawl hanging up in the hall and made her way to the front door.

And if Finlay was here, then his only reason could be that he wished to see her. Why else would he come all this way?

He had not been able to make any promises to her when he had left after their amorous encounter in the stables. And she had not expected him to.

I know you have no wish to marry. That is, a marriage between us would be impossible.

Still, it would have been nice to know when she would be seeing him again.

The cold air hit Rilla hard in the chest as she stepped out into the afternoon air. Goodness, but winter was here.

'Finlay?' she said quietly.

'I'm here,' came the expected answering voice.

Turning, Rilla beamed in the direction of the man she adored. Though the future was uncertain, her connection with Finlay was not one that could be denied. Her prospects aside, she had found what she wanted. True affection, true respect. What could be better?

'I was attempting to consider how I would find you,' came Finlay's voice, which was warm yet stilted.

Because they were in full view of the Wallflower Academy, Rilla surmised. Well, she could hardly blame him. They had done their best to keep their assignation to themselves. It would hardly be possible to keep such a thing under wraps if they were seen together.

'Rilla, I—'

'Why don't we—'

They both halted, and after a brief laugh, Rilla indicated her head to the left. 'A walk would do us both good, I think. Give us the opportunity to…to talk. In private.'

And more, she thought with a flicker of a smile.

Oh, she would hope for more, even if their encounter in the stables was perhaps to be the only time they managed to make love. Though Gwen had managed it with her duke. How precisely she had managed to smuggle the man into her bedchamber, Rilla did not know—had never thought to ask her. And it wasn't as though she could write to the Duchess of Knaresby and ask such a scandalous thing…

'Yes. Yes, a walk.' Perhaps it was her imagination, but Finlay sounded distracted. 'Good. Fine. Yes. May…may I take your arm?'

Rilla beamed, her heart skipping a beat as he once again asked her permission. Oh, it was so delightful when he did that.

'Yes.'

Their footsteps swiftly moved in time, mirroring her heartbeat as they walked around the front of the house and around the side by the kitchen gardens.

Step-step, thump-thump...

This was what she wanted. To be in step with a man she loved. To have him by her side, at all times. To know that if she needed him, he would be right there.

How had she managed to find such a man after all this time? After such a disappointment? After believing that all earls, nay all men, were unworthy of her trust?

'Rilla,' said Finlay in a slightly strangled voice.

Rilla tilted her head towards him. 'Yes?'

There was silence. No, not quite silence. Now she was concentrating, she noticed that his breathing was a little laboured. As though he had run here, which he most certainly had not. Perhaps he was nervous?

Nervous? What did the Earl of Staromchor have to be nervous about?

'Rilla, I... I need to tell you something.'

Rilla's shoulders relaxed. Oh, if that was all, then there was no concern there. This was the great declaration, wasn't it? When Finlay finally admitted that he loved her. Then she could happily tell him that his affection was reciprocated, and then...

Well, what happened after that was a tad vague. But it would not matter. They loved each other. They could overcome anything.

'I had hoped to tell you this in private, but—'

'We are near the gardening sheds, aren't we?' Rilla said, interrupting him.

Finlay stopped and she halted with him. 'How on earth could you tell?'

'I can smell the onions, and there's wild garlic that grows

just outside the potting shed,' said Rilla with a wry laugh. 'Really, it's not that difficult.'

She had expected Finlay to laugh, to admit that once again he had underestimated her. As so many people did.

Instead, Finlay grunted, 'Excellent. Let's go behind here.'

Rilla almost tripped as he pulled her forward hastily, but managed to stay upright as he tugged her around to the left. Then for some inexplicable reason, he released her hand.

Allowing her fingers to move in the space around her, she grazed her palm gently against the wood wall of the potting shed. Fine, that would give her a point to navigate by.

'Finlay,' she said softly.

He sighed heavily, then his forehead was pressed against hers. 'Rilla.'

They stood there in silence and Rilla breathed him in. Not just his scent, though the fragrance was delectable. No, Finlay himself. He was everything to her now. So much of her life she had lived without being understood, and though he had made more than his fair share of blunders, he had adapted.

He had wanted to know how to improve. To know her.

And now they had shared the most precious, the most wonderful thing.

'I have…have something to tell you,' Finlay breathed.

'And I will listen,' Rilla said softly. 'You know you can always talk to me, Finlay.'

It was the wrong thing to say. At least, that was how it appeared. The earl groaned, and suddenly crushed his lips against hers in a potent kiss that pushed Rilla against the shed wall.

It was intoxicating, being pinned against the rough wood with nothing but the softness of Finlay on her lips and the hard wall of his chest before her. Rilla splayed her fingers against his coat and felt the woollen scarf wrapped around his neck.

But she couldn't think about that. She was far more interested in the searing kiss pressing against her mouth, the tease of Finlay's tongue as it slipped along her lips, parting them, the decadent pleasure that poured through her body as he began to ravish her mouth.

Rilla moaned, and that only seemed to spur him on. Finlay's hands were on her shoulders but they slipped to her waist, pulling her closer and making it impossible to escape him.

As though she would want to.

'Rilla, I—'

'I know,' Rilla said in a ragged voice as Finlay started trailing kisses down her neck, her breasts heaving with every arduous breath. 'I know.'

Precisely what he had intended to say she did not know. But she knew what he wanted, was sure that this pressure, this aching need that was throbbing through her was undoubtedly mirrored in him.

And that was why, when Finlay released her and stepped back, Rilla reached out with a whimper of need.

'Finlay?'

'I shouldn't do this. I hadn't intended to. I meant to do something quite different,' came Finlay's voice, rough and coarse.

Rilla's heart skipped a beat. 'What are you— Finlay!'

There was no other option than to cry his name as she felt his hands somehow on her knees. Was he— Surely Finlay could not be kneeling before her?

'Finlay?' she repeated, her voice now a whisper in the hope they would not be overheard.

Being discovered like this, with a man kneeling before her... Surely he was not going to propose?

Rilla swallowed hard, but all thoughts of proposals disappeared the instant another sensation rushed over her knees. This time it was not the warm and steady touch of a gentleman who knew precisely how to please.

No, it was the movement of her skirts.

Then and only then did she get an inkling of what Finlay was about to do.

'Finlay,' Rilla said for a third time. This time her voice quavered with unadulterated lust.

She had guessed right. Kneeling before her, and probably getting damp knees in the process, for it had rained most heavily that morning, Finlay was lifting up her skirts and...

And kissing up her thigh.

Rilla tried to breathe steadily as she leaned against the shed, depending on it for stability as her whole body quaked with mounting pleasure.

Surely he couldn't—he wouldn't? Gentlemen did not do such a thing, did they?

They most certainly did. Before Rilla could even think about telling Finlay to stop—and she definitely did not want him to—his lips had reached between her legs.

And licked.

Shivers claimed her body, making it almost impossible to stand, but the solid potting shed behind her and Finlay's grip on her hips kept her steady.

Though neither of those forces could steady her mind. Whirling, twisting with astonishment at the sparks of pleasure formed with every nibble, lick, suck of Finlay's mouth, Rilla clutched at his shoulders in an attempt to remain upright.

'Oh, Finlay,' she whimpered, the pleasure overwhelming.

It was decadent, it was outrageous, it was scandalous. If they were to be found...

And somehow, the suggestion that they could be discovered at any moment only heightened Rilla's enjoyment. Which was indecent. And delicious.

Finlay's tongue darted inside her and Rilla moaned, the aching heat growing at such a fast pace she could hardly keep up.

'Yes...'

The whisper was not precisely a request, but Finlay seemed to understand what she meant by it.

The intrusion, the welcome intimacy, deepened as his tongue delved into her wet folds, and Rilla's head tilted back against the rough wood of the potting shed as her pleasure built…

'Finlay,' she choked out as her climax rolled over her.

It was short, sharp, sudden. More than she could have imagined, and yet in many ways entirely different from the roll in the hay which they had enjoyed previously. Rilla's body washed with pleasure, the ecstasy hot and burning, exacerbated and fed by the strange sensation of Finlay kneeling between her feet, his head under her skirts.

Just when she thought it was over, Finlay's tongue swirled around the nub of her pleasure and he pushed her higher, thrusting her over a peak she had never reached, and Rilla cried out just as jackdaws squawked and took to the air.

And then she was blinking as the man she loved withdrew from her body, still holding her tight.

It was a wonder, really, she was able to stand at all.

Finlay chuckled as he brought his arm around her waist. 'Steady on there.'

'You think that I can remain steady after…' Rilla swallowed.

It had been difficult enough to keep her voice down as he brought her to such pinnacles of pleasure, but her mouth was still dry and her heart still frantic.

This man—she loved him. And surely he must love her, even if the words themselves had not been uttered between them.

Love was not something one said. It was what one did, and Finlay had proved, several times now that he was a man she could trust. An earl she could trust, far more than she could have believed possible.

And as for the future…

Well, the future would come whether she wanted it to or not, Rilla reasoned as she steadied herself on her feet and slipped her hand into Finlay's arm, feeling the roughness of his coat against her fingers.

What the future would hold, she did not know. The one thing she did know was that Finlay would be in it.

What else could she possibly want?

'I had not intended to ravish you so utterly,' Finlay said in a low voice as they started to walk slowly towards the Wallflower Academy.

Rilla laughed, joy bursting in her chest. 'Oh, I wouldn't say that was utterly.'

Flirting with Finlay was as natural as breathing. So too did it seem natural that his chuckle radiated through her side, making her feel his laughter as well as hear it.

'Well, we are close to the stables.'

'Finlay!'

'Perhaps I can show you just how utterly I adore you.'

Flickers of delight were cascading down Rilla's spine and heat blossomed on her cheeks at the inappropriate suggestion.

'We were fortunate not to get caught the first time,' she reminded him, squeezing his arm.

Finlay sighed dramatically. 'I suppose so.'

'And Miss Pike has decided to ban us from the stables,' Rilla added, recalling the awkward conversation over breakfast.

There was a snort from beside her. 'Dear God, there is no possibility she suspects, is there?'

Heaven forbid.

'No, no,' Rilla said hastily, their feet moving from the grass to the gravelled path. It crunched under their feet as she continued, 'No, this is because of Sylvia.'

Another snort. 'I should have guessed.'

'She is perhaps not the wallflower the Pike envisioned for her Academy,' said Rilla with a grin.

'What has she got up to this time?'

'From what she will admit to me, I believe Sylvia was attempting to steal a horse,' said Rilla in a confidential tone.

She was rewarded by another chuckle from Finlay. 'She didn't!'

'It won't be the first time she's tried to run away from the Wallflower Academy,' said Rilla darkly, though a smile still lingered on her face.

How could it not, when she was with the man she loved?

'Sylvia and her schemes... I tried to talk her out of the last one, but apparently—'

'So it is thanks to Sylvia's antics, then, that we will have to find a new location for...conversation?' came Finlay's low, seductive voice.

A thrill rushed through Rilla as she thought of all the joy and pleasure they had to look forward to in their future. Days and days of it. Precisely what she was going to do when the month was up and her place at the Wallflower Academy was gone, she did not know...but surely Finlay would not allow her to be destitute?

And an idea, a wonderful idea, one she had barely allowed herself to consider but now sparked in her mind as bright as the sun, soared into her consciousness.

Well—they loved each other, did they not? Those words had not been exchanged but they did not need to be. Rilla knew how she felt about him, knew how Finlay felt about her.

He could not marry her—surely he would have offered for her hand if he thought her position appropriate for that of countess—but perhaps that was not necessary.

Rilla swallowed hard. Could she do it? Did she love him enough to become Finlay's mistress?

'Finlay,' she said softly, hardly sure how precisely she was supposed to broach such a topic, but knowing she must.

After all, she had been the one to proposition him to make love to her, had she not? And that had worked out splendidly. More than splendidly. Far better than she could have imagined.

'Rilla,' he said quietly.

A shimmer of need washed over her but Rilla pushed it aside. She needed to concentrate to ask this question.

'Finlay, would you...would you ever consider—'

'Ah, I thought it was you, Miss Newell! And—my goodness. My lord. What an honour!'

And Rilla's heart sank.

Of course.

There was no possibility she could have this conversation without being interrupted. And of all people to interrupt her...

The scent of carbolic soap wafted through the air as footsteps approached them. 'I have just been to the village, my lord, picking up a few things for my wallflowers. I trust you have had a pleasant walk? Where is Miss Bryant? I presume she accompanied you? This is more than a little unsettling, my lord. You hardly need to be schooled in the rules of the *ton*.'

Rilla tried not to permit heat to flood her cheeks, certain her embarrassment would be obvious, but there was nothing she could do to stop it.

Pleasant walk? Yes, some parts of it had been most pleasant indeed...

'You have some beautiful gardens and grounds here, Miss Pike,' Finlay was saying politely. 'I look forward to seeing them in the summer, when the flowers are out.'

'Oh, just a few borders of my own design,' came the immodest voice of Miss Pike. Rilla stifled a smile. 'Gardening is, after all, one of life's most simple pleasures. I typically find...'

Rilla ceased paying attention.

Well, she had heeded the Pike's lectures on the benefits of gardening quite enough times over the years. The woman was hardly going to say something new and surprising after such a long—

'And I do apologize, my lord, I have been most remiss! I have not enquired as to your mother's health. She must be run ragged, preparing for your wedding.'

And all sound disappeared.

It was most disconcerting. Oh, there were sounds, noises in the far reaches of her hearing, but they appeared deadened, as though underwater or a long way off.

I have not enquired as to your mother's health. She must be run ragged, preparing for your wedding.

The words each individually made sense, but as Rilla attempted to weave them together to make sense of them, a dizziness rocked her head and she almost stumbled, leaning heavily on Finlay's arm.

Finlay was saying awkwardly, 'Ah, yes…erm…th-thank you, Miss Pike, for your kind—'

'I had no idea that the wedding was so soon,' prattled on Miss Pike as Rilla attempted to gain her balance. 'Just a few weeks! You yourself must be very busy with the final preparations.'

She must be run ragged, preparing for your wedding.

'Yes, yes, very busy,' came Finlay's voice.

But Finlay was a long way off. Though Rilla still had her arm linked into his, the man was suddenly distant. Unknown to her. A stranger.

Who was this man, then, who purported to be Finlay Jellicoe, Earl of Staromchor?

She had been so certain that she had known him, had understood him. Had cleverly deduced that he was a man to be trusted, a man to whom she could give herself without regret. And now here she was, being forced to listen to the man, whoever he was, talk about his…his wedding?

'I suppose my invitation has been lost in the post…they are getting careless,' the Pike was saying in that delicate tone of self-importance that was all her own. 'Well, I must be off. I have wallflowers waiting for these. Good day, my lord. Come, Miss Newell.'

Whatever 'these' were, Rilla could not tell. She presumed that the proprietress of the Wallflower Academy had showed Finlay something and had not seen fit to bother to explain it to her.

Not that it mattered. Nothing mattered, not anymore. She stepped forward, forgetting for a moment that she was trapped by her hand in his arm. There was nothing in the world that mattered, because the man she had trusted, the man she had been certain she knew—

'Rilla,' said Finlay hastily in a low, urgent tone. 'Rilla—'

'I don't want to hear it,' Rilla said, half in a daze.

She slipped her hand from his arm. It took two attempts as the brigand attempted to clasp her fingers the first time she tried to move away from him, but then she managed it and her hands were on the wall of the Tudor manor.

It earthed her, grounded her, as nothing else had.

So. Everything that she thought she knew about Finlay, as it turned out, was a lie. Once again she had thought herself in love, thought that she could be happy. Once again she had permitted an earl to matter to her, to creep into her heart and have weight with her emotions, and once again she had been disappointed.

She must be run ragged, preparing for your wedding.

Rilla swallowed hard, desperately hoping that the tears threatening to spill would not fall—would not give him the satisfaction of seeing just how hurt she was.

Finlay was to be married. Had been engaged to be married, to another woman, the entire time.

Oh, she had been such a fool.

But no longer. Rilla straightened herself up, ignoring whatever it was that Finlay was saying in a rush of words that made it almost impossible to decipher, and said coldly, 'Stay away from me, Earl.'

Chapter Fifteen

'I do apologize, my lord, I have been most remiss! I have not enquired as to your mother's health. She must be run ragged, preparing for your wedding.'

And that was when Finlay knew he was the absolute worst human being who had ever lived.

Rilla had stiffened in his arms, and though he had turned immediately to her, desperate to show her how remorseful he was, he could not speak.

There were no words.

He had betrayed her, completely and utterly—and the worst of it was that Rilla could not see the contrition on his face. No, she had to stand there in silence and suffer listening to Miss Pike.

'I had no idea that the wedding was so soon,' prattled on Miss Pike, preventing him from saying anything. 'Just a few weeks! You yourself must be very busy with the final preparations.'

'Yes, yes, very busy,' Finlay found himself saying.

Rilla had said nothing, done nothing, merely stood there. Her expression was cold, stiff, as it always was when Rilla was seeking to distance herself from what was happening around her.

And he had done that. Him, and his lies, his deception, his inability to admit the truth: that he was engaged to be married to a woman who was devoted to him.

It pained him as nothing had ever hurt before, but what could he say when Miss Pike was still standing there?

'I suppose my invitation has been lost in the post… They are getting careless,' Miss Pike was saying with a sharp glance in his direction. 'Well, I must be off. I have wallflowers waiting for these. Good day, my lord. Come, Miss Newell.'

She waved the basket under her arm which was full of brown paper parcels, and turned on her heels before walking off.

The instant he judged her to be out of earshot, Finlay brought his mouth close to her ear. 'Rilla. Rilla—'

'I don't want to hear it,' Rilla said dully.

That was when she tried to pull free of him. Finlay attempted to hold on to her, desperate not to lose the connection they had, that they shared—emblematic of the closeness he was terrified to lose.

But he could not, would not hold her against his will. He was not that sort of man. He would not demand a woman's intimacy when she so clearly wished to revoke it.

It was as though he had been punched in the gut as Rilla took a step back from him, clinging to the wall of the Wallflower Academy as though it was the only dependable thing in the world.

Nausea rose in Finlay's chest. What had he done?

She must be run ragged, preparing for your wedding.

If only Miss Pike had not been foolish enough to mention the wedding.

But no, Finlay could not blame her, much as he might wish to. It had been his choice to keep such a thing secret, his decision not to inform Rilla of his betrothal.

He had been the one to accept her offer of lovemaking. Dear God, he had been the one to lick her to ecstasy just minutes ago.

And despite his best intentions, which had been to come to the Wallflower Academy and finally admit to Rilla that he had a prior commitment and could no longer enjoy her company as he would wish...

Despite all that, it was Miss Pike who had revealed the truth. *Hell.*

Finlay's gaze raked over Rilla's face and saw the devastation he felt. Christ, she was trying not to cry; he could see the tension in her temples as her eyes sparkled.

He was the lowest of the low. He had to explain.

'I know I should have told you from the start and I had intended to but I was in too deep before I realized what I was about and it grew harder and harder to—'

The words tumbled from his mouth, almost nonsensical in their speed, and evidently Rilla was not interested.

She had straightened up, back against the wall, as she said, 'Stay away from me, Earl.'

Mortification rushed through Finlay's chest.

Oh, it was not bad enough that he had completely destroyed all faith and trust between them. It wasn't enough that he had lied, and had now been caught out in said lie in a most shameful way.

No, it was worse than that. He had manged to confirm to Rilla just what she had believed when they had first met: that earls were not to be trusted.

'I should have told you earlier.'

'You should have,' said Rilla quietly, her voice distant, as though they were discussing the weather. 'And yet you did not.'

Finlay swallowed. This would have been a much easier conversation if he could have arrived with his engagement broken completely, Isabelle Carr nothing more to him than an acquaintance he used to know as a child.

Oh, hell. How had he managed to create this situation? One bad decision after another, but each one made because he had thought it was the best thing at the time. The best thing for Isabelle.

How had he managed to get this so wrong, hurt so many people?

'Who is she?'

Finlay winced. The ice in Rilla's tone was surely merely a front, something designed to keep her true feelings at bay, but after all they had shared it was excruciating to hear all warmth gone.

Less than an hour ago, they had been happy. But that time was over.

'Her name, please, my lord,' said Rilla, as though she were merely enquiring about a pair of kid gloves.

Finlay took a deep breath. 'Isabelle. Isabelle Carr.'

'Carr?' Rilla nodded slowly. 'Ah, I see. Cecil's sister. You must care for her very much.'

'It's not like that.'

'Then why are you marrying her?' Rilla said, cutting him off.

Finlay attempted to gather his thoughts, flying about him with no consideration for his exhausted mind.

Why was he marrying her?

A fortnight ago he would have said it was nothing more than a marriage of convenience. Something required as a man of honour, not because he had ruined Isabelle's, but because she had precious little else to sustain her.

And now...

Now there was guilt. Oh, there was guilt. He should never have listened at the drawing room door, but he could not forget what he had heard.

His happiness is... It is the most important thing to me. There is not a single day that does not go by when I do not think of him.

She loved him, depended on the marriage going ahead. The true affection had been so potent that he had not needed to see her speak to believe her words. And he could not cause that woman any more grief. She had already suffered enough.

'It… She…' Finlay pulled a hand through his hair, desperately attempting to marshal his ideas. 'It was a marriage of convenience.'

'Was?'

'I offered her marriage when her brother—when Cecil died,' Finlay said, rattling on hastily in the hope it would be less painful that way.

The wind blew between them, a chill in the air. It would snow soon.

'Why would you do that?' Rilla's voice was calm, as though attempting to discover why a friend had chosen a particular hue for a painting.

If only he had time to think—if only his frantically beating heart would give him solace, rather than course panic through his veins with every squeeze!

'I— It's hard to explain.'

'You said it was a marriage of convenience.' Rilla's hands were clasped before her. 'Was. What is it now? Are you in love with her?'

'No,' Finlay said immediately. Of that, he was sure.

'And yet you will marry her.'

'I— It's not as simple as…' His voice trailed off as he attempted to think.

It was his own fault. If he had just been open about Isabelle's existence at the beginning…

Finlay's shoulders sagged. But he had so swiftly been caught up in Rilla's presence that all thoughts of Isabelle were entirely forgotten.

He swallowed hard. 'She loves me.'

'Ah, there it is,' said Rilla darkly, in a sardonic tone that cut straight into Finlay's chest. 'Of course she does! What woman would not fall in love with the charming earl?'

'It isn't like that,' Finlay snapped.

'Isn't it? You are engaged to be married, you absolute cur, and you knew that I had once—that I had almost married. Was it not enough to make me the laughingstock of the whole Wall-flower Academy? How can I ever trust—'

Rilla's voice broke off as she raised a hand to her mouth, forcing down a sob that broke Finlay's heart.

He had done this.

Rilla was right; he had known her history with the Earl of Porthaethwy and he had ploughed on regardless. He had wooed her, flirted with her, charmed her, and he had known at every turn that nothing could happen between them.

Nothing that would last, at any rate.

'I wanted to end the engagement,' he said, his voice cracking.

Rilla snorted. 'But you have not.'

Finlay closed his eyes, desperately forcing the tears away. 'No—not yet! I intended to last night, but she was out, and… I will. I will, I promise.'

Oh, God, he sounded like such a scoundrel saying that.

But Rilla had not heard Isabelle talking so passionately about her affection. She had lost her brother—they had both lost Cecil, but Isabelle was the one alone in the world.

What, was he to deny her any happiness whatsoever?

But there could only be one happy woman: Rilla or Isabelle. Finlay knew he had been forced to choose between them.

And there was only a wrong choice.

'I… I made you no other promises,' Finlay said, grasping on to that fact like a lifeboat in a storm. 'I never intended for you to care.'

'You have broken no vow, either,' Rilla retorted. 'Do you feel proud of yourself?'

Finlay's jaw tightened. 'No.'

'Oh, God, I said to you before that I was more than a match for an earl, and yet here you are, proving me wrong!'

'No, Rilla, I—'

'I am worth far more,' she said imperiously, holding her head high. 'I am certainly worth more than this.'

How could she say that? How could they even be having this conversation here, right in front of the Wallflower Academy, where anyone could see them?

Oh, God. Where anyone could see them.

Finlay turned away from Rilla for a moment and saw precisely what he had hoped not to see. There, in the large bay window that jutted out from the morning room, and therefore where there was an excellent view of the front of the house, was...

A troop of women. He recognized Sylvia and Daphne, but there were also half a dozen other ladies, all goggling. Hell. There must be an afternoon tea or something. Of course there was.

Finlay swore under his breath.

'There is no need for language like that!'

'No, it's just—'

'And I did not demand any promises,' Rilla said, countering his earlier point.

'Rilla, there are people watching.' Finlay tried to take her arm to pull her away from the window and the gawping gazes of the wallflowers, but she continued on, her voice catching as words spilled out.

'But I presumed that friends—lovers—had an unspoken expectation of honesty. More fool me.'

Finlay's jaw was tightening again, causing a throb of pain to stretch to his temple. This was all going wrong, but he had to admit, even if it were only to himself, that there was no possibility of it going right. He had made this decision. Now he was having to face the consequences.

'You should have been honest with me,' Rilla said quietly. 'You should have said... That poor woman, and here I am... I would have wanted to know if there was no future for us, of any kind.'

That sparked indignation in Finlay's chest. 'I did. You said that you knew we could not wed!'

'But I hadn't thought about marriage, not really,' she said fiercely, and Rilla actually took a step towards him, her body seeming to thrum with certainty. 'I hadn't expected *that*! When I thought about our future, I thought… I hoped…'

Finlay's stomach lurched.

Was it possible? Could it be that Rilla had considered becoming his mistress?

They could have been together in a small way. He could have found his joy and happiness with her while Isabelle…

The thought of his future bride poured cold water over that idea.

He was no rake. He could not take one woman to the altar, knowing that she was desperately in love with him, then betray her with another woman.

His stomach twisted painfully. Though hadn't he done just that? Self-loathing and regret mingled with pain in his chest. How had this gone so wrong?

Finlay took in a deep breath and rubbed his chin, his jaw tight. 'I know you probably think very little of me in this moment. I may not love her, but I have to respect her. Respect her feelings.'

'Like you respected mine?'

He hung his head, shifting on his feet. 'You…you're right. I lied to myself, Rilla. I made myself believe this whole damned situation wouldn't hurt anyone. And I've hurt you, and I'm so sorry, you're the one I would least like to hurt, Rilla, I—'

'Don't call me that,' she said sharply.

Pain flared in his chest, but it was quickly subsumed by despair. 'I was weak, Rilla, I was a fool, but you have to believe me, no one can loathe me more than I loathe myself! You've never made a mistake? Rilla—'

'I told you before, my friends call me Rilla,' she said, and now she was crying, tears gently falling down her cheeks, and Finlay's heart twisted in agony. 'You may call me Miss Newell, for the purposes of this conversation.'

A flicker of hope. 'This conversation? And after?'

'Oh, there won't be an after,' Rilla said with a sniff. 'You think I wish to speak to you again after this?'

Finlay turned away for a moment in an attempt to gather his thoughts. If only there was a way to prove his affections… but what was the point? He would be Isabelle's groom in ten days. Ten days—that was all—and he would be parted from Rilla forever.

Though he wasn't sure they could be much more parted than this.

She was closing herself off from him, distancing him from her true self, and there was nothing he could do but watch it happen. Hate it happen. Hate that he could do nothing about it.

'I… I hoped—'

'When you said that you were not getting married anytime soon, that was a lie,' Rilla said, speaking over him as a cloud shadowed the sky. 'Your friendship, our connection, whatever… whatever this is, it was all based on a lie. Did you think you could lie to my face because I can't see?'

Revulsion poured through Finlay's chest. 'No.'

'Yet you did so anyway,' Rilla said with a nonchalant shrug that cut to his very soul. 'I wasn't important enough to tell the truth to just a wallflower, no prospects, no family—'

'I love you!' Finlay blurted out.

He had imagined a completely different moment when he would tell her this. When they were in each other's arms, perhaps. When they had just finished kissing. Maybe when he had just finished feeding her strawberries, Rilla's lips stained with the juices and his own lips hungry for hers.

He had certainly hoped for a different response.

Rilla snorted. 'Don't be ridiculous.'

'I am not being—'

'A man in love doesn't hurt the person he purports to love,' Rilla said, and there was pain in her voice, which Finlay hated to hear. 'A man in love—a gentleman!—does not lie about his marital prospects!'

'I never lied. I just never—'

'Told the truth?' she said, finishing the sentence for him.

Finlay turned away for a moment, trying to collect himself, but when he turned back to her she was still standing there, still Rilla, still perfect.

'I should have known,' Rilla said softly. 'Never trust an earl.'

And the fire that flared in his chest had nothing to do with Isabelle, or his upcoming marriage, and had everything to do with Rilla's words.

'I'm not saying that I am a paragon of virtue,' he said quietly. 'But blame me for my actions, not my title. You were just as guilty of treating me poorly when we first met.'

'You made me think you were a footman!' Rilla interjected hotly.

'I thought we had moved past our assumptions about each other, but clearly I was wrong!' Finlay said bitterly before he could stop himself.

Regret soared through his heart immediately.

What did he think he was doing, speaking to a woman like that? Speaking to Rilla like that—to anyone like that?

Finlay's head hung low.

Dear God, he was just as bad as she thought he was. Perhaps worse.

But there was still something he could do, if he could just kiss her, show her…

'Rilla…'

'Rilla!'

Finlay stepped back hastily as he glanced over his shoulder to see Miss Smith, her blond hair now paired with scarlet cheeks, staring at the two of them.

'What are you doing to her?' she said, a mite accusingly.

'Nothing,' snapped Finlay, knowing he should be more patient, knowing the poor woman had no idea what was truly happening, but unable to restrain his ire. 'I'm not doing anything.'

'That is precisely right. His Lordship is doing nothing,' said Rilla with a sardonic smile. 'Go on in, Daphne. I will join you presently.'

The wallflower did not seem particularly convinced, but she did not appear to have the force of character to disagree. She turned slowly, fixing her eyes for the longest moment in a stare, then trotted up the steps to the Wallflower Academy.

Only when the door closed did Finlay take a deep breath. Now to show not tell Rilla precisely how he felt.

'And on that note, I will bid you good day,' Rilla said darkly.

She had managed to take three steps before Finlay grabbed her arm. 'Let me help.'

'I have had quite enough of your help, thank you,' she snapped, wrenching her arm away. 'Don't touch me!'

'But I can help you up the steps,' Finlay persisted, walking alongside her.

He was bound to her in honour, even if he could not be bound to her in any other way. Did she not know that? Could she not see that he adored her? Had she not listened when he had said that he loved her?

'Oh, I know this path,' Rilla said with a laugh that held no mirth. 'I know this path well. It is one I have walked for many years—alone.'

Finlay swallowed, wishing he could console her, wishing things could be different.

'At this rate, I will be walking alone for many years to come,' Rilla said as they reached the steps up to the Wallflower Academy. 'But you know what, Finlay?'

Her voice had modulated, calmed. Hope, pathetic and small, rose. 'What?'

'I would rather walk it alone than with you,' Rilla said sweetly before she turned, walked up the steps, and slammed the door behind her, leaving Finlay standing before the Wallflower Academy entirely alone.

Chapter Sixteen

Staying in one's room for three days and requesting meals to be sent up to you was the sort of thing that great ladies did, Rilla reflected as the haze of light she could just perceive moved slowly across her bedchamber.

Still. That did not prevent her from doing it.

After all, it was not as though there was anything downstairs that she wanted. Company was abhorrent to her. The well-meaning questions flying about the place were anathema to her, and Rilla had already suffered the curiosity of those who had spotted herself and...and the Earl of Staromchor arguing.

A tear crept from her eye, sliding down her face and onto the bedlinens. Rilla did not bother to contain it. What was the point? There was no one here to see it, no one to judge her for making such a foolish choice as to trust an earl.

Not that she didn't judge herself.

I should have known. Never trust an earl.

A second tear followed the first one. She had fallen in love with Finlay Jellicoe, Earl of Staromchor, and try as she might she could not just cease loving him because it was inconvenient. Because he was marrying another woman. Because they were to be separated for the rest of their lives.

Rilla swallowed. What she had expected from him, she did not know. It was all so clouded now, clouded with the confusion of pain and their argument.

A man in love doesn't hurt the person he purports to love. A man in love—a gentleman!—does not lie about his marital prospects!

I never lied. I just never—

Told the truth?

And now all she could think about was Finlay and the woman he would marry. Was she beautiful? Did she sing well, play the pianoforte, embroider cushions and dance elegantly while listening to Finlay's words?

The knot in her stomach twisted most painfully.

Because it did not matter, did it? Finlay had made a commitment to that woman, and in all honour he certainly should continue with it.

Even if it hurt.

The pain of losing him was exquisite. Rilla had known hardship, known pain, known the separation between people you loved...or thought you loved. She had known betrayal. She was hardly new to expecting the worst in people.

Yet he had somehow wormed his way into her heart and now she was crippled by the affection within it that she could no longer give. It was a physical ache in her chest, as if a heavy weight had been placed there, and no one but Finlay could remove it.

But she couldn't just stay up here moping. Rilla knew, better than anyone else at the Wallflower Academy, just what was at stake if she did not find herself a situation.

I refer, most unwillingly, to the fact that your father will cease to pay for your place here at the Wallflower Academy at the end of next month.

Taking a deep breath and propping herself up against some pillows, Rilla tried not to think about the Pike's latest recommendation.

'A perfectly good school not ten miles away,' the woman had shouted through the keyhole only last night. 'They are looking for a well-bred, elegant woman to take charge of literature and history, and I thought—'

'They won't want a woman like me,' Rilla had shot back at the proprietress through the door.

Which had been a mistake. It had only encouraged Miss Pike to rattle on about how she was the daughter of a baron and an honourable and there was nothing anyone could dislike about her.

As if she did not know what Rilla meant.

The trouble was, the idea had kept Rilla up all night. It was a good situation, two hundred pounds a year, and bed and board included; it would certainly afford her a comfortable life. She may even be able to put a little aside for the future. For when she would be no longer useful, and therefore have nowhere else to go…

Rilla had finally arisen that morning with a headache and no clear direction. If only he hadn't—

Pushing thoughts of Finlay aside was getting harder and harder. Intrusive, warm thoughts about how comforting it was to find herself in his arms, how strong he was, how she had sunk into his embraces and kisses…

Sighing heavily, Rilla turned onto her other side. Today was the last day she would permit herself to lie about the place, she promised herself.

Tomorrow she would rise and tell the Pike that—

A timid knock on the door made Rilla jerk her head in that direction.

'Go away.'

The knock was repeated, louder this time. Rilla sighed and fell back onto the bed. The Pike had been sending wallflowers almost hourly since she had flown upstairs after the argument with Finlay.

She did not want to see anyone.

But that did not appear to matter. The Pike was determined that Rilla entertain, God forbid, and that was the direction her requests—demands—tended.

Come and converse with the wallflowers.

Come and sit with the wallflowers.

Come, tell the wallflowers the pitfalls of losing one's heart to an earl...

Another knock, this time even harder.

'I said, go away!' Rilla said sharply.

'I knew you would say that,' came the wretched voice of Daphne Smith. 'I told the Pike you wouldn't want to see me. No one ever does.'

A shard of guilt slid into her heart.

Oh, very clever, she thought darkly. *Well done, Miss Pike. You knew I could not be angry at someone like Daphne Smith.*

'Come in,' she said wearily aloud. 'The door is unlocked.'

Rilla never locked her door now, not after the key was once jostled from the latch and it took her over an hour to find it. The sense of being trapped, of being unable to escape, had been formidable.

The click of the door opening, then the snick of it closing again, sounded around the little bedchamber. Rilla pulled herself into a proper sitting position on the bed and looked defiantly in the door's direction, not bothering to wipe away her tears.

She could sense the hesitation of her friend. One of her two friends, really—being a wallflower at the Wallflower Academy naturally led some to a competitiveness that Rilla simply did not care for.

But Daphne was not like that. She was a true wallflower, a woman who hated being the centre of attention for more than five minutes.

Even when it was just the two of them, she was hesitant.

'I suppose the Pike wants me to come downstairs,' said Rilla into the silence. 'Please, sit.'

The creak of the wicker chair in the corner suggested that Daphne had accepted her invitation. Her assumption was confirmed when her friend spoke, the words coming now from the corner rather than the door.

'We are all very worried about you.'

Rilla snorted. 'I doubt that.'

It was perhaps a tad cruel, but it was also the truth. The Pike would be worried, certainly, but about what on earth to do with her when the money ran out, not about Rilla herself.

'I am very worried,' came the tentative voice of Daphne. 'Worried for you. No one should feel alone.'

And some of the bitterness and resentment against everyone in the world melted away.

'Thank you,' Rilla said awkwardly. 'You... Well, you did not have to trouble yourself.'

'I am happy to do it,' said Daphne softly. 'I never had a sister, and I thought— Well, when I was sent to the Wallflower Academy, I hoped...'

The trailing off of her words was in some way worse than her actually saying them.

A twist of discomfort surged in Rilla's chest. She and Sylvia had always been close, and Gwen had joined them for a time. Daphne was always on the outside looking in. She was a naturally shy woman who could not compete with the rambunctious Sylvia or the dry-witted Rilla.

It was not a pleasant thought, to believe she had left out someone who had so desperately craved friendship.

'I would like to be a friend to you,' she said awkwardly.

There was a slight chuckle from the corner. 'I don't want your pity, Rilla.'

'I did not mean it like that.'

'I know, and it speaks well of you that you would wish to... well, make amends is not quite the right phrase, but I do not know what is,' came Daphne's quiet voice. 'And I would like to be a friend to you. I would like to help, if I could. If you wished to talk to me about...about him.'

Him.

The entire Wallflower Academy had apparently watched her argument with Finlay with open mouths, from what Sylvia had said through the door yesterday. It showed great restraint on Daphne's part, Rilla thought, that she did not say his name.

'There's not much to say,' she said swiftly.

Not much that she was willing to say, anyway.

Rilla's fingers tightened around the bedlinen, the comfortingly familiar weave of the fabric grounding her.

'I suppose not,' came Daphne's soft reply. 'And I have no wish to force you.'

And it was precisely because Rilla knew that Daphne would never consider forcing her to spill her secrets that she felt as though she might.

After all, thoughts had been whirling around her mind for days and she had gained no relief from them. It was frustrating to the extreme to think that she may never fully understand why Finlay had done what he had done. She might never get the answers she sought, never again feel the brush of his fingers along her arm...

Rilla swallowed. 'It's...complicated.'

There it was again, another chuckle from the wallflower. 'I presumed that.'

Laughing despite herself, Rilla sighed. Opening up to anyone wasn't exactly the sort of thing she typically did. It was always easier to hold herself at a distance, to allow the cold and stiff expression on her face to keep others away.

Once bitten, twice shy.

But it was more than that. Rilla had never noticed it before, but the three years she had been at the Wallflower Academy had reduced her somehow. She had squashed herself, forced down her instincts, her personality, made it almost impossible not to succumb to the fear of...

Fear of what?

Rilla could not articulate it. Fear of what had happened, happening again.

But now the very worst had happened. She had fallen in

love, truly, for the first time, and that love had been betrayed. Nothing could be worse than that, could it?

'I trusted him,' Rilla found herself saying, her voice breaking.

She sensed a creak of the willow chair, a footstep, and then a depression on the bed near her feet.

'Tell me about it,' said Daphne softly.

And she did.

The words came slowly at first. It had been many years since Rilla had been open, truly open, with anyone. Besides, it was shameful, to reveal just how easily she had been taken in.

I know you have no wish to marry. That is, a marriage between us would be impossible...

The only parts of the story she neglected to mention were...

Well. Daphne did not need to know about that particular moment in the stables, did she? Or the proposition that came before it. Or the moment of intimacy by the potting shed near the kitchen garden.

Rilla swallowed.

No. Definitely not.

Daphne was an excellent listener. Rilla supposed it was due to the fact that the wallflower was often excluded from conversations—a thought that made her cringe with shame.

And before she knew it, she was nearing the end of her tale.

'And Miss Pike enquired about his wedding,' Rilla said miserably, her chest tight just thinking about it. Her hands had moved to her lap, clasping and unclasping. 'His wedding. And it was—oh, Daphne, it was so humiliating! To know I had given my...had given my heart to him, and he had known all the while that he was betrothed to another...'

That was when her voice faded into nothing.

Rilla swallowed hard, but there was no force left in her tongue.

What else was there to say? She had been taken in, and cruelly, but there was no brother to defend her and her father would surely not disgrace the family name again by intervening.

Miss Pike would merely censure her for getting entangled with an engaged man, Rilla thought darkly, and Sylvia—

Well. Sylvia would probably bodily attack the man, which wouldn't help, either.

What she needed, Rilla thought darkly, was for Finlay to wake up one moment and realize he had changed his mind. That he could not, would not go through with the wedding. That he would—

Carr? Ah, I see. Cecil's sister. You must care for her very much.

Her stomach lurched.

What, would she take a man like Finlay away from a woman who had, by the sound of it, already gone through so much?

'I am sorry,' came Daphne's soft voice.

Rilla laughed ruefully. 'As am I.'

'It seems a most unfortunate situation.'

'Most unfortunate, yes,' she replied sardonically. 'An earl who took advantage of me—which should not have surprised me—who is going to go and marry a woman he…he doesn't even love.'

Which was another reason why the whole blasted situation was such a disaster, Rilla wanted to say, but couldn't bring herself to.

Finlay was going to be miserable.

There was no doubt in her mind: he did not love this Miss Carr. He was only marrying her for some strange sense of duty. Did they both have to be miserable?

'I wish there was an answer,' came Daphne's gentle voice. 'I suppose in times like this, there is no one solution, no way to make everyone happy.'

Rilla blinked away tears. Daphne was surprisingly astute. 'N-no. No, there isn't.'

Finlay could only wed one woman and he had made his decision. It was one he may regret, in time. She regretted it already.

Could he not see—did he not understand how happy they could be?

'Unless…' Daphne said slowly. And then she said nothing.

Impatience flared in Rilla's chest. 'Unless what?'

'Well, it was just a passing… I would not like to presume… but—'

'Really, I must insist that you— Ah, Miss Smith. Miss Newell, I see you are feeling better,' uttered the voice of Miss Pike, coinciding with the snap of the door being thrust open. 'Excellent.'

Rilla sighed.

The Pike meant well. She knew it, all the wallflowers knew it. But the woman had no sense of timing.

What had Daphne been about to say?

'Now, I have not wished to press you while you were…unwell,' said Miss Pike sternly, stepping towards the bed and halting somewhere nearby. 'But as I can see that you are now entirely better—'

'Miss Pike,' Daphne said softly, but she was entirely ignored.

'I have come here to request your decision,' Miss Pike continued firmly. 'I believe you have had sufficient time, and time is, as it were, not your friend in this matter.'

Rilla winced. Yes, the proprietress of the Wallflower Academy certainly had a way with words. Not that Rilla could deny anything the woman had said. Time was certainly not her friend in this matter, and a decision was needed.

There was not much of a choice. Teaching, or penury on the streets?

'Well, you will be delighted to hear I have made a decision,' Rilla said stiffly. 'I will accept a post anywhere away from here. Where he can't— Where I won't have to meet—'

'You will?' came the delighted tone of Miss Pike.

'You will?' repeated Daphne, evidently confused. 'What post?'

'If you had wished to teach here, I would have welcomed that, naturally,' the Pike continued, once again ignoring the shy wallflower. 'And I am confident you will make an excellent teacher at—what was it called? I can't remember, I've got it written down somewhere. Arrangements will have to be made. You can take the Wallflower Academy carriage most of the way...'

Rilla allowed the words to wash over her as a dull sensation settled in her chest.

So, it was decided.

She would be leaving the Wallflower Academy and not to be married, as her father and the Pike had so desperately hoped—but to be a teacher. To accept that she required wages now to live.

'I'm sure some of the reports of the fractious nature of the pupils are completely fabricated.'

Rilla's shoulders tensed. But she couldn't fight any longer. She had no one on her side, supporting her cause. Her father had no interest, and Finlay...

She blinked back her tears furiously. Finlay had made his choice. He would be marrying Miss Isabelle Carr, and she was certain they would find a way to be happy together.

Could she have been happy with him?

Some moments, Rilla could not understand him. A man who had everything, a title, a position in Society, a fiancée—why had he dallied with her?

And then she recalled the openness in the garden, the closeness they had shared, the knowledge, knowledge she had felt in her bones, that she was the only one he cared about.

Oh, it was all such a confusion.

'So you can be gone within a week,' the Pike finished with a falsely bright tone. 'Won't that be nice?'

A wave of nausea flooded through Rilla at the thought.

Leaving the Wallflower Academy was an inevitability—she knew that—but leaving its comforting, familiar halls would be a wrench.

'Very nice,' she said aloud.

'Yes. Well. Right,' said Miss Pike, perhaps a little rattled by Rilla's lack of fighting spirit. 'I'll leave you two alone, then.'

Footsteps sounded, and a flutter of carbolic soap wafted through the room before the door snapped smartly behind her. The departing footsteps grew fainter on the other side of the wall, and then there was silence.

Silence, that was, until Daphne cleared her throat.

Rilla jumped. Goodness, she had almost forgot that the wall-flower was still there.

'Why did you not argue with her?' Daphne asked. 'I… Well, I do not mean to presume, but I did not think you wished to be a teacher. I have heard you and the Pike argue about it before.'

'What choice do I have?' Rilla said dully.

A woman without choices—most women, now she came to think about it. Choices were made by a father, brother, husband, someone else. Or there were no choices at all.

'But—'

'Daphne, I have no choice,' Rilla said sharply. 'Finlay, the Earl of Staromchor, is wedding someone else. I don't have a home to go back to, my father won't welcome me at home, and with no money to pay for my place here at the Wallflower Academy… I have nowhere else to go.'

Chapter Seventeen

Finlay pushed open the door, ignored the bell, ignored the astonished gasps from the customers about the place, and did what no gentleman had ever done before.

He marched past the modiste's assistant and into the fitting area.

'My lord!'

'Sir, please, you cannot go back there, it is for the ladies—'

But Finlay did not care.

He had taken three days to think it through. Three days, he had reasoned, was enough time to truly sit with the decision he wished to make. Time to consider if it was truly what he wished to do. Whether it was something he could live with.

And no matter how much time passed, his resolution remained: he had to marry Rilla Newell.

The instant he had come to the decision, he had to enact it—and this was the first step. To be sure, when Turner had said that his mother and Miss Carr were out, he had presumed they were at Hatchard's, or a bakery, or Twinings tea shop.

Still. Once he'd made the decision, nothing was going to hold Finlay back. Not even—

'Really, sir!' Another modiste's assistant, an apron over her gown and a wide-eyed expression of horror on her face, attempted to bat him away. 'This area is for ladies. There is a young Miss here for the final fitting of her wedding—'

'I know,' said Finlay sharply. 'She is my betrothed.'

Or at least, she was for the moment. A moment that would not last very long.

Ignoring the startled expression on his mother's face, Finlay marched past the two sofas and an armchair which were evidently there for the friends and family of whoever it was being fitted, and approached a screen.

'Isabelle?'

There was a startled yelp, a genteel curse, and Madame Penelope's head appeared around the side of the screen.

'You have made me prick my thumb,' she said darkly. 'I hope you have a good reason for barging in here, my lord.'

'I quite agree with you, Madame,' came the dour voice of the Dowager Countess of Staromchor behind him. 'I do not understand, Staromchor, why you suddenly have lost all sense of decorum. Really! A modiste's!'

Finlay ignored them both.

Well, he ignored them both as much as he could. It was impossible to prevent his ears from pinking. Especially as now he looked around him, he could see... Ah.

His mouth went dry.

Well, it was a lady's domain, he supposed.

The chintz everywhere was not his style, nor were the delicate shades of pink and leafy green that Madame Penelope had chosen to decorate the place with.

It looked more like a boudoir than a shop.

And it was even more like a boudoir, Finlay realized with growing apprehension in his lungs, because on display just to his right were a number of garments that were designed ... well, to be underclothes.

His face was now burning.

Hell's bells, but he hadn't expected this.

What man knew anything about the attiring rooms of a modiste's?

Finlay turned to his mother, who raised an eyebrow.

'I hope you are satisfied,' she said calmly, looking up from a pamphlet with a variety of different styles of gowns printed on its pages. 'I suppose this will be the talk of the Town, you forcing your way into a modiste's and risking seeing Miss Carr's wedding gown, too.'

It was the mention of the wedding gown that stiffened Finlay's resolve.

He had to finally speak his mind about this wedding. It had gone on for too long. He was starting to think, in truth, that he should never have made the offer to Isabelle in the first place.

The instinct had been a good one, Finlay knew, but it was not one which he could surely be expected to hold for the rest of his life.

I did not demand any promises... But I presumed that friends—lovers—had an unspoken expectation of honesty. More fool me.

His shoulders snapped back and he held his head high. No, mortified Madame Penelope and irate mother aside, he had to speak his mind.

He had not expected to do so in front of so many people, of course...

Finlay looked around and spotted no less than three assistants, one holding a plethora of ribbons, another merely blinking in astonishment.

Right. First things first.

'I wish to speak to Isabelle—to Miss Carr,' he amended hastily, in a voice he hoped was both commanding and charming. 'Alone, if you don't mind.'

The three assistants scampered away, but his mother rose and drew herself up in a most impressive manner.

'I do mind,' she said sharply. 'I cannot just permit you to be alone with Miss Carr. That would be scandalous. The very idea, a gentleman and a lady together, alone—and unmarried!'

Try as he might, Finlay was unable to put aside all thoughts of Rilla. Of the time they had spent together alone, of the things they had enjoyed while alone…

Perhaps his mother was right.

'My lord?'

The voice was gentle, and nervous, and it came from behind the screen.

Finlay's stomach twisted in a painful knot but he could not turn back now. He had to act. He had to have this…this show-down, for want of a better word.

He had hoped to speak with Isabelle at her lodgings, but the housekeeper had said she was getting her wedding gown fitted and—

Well. He had rather lost his head. The idea of Isabelle, a woman painfully in love with him, having her wedding gown fitted before he could speak to her…it could not be borne.

Which had led him, circuitously, to this awkward conversation.

Madame Penelope disappeared for a moment behind the screen again, and when she emerged she was not alone.

Isabelle Carr stood there, gazing with a curious look.

Finlay's heart skipped a beat.

Not because affection had suddenly welled in him—quite the opposite. A part of him, and he had not realized it had even existed until this moment, had wondered whether he would eventually fall in love with her. Whether the Isabelle he had once known would resurface, once they were married, and they could enjoy a sort of companionable respect in their marriage.

But seeing her like this, dressed in her finery, the elegant blue silk gown delicately fitted around her bust, her hair taste-fully shaped upon her head…

It was nothing. She was nothing compared to the sight of Rilla, straw in her hair and her unseeing gaze trusting.

Finlay swallowed.

There was no easy way to do this. Best to just get it over with.

'I can't marry you,' he blurted out.

The silence that followed this pronouncement was absolutely excruciating.

At least, Finlay had thought so. It was only then that he realized that the scream of astonishment from his mother was perhaps worse.

'Not…not marry her?'

'Ah, I think I hear a customer calling,' murmured the modiste quietly. She stepped past Isabelle, past Finlay, and out into the shop proper.

At least, he presumed that was where she went. Finlay had not taken his eyes from the woman who, until a minute ago, had been his betrothed.

Isabelle's eyes were wide and her lips had parted in silent shock. Evidently his statement had made it impossible for her to speak.

Wretched guilt tore at Finlay's heart. This was his fault, all his fault. If he had not been so charming, so polite—if he had not attempted to make Isabelle comfortable in the marital decision they had taken, she would not have fallen in love with him.

And now he would have to stand here and watch her crumble.

'I know I should have said something sooner,' Finlay said awkwardly, taking a step forward and ignoring the impassioned speech from the dowager countess behind him.

'The scandal sheets! The whole of the *ton* will be filled with the news that my son has abandoned his bride.'

'I offered you marriage out of convenience. We both agreed to that—to provide you with a home,' Finlay said stoically, not taking his eyes from Isabelle. 'And though I fully intended until just a day ago—'

'Disgrace upon our name! No one will ever touch us again. We'll be forced to—'

'Once I realized that I could not marry you, I knew I had to tell you instantly,' continued Finlay doggedly.

Oh, Lord, only his mother could make this situation about herself.

'And I am sorry…truly sorry, Isabelle.'

'Why?' breathed the young woman, her face pale. 'Why won't you marry me?'

Finlay winced. But this was the decision he had chosen, and he could not back away from it now just because it was uncomfortable. 'Because…'

'I shall lose my voucher at Almack's and then what will I do? Oh, the shame of it all!'

Finlay squared his shoulders and ensured that he looked Isabelle directly in the eye as he said the words he knew would cut the deepest. 'Because I am in love with someone else.'

That cut his mother's tirade short. 'And I… Wh-what?'

He did not look around. He could console—or attempt to console—his mother later. He would have all the time in the world to do that, and to acclimatize her to Rilla, if she decided to take umbrage at the fact that he had chosen his own bride.

Oh, please God, let Rilla accept him.

Yes, the dowager countess could be calmed another time, but Isabelle?

Finlay did not look away from the young woman. A young woman who had lost her only family and had no one else to turn to. Who would now have nothing to live on, no one to protect her…

'Isabelle,' he said, taking a step forward. 'I will still help you—'

His words were cut short by such a bizarre occurrence, all words fled from his mind.

Isabelle raised both hands to her face, covered her eyes, and…laughed.

It wasn't a snort of panic or the beginnings of tears—at least, he did not think it was. No, her shoulders were shaking from the fit of giggles she appeared to be experiencing.

Finlay swallowed awkwardly. She was having a most strange reaction to the news, but then perhaps this was just her way of attempting to understand what was happening to her. It was hardly an everyday occurrence, a broken engagement mere days before the wedding itself.

Right, now, what had he decided? Oh, yes.

Finlay stepped forward, awkwardly patting the arm of the now hysterically giggling woman. 'Please do not concern yourself. I have thought long and hard about it, and I will give you a thousand pounds.'

'Finlay Jellicoe!'

'A thousand pounds,' continued Finlay, throwing a dark look at his mother over his shoulder. 'That should be more than sufficient for your needs for the rest of the Season, at least I think so, and I am sure that by that time you will most definitely have found another man to marry you.'

Which would be a relief from his shoulders, he thought woefully, hating that he had placed her in such a terrible position.

First the loss of Cecil, and now the loss of him. Would it be any wonder if Isabelle decided to leave the marriage mart and take a Grand Tour on the Continent?

Perhaps an Italian prince or a French count would take pity on her. Perhaps she would become someone else's problem.

Finlay instantly felt guilty for such a thought, but he could not blame himself. He had taken the weight of responsibility of caring for Isabelle Carr without considering just how heavily it would press upon him.

Now he had just informed her that the safety and security of marriage had been, at least from him, removed.

No wonder she was so hysterical.

'Please, Isabelle,' Finlay said in a low voice, patting her self-consciously on the arm again. 'Do not distress yourself.'

'The woman can be distressed if she—'

'I know you are deeply in love with me,' he said, hoping to goodness that she did not mind him revealing that he knew of her feelings. 'But your affections... I am sure they will fade with time, and it will be as though you never cared for me in that way. I hope... I trust that we will be able to return to being good friends. As we once were.'

As I thought we would be forever. You and me and Cecil and Bartlett. God, what had happened to us?

At his words, Isabelle dropped her hands from her face, and Finlay was astonished to see that she was...smiling?

Perhaps she was in shock. Perhaps after losing Cecil, she had no other way of accepting difficulty than through laughter. It was odd, to be sure, but—

'My dear Finlay,' said Isabelle with a broad grin. 'Please do not concern yourself.'

One may as well tell paint not to dry. 'But—'

'I am in love with someone else.'

This time it was Finlay's turn for his lips to part in astonishment.

I am in love with someone else.

It wasn't possible—no. He must have misheard.

Finlay cleared his throat as tingles of anticipation washed over his body. 'I do apologize. I do not think I heard you.'

'I am in love with someone else,' repeated Isabelle, soft pink tinging her cheeks. 'Someone who wants to marry me.'

It could not be happening.

Finlay did not understand—he had heard her most clearly, had he not? Isabelle had been effusive in her regard, passionate in her affection, far more than he could have imagined.

Oh, I could never speak to him about the depths of my feelings. Besides, I do not think it would be appropriate. He does not expect it. He would not... I do not think he would wish it.

I love him, my lady. Everything he says is music to my ears, everything he does is the best thing a man has ever done!

He could not have misheard, nor misunderstood, all that. 'But...but...'

'And why you believe that I am in love with you, I really do not know,' continued Isabelle blithely, a small line appearing between her brows as she frowned. 'I do not believe I have ever given you cause to believe that from my behaviour.'

Finlay's mouth dropped. 'But I heard you!'

It was probably not the politest thing he could say, and he was not surprised when his mother behind him snapped, 'I beg your pardon?'

'I heard you, the two of you, talking,' Finlay said, a shade discomforted at having to reveal that he had been eavesdropping. 'I assure you, I did not intend to—'

'And you heard what?' asked Isabelle.

Hell's bells, why did it feel so awkward to repeat this?

'Well, a lot of talking about...about being in love with me. How deeply you felt, how you adored me.'

Whenever I am with him, I can think of nothing but the pleasure I gain from being in his presence.

It had been strange to hear, but it was far more mortifying to repeat. Finlay hardly knew where to look, but as his gaze eventually returned to Isabelle, she...she was laughing again.

Laughing, at him?

'Look, I know this has all been very difficult for you,' he said a little stiffly. 'But—'

'Oh, Finlay, you dear sweet man,' said Isabelle, shaking her head with a laugh. 'You presumed that I was speaking of you, then?'

A flicker of uncertainty awoke in his chest. 'Well...well yes, obviously. Who else could you be speaking of?'

And the pink tinges in her cheeks darkened as Isabelle held his gaze. 'Why, George of course.'

George. George? They did not know anyone called George. Finlay blinked. 'Who the devil is George?'

'Lord George Bartlett,' Isabelle said, her eyes shining.

Bartlett.

Bartlett? What the hell was going on?

And then the memory of their conversation that late night resurfaced in Finlay's mind. Bartlett had been concerned, had he not, very concerned about Isabelle's well-being? They had discussed her in depth and the man had been worried about her.

Far more worried than he himself had been, now Finlay came to think about it.

Bartlett and Isabelle?

'And I have been feeling so guilt-ridden, all these weeks,' Isabelle was saying as Finlay forced himself to pay attention. 'I have been spending every moment with him that I could, and yet my remorse about lying to you, about keeping this hidden—'

'Why on earth did you not say something?' Finlay said, a slow smile starting to creep across his face. 'Do you mean to tell me that the blackguard is in love with you?'

Isabelle's expression was warm. 'He tells me so.'

'Then why—'

'I did not know of his feelings before...well, before you offered me marriage,' Isabelle confessed, hugging herself as the evident regret of her actions rose. 'I thought— Well, I had no other choice.'

'Charming,' muttered Finlay, his smile broadening.

Isabelle shoved him hard on the shoulder, and there she was, the Isabelle he had known, the one who had pushed him about when they were younger and had thought nothing of cutting off her own hair so that she could play pirates with them.

The three of them. The three boys: Cecil, himself...and Bartlett.

'When a woman has few options, she takes the option presented to her,' Isabelle said with a snort. 'Even if it was you.'

'Outrageous!'

'And before I knew what was happening, George and I… Well, there it was. You had paid off so many of my debts.'

'I had not bought you,' Finlay said sharply.

Isabelle nodded. 'I know that, but you must admit, it put me in rather a delicate situation.'

He supposed it did. That was the trouble with money; it always ruined perfectly good friendships.

Still, it did not explain why Bartlett was so damned silent about the whole thing. 'And Bartlett never thought to say anything?'

'Neither of us wanted to offend you, and though George was certain you were not in love with me—'

Dear God, it was so obvious, Finlay thought with rising disbelief.

Had not Bartlett asked closely about his feelings for Isabelle? Had he not been most interested to discover whether Finlay had fallen in love with her?

'But I wasn't sure, and just when I was attempting to tell your mother that I was in love with another—'

'Mother!' Finlay turned around, nettled. 'You knew?'

The Dowager Countess of Staromchor shrugged. 'I knew she cared for another, but that is by the by.'

'Mother!'

'You think every marriage is made between two people who love each other? Come now, Staromchor, I raised you to be smarter than that,' said his mother in a cutting tone, seated still on the sofa and with the pamphlet open in her lap. 'Hardly anyone marries for love. I knew you would be a good husband to Isabelle, so what did it matter if she had feelings for another? Those feelings would fade.'

'They will not,' Isabelle said sharply, and Finlay grinned as the rambunctious tomboy he had known sparked back to life once more. 'I happen to believe that if love can be found, then it should be grasped as tightly as one can. How often does love arrive? Should we not seize it when it does?'

Finlay swallowed.

I love you!

She was right. Both of them. He should have offered Rilla his heart the moment he had realized it belonged to her. And now…

There was still a chance it was too late, even with the complication of Isabelle removed from him.

It was removed, wasn't it?

'Just to be clear, then,' Finlay said hurriedly, and Isabelle's attention moved back to him. 'Our engagement is at an end, and you are…happy?'

'Ridiculously so.' His previously betrothed beamed. 'No offence meant, you understand. But I wish to marry the man I love.'

There was a loud sob that filled the modiste.

Finlay blinked. He had not made such a sound, and neither had Isabelle. Which could only mean…

The two of them turned around slowly, Finlay hardly able to believe his eyes, as he saw his mother sobbing on the sofa.

'Mother?' he said weakly.

'I… I am in love with someone, too!' declared his mother, tears rolling down her cheeks. 'And I declined him b-because… a small scandal, but that was twenty years ago. I want to marry him, but I said no, I do not know why!'

'Mother?' Finlay repeated again, hardly able to keep up with all this change.

'Right, I had better go,' said Isabelle smartly, starting to pull her gown off.

Finlay snapped a hand over his eyes, now utterly bewildered. 'Where are you going?'

'Why, to find George and make him marry me, of course,' Isabelle said lightly. There was the sound of fabric pooling to the floor, and Finlay wished to God she had stepped behind the screen. They weren't seven years old anymore. 'And what about you, Fin?'

It was the childhood name they had all used, and its utterance here, at Madame Penelope's after his engagement was put to an end, was a moment of realization for Finlay.

He dropped his hand and grinned at the troublemaking Carr that he and Bartlett—he and George, heaven forbid—still had in their lives. 'Good luck.'

'You, too,' said Isabelle, pulling up a sprigged muslin gown and hastily doing up the ties.

'Me?'

She snorted and laughed as she marched out of the modiste's. 'Did you not say you were in love with someone else?'

And a moment of clarity dropped into Finlay's mind as he realized what he had to do next. 'Rilla.'

'And now he might not marry me! Why did I decline…? My fear of scandal… What was I thinking?'

After, that was, he had comforted his mother.

Good grief.

Chapter Eighteen

'Here we are, then,' said a gruff voice Rilla knew well, and strangely thought she would miss. 'The Markhall School for Girls.'

Rilla had felt the carriage slow five minutes ago, the surface of the road shifting from the rough country lane to the slightly smoother gravel path.

They had arrived, then.

'C'mon,' the driver snapped gruffly.

Rilla bit back her tongue and forced down all the explanations that she had already made to the unfeeling and unpleasant man. Her fingers curled around the unopened letter she could not see. She was depending on the driver to guide her in and out of the carriage; this was all new to her, and she did not know where she was going.

A heavily gloved hand grabbed her own.

Trying not to cry out with the discomfort of someone suddenly touching her, Rilla allowed herself to be tugged forward in the carriage, moving in a haze of uncertainty and distrust.

'Step,' snapped the tired voice.

She had tried to be patient. She would certainly not like to be a carriage driver, spending hours and hours out in the elements, freezing in the winter and baking in the summer sun. The wind was surely a cruel whip across one's face, and one's fingers and toes were doubtless ice in this weather.

But that was no call for rudeness.

'Oh,' Rilla muttered as her foot caught on the first step. Then she had her bearings and was able to descend from the carriage with relative decorum.

The instant her booted feet crunched on the gravel she gained her equilibrium, she snatched her hand away from the driver.

'Thank you,' she said ungraciously.

It did not appear that he had noticed. His footsteps, heavier than hers and faster, had moved around to the side of the carriage, and soon they had returned. The hearty thud of her trunk being dropped beside her was unmistakable.

'Nice place,' the carriage driver grunted.

Trying her best not to be sarcastic, Rilla shrugged. 'It makes no difference in the end.'

And it didn't. Whether or not the Markhall School for Girls was pleasing to look at was neither here nor there.

Even if she could see, Rilla could not help but think darkly, the place was not going to be improved by fine stonework.

No, she was here to do a job. The students of the Markhall School for Girls were the important factors to secure her future happiness, and she would not know that for some time.

She would simply have to hope, to trust, that they were not as odious as she feared.

'Y'want yer bonnet?'

Suppressing the desire to point out that if she'd had any warning that she was about to be dragged out of the carriage, she would certainly have picked up her bonnet, Rilla said instead, 'Yes, if you please.'

Her courtesy was not returned. The bonnet was thrust into her hands, the surprise at the sudden movement meaning that she almost dropped it.

Then the door snapped shut behind her, and there was a creak of wood and leather.

'Good luck, Miss,' grunted the man.

Rilla turned immediately, real panic flaring now in her chest. 'But Miss Pike instructed you to—'

'I reckon as you can find your own way in,' the driver said curtly, jerking the reins and causing one of the horses to neigh in indignation. 'Night is drawing in and I want to be on my way afore dark. Good luck, as I say, Miss.'

'But—'

Whatever words of remonstrance she had intended to utter would have made little difference, Rilla was sure, even if the man had heard them. As it was, he had urged the horses on and the rattle of the carriage made her attempts at speech completely moot.

Only when the sound of the carriage had entirely died away did Rilla swallow and allow the emotions flooding through her veins to appear on her face.

Oh, damn.

Her cane was still in the carriage.

She'd accidentally left it in the carriage when she arrived… and now it was rattling on its way back to the Wallflower Academy.

Ah, well. She would have to learn quickly, that was all.

Rilla had known, from the moment that the Pike had suggested that she go and become a teacher for a school, that leaving the Wallflower Academy would be a deprivation.

None of them could truly understand. It was like having her right arm cut off, the familiar sensations of the Wallflower Academy removed from her.

This gravel was different. It crunched at a different pitch when Rilla took a hesitant step to where she believed her trunk had been deposited. It took her three attempts to kneel and find the blasted thing, and in the end, it was only when her toe clipped the corner that she was absolutely sure.

Straightening up and holding the handle of the trunk in her

hand, Rilla rammed her bonnet on her head and turned her face up to what she presumed was the school.

And then she swallowed.

How had she managed to learn the routes and routines of the Wallflower Academy? It had all seemed so long ago now, she could barely recall. It was as familiar to her as her own limbs.

Well, she had to start somewhere.

With a sinking heart that was partly to do with her practical predicament, and partly to do with the unopened letter clutched in her hand, Rilla took a step forward. Hating that she had to do this, she put out a hand.

Then she halted.

Rilla turned, back to the direction the dratted carriage had gone, and swore under her breath.

It took five minutes of careful exploratory stepping for Rilla to find the portico, then another minute to navigate the six steps whilst holding on to her seemingly increasingly heavy trunk.

By the time she had deposited it on the stone before the front door, Rilla's shoulders ached and her temples were starting to throb.

It had been a long journey, and now…now the difficult part was about to begin.

She did not irritate herself by seeking a doorbell. Instead, Rilla rapped hard on the door with her fist.

It would have been far louder with a cane, she could not help but think, *but there it was.*

The door did not open for several minutes. When it did, a voice far sharper than Miss Pike's snapped, 'Yes?'

Rilla curtsied, hating that she had no idea if this woman was a maid or the headmistress. 'Miss Marilla Newell, at your service.'

'Miss Marilla— Dear God, you're the teacher?'
Still no real clue as to the voice's owner, Rilla thought darkly, though it was not a good sign, whoever it was.

'Yes,' she said aloud.

The owner of the voice sniffed. 'I should have informed your previous headmistress…teachers are supposed to come around the back.'

Like a servant, Rilla thought with an ever-sinking heart. That was indication enough that this place was not going to be the haven of learning and new home she could grow comfortable in as she had hoped.

Still, she was far away from everything and everyone that she knew. If there was ever a time and a place for a fresh start, it was the Markhall School for Girls.

No Sylvia, no Daphne, no Miss Pike, and no…no Finlay Jellicoe, Earl of Staromchor.

Which was all to the good. Of course. There was no reason that she would want to see them, especially not the latter. No reason at—

'Well, don't just stand there—come in,' sighed the voice. 'I am Miss Hennessy. You may call me ma'am.'

Rilla nodded, apprehension flowing through her veins. 'Shall I just leave my trunk—'

'You can bring in your trunk. Our teachers don't have airs and graces,' said Miss Hennessy curtly. 'Honestly, what did they teach you in your last position?'

It was only then that Rilla realized just what a false reference Miss Pike had provided.

Dear Lord, had the woman intimated that Rilla had already been a teacher?

What on earth was she supposed to say?

'It was…a very different establishment,' Rilla said demurely, leaning to pick up her trunk as her shoulder protested.

Miss Hennessy sniffed. 'So I see. Come on.'

Her footsteps on what sounded like hardwood floors immediately began to move away, and Rilla hastened to follow her.

If only there had not been such a large step into the building.

Careering forward and only just managing to prevent herself from smashing her nose onto the floor by whirling her arms like a windmill, Rilla's heart was thundering painfully by the time she righted herself.

'No time for fun and games,' came the distant voice of Miss Hennessy. 'Honestly, were you always larking about at your old place? We don't have much time for that here.'

Rilla swallowed her irritation as she turned vaguely in what she presumed was a hall. 'Miss Hennessy, I do not know what the Pike—what Miss Pike—told you about me in her letter to you, but—'

'Not much, scarce enough to place you with a subject.' Miss Hennessy appeared to be moving away, though where precisely, Rilla could not tell. 'Keep up, will you?'

'The reason I mention this,' Rilla continued doggedly, putting her trunk down and deciding once and for all that she was not going to cart it about like a servant, 'is because Miss Pike appears to have neglected to tell you—'

'I am sure there are many things your precious Pike hasn't—'

'To tell you that I am blind,' Rilla said, with the patience of a saint.

Miss Hennessy's voice immediately disappeared.

And there it is, Rilla thought dully as the silence elongated most painfully.

There was always the awkward silence after a statement of that nature. Next would be the frantic apologies, then the questions about precisely how it happened, and what she could see, and whether she had seen a doctor...

'I beg your pardon, I'm sure,' said Miss Hennessy, her voice growing in volume as her footsteps echoed towards her. 'Why on earth didn't you say?'

'I... I presumed you knew,' returned Rilla, slightly dazed.

Where was the apology? Where were the questions? Where were the recommendations of different eye drops, poultices, and for some reason, liquors that different people had recommended her over the years?

'Honestly, why would you presume that? I am glad you told me, though,' said Miss Hennessy briskly. 'It makes things a good deal clearer. Do you want my arm?'

Rilla's mouth fell open.

It was...refreshing.

Miss Hennessy would never gain many friends, not with that acidic nature and sharpness of tongue—but it was far pleasanter to be subjected to that than the pity she'd expected.

Despite herself, a wry smile crept over Rilla's face. 'That would be most welcome, thank you.'

It was not the softest of touches when Miss Hennessy pulled her arm into her own, but at this point, Rilla did not care. Perhaps this place, though strange and unfriendly at first, could become a kind of home.

Exhausted from her journey, Rilla did not attempt to memorize the path from the hall to whatever place it was that Miss Hennessy was taking her. Left, right, up a flight of stairs then down a few steps, the place appeared to be a maze.

'Here we are,' came Miss Hennessy's voice, accompanied by the click of an opening door. 'Your schoolroom.'

Rilla's stomach lurched as she was guided into a place that was far lighter than the corridor before it.

Her schoolroom.

Well, the Pike had been attempting to convince her to become a tutor at the Wallflower Academy for...how long now? Eight months? Longer?

Perhaps she should have known from the very beginning that she would end up here, Rilla thought darkly.

In a schoolroom, in an unwelcoming school, in the middle of nowhere.

'Most people don't want to teach here,' came the sharp voice of Miss Hennessy as she released Rilla.

Rilla raised an eyebrow. 'Oh?'

It was as non-committal an answer as she could manage, without giving offence or leading to further questions.

Miss Hennessy's sniff occurred from several feet away now. 'Yes, we are too far from London to be of interest to most.'

The words slipped out before Rilla could stop them. 'I have no wish to be near London.'

'Really,' came Miss Hennessy's wry response, no question within the word. 'I thought as much.'

Heat burned Rilla's cheeks, but there was nothing she could do about it. She was not about to bare her heart to anyone at the Markhall School for Girls, much less Miss Hennessy, who had still not clarified whether she was housekeeper, fellow teacher, or headmistress.

No, the sorrows that plagued her heart were hers alone, and she would bear them as best she could.

Even if it meant pain beyond what she had ever known.

'I suppose it was a great wrench,' came Miss Hennessy's next words. 'Leaving your previous position.'

A far greater wrench than Rilla had expected. Until the very moment of departure, she had considered the Wallflower Academy to be what it was for so many: a strange sort of prison, attempting to mould the women termed wallflowers into something that the *ton* preferred.

Only when she had left it did she realize just what a sanctuary it was from the world.

And now it was gone—or more accurately, she had gone, and now her very independence had been similarly taken from her.

'Is that a letter?'

Rilla's hand tightened around the paper. 'Yes, it is.'

'But how do you…?'

The question was left delicately on the air, as though that would make it less distasteful. In truth, Rilla could hardly blame her. It was a question borne of curiosity, not malice, and it was not a difficult one to answer.

'I cannot read,' Rilla said airily. 'I usually have a friend read my letters to me and then I memorize them. It is easier that way.'

She really should have asked Sylvia or Daphne to read it for her before she left. Rilla's finger stroked along the soft grain of the letter. There hadn't been time.

Lying to herself, now, was she?

She hadn't wanted to see them. Hadn't wanted to hear the disappointment and the disgrace in their voices. Would they treat her differently? Had they forgotten her already?

'And who will read your letters now?' came the voice of Miss Hennessy.

Rilla swallowed. Well, there was no time like the present for trying to make new friends. Goodness knew, none of them here could be as shy as Daphne nor as wild as Sylvia.

'If you would do me the honour?' she said formally, holding out the letter.

Miss Hennessy did not reply in words, but perhaps that was unnecessary. Her eager steps forward and the way she half took, half wrenched the letter from Rilla's hand suggested her nosiness was perhaps on par with Sylvia's after all.

Rilla was silent as she heard the breaking of the seal and the unfolding of the page. It had been good paper, a high quality; her fingertips had told her that much. Her father had perhaps wanted to wish her good fortune on the start of her new endeavour. It would have been more pleasant if he had visited, but—

'"My dear Rilla…"' said Miss Hennessy aloud. 'Rilla?'

Her stomach lurched painfully. 'It is what my family and some close friends call me.'

I told you before, my friends call me Rilla.

It was impossible to tell whether Miss Hennessy approved of this. With a sniff, she returned to the letter.

'"My dear Rilla, I am so sorry that I was not able to see you before you left the Wallflower Academy. It had been my intention, but as you can imagine, I have had a few important things to take care of before then."'

Rilla forced her expression to remain still.

Of course her father would put almost everything before her. Why was she surprised?

"'Having discovered that you will be leaving before I can return, I hope you will do me the honour of receiving me at the Markhall School for Girls, and we can continue our very important discussion then,'" Miss Hennessy read.

A frown puckered at Rilla's forehead. Important discussion? It had been a good many years now since she and her father had had a discussion of any description. What on earth did he mean?

"'Your very faithful Finlay.'"

Rilla staggered, the weight of the name Miss Hennessy had just read unsettling her to such an extreme that her knees buckled. 'Wh-what did you say?'

"'We can continue our very—'"

'After that,' Rilla snapped.

She was undoubtedly offending Miss Hennessy, the only person at the Markhall School for Girls she knew, but that did not matter. Not with those words ringing in her ears—words she could not have heard.

"'Your very faithful Finlay,'" repeated Miss Hennessy in a bemused voice. 'Who is that—a brother?'

There had never been anyone less like a brother in her entire life.

Despite the fact that her head was ringing and her knees felt as though they were about to collapse at any moment, Rilla managed to say, 'No, a…a friend. Thank you, Miss Hennessy, I will have my letter back now.'

The accompanying sniff was unwelcome, but expected. 'Well, I'll leave you to get accustomed to your schoolroom. Just ring the bell by the blackboard, and I'll send someone to show you up to your room. Good evening, Miss Newell.'

'Miss Hennessy,' Rilla said in a hoarse voice.

The door snicked shut behind her, and Rilla staggered back until her fingers found a wall. Then she leaned against it and closed her eyes.

He was being cruel.

All that talk about continuing their discussion—there was nothing more to discuss! Finlay was not truly in love with her, and though he was not in love with Isabelle Carr, he was about to marry her.

What else was there to say?

'He is not coming back,' Rilla said into the silence of the room. 'And you would be a fool to wish for it.'

A fool to wish for greater heartache. A fool to hope for something that simply could not be.

The door to the corridor clicked open.

Rilla straightened as best she could. Well, she did not want Miss Hennessy to think she could be so easily exhausted. Her place here was only secure if she could teach all day, after all.

'I am quite well,' she said firmly in the direction of the door. 'In fact, I do not believe I have ever been better.'

'Excellent,' said the voice of Finlay Jellicoe, Earl of Staromchor. 'I am delighted to hear it.'

Chapter Nineteen

Finlay had to put the past behind him and attempt to make those things right. He had already given Bartlett and Isabelle their wedding present—an impressive gold clock—and had managed to calm his mother sufficiently, though he had still not gained a clue as to who this gentleman was that she was supposed to have fallen in love with.

Now it was time to tend to his own affairs.

Swallowing hard, wishing to goodness he had a speech prepared and certain that merely seeing Rilla would thrust it out of his mind anyway, Finlay opened the door.

When he stepped into the room, his breath was quite literally taken away.

There she was. Rilla. The woman he loved.

He had never seen her quite so downcast. Her travelling pelisse was stained with mud at least three inches deep, and her bonnet was askew, as were her dark midnight curls. There was a look of pain in her expression that even her straightening up against the wall she had been leaning against could not distract from.

And then Rilla spoke.

'I am quite well,' she said, turning to him and evidently presuming he was someone else. 'In fact, I do not believe I have ever been better.'

And Finlay's heart stirred as it had never stirred before.

She was so brave. Here she was, to all intents and purposes alone, with a new life ahead of her—one Rilla had not chosen.

And still she was determined to face it head-on.

It was all he could do to keep his voice steady. 'Excellent. I am delighted to hear it.'

Finlay was gifted a brief moment of satisfaction. There was nothing quite like the woman you loved gawping at you, utterly confused, her jaw dropping and her fingers tightening on—

Was that his letter? Was the fact that Rilla was still holding it a good sign?

No, it could not be that simple. Within a heartbeat, Rilla's expression had transformed into one that was stiff, polite, and worst of all, aloof. He knew she only put on that appearance when she wanted to be distant from the person with whom she was conversing.

So, he had a great deal of ground to cover. There was a chance, perhaps, that she would not forgive him at all.

Though the thought of being separated from Rilla forever was bitter bile on his tongue, Finlay had to accept it was a possibility. There was nothing he could do here, save tell the truth.

And apologize. Dear God, she deserved an apology.

'Rilla, you have to let me explain,' Finlay said hurriedly, launching into a declaration that his mind managed to drag up from the depths of his imagination. 'I know you probably don't want to hear it.'

'You're right,' came Rilla's curt reply. 'I don't.'

Finlay only hesitated for a moment, then forced himself to take a step closer. If he could only tell her everything he had done since he had last seen her, then surely she would understand.

She may still not wish to have anything to do with him, but she would at least understand.

'I'm afraid I'm going to tell you anyway,' said Finlay, cringing at the inelegance of his behaviour. Most unsuitable for an earl. 'The moment you left me standing outside the Wallflower Academy—'

'Which you rightly deserved.'

'Which I deserved,' Finlay accepted, trying not to allow himself to get drawn into a debate.

He could see what was happening. All Rilla wanted to do was protect herself, prevent herself from ever feeling hurt again.

And he knew why. Finlay had hurt her. He had hurt himself, too, but that had been different; he had been in possession of all the facts. It had been Rilla who had been thunderstruck by the revelation that he had been engaged to another.

Now he had to make it right, push through Rilla's defences one last time, make her see his bruised and battered heart, and...

Wait for her to make her decision.

'I wanted to tell you everything, but I had to—'

'What are you doing here?'

'I'm trying to tell you,' Finlay said, his voice rising in volume. 'If you would just let me—'

'Are you the new footman?'

Finlay whirled around. There stood a woman who could only be a teacher at the Markhall School for Girls. She was wearing a very masculine-styled gown with a sort of fitted waistcoat around the bodice, and her spectacles were topped by a pair of frowning brows.

'F-footman?' he spluttered.

Then a noise caught his ear—a noise he had not expected, but nonetheless lifted his spirits magnificently.

Rilla was laughing.

Finlay turned to her, delight soaring through his chest as he watched the woman he adored giggle with unrepressed laughter.

'I do not see what is so amusing,' sniffed the woman who had stepped into Rilla's new schoolroom. 'I only asked—'

'Miss Hennessy, this is the Earl of Staromchor,' said Rilla with a grin, managing to stifle her laughter long enough to speak. 'I apologize for laughing, but the misunderstanding—'

'Oh!' Miss Hennessy went scarlet.

Finlay waved a hand and cast her a charming smile. 'Please, do not concern yourself. It happens all the time.'

Rilla snorted with laughter behind him.

'Well, I— Right, so… Your Lordship is an acquaintance of Miss Newell?' spluttered the teacher.

Finlay swallowed.

An acquaintance?

Oh, they had shared so much more than mere acquaintance-ship…but at the same time, he could hardly describe Rilla as a friend. Not in this moment. Not when he was uncertain whether or not she would even permit him to attempt to explain…

'Something like that.' Rilla's dry voice held no hints as to whether she would let him continue, but her next sentence did. 'Please excuse us, Miss Hennessy. I believe the earl has some-thing important to tell me. If you would be so good…'

It was delicately done, and Finlay had to remind himself once again that Rilla, far from being an abandoned wallflower in the Wallflower Academy, was the Honourable Miss Newell.

Dear God, there was so much of her he still had to learn. So much more of Rilla to discover.

If she would let him…

Miss Hennessy was all awkward apologies, curtsies, and kowtowing. By the time she had shut the door with as genteel a click as she could manage, nerves had once again seized Finlay's heart.

He turned back to Rilla, who was now staring with a bold-ness typical of the woman he cared so deeply for.

For a moment, silence hung between them.

Then their mutual laughter echoed in the otherwise empty room.

'A footman,' Finlay said dryly. 'I must just give off that sense.'

'I think it more likely that anyone in my presence immediately becomes more servile,' Rilla said dryly.

Finlay winced, but only for a moment. Rilla was a woman, he knew, who could quite happily laugh at herself. If she were saying such things, it was because she felt comfortable doing so.

'Look,' he said quietly.

The laughter left Rilla's lips, but her openness appeared to remain.

Finlay took a deep breath.

Well, here goes—everything.

'It is true that the initial flirtation I enjoyed with you was never meant to mean more,' he said quietly, then hurried on, 'but I promise it was not nearly so bad as you probably think.'

A sardonic eyebrow rose. 'You have no idea how bad I think it was.'

'Oh, I can probably guess,' Finlay said darkly.

After all, had he not heard some of the lewd things the members of White's had suggested about innocent and largely unprotected ladies of the *ton*? There was a reason he had moved clubs.

'Was that all I was?' cut in Rilla, her voice once again harsh. 'A bit of fun?'

'Not in the slightest. Well, yes,' Finlay said, stepping forward and wishing to goodness the woman before him could see how contrite his expression was.

Her frown deepened. 'Well? Which is it?'

'Both, I suppose,' he said awkwardly, twisting his fingers before him as his heartrate started to quicken again. 'It *was* fun, talking to you. I had never experienced so much joy in the presence of a stranger.'

It was difficult to admit such a thing, but far more difficult to see the complete distrust on Rilla's face. 'I find that hard to believe.'

'I am telling you nothing but the truth,' Finlay said simply. 'Bartlett's encouragement to flirt with someone before I was chained to Isabelle…it was the perfect excuse. I already wished to know you better.'

That was clearly not something she had expected to hear.

Rilla's expression softened, just a mite. 'You…you did?'

'I did,' said Finlay, taking another step forward. A great expanse still separated them from each other, an expanse he did not believe he could yet cross. But perhaps, with enough time, enough trust…

'And our conversations swiftly became so much more than that—more to me, at any rate.'

'You think they did not mean anything to me?' Rilla's whisper was full of heartbreak.

Finlay swallowed, crushing the instinct to pull her into his arms and kiss away all the misunderstanding, the mistrust.

He would not do that to her. Rilla would not be touched by anyone, including him, without her permission.

'Our conversations, our time together… I have never felt so…so seen,' Finlay said, conscious of his poor choice of words. 'Dammit, I cannot explain.'

'I know what you mean. At least, I think I do,' said Rilla quietly.

Her hands had left the wall, as though it was no longer required to sustain her. Was that a good sign? Finlay's head was spinning so rapidly, the room almost swaying before him, he could not really tell.

He swallowed. 'Our connection has meant so much to me that I have… I have broken off my engagement.'

His heart rose to his mouth as he waited for Rilla's response.

It did not come. She merely stood there, still as a statue, as though she had not heard his words at all.

Finlay cleared his throat. Rilla said nothing. He shifted from one foot to the other, certain she would be able to hear the movement. Still she was silent.

When he could endure the silence no longer, Finlay said, 'It was really only a marriage of convenience, as I told you. Yes, I paid off her family debts, and I felt a debt of honour, but… but that is nothing compared to you.'

He had presumed such words would inspire a response, but still Rilla remained taciturn.

And though his instinct was to speak, to fill the silence, Finlay forced herself to remain quiet. This was all new information for Rilla, information she surely could not have been expecting. The very least he could do was give her the chance to absorb it.

When he truly felt as though he would burst with the unsaid words rolling about his chest, Rilla said quietly, 'Will… will Miss Carr…will she be able to live? Without the money and protection, I mean, of your name?'

'If anything, I believe I was holding her back,' Finlay said wryly, a spark of mirth in his lungs. 'She had already fallen in love with someone else. Their engagement will be announced tomorrow.'

'But…but you said…you said she was in love with you!'

'No need to sound so surprised,' Finlay said, a dart of pain searing his heart. 'I had thought, but I was mistaken. It appears that another man, a better man in my estimation, captured her heart months ago. It was only our arranged marriage that was preventing them from being together and now…now that is at an end.'

And his heart leaped as Rilla did something he could not have imagined when he first entered the room.

She took a step towards him.

'This…this bet. Was it to bed me?'

'No!' Finlay was horrified at the insinuation, that she could believe such a thing of him.

Dear God, had he proved himself to be the rake he had never thought he was?

'Absolutely not!'

'Because I can imagine two gentlemen, an earl and a…?'

Finlay winced. 'A viscount.'

'An earl and a viscount, from my experience, would have few qualms in—'

'Bartlett—Lord Bartlett—is not like that,' Finlay said firmly. 'In truth, I cannot think of anyone less likely to do such a thing, or even think such a thing. No, it was…it was to charm you. To flirt, to enjoy a woman's company.'

Rilla breathed a wry laugh. 'And we have done so much more than that.'

'And I want more,' said Finlay, his mouth dry as he tentatively approached the crux of the conversation. The centre, the part that mattered the most. 'So much more.'

He took a step towards her, making sure his footstep was heavy. She did not blanch or move away.

Finlay's heart skipped a beat.

He was going to do it.

'Rilla— Marilla, I suppose I should say—'

'You're not going to…are you?' Rilla peered in his direction with flushed cheeks.

And that was when he knew. Finlay could not have known beforehand, not in advance of turning up at the Markhall School for Girls and hoping to goodness that whoever opened the door would let him in.

But in this moment, he knew.

She loved him. She wanted him, had been devastated not just because of the lies, but because Isabelle Carr's existence would make it impossible for them to be together.

And the affection he felt for her stirred so powerfully, it

was almost as though it was pouring out from him, invisible perhaps to the naked eye but perfectly evident to Rilla Newell.

'Goodness, I love you,' Finlay said simply.

Rilla's pink cheeks turned red, but she took a step towards him. 'And I love you.'

The simplicity of it all—that was what he loved. The fact that loving each other did not have to be difficult or complicated. Life might make it so, but at the very centre of who they were was love. Love for each other. Love for what mattered.

Finlay grinned as he caught Rilla's hands in his own, and she did not pull away. 'When we are married—'

Rilla snorted. 'I never had the impression you were particularly fond of the married state!'

'I did not want my life chosen for me, dictated by honour and forced down a particular path,' Finlay quipped, warmth spreading from the connection of their fingertips. 'And it's not. This is my choice—you are my choice. And yes, it may perhaps shock the *ton*.'

'Oh, good,' said Rilla darkly. 'Another scandal.'

'But as long as I have you, I don't care,' Finlay finished seriously. 'Rilla, you said before that you were more than a match for an earl.'

'Oh, don't repeat what I—'

'And you were right. You're more than a mere match—you… you are everything,' he said, taut emotions finally pouring out of him. 'My better half, my best friend—the one woman in the world who makes me laugh and makes me think, usually at the same time. More than a match? You're more suitable a match for me than anyone I've ever met.'

The woman he loved tilted her head as she laughed. 'You were never going to take no for an answer, were you?'

'I would always take no from you, if you do not wish it,' he said quietly. It was important she knew that. 'Even as my wife, you will never get dictated to, Rilla.'

Her twisting smile aroused his manhood. 'And what would you have done, then, if I had rejected you?'

Finlay stared. Then he pulled Rilla into his embrace and she stepped willingly into his arms. 'You know, it did not even cross my mind.'

Their kiss, when it came, had been awaited forever—and as Rilla melted into his passionate affection, Finlay was certain he would never see the world the same again.

Epilogue

Her hands were shaking as they carefully smoothed her gown, but there was a smile on Rilla's face that had been there from the very moment she had awoken.

It was, after all, her wedding day.

'Such an exquisite gown,' Daphne said softly just behind her. 'You look wonderful, Rilla.'

Rilla's smile did not shift as she shrugged. 'I suppose so.'

What she looked like did not matter, not really. Not when she was going to become the wife of the best man she had ever met.

'And the service! Oh, it will be beautiful,' continued Daphne in her soft, shy voice. 'I have stuffed not one, but two handkerchiefs up my sleeve, just to be sure.'

And it was indeed most pleasant.

Finlay had surprised her with some careful planning that had brought such joy, Rilla had been unable to express it as they had left the church. Only when the wedding party had entered the Wallflower Academy and stepped through to the ballroom, where the wedding reception was being hosted, had Rilla managed to find time to thank her husband.

'You were so thoughtful,' she said between two hasty kisses.

Finlay had laughed. 'Well, I thought you deserved to have a little beauty in your day, Lady Staromchor. Your special day.'

'It is special because I am marrying you,' Rilla pointed out, splaying her hand on her husband's chest and being rewarded by the *thud-thud-thud* of his heart.

Lady Staromchor—she was the Countess of Staromchor. Now, that was a strange thought.

'You're the reason this day is just perfect.'

But his decisions had not hurt. Instead of going for the traditional roses, he had told her as they had walked from the church to the Tudor manor of the Wallflower Academy, he had instead instructed the florist to select those with the headiest scents.

Oh, the church had smelled divine.

'Isabelle helped,' Finlay said, his voice quavering as he said his previously betrothed's name. 'Which was to her credit, I must say.'

Rilla's stomach lurched, but only slightly.

It was perhaps fate that the two of them should find each other after both exiting an engagement—although of course, for very different reasons.

From the little Rilla knew of Miss Isabelle Carr from the single meeting they had shared, she seemed a very pleasant kind of person. It was natural, surely, for there to be awkwardness between them. They had, after all, both been engaged to the same man.

'I hope she will be happy,' Rilla said aloud.

'Oh, she will be.' Finlay's voice was confident, with none of the wavering that had accompanied it when he had been asked by his mother days ago whether he preferred the cream linens or the champagne for their wedding reception. 'Bartlett will take good care of her. Far better care than I could—that is certain.'

Rilla was not sure about that, but then she was hardly going to argue.

'And…and Nina? Your other sisters, your father? You have spoken to them to your satisfaction? I had no wish to intrude when I saw you together…' Her new husband spoke quietly so that, in the hustle and bustle of the ballroom, only she could hear him.

Trying her best not to disturb the pins Sylvia had dug into her midnight curls, Rilla nodded. 'And they were most gracious in their congratulations, too. I think... I hope that this is the beginning of a renewal. Of an understanding between us that has been lost for many years.'

It had been an awkward conversation. Rilla had almost been surprised that her family had bothered to come—but then, an earl was an earl. She had finally done what they had wanted, but she had done it on her terms, and to an earl who was far superior to the one they had initially chosen.

And Nina had listened to her apology.

Rilla let out the breath she had not known she had been holding. A new beginning.

'Oh, dear, it looks like one of the hired footmen is lost,' Finlay's voice said wearily.

Trying to stifle a grin, Rilla said, 'Well, you had better go and assist him, my love. After all, you were a footman the first time we met.'

His hasty kiss was followed by a snort of laughter, one that grew quieter as Finlay stepped away, leaving Rilla to stand alone.

But this time, she did not mind.

Finlay may not be standing right beside her, but she was still strengthened by his love, his adoration. Knowing that he cared about her so, that she had nothing to prove to anyone, to the world, was enough to keep her head as high as her spirits.

'I have an announcement to make!'

Rilla knew that voice, and tried not to groan as silence filled the ballroom of the Wallflower Academy.

The Dowager Countess of Staromchor. Finlay's mother. Her new mother-in-law.

She was a difficult woman to be around, to be sure, but as

she now had a lifetime of being her daughter-in-law, Rilla supposed she would have to attempt to get used to her, if she could.

If she could.

'I have an announcement,' repeated the dowager countess. There was another sound, something that sounded like tinkling glass. Was she tapping on a champagne glass?

A hand slipped around hers, and Rilla squeezed it immediately. She knew that hand.

'What on earth is my mother doing?' Finlay breathed into her ear.

Rilla ensured to keep her expression steady. 'I have absolutely no idea. I thought you would.'

'There is no announcement as far as I know,' he said softly as curious chatter rose up around the room. 'Isabelle and Bartlett have eloped.'

'Eloped?' Rilla repeated, perhaps a tad louder than she ought.

She did not need to see to feel the stares pressing against her skin. Well, she could not help it—anyone would have responded loudly to a remark like that.

Besides, it was her wedding. Her wedding, to Finlay—a man she loved, and who she had never believed could love her in the same way she loved him. It was understandable that people would be looking at her.

Staring at her, no doubt.

Finlay's chuckle was light. 'I should have known they wouldn't be able to wait for the preparations of a wedding. They had kept their affection hidden for so long, they simply could not prevent themselves from heading in a carriage to Gretna Green.'

A slight tinge of envy crept through Rilla's heart. 'What an excellent idea. We should have done such a thing.'

Her new husband nudged her shoulder. 'Don't be daft—and miss whatever spectacle my mother is going to make of herself?'

Rilla groaned, but kept it as quiet as she could as her new mother-in-law cleared her throat loudly.

'This is a splendid day for the Staromchor family,' the dowager countess said in that grand voice she had. 'But I could not let this moment of happiness go by without revealing…without saying… Well, I am to be married!'

Somewhere in the ballroom, someone dropped a glass. It smashed, the sound a mixture between tinkling and shimmering, and Rilla's mouth fell open.

The Dowager Countess of Staromchor…was engaged to be married?

'What the—' breathed Finlay.

He was not the only one. A great deal of consternation appeared to be fluttering through the ballroom, from what Rilla could sense.

'Mother!' Finlay hissed. The dowager countess must be close to them, then. It was hard to tell, since the woman always spoke so loudly. 'What are you saying?'

'I am saying, dear boy, that there is no reason why Lord Norbury and I—'

'Father!' gasped Daphne from just behind them.

Rilla could hardly breathe.

Finlay's mother—and Daphne's father?

She turned, eager to assist her friend in what must be a mortifying and astonishing situation, but without the knowledge of precisely where she was there was no chance of finding Daphne. There was almost a stampede of well-wishers marching on the dowager countess, pushing past Rilla, jostling her, making it almost impossible to stay upright.

Panic welled in her chest and she instinctively cried, 'Finlay—'

He was by her side in an instant. 'I have you.'

His steady, comforting hand was already on her waist and Rilla reached out for him, love blossoming once more in her chest. 'Did you have any idea—your mother and Daphne's father?'

'Not a clue,' Finlay said darkly. 'I suppose I was too wrapped up in my own complicated romance that I became blind to my mother's.'

Rilla snorted.

'Ah— I mean…'

'I know what you meant,' Rilla said hastily. 'Of all people in the world, I know to trust your intentions. Can you see Daphne? Is she quite well?'

'She…' Finlay's voice trailed off.

Concern gripped her stomach. 'Well, is she?'

'She has left the room,' her husband murmured in her ear, lowering his voice. 'Looking quite distressed, I think. Sylvia has gone after her.'

Rilla relaxed. It wasn't as though she could do much for her friend, and Sylvia was far better at comforting people than she was. The young woman would soon have Daphne laughing again.

It was a shock, to be sure. It would also make Daphne her… her step-sister-in-law?

All thoughts of attempting to calculate just how the Staromchor family would now be formed were scattered, however, as Finlay pressed a kiss to her temple.

'You look radiant.'

'You know, I feel radiant,' confessed Rilla with a shy smile.

'And that is the most important thing,' Finlay said, his voice full of pride.

Pride in her.

She could hardly believe it. There was such joy in her heart it was overflowing, spilling out whenever she spoke to anyone, making it impossible for dour worry to overcrowd her heart.

She was loved. She loved a man who was good, and noble, and who felt things so deeply. Finlay was a man not made for her, but who had made himself what she wanted, what she needed.

A life full of richness and meaning was ahead of her, a life Rilla could never have imagined, let alone presumed to claim.

She would be leaving the Wallflower Academy after all, but she now had a home, a heart quite given over to her, to fill her life.

'Miss Pike appears most disconcerted,' Finlay said, narrating the room's surroundings as he knew she appreciated. 'A few guests have accosted Lord Norbury, who looks pleased yet red-faced. My mother is adoring all the attention, as you would expect, and I—'

'Yes, how are you?' Rilla said, a teasing lilt in her voice.

Another kiss was brushed against her temple. 'You know full well that I would much rather take my wife home and ravish her than stand about with all these people.'

Rilla shivered. She was quite aware of her husband's mind, in truth, but she knew what was expected of them, even if neither of them wished it.

They would remain here, at the wedding reception, for another hour at least. Then, and only then, would they be permitted to depart.

Depart, and start the beginning of a happy life together.

'Ah, I see Miss Pike wishes to distract people,' came Finlay's laughing voice. 'She's about to instruct the musicians to— Yes, there they go.'

Music expanded just to Rilla's left. She had attempted to convince the dowager countess and Miss Pike that a dance at their wedding reception was most unnecessary, but they had both discounted her objections. The dowager countess said she wished to dance, and Miss Pike said it would be a wonderful opportunity for her wallflowers to gain practice.

'After all, the gentlemen your future husband will be inviting to his wedding will doubtlessly wish to dance with my wallflowers,' Miss Pike had said only the previous day. 'Will they not?'

Whether Rilla herself would dance apparently had not occurred to either of the women. In truth, it had not occurred to her.

But she smiled broadly as Finlay squeezed her hand and said, 'My darling wife. Will you give me the honour of this dance?'

This dance, and the next, and the next, she wanted to say. *All the dances of my life, for the rest of my life. And all the days, and all the nights, all the griefs and all the joys. The moments I never thought I could share with another. And all the rest.*

'Yes,' Rilla breathed. 'With all my heart.'

And as they stepped forward, her arm in Finlay's, Rilla did not care whether anyone was watching. The whole wedding celebration party could have melted into thin air and it would not have mattered.

What mattered was the man beside her. The man who would be by her side for the rest of her life.

Being safe, being loved, being adored in his arms was the only way she knew how to live—and as Finlay placed her in the set and whispered, 'I love you,' Rilla knew nothing could compare to this. Nothing.

Except, perhaps, the next dance. And the next. And the next...

* * * * *

If you enjoyed these stories, look out for more escapades from The Wallflower Academy coming soon from Emily E K Murdoch and Mills & Boon Historical!

MILLS & BOON MODERN IS
HAVING A MAKEOVER!

The same great stories you love,
a stylish new look!

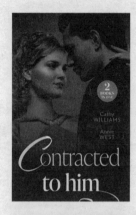

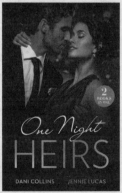

Look out for our brand new look
COMING JUNE 2024

MILLS & BOON

LET'S TALK

Romance

For exclusive extracts, competitions and special offers, find us online:

- Ⓕ MillsandBoon
- 𝕏 @MillsandBoon
- ⓘ @MillsandBoonUK
- ♪ @MillsandBoonUK

Get in touch on 01413 063 232

For all the latest titles coming soon, visit
millsandboon.co.uk/nextmonth

afterglow BOOKS

Afterglow Books is a trend-led, trope-filled list of books with diverse, authentic and relatable characters, a wide array of voices and representations, plus real world trials and tribulations. Featuring all the tropes you could possibly want (think small-town settings, fake relationships, grumpy vs sunshine, enemies to lovers) and all with a generous dose of spice in every story.

♪ @millsandboonuk
◎ @millsandboonuk
afterglowbooks.co.uk
#AfterglowBooks

For all the latest book news, exclusive content and giveaways scan the QR code below to sign up to the Afterglow newsletter:

SCAN ME

MILLS & BOON

THE HEART OF ROMANCE

A ROMANCE FOR EVERY READER

MODERN

Prepare to be swept off your feet by sophisticated, sexy and seductive heroes, in some of the world's most glamourous and romantic locations, where power and passion collide.

HISTORICAL

Escape with historical heroes from time gone by. Whether your passion is for wicked Regency Rakes, muscled Vikings or rugged Highlanders, awaken the romance of the past.

MEDICAL

Set your pulse racing with dedicated, delectable doctors in the high-pressure world of medicine, where emotions run high and passion, comfort and love are the best medicine.

True Love

Celebrate true love with tender stories of heartfelt romance, from the rush of falling in love to the joy a new baby can bring, and a focus on the emotional heart of a relationship.

HEROES

The excitement of a gripping thriller, with intense romance at its heart. Resourceful, true-to-life women and strong, fearless men face danger and desire - a killer combination!

From showing up to glowing up, these characters are on the path to leading their best lives and finding romance along the way – with plenty of sizzling spice!

To see which titles are coming soon, please visit

millsandboon.co.uk/nextmonth